BALLISTIC

BAEN BOOKS by TRAVIS S. TAYLOR

THE TAU CETI AGENDA SERIES
One Day on Mars • *The Tau Ceti Agenda*
One Good Soldier • *Trail of Evil*
Kill Before Dying • *Bringers of Hell*

WARP SPEED SERIES
Warp Speed • *The Quantum Connection*

WITH JODY LYNN NYE
Moon Beam • *Moon Tracks*

WITH JOHN RINGO
Into the Looking Glass • *Vorpal Blade* • *Manxome Foe*
Claws That Catch • *Von Neumann's War*

WITH MICHAEL Z. WILLIAMSON, TIMOTHY ZAHN, KACEY EZELL, AND JOSH HAYES
Battle Luna

WITH LES JOHNSON
Back to the Moon • *On to the Asteroid* • *Saving Proxima*

BAEN BOOKS NONFICTION BY TRAVIS S. TAYLOR
A New American Space Plan
The Science Behind The Secret
Alien Invasion: How to Defend Earth (with Bob Boan)

To purchase any of these titles in e-book form,
please go to www.baen.com.

BALLISTIC

TRAVIS S. TAYLOR

A Baen Books Original

Baen Publishing Enterprises
P.O. Box 1403
Riverdale, NY 10471
www.baen.com

ISBN: 978-1-9821-9202-0

Cover art by Kurt Miller

First printing, August 2022

Distributed by Simon & Schuster
1230 Avenue of the Americas
New York, NY 10020

Library of Congress Cataloging-in-Publication Data

Names: Taylor, Travis S., author.
Title: Ballistic / Travis S. Taylor.
Description: Riverdale, NY : Baen Publishing Enterprises, [2022] | "A Baen
    Books Original"—Title page verso.
Identifiers: LCCN 2022019109 (print) | LCCN 2022019110 (ebook) | ISBN
    9781982192020 (hardcover) | ISBN 9781625798725 (ebook)
Subjects: LCGFT: War stories. | Novels.
Classification: LCC PS3620.A98 B35 2022 (print) | LCC PS3620.A98 (ebook)
    | DDC 813/.6—dc23
LC record available at https://lccn.loc.gov/2022019109
LC ebook record available at https://lccn.loc.gov/2022019110

Pages by Joy Freeman (www.pagesbyjoy.com)
Printed in the United States of America
10 9 8 7 6 5 4 3 2 1

This book is dedicated to the myriad of workers—military, civilian, and contractors—who have labored for decades to create a defense against missile attacks, be they from superpowers or rogue states and rogue actors. These great and brilliant people have fought through constant political whirlwinds and upheavals in their program funding and job security but they have continued to press forward with technologies that someday might prove to be the shield a free world needs to protect itself from madmen. Keep up the good work, folks.

PROLOGUE

ᘇᘏ

Somewhere near the Southwestern United States and
Mexico Border
One Year Ago

"THE TETHER IS SECURE. WE'RE CLEAR TO EGRESS TO THE ENTRANCE."

"Copy, J." M slid slowly across the tether under the power of the water jets on the mockup suits. He landed against the hull with a muted *thud* as his boots made contact with the ceramic composite hull just above the large three-meter-diameter hotel window. He quickly attached another tether to a handhold to keep himself in place, realizing that his maneuvering in space would be much more uncontrollable as there would be no water viscosity to slow his movements and reaction forces. "Removing outer casing cover and setting the hull-clamp."

"Good, M," J said while doing his best not to be distracted by the bubbles rising from the rear of the mockup space suit's automatic buoyancy compensation device, or ABCD. "We'll have to be careful here or we could explosively decompress the chamber."

"Doesn't matter at that point," M said. "We just won't have any survivors inside the hotel is all."

"Is that a good thing or a bad thing?" V sounded sincere as he tethered himself beside his companions. "I'm just asking, comrade."

"Just a thing," M said. "Initiating impact driver now."

1

M pulled a cover from the metallic device revealing two toggles and one red-light push button like an old-school video game cabinet. The device was approximately eight centimeters thick and twenty centimeters on a side. It was somewhat heavy on Earth and underwater but in space that wouldn't be an issue. In fact, it was more likely that it would be molded in place or bolted to the structure. Inside the box there were several mechanisms. A tubular U-shaped handle protruded from the middle of it, large enough to get a space-suit gauntlet around.

"Firing." M flipped both toggles and then hit the red push button. Four spring-loaded pitons fired simultaneously inward into the handle mechanism, releasing the box from the ceramic and aluminum layers of the airlock door, generating a slight surge in the water around it. "J, ready to blow the hatch mechanisms."

"Copy," J replied. He'd already placed the charges in the predetermined critical points along the periphery of the Davidson-Schwab Inflatable Hotel Module—DSIHM—airlock door and was ready. The door was almost two meters in diameter and had been designed for egress and ingress of Orlan space suits. If it explosively decompressed it could kill them instantly from impact. "Stand clear. Three, two, one."

Pop!

"Okay, ready to pull the hatch to the DSIHM airlock," J instructed.

"Okay in three, two, one!" M said, giving the handle on the interior door a twist and then pushing against it with his jets in the forward position. He pushed until he felt it give and then the hatch let loose, releasing large air bubbles from a trapped air pocket inside. The bubbles floated out and upward to the surface of the large rock quarry. Once the hatch was blown clear, he hit his mockup thrusters and entered feetfirst, waiting for his boots to make contact with the bulkhead nearest him. He fired a burst from the modified underwater pseudo-recoilless paintball gun at a mannequin just inside the airlock compartment, hitting it in the chest with a blue spatter. He quickly tethered off to the main entrance hatch.

"Interior breached. Seal off the outer hatch!" M said.

"Got it." V thrusted into place slowly and sealed the hatch with a metallic *thunk* that was muted due to them being underwater. Had they been in space it would have been silent.

"Okay, at this point, either the door to Node three is opened from the inside, or it isn't," M said. "Either way, we're going in. J, while we secure the platform start installing the launcher and secure the warheads to the DSIHM bulkheads."

"Copy that," J replied.

"Command? K? Initiate the startup sequences for the launcher and begin the restart of the platform systems."

"Roger that, M. Initiating the launcher startup sequences. Let me know once they are installed on the DSIHM exterior," S replied.

"Copy, M. Platform computer system restarting...now." K said.

"Good..." M waved V and J into the now open platform hatch.

"Take the hill?" V asked.

"Take the hill," M said.

CHAPTER 1

ۈ

Undisclosed Location
Southern Russia Border
Tuesday (Present Day)
1:03 A.M. Coordinated Universal Time
6:03 A.M. Local

COLONEL VLADIMIR LYTOKOV SQUINTED A BIT AS THE RISING SUN glared against the windshield, exacerbating the mild hangover he was struggling with. The oranges and reds were beginning to spread across the sky and shine over the tops of the taller birch and pine trees along the ridge ahead of them. He reached in his shirt pocket for his sunglasses and fumbled with them as the vehicle bounced like a kicking mule, almost dropping them twice before he could get them in place. A brief memory of his days flying MiGs flashed in his mind, but the fighters had never made him nauseous. Vladimir had spent more than seven thousand hours in the Mikoyan and Gurevich creations including his favorite, the MiG-35. He'd done bombing runs over most of the former southern Soviet states and even been a test pilot with the MiG-41 program. He'd been through high-gee maneuvers, flat spins, and had to punch out on three different occasions. Even the concussion he'd gotten from the latter was no match for his current hangover. But, it was only a "mild one."

Vladimir swallowed the lump in his throat, drawing a smirk

from his subordinate seated in the driver's position. He choked back a retort along with the bile rising in his esophagus. His face was oily and covered with a light sheen of sweat. He white-knuckled the armrest briefly before massaging the bridge of his very Russian nose and then placing the shades on. The lenses powered on and quickly adjusted the tint until the optical recognition chip saw his squint wrinkles relax and his pupils adjust to normal. Vladimir could hear the *ding-dong* doorbell sound telling him that the glasses had made the local connection with the audio implant behind his ear. The heads-up display, or HUD, window view through the virtual glasses would kick on if there was any important information for him to see. There was.

The MZKT-79221 mobile transporter erector launcher—"TEL" rhyming with Hell, as the Americans had coined it—was one of the most rugged, versatile, and capable vehicles on the planet. If there was such a thing as being more of a "tank" than an actual tank, the TEL was it. A history that had turned out to be the ultimate battle of strategic wits, a chess match of warfare and super technologies, had forced the vehicle into being. Decades of Cold War pressures to technologically and militarily overpower the Americans had forced an environment where pure and simple Russian, hard-nosed, devil in the details, bang on it until you make it work or go to the gulag, rocket science and engineering had led to a solution that worked, and worked well—in fact, worked better than any other system similar to it on the planet.

The sixteen-wheeled vehicle rolled through the rough terrain across the uneven hillside so close to the southeastern-most Russian border near northeastern Oral, Kazakhstan, that at times Vladimir wondered if half the truck wasn't across the mostly imaginary country borderline creating imminent diplomatic issues with what was left of NATO, the World Security Council, the Ukrainians, the Europeans, the Kazakhstanis, and, mostly, the Americans. But Vladimir didn't care. He had a job to do and he was going to do it come Hell or winter blizzards—fortunately, spring was approaching and most of the snow had melted.

The TEL plowed over saplings of ash, pine, and maple trees along the way, tearing such a large path in the greenery that, if anyone were looking, one could compare their path to borders on the map. Most certainly the Americans were looking, or at least they would be in about nine minutes and thirty seconds.

Of course, it was all a show for the United Nations Security Council. The Russian president had for more than a decade been posturing and showing off the nation's military might, especially their nuclear one, and the MZKT-79221, with a Topol-M on it at the southern border for all the world's spy satellites to see, was the ultimate flexing of those muscles. The Russian president had made a show of making comments about placing the missiles in Canada, but that was certainly show. That would be as bad or worse than the Cuban Missile Crisis.

The Topol-M had no need of being deployed in Canada. From the TEL, the Topol-M could hit anywhere in the world undeterred in about thirty-two minutes or less if so desired. Vladimir and his crew were simply playing a part on the global diplomatic and strategic stage.

His team was just one of many across the country posturing and, for all intents and purposes, vainly showing off. Vladimir also knew from intelligence briefings that the Chinese Communist Party (CCP) was doing exactly the same thing and only "sort of" hiding what they were doing. They weren't moving TELs. Instead, they were building launch sites for the Deng Fong rockets that could go orbital and carry nuclear weapons. The world was becoming more and more dangerously close to the threat of something bad.

The current showing of military might on the world stage was more heated than it had ever been during the Cold War era, and the only thing keeping the world from the brink of nuclear war was the fact that all the world liked having "stuff" and doing "things." From the old guard Soviet KGB that was still secretly running Russia to the CCP, all of the current figureheads enjoyed their lives of luxury too much for the lean times of global war. But that type of world peace, Vladimir knew, was a threadbare tapestry—and one only needed to know which thread to pull to unravel it.

Vladimir checked his watch and noted the time and relaxed as best he could while being thrown around in his seat against the restraints. He had to gulp down the lump in his throat, again. While the MZKT-79221 was a marvel of Russian engineering it was also a testament to the Russians having little care for creature comforts. The ride was rough as hell and then some. There was no comfort to be had.

They didn't need to be caught over the border by a spy satellite photo that could be embarrassing for the Kremlin, at least those were their standing orders. Kazakhstan was its own sovereign country with its own demarcated and established borders. But as far as the Russian government was concerned it was still a part of the empire that might have to be "reintegrated" back into the homeland someday and therefore the Russian president had told them to "push the boundaries to the edge of unclassified GLONASS positioning capabilities." That was a farce, he knew. The Russian Global Navigation Satellite System was just as capable as anything the American Gobal Positioning System satellites could do. GLONASS could put the TEL within a meter of where it needed to be. But, diplomatically, one could always argue loss of satellite connectivity. They might get away with as much as a kilometer across the border—the key word being "might."

As far as Vladimir was concerned there was little that would stop the Russian military in an all-out war, perhaps not even the Americans and CCP combined. But there was no chance the Chinese would align with the West. They'd damn near toppled them economically during the first pandemic invasion. No, there was little might that could stand against Mother Russia.

The RT-2PM2 Topol-M nuclear missile sitting behind him was a testament to his sentiment. The missile itself was a brilliant piece of Russian rocketry and the reentry vehicles and single warhead—treaty allowed them to carry only one—couldn't be targeted by American antiballistic missile defense systems, at least not as far as any intelligence briefings had said. The Topol-M was state of the art more than a decade prior and was still unrivaled by any other nation and yet the Russian military had produced an even better one, the RS-28 Sarmat "heavy," which had recently just replaced the R-36M the Americans called "Satan." This new one was often referred to as the "Satan-2." The fact that an ICBM more threatening to the Americans than "Satan" himself was being deployed excited him. Vladimir really hoped to get a close up look at one of them someday. Someday, soon.

But for now, the mobile TEL and the Topol-M were impressive enough. The ninety-foot-long hunter green diesel truck rolled and bounced unhindered by anything in its path. Directly behind them rolled the Launch and Mission Command Center vehicle. Several other vehicles also made up the convoy. The security detail vehicles behind, to the sides on each flank, and far out in front kept precise formation around the TEL and Command vehicles. The squad of Russian specialists and officers were well trained and patriotically driven to do their jobs as well as any soldiers on the planet.

Vladimir appreciated that and respected it. In decades past the TEL would have been housed in a special facility and only brought out during times of show or potential world crisis, but the last few years had brought back the Cold War style of preparedness. The missiles were moved about, some hidden, and some in plain sight, just to keep the Westerners on edge. At the moment they weren't the only ones driving nuclear weapons about the Russian countryside and borders.

"Take it easy on the pedal, Pyotr." Colonel Vladimir Lytokov looked at his young junior sergeant and smiled. "We are way ahead of schedule, comrade."

"I would think such a decorated MiG pilot as yourself wouldn't be so, uh, unsettled by a little truck ride, Colonel." The junior sergeant smiled and goosed the throttle of the TEL purposefully. The noncommissioned members of the unit had likely heard of the drinking binge the officers had been at the night before.

"MiGs typically do not have six one-hundred-and-twenty-kiloton warheads strapped to them. And they ride much more smoothly." He smiled sardonically.

"One. Colonel," Pyotr replied.

"Begging your pardon, Junior Sergeant?"

"MiGs typically do not have one five-hundred-and-fifty-kiloton warhead strapped to them." Pyotr flashed a smile at the colonel. "Treaty only allows for one warhead, sir."

"You keep believing that, Pyotr. Of course, there is only one warhead on our missile back there. Just one." Vladimir smiled back at either the naivete or excellent security training of the young soldier. Not only were there six warheads that would yield over one-hundred-and-twenty-kiloton explosions each as payload of the missile, Vladimir also knew that the missile was loaded with decoys, chaff, and radar flares. Indeed, their cargo was the full-up and ready-for-a-hot-war real deal. Whether NATO or the United Nations Security Council knew this was a whole other matter. And unless the Americans had invented some sort of magic, all the spy satellite photos were going to tell them was that the TEL was in the location as laid out by the treaties and that it was likely a standard Topol-M. The Americans called it an SS27. He had also heard it referred to as a "Sickle-B" in the counterintel briefings.

"Two minutes to GLONASS coordinates, Pyotr. You can slow down." Vladimir double-checked the readout on the Russian Global Navigation Satellite System and compared it to the American satellite orbital tracking information. Both pieces of data were extremely classified yet the Russians and the Americans knew them whether they wanted to admit that or not.

"Standard approach and setup, Colonel?" the junior sergeant asked.

"Affirmative."

"Very well."

Vladimir held the armrest of his seat tightly and closed his eyes for the remaining two minutes of the drive. Once he felt the engine throttling down, he breathed a sigh of relief. The TEL rolled to a stop on nearly level ground by a small stream and an outcropping of pine trees nearly twenty meters tall. He rolled the window down and cautiously scanned the terrain and only briefly glanced down at their coordinates. They were right where they were supposed to be.

"This is good, Pyotr. Level the rig and lock it down. Have the convoy close in and I want all the troops outside their vehicles for the satellite images so they can get a full head count in the spy satellite images. We should all smile big for the Americans, yes?"

"Yes, Colonel." Pyotr smiled in response. "You would think we would want our missile locations a secret from our enemy."

"We must hide some of them in plain sight so they can count them. The treaties only allow so many. We must show them those are all that we have. It is a cautious balance of peace," Vladimir explained. "Now get to work."

"Yes, Colonel. But I still don't think it makes any sense." Pyotr shrugged as he moved to the back of the rig to start the leveling procedures as if they were actually going to launch the missile.

"Me either, my friend. The peaceful balance is just an appearance that keeps the world calm." Vladimir knew that of course there were other missiles unaccounted for. After he'd left the test pilot program and became part of the Strategic Rocket Forces of the Russian Federation he had been briefed into the various strategies of the homeland's nuclear arsenal. He was well versed in the details of those missiles that the world knew about—and those it didn't. The garages that were built for the TELs were never empty even when "all" the TELs were deployed out in the open. "We must keep up appearances."

The six other vehicles had closed in ranks and the men had filtered out of them, taking up casual positions about the missile TEL; several of them had lit cigarettes. Vladimir had decided to pull his thermos from within the vehicle and leaned on the back of the TEL beside Pyotr, having a cup of extremely black and bitter French roast coffee that had just a hint of vodka smell mixed in. He couldn't remember if he'd held a bottle of Kahlua anywhere near the thermos or not, but it was as close a rendition to a hot "Black Russian" as he cared for.

"'Hair of the dog,' you Americans would say," he whispered to himself as he toasted the sky with the thermos cup.

The availability of goods in the present, post-pandemic but pre-next-pandemic "world economy" at least still managed to have some positive benefits despite all the global supply chain issues. Coffee had never been in shortage that he knew of. The aroma, heat, and the bitterness on his tongue were enough of a sensation to bring his mind close to fully awake. There was just enough alcohol to calm his nerves. He wasn't really a morning person and, after nearly thirty years in the military, he'd become dependent on coffee's bitter pick-me-up to make it through them. He'd only recently added the vodka. In the earlier days, the blend was a very sad and strong version of coffee that was whatever the Russian economy allowed. The world had changed. It had only been the last few years where he had become a fan of the stronger French roast. The brand of vodka didn't matter. As far as he was concerned, vodka was vodka. Cognac, on the other hand, well, that required more of a delicate choosing. But cognac wasn't for hair of the dog; it was for more special occasions. He sipped the coffee as the countdown timer in the virtual view of his sunglasses continued toward zero.

"Everybody smile for the Americans," Vladimir said as he held his cup upward again as if toasting the spy satellite. "What is it they say?"

"Cheese, Colonel." Pyotr laughed with him. "They say 'cheese.'"

"Ah, yes. Ha-ha. Say 'cheese,' my friends." He let out a very fake laugh and acted as if he were looking at his wristwatch for the timing of the satellite flyover for his troops to see. The countdown timer in his virtual glasses continued to tick downward.

There would just be a couple of minutes longer until the American spy satellite pass was over. He lit himself a cigarette to pass the time and to go with the coffee mixture. They just might get him through the morning, he thought. The stopwatch timer on his wristwatch counted down from twenty seconds and then beeped the last three as he counted them. "... and three, two, one! We should be out of their prying view now. We can rest here for a few minutes and then prepare to move to the next location."

Vladimir purposefully reset his wristwatch for all the team to see and then turned to the young junior sergeant as the countdown in his virtual glasses approached zero. He smiled at the man and gave him a nod. "Good job, Pyotr."

"Thank you, Colonel, I, uh—" The Russian soldier stopped midsentence and looked at his chest as red flowed across the uniform; he slumped and fell forward to his knees into the colonel. The *schzipp, schzipp* of suppressed rifle fire continued. Three of the men to his right were hit in the head almost simultaneously by very-large-caliber rounds practically tearing out the backs of their skulls, flinging gray matter and bright red blood across the hunter green truck behind them.

"Fifty caliber—" One of the soldiers didn't finish before being hit.

Vladimir dropped to the ground and crawled up underneath the truck as the previously silent sniper fire either became, or was supplemented with, automatic weapons fire. The clear sound of 5.56 by 45 millimeter rounds being fired from the distance was unmistakable. The *ping*ing of rounds against the heavily armored TEL and flying rocks and dirt around them gave Vladimir the impression that there was little intention of the attackers to leave behind any survivors.

"NATO rounds, Colonel!" one of the soldiers said. "Americans here?"

"I doubt it." Vladimir grunted while doing his best to crawl to cover as close to the truck as he could manage. "NATO, Russian, Chinese, doesn't matter if it hits you! Get down!"

The remaining convoy soldiers took cover behind the vehicles and scrambled for their weapons. One of the men crawled beneath the vehicle adjacent to them and began returning fire rapidly.

Vladimir worked his way to the opposite side of the TEL and knelt against the giant wheels in cover position. Two of the other soldiers dove in beside him.

"What is happening, Colonel?" one of them asked. Vladimir could see the man's hands shaking so fast that he couldn't hold his pistol.

"Clearly, we are under attack," Vladimir said nonchalantly over the cigarette stuck in the corner of his mouth. He took a last draw from it, tossed it aside, brought his pistol up to chamber a round, held it up and around the edge of the TEL's rearmost wheel, and fired twice in the general direction of the incoming fire. Several rounds dug up the ground near him, startling him to the point that he lost his footing, his left bootlace entangled itself with some of the underbrush, and he fell over backward clumsily.

"Colonel! Are you hit?"

"No. Return fire, men!" he ordered as he regained his composure and scrambled for cover once more.

"Good shot, Amir. The rest of you move in on the flanks now before they decide to start really shooting back," Michael Tarin subvocalized on his throat mic. "I'll take the package. Jamal, you're with me."

Several of the mercenary team members moved in from the hillside through the trees nearest the forward vehicles. Several AK-47 bursts tore dirt up around them and threw splinters from the maple and fir trees near them, but it was clear that the inexperienced soldiers firing back in their direction were only firing scared and randomly from under their cover positions. They were not even shooting at specific targets. Michael heard four single shots fired to his right. Then the action settled. It would be a shame what they had to do next. But it had to be done for the bigger picture.

"Clear west."

"Good work, Overtund. Hold the position. Amir, shots as available."

"Of course," Amir said. He heard the wet slapping sound of the high-caliber sniper round impacting a body. The sniper was very good at his job and certainly had come to grips with any moral questions as to what he did. "That is another one."

"Jamal, let's get on with this." He moved to the front side of the TEL, taking cover behind one of the giant wheels on the opposite side of the soldiers who had previously fired at him. Automatic weapons fire continued as fast as the soldiers could reload and the Russians continued to randomly spray the ground and trees nearby, not even getting close to one of them. "Stupid kids aren't even getting in the ballpark. Such a shame to do this. Shit, a job's a job. Eyes on the prize."

"They're tucked in behind the truck, Michael. I have no shots," Amir said.

"Grenade?" Jamal tapped at the bandolier on his webbing where the grenades were attached. He fingered the pull-pin on one of them.

"Are you actually being serious right now?" Michael whispered. "You do see the nuke, right? This big missile-looking thing right over our heads?"

"Just sayin'..." Jamal frowned. He was clearly disappointed.

"Just keep my backside clear. And, I'm serious about this, no grenades!" Just as the words came from his mouth several rounds dug into the tire and dirt around them. Dirt flew up with each impact and white-hot sparks showered into his face, startling him more than they stung. Michael hugged the wheel even closer. "Shit! Sandy! Taking fire from the east! Where the hell are you?"

"Right where I am supposed to be," a female voice said over the comm channel as Michael searched the hillside for her. Finally, he could see the bright auburn color of her hair whipping about in the morning sunlight. The Ukrainian mercenary seemed to have appeared from nowhere, moving like a blur, wielding a bladed weapon in one hand that glinted furiously as she slashed it about and an AR platform pistol in the other that was firing in controlled bursts. The muzzle flashes were still visible in the morning light. Michael heard several other shots but not in his direction. Then Sandy dove for cover as someone laid down cover fire from the other side of the TEL.

"A little help, gentlemen?" she said calmly and very properly. "There seems to be someone impeding my progress."

"Go, now!" Michael nodded westward in the direction of the front of the truck to Jamal. "I'll go east."

The two of them went in opposite directions about the giant vehicle, M4 carbines in the ready positions. Michael turned the corner underneath the nozzle end of the missile TEL with his back against it. He was starting to sweat underneath his body armor even though it was so cold that he could see his breath. The sound of the cover fire was deafening as the barrel of an AK-47 protruded from the edge of one of the giant wheels just inches from his head. He covered his ears and waited for the shooter to release the trigger and then ducked under it, slamming the muzzle upward with his M4 and at point blank pulling and placing his Colt 1911 .45 automatic pistol in the young soldier's sternum, releasing two rounds. The soldier, not wearing body armor, was down almost immediately and bleeding out if he wasn't already dead.

Jamal was there just in time, dropping a second soldier from behind. The hillside was suddenly quiet again. Michael scanned about at the bodies of the soldiers nearby. There was no further movement. The countdown clock on his sunglasses showed one minute and thirty-seven seconds and counting upward.

"Report."

"Clear West. The Command vehicle is ours," Sandy said.

"Clear East."

"Talk to me, Amir." He hoped his sniper in place at the hilltop had a clear view of the sight.

"I'm getting no further motion. Hilltop is ours."

"Alright, bring in the vehicles and let's get to work." Michael nodded at Jamal. "Go. I'll start here."

"Right." Jamal grunted and turned up the hill in a light jog.

"So, where was your officer?" Michael kicked gently against one of the soldiers lying lifelessly on the ground. Kneeling down beside the young soldier he started rummaging through his pockets for any paperwork, when suddenly a barrel of a Makarov pistol pressed against the base of his skull. Michael couldn't believe he'd been so careless.

"Don't move!" a frightened voice ordered him. Michael slightly turned his head enough to see from his peripheral vision that it was one of the troops he'd assumed was dead. He did his best to stretch his neck to get a better view but the Makarov dug painfully deeper at the base of his skull. He could feel it shaking against him and was sure it wasn't due to the cold. "I said don't move or I will shoot!"

Bang!

Michael almost pissed in his tactical pants as the Russian soldier's body fell limp to the ground beside him. Most of the front of his forehead had been blown out. The ground started to turn red around the soldier. Michael looked away and turned, placing his hand on his 1911.

"Take it easy, comrade." Vladimir stood with his own Makarov pointing upward at the sky. Smoke still swirled from the muzzle. Vladimir blew on the end of the barrel, making a deep flute sound, and then holstered it. "You are getting careless, my friend."

"Jesus, Vlad! You scared the shit out of me." Michael accepted his friend's hand up and reached into his pocket for his smartphone. He fingered at it for a second, looking over blueprints and instructions. He tossed them up to his glasses' view. "We've got to disconnect the tracking system and get moving."

"Relax, Michael. I estimate we have an hour or so before anybody even expects a call in from us. I will make that call and tell them all is well. From there, we'll have another four to five hours before another check-in. We have enough time." Vladimir leaned down and picked up the thermos he'd dropped at the beginning of all the ruckus. He brushed it off and filled the top with some of the coffee and vodka mix. He took a long swill from the cup and sat it on the TEL near one of the large tires. Then he slipped a pack of cigarettes from his shirt pocket and tapped one out, pulling it the rest of the way out with his lips. He offered Michael one. "Yes?"

"You know I don't smoke."

"I keep hoping, one day." Vladimir laughed. "About now, I'd think, we should look up."

"What?"

"Look up." Vlad pointed up and southward. The countdown clock in his glasses reached zero. There was just enough light that only Venus and the Moon were still visible in the sky, but then a very bright star began moving across the sky, getting brighter the closer it got to directly overhead.

"Right." Michael smiled and patted the Russian missile TEL. "Let's get this baby moving."

CHAPTER 2

੭੭

Low Earth Orbit
Approximately 400 Kilometers Above Southern Russia
International Space Station
Tuesday
2:07 A.M. Coordinated Universal Time

"HEY, THERE IS SIBERIA, ALLISON." DR. PETER SOLMONOV WAVED to the Earth below as it passed underneath. Allison laughed and waved as well. "I used to live there, you know."

"I seem to recall you mentioning that about ninety minutes ago, Peter," United States Space Force Major Allison Simms replied. "Our next orbit will be farther east so you'll have to wait a while to tell me again."

"You should be right over it now," Royal Canadian Navy captain Teri Yancy, their Canadian mission commander, interrupted their conversation.

"Uh, roger that, Teri." Allison backed off on the jets from her extra-vehicular activity suit. The manuals called the suit a Simplified Aid for EVA Rescue Extravehicular Mobility Unit, but the astronauts called it either a SAFER EMU or simply a "jetpack."

"I can see gas venting." Peter stopped his jetpack thrusters and tethered himself close to the leak. Then he reached up and took Allison's tether as she closed the distance. "It is bigger than we thought. I am not so sure it was just a micrometeorite."

17

"Yeah, from the looks of it, I'd say we hit some debris the size of a washer or small bolt." Allison reached to her belt level harness and detached the long pack there. "This is gonna be at least a Type II patch, boss."

"You're going to have to get to it from there because it is behind a bulkhead in here. No way to get to it," Commander Yancy told them.

"Allison, I'll take the prep kit. You prepare the gun." Peter reached toward her to take the patch kit package from her.

"Type II."

"Yes, at least," he agreed with her.

"Mission Control, you copy that? Type II fix up here," Yancy repeated.

"Roger that, ISS. Go for Type II repair."

"Looks like it went clean through the outer hull into the multilayer insulation and kept on going. We're still venting, it appears. That would explain the overtaxed environmental systems alerts," Solmonov said without attempting to look up at Allison. She watched him out of the corner of her eyes as she prepared the patch injector gun.

"Yes, I see. Prepare the cover plate while I prep the gun."

"Copy that, Major. Prepping the Type II cover plate."

The patch kit was the latest version developed in Huntsville, Alabama, by some graduate students at the local university and one of the many aerospace and defense firms there. Versions of the kit had been deployed since the very first module of the International Space Station was launched into orbit, but the kit had evolved dramatically over the years—and so had the space station, for that matter. The modern-era patch gun looked more like a fancy caulking gun crossed with a ray gun from old science fiction movies than it did anything else. In cases where the damage wasn't all the way through the hull, forcing the environmental system to work overtime, the robot "Dextre III" could be slid into place to fix the damage. But with an extremely critical commodity, oxygen, leaking out into space, astronauts and cosmonauts were the quickest repair approach. And the human component of the crew had yet to completely trust a robot to keep their precious oxygen in place when it didn't breathe. The robot was only motivated by software, whereas the humans, well, they were motivated by something much more imperative. Besides, it took hours to place the robot where it would need to be for such repairs. By then, the amount of oxygen leaked would be critical.

"Cover plate is ready, Allison." Peter carefully pressed the ten-centimeter-diameter clear spaceglass plate over the venting hole.

The plate had an aerospace-rated 7075-T6 tempered aluminum ring on the outer circumference, about three times thicker than the spaceglass. Once Peter pressed it against the hull of the space station it looked like a raised glass portal one might see on a naval vessel—but there was one slight difference. The portal-looking fixture also had a nipple valve located on the aluminum ring. The nipple was there to attach the glue gun to, but not until the cover plate was bolted down.

"Plate is in a good position, yes?" Peter asked her.

"Yes." She used the glue gun to fill the first pilot hole on the ring with the space adhesive. "Preparing screw gun for hole one."

Allison let the glue gun dangle from its tether and then pulled the screw gun from the magnetic mount on her hip. She tapped the screw-load button on the side and then placed the tip of the space-rated sheet-metal screw into the pilot hole on the aluminum ring. She held the gun in place carefully as it started spinning the screw. She could feel it bite into the outer hull surface of the space station and then the torque limiter on the screw gun stopped the spinning. The adhesive expanded around the screwhead and then hardened quickly. There was no time for dilly-dallying around with that adhesive.

"Preparing hole two . . ." she said.

"Plate is secure, Peter." Finally, the cover plate was secured with screws to the ISS and Dr. Solmonov could take his hands off. There were still safety straps in place. Astronaut hands were a tertiary safety protocol.

"Great, Allison, I was beginning to grow tired." He laughed. "Ready to remove the fill cover, yes?"

"Yes." Allison waited as he pulled the tab that would activate the fill valve. She realized that she had nodded inside the helmet, but at the angle Peter was from her it was unlikely he saw the gesture.

"Valve is active," Peter stated.

"Roger that." Allison snapped the end of the glue gun onto the valve's nipple fitting, applying pressure with her right hand until it locked into place with a good solid clicking feel—there was no sound. She then used her left hand on the threaded fastener and turned the locking ring to hold the glue gun in place on the nipple fitting. She twisted the fitting, as the manual said to "hand tight," which she had done many times. Once the gun was snapped tight to the nipple she then triggered the locking mechanism that would keep it from being blown loose from overpressure.

"Is Type II patch plate nipple securely fastened to the glue gun assembly, Allison?" Peter asked, reading from the checklist that was up on both of their helmet visor heads-up displays.

"Glue gun connected, sealed 'hand tight,' and locked."

"Check. Proceed with glue injection."

"Here we go."

Allison squeezed the trigger of the gun, releasing the gas pressure from the canister of stored accelerant into the piston that forced the glue from the disposable tube. The bluish-white glue began to fill the volume underneath the cover plate with pressure greater than the outgassing and leaking air. She held the trigger until the red light turned green, indicating that an overpressure was forcing the sealant into the bulkhead hole. The indicator began blinking green and the glue stopped flowing into the patch volume.

"Patch volume filled."

"Prepare for glue gun assembly detachment," Peter read aloud.

"Disconnecting the gun. Hole appears to be patched. How does it look from inside?" she asked over the comm line.

"Copy that, Allison," Commander Yancy replied. "The gauge has stopped spinning. Looks like that did it."

"Great. What next?"

"That's it, you two. Dextre can handle the rest for today. Besides, you need to get inside and finish your sleep cycles. We'll have to get up early and prep for docking. We've got that space tourist tagging along behind us that's been waiting to dock since the repair procedure started."

"Tourists," Allison grunted with disdain. "Peter, I believe your people would sell tickets to Armageddon."

"Not sure what you mean, Allison; space tourism helps keep us all in jobs." From his tone of voice, Allison could tell he didn't get the humor.

"Sarcasm, Peter."

"Ah, Americans and sarcasm," he said. Allison could imagine the shrug he was making inside his suit. "And, that isn't such a bad idea. I'm sure we could charge very much for front row seats to the end of times. Maybe the view of Armageddon from space would be a premium ticket?"

"Yeah, but then where would you spend the money?"

"Pesky details. You Americans are always concerned with such details."

"Soyuz, you are go for docking procedure," Commander Yancy announced over the interlink between the ISS and the manned space capsule a few thousand meters below them.

"Copy that, Alpha. Go for docking procedure." The thick Russian accent from the cosmonaut was unmistakable.

"LIDAR and Image Automated Guidance Systems are handing off, now, now, now." Yancy said.

"LIAGS handoff is in the green, approaching now."

Allison floated motionlessly watching the screen in front of her as the Soyuz capsule connected itself to the ISS. The Russian cosmonauts had been doing that for more than three decades and had become quite good at it. Well, she knew that nowadays the procedure was ninety-nine percent automated and controlled by a computer, but nevertheless, it was still always an impressive and exciting procedure to watch. She could only imagine what it must have been like for the first astronauts in the previous century flying the craft and docking them by hand. That had to be an adrenaline rush.

She could feel the module clanking into place with the Docking and Storage Module just beneath the Control Module and then she could feel the hatches opening and the valves regulating and equalizing the pressures between the vehicle and the station.

"You coming, comrade?" Solmonov nudged her as he floated by. Calling her "comrade" had been a running joke of theirs for the more than two months that they'd been on board together. The two of them had trained together both in Houston and in Kazakhstan. They had known each other for years.

"I'm right behind you, cowboy." She pushed off her console to give her momentum in the direction of the Control Module.

"Always fun to see the newcomers," Solmonov said over his

shoulder at her as they made their way to the opening of the hatch into the Docking and Storage Module in the Russian part of the space station. It took them several more minutes to equalize the air lock, remove the SAFER EMUs and stow them, and then ingress into the normal interior of the ISS for the second time in the past seven hours. Following the initial patch procedure, they had cycled back in and finished a few hours of their sleep cycles. By the time they were awakened there was a scheduled electrical repair on one of the Russian solar panels. That EVA had taken the better part of the morning before the trailing cosmonauts could approach and dock.

Once the repair had been completed and Solmonov and Simms had locked back in, their approach began. Allison and Peter then had to remove and stow the jetpacks and suits, remove the liquid cooling garments, get dressed, and then head down to the docking module. By the time they got there, Yancy was already greeting the new crew of two and the one space tourist.

"I'm Mission Commander Teri Yancy—people usually just call me 'Teri' or 'Yance' or I'll also answer to 'Commander.'" She smiled while shaking the new crew members' hands one by one as they floated through the hatch into the Control Module. "Aha, this is Dr. Peter Solmonov and Major Allison Simms."

"Greetings," Solmonov said while making the Vulcan hand gesture for "live long and prosper."

"Don't mind him. Not only is he a total cliché, he's also a big nerd." Allison held out a hand to shake with the first person who passed the commander.

The Soyuz commander and pilot introduced his crew. Of course, they all knew who was coming and what their jobs would be, but tradition was to make introductions to the commander of the station upon entry.

"Pilot-Cosmonaut Vasiliy Nolvany, Russian Federation. Nice to meet you, Major Simms. Allow me to introduce U.S. Space Force Captain Ramy Alexander." He paused and then motioned to a man wearing some sort of active glasses that were clearly holding his attention. Allison recognized the billionaire from social media and news vids.

"And this is Dr. Karl van der Schwab of Austria. I'm not sure you'd say he's a space tourist, more like a space entrepreneur with some interesting experiments he plans to oversee and consult on.

Plus, he's the partner-owner of the Davidson-Schwab Inflatable Hotel Module attached to Node 3, which I'm most certain you already know."

"Can someone please show us our personal spaces, please?" Dr. Schwab asked. "I'm anxious to see my hotel room."

"Captain Alexander." Major Simms returned the salute to her fellow service member. "Great to have another Guardian up here."

"Yes, ma'am."

"Unless we're on open channels with command, 'Allison' is fine."

"Understood, Major—uh, Allison. I'm Tom."

"Tom?"

"My middle name, ma'am. My father's name was Ramy and to avoid the confusion or being called 'Little Ramy' or 'Junior' I've gone by my middle name, Thomas or Tom, all my life," the USSF captain explained. "I explained this to Vasiliy, but you know Russians and their rank formalities."

"No, probably just Vasiliy messing with you. He was captain on my first international mission and almost everything to him was done with designs on a future joke or humor. Just his personality, I guess. Very well, then. Just think, after this mission you're likely to be Major Tom. How about that?" Allison grinned, showing pride in her humor.

"Not the first time I've heard that one, Major." He grimaced at her.

"Right. Maybe I should have ordered you to laugh. Rank does have its privileges." Her smile quickly faded to a smirk and a raised eyebrow. "Let's just get y'all situated and moved in. Shall we?"

CHAPTER 3

ᠺ

Republic of Vanuatu Islands, South Pacific
Tuesday
9:00 P.M. Local Time

KEENAN JAMES INGERSOL SAT IN HIS MODEST ISLAND BEACH HOME,
paying no attention to the beautiful blue ocean waves gently
breaking onto the white sand beach just meters from the full
glass wall overlooking it. The view was stunningly breathtaking.
The sun was beginning to set just over the horizon, casting reds
and oranges in a brilliant display of colors that would generally
impress almost any onlooker. Not Keenan.

Keenan wasn't really excited about the beach life although he
had to admit the occasional people-watching opportunities were
interesting. The island he lived on was very sparsely populated,
but every now and then some visitors to the resort a kilometer
down the beach would wander by. Most of the times the wander-
ers were fully nude. Again, that was mildly interesting to Keenan.
But he really didn't care for the beach. And there was nothing
he'd see walking down the beach that he couldn't find online.

What he did care for was that the Republic of Vanuatu Islands
had no extradition treaties with the United States of America.
After he'd had to make a fast exit from South Texas between El
Paso and Las Cruces, New Mexico, where he used to live, he'd
bounced around the globe until he managed to make it to the

islands. It had taken him the better part of the past year, with help from some friends, to rebuild his computer system and his hacking infrastructure from the middle of nowhere in the South Pacific Ocean. But his work was important and his friends needed him for things that only he could do and, so, they kept him funded as needed.

Keenan had been staring at the various computer screens for more than thirty-six hours, using every trick he knew to hack into the mainframe system at the 33rd Guards Rocket Army Headquarters in Omsk, Russia. With some help from a Russian insider, he'd managed to find a backdoor through the security firewalls. But finding what he'd been looking for was the hardest part. Mainly because he didn't speak Russian, though he could read it some. That made his job harder. Almost with every command input he'd had to run a translator program. That slowed his progress tremendously. So, he'd ended up modifying one of his standard artificial intelligence dictionary search programs to interact with the translator program to speed up the process. After all, data was data no matter what language it was in. And nobody but nobody could keep data from Keenan.

And finally, there it was. RT-2PM Topol and RS-24 Yars maintenance records, manuals, and videos. There were others there, including the Sarmat missiles and the R-36M2 silo-based systems. There were records for TEL movements and plans that were all highly classified. He'd hit the mother lode. His friends were going to pay millions for the data he'd just mined.

Working as swiftly as he could, Keenan started downloading the files through multiple dummy IP addresses and nodes to multiple virtual server locations that only he had access to. While the more mundane files, like repair manuals for a nuclear missile, downloaded, he poked around for anything that looked like something a little more fun. He found a personnel roster that might come in handy in some future endeavor. There were some data files with personal information of some of the troops that might also be worth something to somebody someday. But other than day-to-day military information and things that only people interested in geopolitical intrigue would care about, he found nothing exciting. There was one file marked with the Russian equivalent of "UFO" that he made a point to download to read through when he was bored.

The download of the files continued for several minutes and then a window popped up on his screen telling him the program was complete. Keenan added a few extra backdoors on his way out so he could come back when he wasn't pressed for time and look about more thoroughly. He then carefully covered his tracks as he disconnected from those particular servers. He stretched and reached for the can of energy drink next to his mouse, but it was empty. He turned and looked at the glass door fridge a meter from him but there were no more of them there. He looked across his open floorplan to the kitchen area and saw only stacks of bottled water and empty cases of the drink. Delivery to the island without the pandemics affecting the supply chain was slow enough. It might take a month to get more of the drinks if they didn't have them down at the resort.

"Damn it. Better order some more of those." He reached in the minifridge and took out one of the soft drinks there and opened it. "Better than nothing, I guess."

He sat the can down and looked out the window down the beach, partially distracted by a nude couple walking hand in hand, and shook his head.

"If they only knew," he said. Then he tapped the blue-blocking big-lensed glasses he wore, opening up the virtual display. Icons filled his field of view. He tapped the messenger icon and opened it. He quickly typed out a message and sent it to one of his "friends."

> S,
>
> *Here are the manuals and design diagrams you needed located at the link here. Encrypted the same as always. You know the drill. I think this will give you all the information there is on these things. I could use another seven figures of crypto to purchase that processing system we spoke about last time. I hope this gets us to the finish line. Also, I set all the cameras and sensors along the pipeline as per the plan. Please pass that along to M. Tell V, thanks for the assist.*
>
> *You're welcome,*
>
> K

CHAPTER 4

Ꮼ

Russia-Kazakhstan Border
Uzen-Atyrau-Samara Pipeline
Tuesday
1:19 P.M. Local Time

IT HAD TAKEN ALMOST FIVE HOURS TO DISCONNECT THE WARHEADS from the missile, safe them, load them on the trucks, make the drive through the rugged terrain to the pipeline access roads, make contact with the "right" pipeline access security team, and then get through the border and on their way. One of their contacts had hacked through most of the security and street cameras along the way, erasing them as needed and covering their tracks. It was good to know competent people and to have a well-thought-through plan of action.

Michael and Vladimir couldn't have pulled this part of the plan off without the right people—people who were very influential politically, well connected across multiple business avenues, and very rich. It was the right kind of help, in the right ways, at the right times and places that made the plan possible in the end. And this particular part of the plan had been in motion for more than six years. The overall plan, well, that had been in the works since before the first pandemics. In fact, if the pandemics weren't actually part of the plan, they had certainly been useful along the way. But Michael couldn't get an honest answer from his well-placed and connected partners as to whether they had been integral in the pandemics or the plagues had been mere serendipity. Michael didn't believe in coincidences. But he also had a hard time believing in conspiracies, unless they were his.

One of the big benefactors of the plan was a major shareholder in the oil fields of the Russia-China "new silk road" and therefore had unbridled access to the pipelines and the maintenance contracts. That had come in very handy for Michael and Vladimir. As it turned out, they were in actual maintenance trucks with all the right papers and even the yellow flashing caution lights on top whirling about. Not only did they look official, they *were* official, and were supposed to be on the road according to all the pipeline management and security paperwork and software. They truly did have friends in high places.

"We'll have to thank Marcus for building us such a nice road to drive our stolen nuclear warheads on," Vladimir said with a laugh. "It must have cost him millions to build them."

"Six hundred and fifty million American according to a Reuters article I read a few years back. That's only a drop in the bucket for what he spends on election rigging and currency devaluation around the globe," Michael replied from the driver's seat as he kept a wary eye on the side and rearview mirrors. The three chase vehicles with the rest of the team were following closely and, so far, there had been no issues. Michael didn't like issues.

"Indeed," Vladimir responded and added a Russian curse Michael had heard him use before but never quite understood. He figured it was a bit like when he used the MFer-word as a positive adjective. To Russians there was nothing that directly translated the sentiment, and when he used it, they only saw it as a terrible incestuous comment.

"He managed to get Chinese, Russian, and Kazakhstani investors to pay most of the pipeline—that's several billion. He also got the Turks and the Russians to help pay for the port we're headed to. According to *The Economist*, he was in for an undisclosed large amount on that too. I suspect he was in for about a billion U.S. dollars total said and done. I managed to make about seven hundred and eighty thousand on the deal. Helps knowing which politicians are paid off and what companies will get the contracts."

"I could have used this information, my friend." Vladimir grunted disapprovingly. "You know, I like money too."

"I didn't quite know you then," Michael replied. "With hindsight, sure. Sorry."

"Marcus did. I had already been interviewing with his company to be his test pilot. He could have vouched for me," Vladimir said.

"Yeah, I know. He had me and Sandy do your background check. But that didn't mean that I trusted you to help me hide a body."

"Didn't know that." Vladimir shrugged. "And I guess I can see it from your point of view."

"I thought you did."

"Did what?"

"Know that Sandy and I did your background investigation."

"Oh, no. I didn't. No matter." Vladimir waved it off as unimportant.

"So, anyway, I know where all *your* bodies are buried." Michael laughed halfheartedly.

"Not all of them, my friend. Not all." He paused for a dramatic smirk. "And I didn't bury all of them."

"Hahaha." While Michael hadn't truly known him at the time, he did now. He trusted him now and had, in fact, helped him bury a few of those bodies over the past few years. Vladimir was as much of a friend as he'd ever had and was as much in on the plan as he was. Michael also now knew that Vladimir was willing to go all the way to the wall, or die trying, to get to their end goal. Or, as Marcus had often said, "to the beginning."

"Fortune..." Vladimir said almost under his breath, "...favors the bold, comrade."

"Hey, man, no worries. We've got all the fortune in the world in the back of this truck." Michael watched the timer in his virtual glasses telling him that they were currently "on schedule." He didn't like being "on schedule." There were still hundreds of kilometers to go to reach the pipeline junction with the Caspian Pipeline Consortium just north of the northern shore of the Caspian Sea. There it would be a "scheduled" turn to the east to follow that line all the way across the Russian lands between the Caspian Sea and the Black Sea to the oil shipping port at Novorossiysk.

"Yes, my friend, we have the fortune," Vladimir said. "Now it is time to be bold."

"Soon enough, V. Soon enough."

The port where the pipeline hit the Black Sea was where they'd take to water and be less likely to be discovered. The plan was to keep the nukes belowdecks and beneath shielded water tanks on a specially designed high-end yacht until they met up with other means of transportation. Until they got to the water, there was always the chance that somebody might want a peek inside the truck. If that were to happen, well, Michael eyed the M4 sitting next to him and noted the rest of his team in the rearview mirror.

While they were "official" pipeline contractors, there was always the chance Murphy's Law could rear its ugly head. Michael would have preferred to be "ahead of schedule" just in case any nonsense, such as Murphy, got in their damn way and delayed their progress. He wanted to get this part of the plan behind him as soon as possible. They were sitting on the hottest commodity in the world right now and soon everyone on the planet would be looking for them.

"Fortune. Bold. Bah." Vladimir took his shades off and rubbed the bridge of his nose. He took in a long breath, held it for a moment, then exhaled between pursed lips, making a motorboat sound. "I'm more interested in the fun. Life gets... boring, sometimes. I hate boring."

"Well, we have a very, very long drive ahead of us and I, honestly, am hoping to avoid as much 'fun' as possible. 'Fun' wasn't accounted for in the schedule. In case you have forgotten, we have a boat to catch and a whole lot more, which *is* on our schedule. We don't need any 'fun' today. Actually, I hope today turns out to be... boring... as hell. I adore boring." Michael didn't bother to look away from the road as he responded.

Yellow caution lights flashed across the pipeline to the right then to the trees on the left and rotated back again. Knowing that there were six nuclear warheads in the back of the truck made the caution lights almost humorous to him. But now wasn't the time for humor. He checked the schedule clock and the map in his virtual view again almost obsessively and compulsively.

"I suppose in this particular instance, Michael, I agree with you. The fun will start soon enough." Vladimir grinned and nodded. Michael managed to match his colleague with a half-upturned corner of his mouth and a raised eyebrow. He pulled his coffee mug from the cupholder on the dashboard and raised it to his friend. Vladimir followed suit by grabbing his mug.

"To soon enough," Michael said.

"I'll drink to that. Soon enough, my friend." Vladimir sipped from his coffee mug. It was mostly coffee now, which he hoped to soon remedy. "Soon enough."

CHAPTER 5

∾

San Jose, California
Blue World Space Industries
Wednesday
9:00 A.M. Pacific Time

MARCUS JEFFERY DORMAN SAT IN THE CORNER SUITE OF AN ALL-glass exterior walled office atop the Miro hi-rise building. He looked out the side window down at the people scurrying about East Santa Clara Street. The sun was just high enough to cast bright rays of golden light between the alleyways, accentuating the newness of the district. With the new editions to the skyline from the latest multibillion-dollar big tech industries, San Jose was an even bigger hotbed of brainpower than it had been in the previous few decades. Just down the way Marcus could see the edge of Modera San Pedro Square and the top of the Tabard Theatre. Though he preferred the theater at Invicta, he'd helped pay for the Tabard updating and a lot of the recent buildup of the infrastructure for the "Square." After all, the Silicon Valley billionaire had to keep the local politicians happy and show he was an upstanding pillar of the valley community—and the right politics had to be played in order to achieve his endgame goals. Politics always had to be played out and paid for.

Marcus leaned back in his desk chair, staring off into the city, but he was really not paying much attention. The icons floating about in front of him via his active-glass contact lenses and the conversations going on in his ear implants were holding his attention. The contacts acted as a transparent computer monitor that wirelessly connected to the next-generation computing system-slash-phone-slash-gaming console-slash-everything else that would be his next multibillion-dollar connectivity platform—he was tentatively calling it "Moebius" for now. The contacts wouldn't come out with the Moebius platform for many years—at least not in the United States until he managed to pay off the right officials at the Food and Drug Administration and the Federal Communications Commission. The initial system would be able to connect to any wireless monitor, VR style goggles, and the new Moebius Shades that would be another very expensive item everyone would have to have. After he'd made billions from the glasses through several iterative versions—glasses 2.0, glasses 3.0, etc.—then, and only then, would the contact lenses be released. By then, he planned to have permanent lens replacement done to his eyes. But those were still very experimental—even too experimental for him to implement.

For the time being, audio would be through wireless earbuds, but Marcus had plans for the future to sell the implants that he had put in himself and a few close, um "friends," over a year prior just behind his earlobes that gave him always-on wireless audio connectivity to the various information networks available. He thought of them as his personal superpower gadgets for now. And, he could "think" to them to do data searches. He was a killer at trivia games. Once he had the eye implants too, he'd be unstoppable, in more ways than one.

Marcus reached out before him and moved some virtual icons about and then leaned forward to type out a message on the virtual keyboard. So far, the morning had been very mundane and ordinary, but he had high hopes, when suddenly a flashing red notification told him that an encrypted email from the dark web many layers deep in the "Onion" had arrived in his highly encrypted and hidden inbox. He tapped the email open and then input his decryption key. The message was still quite cryptic:

M,

We have the Means, now. Make certain the Method will be available as planned. BTW, nice boat.

Regards,

V

Marcus smiled excitedly and then typed in a response.

V,

All is going as crafted. There is Method to the Madness just waiting for the right person to come along and take it.

M

Marcus leaned back with a very big smile across his face. Those politics he needed were getting closer and closer to being achieved. Within seconds of the email from V, the alert flashed again, showing an encrypted message. Marcus tapped it and thought in his PIN.

M,

Here finally! Settling in. The app you sent me stopped the motion sickness completely, but only while wearing the glasses. Very clever, my friend. I'm compiling the data we need along with crew rosters and such. I may need a hand with some encryption breaking in a bit. Forthcoming. In the meantime, the hotel is in great shape and the mounting brackets can be seen from the window view. Build back better, my friend!

K

Marcus smiled at the way K had used the World Economic Forum's slogan for the Great Reset, as they had called it. They had used the pandemic invasions to destroy most of the world's previous economic systems and usurped over eighty percent of the world's wealth, and therefore, power. Marcus, while a part of the WEF by necessity and design, didn't care a lot for the so-called Party of Davos. But he never let on to them such sentiments because that bunch of oligarchs represented most of the world's money and power structure. He'd never let on that, when it came to the original Great Reset, he didn't like how they had handled things. His plan was better, bolder, and he was going to usurp it all from the usurpers. He was going to snatch it right out from under them without them ever suspecting a thing. He worked out a quick response and thought it to words.

> *K,*
>
> *Glad the app helped. Will have to market it to sailors or cruise ship passengers somehow in the future. Might be some coinage there. Looking forward to the data you are collecting. Note: V is building back better as we speak! The plan is in motion.*
>
> *M*

Marcus leaned back in his chair and swiveled it around a full three-hundred-sixty-degree rotation before letting his feet back on the ground. He could feel the hardwood of his office floor slide beneath his Armani loafers as they slowed his rotation to a stopping position, giving him a clear view out the window again. He looked up and wondered where his friend was about now. That thought led him to the motion sickness app. He made several mental notes in his notepad and then emailed that to his legal assistant to start on a marketing campaign for it. He'd have to make a low-budget version that worked on a standard monitor, but that was easy enough. Maybe some glasses that displayed just the app would be version 2.0.

Marcus then turned his attention to the news feeds across the Onion, looking for any reports from Russia or other intelligence organizations for anything interesting. So far, there were no reports, but he knew that it was just a matter of time before that changed. He'd have to reach out to his spies in the intelligence committees for more information. Or he could always just call the White House.

Then he tapped into his online stock apps and pulled them up in spreadsheet fashion, showing the growth from all of his aliases and shell companies as well as his actual known and "taxable" wealth. Everything looked like it was supposed to. The buildup of his portfolio in certain services, technologies, and providers continued as it had for the more than six years he'd been building this plan. He had been building very large ownership in just the right industries. He'd shifted precious and standard metals' and minerals' futures about and collected major shares in the major mining interests. He'd collected as many of the finite crypto currencies as he could manage, because when fiat money collapsed around the world, crypto and precious metals would become the real global currencies. He approved of his current portfolios. For today, everything was right where he wanted it, but soon, very soon, he would need to shift some investments to match the events that were coming.

His mental focus was broken by an incoming-message alert in his virtual view. His secretary was trying to reach him. He used his mental mouse to click open the channel.

"Yes, Meena?"

"Mr. Dorman, Senator Shamus Kennedy and Congresswoman Roberta Young are here for your 9:15 appointment," she reported through the audio link.

"Show them in, Meena, don't keep them waiting."

"Right away, sir."

Marcus adjusted his tie just a bit, an old nervous habit, then spun back around toward his desk. He accidentally toppled a small plastic figure of Minecraft Steve that he kept there as a memento. The blue, green, and very blocky action figure was mounted on a plexiglass block with a signature on a napkin displayed within it. The signature read:

To Marcus,

Keep crafting and world building.

Markus Persson

He righted the figure just as the door opened. He put on a fake smile to appear as if he was happy to see his visitors. *Politics had to be paid for.* In truth, he really was happy to see them, but not in a friendly way. Instead, the visit meant one more piece of his new world map was falling into place. They were, indeed, an integral part of the plan even if they had zero idea of there actually being some plan.

Marcus had long understood something that the Party of Davos had missed. He realized one very important thing. And that thing was that the world's power ran on, well, power. And politicians craved power, but of a different kind. And they needed money to gain political power. Marcus had money to burn, literally. And the respective chairpersons of the United States House of Representatives and the Senate energy committees had just sat down in his office needing to burn some of it for him in exchange for, well, literally power. *And money to burn.*

"Congresswoman! Senator! Please, please, come on in and have a seat. Meena! You didn't keep them waiting long, did you?" He knew she hadn't.

CHAPTER 6

⁂

Fort Belvoir, Virginia
Defense Threat Reduction Agency
Wednesday
10:27 A.M. Eastern Time

"JUST GOT THE IMAGERY DATA FROM SPACE COMMAND IN COLORADO Springs, Admiral. Second source verified with NRO imagery and radar from various assets. Third-source verification from CIA has intercepted communications between the Russian Space Force commanders and the Kremlin. I've asked NSA for fourth-source verification and waiting. But, as far as I can tell, this is very real, ma'am." United States Navy SEAL Special Warfare Development Group (DEVGRU) Chief Warrant Officer 4 Wheeler "Mac" McKagan tapped in his password and drove the mouse cursor over the large screen with big red letters TOP SECRET across the top and bottom. The computer processing circle spun a bit and then his desktop appeared. "Got the link to the imagery just now if you want to see it all, ma'am."

"Let's see it, Mac," Rear Admiral Lower Half Tonya Denise Thompson leaned forward on her elbows onto the secure conference room table to get a better look. Mac could tell by the look on the admiral's face that she was as nervous about this as he was. "What did the intercept from CIA say?"

"Right, here it is," Mac said. Then he pulled up a classified email on the screen and read it out loud. "I checked with a buddy of mine at SAC/SOG"—Special Activities Center/Special Operations Group—"at CIA and he verifies it. Starts with... unknown speaker number one: 'There were heavy casualties. No survivors.' Then the source from Moscow voice replies: 'Was Colonel Lytokov among the casualties?' Unknown speaker number one then replies: 'No, sir. His body was not recovered or any sign of it on the site.' Moscow voice replies: 'Damn fool Lytokov! Is the missile intact?' Unknown speaker number two, a new voice, says: 'No, the warheads are missing and the missile has been scuttled, sir.'"

"Jesus Christ, Mac!" RDML Thompson gasped. "Warheads? Do we know what they are?"

"Well ma'am, from the imagery here..." Mac tapped away at his keyboard. Satellite imagery appeared on the screen showing an area that appeared to be sparsely populated with maple and fir trees, a couple of trucks, a command center vehicle, and one very large modern-era Russian ICBM on a transporter erector launcher vehicle. He smiled to himself. This was right in his wheelhouse and what he had personally trained for all those years with DEVGRU—what some people, wrongly, referred to as SEAL Team Six. He specifically had trained for just this type of event. "It's a Topol-M was my first guess, ma'am. By treaty, it is only supposed to have one nuke on it. But they did say 'warheads' with an S. Or, at least the translators said it was plural. If plural as translated, then that suggests it is a MIRV-carrying variant like the Topol-MR, also known as an RS-24 Yars. But Topol-M will do, that's the generic description or class of missile. You might hear some analysts and historians in missile technology and defense refer to it as the Sickle-B. I just say Topol-M."

"How many warheads, Mac?"

"As many as six, ma'am. Eighty to one-hundred-fifty kilotons' yield each. Some variants of the missile have been rumored to be capable of carrying eleven, but I don't think this is that variant."

"Jesus Christ!"

"Yes, ma'am. My sentiments exactly, ma'am. Should I alert the Teams?"

"Not yet, the Joint Chiefs may want to handle it differently. I've got to get this to the J2 immediately! Put this in a neat package for me. I'll try to get on the J2's calendar within the next hour or so. I'll need the package by then. Just drop it in my folder on the shared drive. ASAP!"

"Yes, ma'am."

✧   ✧   ✧

It had taken Tonya almost two hours to get onto Vice Admiral Frank Whitburn's schedule. Atop that the traffic going north on I-95 was a total pain in the ass. Tonya was beginning to wish she'd parked at the Park'n'Ride D.C. Metro stop at the bottom of the yellow line in Franconia-Springfield and just taken the damned Metro from there. She'd probably have been at the Pentagon thirty minutes earlier. As it currently stood, she was just now badging through and passing by the cafeteria, stores, and shops. She had been there so many times during her career that she had worked out multiple ways to get where she needed to be quickly. But then again, maintenance was always adding and removing walls and there were stories about ensign junior grades getting lost and walled in and never being heard from again. The Pentagon was a rat maze if there ever was one. Some said it was by design. Tonya was fairly certain it was due to a lack thereof.

Tonya had gone up stairs, down corridors, then down stairs, down another corridor, then back upstairs until she got to the right place. She could tell she was getting closer to the part of the ring where the Joint Chiefs were as the paint, décor, and even the furniture she could see in the office spaces looked nicer.

"Okay, here we go," she whispered to herself as she read the placard outside the door just as she'd done some many times before. "The J2 Defense Intelligence." It never got old being where she was and seeing what she got to see. Maybe today was the day that sentiment changed.

Tonya buzzed in and was let into the office waiting area.

"Can I help you, Admiral?" A new navy lieutenant commander sitting behind the desk rose. Tonya had never seen this one. *He must be fresh in on his rotation*, she thought.

"At ease. RDML Thompson for 13:10 with the J2."

"Yes, ma'am." The young lieutenant commander sat back down and tapped nervously at his console, reaffirming the appointment, and then looked up at her. "Did you send briefing materials?"

"Yes, I sent it on JWICS about an hour ago."

"Hold one second, ma'am." Tonya could tell he was searching for the email she had sent him over the Joint Worldwide

Intelligence Communications System, which everyone simply called "jay-wicks."

"Yes, ma'am. IT has already got them ready." He stood to escort her. "This way to the conference room. Would you like some coffee or water or something, ma'am?"

"No, thank you. I'm good." Tonya had been to the J2 conference room many times in her career and didn't need the hand-holding. But this young naval officer didn't know that and there was no need in explaining it to a sailor just doing his job.

"Right this way. Have a seat and he'll be right with you." The lieutenant commander turned a touch screen in the middle of the conference room table around and tapped at it. Then the monitors on the walls showed a classified computer desktop. A few seconds later Tonya's briefing was on the screen. He handed her a remote. "This moves the slides forward and that one backward. This room is now at the level of your briefing and nobody uncleared will be allowed in. Any questions?"

"Got it. Thank you."

Tonya sat patiently for about ten minutes, all the while going over the data in her mind. It was almost unfathomable. What was this Russian going to do with these nukes? To what endgame? These would be the hottest stolen goods ever and couldn't just be fenced through some gunrunner or warlord. That really suggested to Tonya that the Russian and whoever else was with him planned to *use* these nukes. Jesus Christ...

One of the maple brown walls opened, revealing a door at the end of the room and on a side wall. The protocol was clear, as always. Tonya jumped to her feet at attention. A navy captain entered and announced, "Vice Admiral Whitburn." The captain then stood at attention until the three-star director of the Directorate for Intelligence, J2, support to the Chairman of the Joint Chiefs of Staff, the Secretary of Defense, Joint Staff and Unified Commands, Vice Admiral Frank Whitburn walked in swiftly and stood at the end of the table.

"At ease. Sit down, Tonya." VADM Whitburn turned to the navy captain. "Thank you, Thomas." That was clearly the order to the lower rank that this was an admirals-only meeting. The VADM waited for the doors to close. The mahogany leather chairs squeaked as they settled into their seats.

"Okay, Tonya, now what is so damned urgent that..."

CHAPTER 7

∽

Washington, D.C.
The Pentagon
Wednesday
4:27 P.M. Eastern Time

"MS. THOMPSON, ARE YOU TELLING ME THIS IS VERIFIED DATA?"
Four-star Navy Admiral Tommy James Bristol was almost in a
panic. While the other service chiefs looked back at her as grimly
as the admiral, they remained quiet. Tonya knew that if her data
was the slightest bit wrong and the Joint Chiefs briefed this up
to the SecDef and the president that she'd never see a second
star on her shoulder. She looked over to her direct line boss,
VADM Whitburn, who slightly nodded his head in reassurance
to her. Tonya turned back to the Chairman and answered slowly,
choosing each word very deliberately.

"Sir, this is four-agency and four-sources verified. This is real.
We have a rogue Russian officer and a team of very well-trained
unknown mercenaries somewhere out there with as many as six
nuclear warheads of up to one-hundred-fifty kilotons each. The
Russian government had this specific missile TEL Treaty Desig-
nated as one of the Topol-M sites with nuclear capabilities. Realizing that the Treaty only allows for one warhead per Topol-M
puts them in a precarious spot diplomatically. That assessment
is in the brief only for a notice to the State Department. From a

military intelligence perspective, we must assume they have more than one." Tonya pointed out the dismantled nosecone of the now scuttled ICBM with the wireless mouse pointer. The Joint Chiefs of Staff conference room was even larger and nicer than the J2. She'd briefed the chiefs, or at least some of them, at times, but never like this with a real immediate looming threat. "This team knew what they were doing and they did it fast."

"Do we have any idea where they are now?" Army General Harold "Harry" Galveston asked. "Any word on a buyer?"

"No, sir. We've been reverse tracking back to the event with assets of every type, but the culprits were smart. They knew when we would have assets in view and they waited for them to pass overhead before they attacked. The next pass of an asset was eighty-seven minutes afterward, and they were out of sight, hidden, or gone by then." Tonya paused for that to sink in.

"Eighty-seven minutes to pull up to six warheads?" Admiral Bristol exclaimed rhetorically.

"That sounds impossible." USSF General Kimberly Hastings added her skepticism.

"Well, General Hastings, I'd agree, but our expert USN CW4 McKagan from DEVGRU believes it is doable with two highly skilled teams and knowledge of the vehicle design. He says he could train his team to do it. But the CW4 has another thought about this, sirs."

"Go on."

"Well, if you look at this first image from our overhead asset, just around sunup, there are seventeen Russian Space Force soldiers practically posing for a spy satellite image. In this next image, eighty-seven minutes later, there they are again, including the Russian colonel Lytokov, and appear to be posing again. But note, there are only six soldiers in view. While they could be inside the vehicles, it is possible they had been killed and hidden out of view. The next image was from a polar orbiting asset almost two hours later and here you can see the dismantled nosecone image I showed you just a moment ago. It was taken from this asset almost five hours after the initial image. My analysts and the CW4 all agree that a small well-trained team with inside design and repair knowledge could accomplish this and get away with the warheads intact in five hours."

"Five hours is more believable than eighty-seven minutes," the Army four-star added.

"And what's more, sirs, ma'am, is that I don't believe they could sell these warheads, not with the U.S. and the Russians looking for them."

"Then what is it you 'believe' they plan to do, Admiral Thompson?" General Hastings asked.

"Well, ma'am, I think they intend to use them, or at least one of them. They have to know they can't sell them and can't hide them forever. I'd guess we only have a few days to a couple weeks at best before they can reconfigure at least one of them in a way to detonate it." Tonya almost held her breath and bit her tongue after saying that out loud.

"Jesus Christ!" General Hastings exclaimed. Tonya had been hearing and saying that a lot today. In fact, she believed she'd heard it more in this one day than during her entire career with the Joint Intelligence and DTRA—the Defense Threat Reduction Agency.

"I agree, General. This appears to be an inside job so the engineering and maintenance knowledge of the missile would have been available." Tonya paused to give the room time to absorb and assimilate the data she had given them. "Sirs, ma'am, to recap, my team and I have no idea to what end the mercenaries are after here, but we do know that now they have at least one nuke, and maybe a half dozen, as means toward whatever that end is. This was done so swiftly and professionally; they were most certainly highly skilled and funded, and on the inside of the Russian Space Force infrastructure. This was no simple 'arms grab-n-go' for the warlord markets. There must have been nuclear missile scientists or engineers or at least skilled techs involved. And we know they have one long-term career, highly trained, and perhaps disgruntled, Russian Space Forces colonel with them."

"Disgruntled, Tonya?" the admiral asked.

"Um, yes sir. Our intel package on Colonel Vladimir Lytokov shows that he was hopeful to be in the Roscosmos Cosmonaut Corps but for—and the intel is sketchy on this—political reasons...and just maybe he couldn't get out of his own way...he was transferred away from flying to the missile group. Basically, a transfer to Siberia, sir. As far away from the Moon as you can get if you're a cosmonaut."

"I see..."

"Who are we putting on this?" U.S. Marine Corps General Alton Cole asked.

"Right now, the CW4 is the only operative I have on it. CIA has put operatives from SAC/SOG on it but are coming up dry. Chief McKagan is on special assignment to me and not active with the SEAL Teams right now, but has requested to put a special team on this, sir."

"Admiral, no offense to your warrant, but I know just the man for this," General Cole said.

"Do I pull the chief then, sir?"

"No, we need all the smart eyes and ears on this we can get. Have your warrant connect with my guy and give them all priorities and accesses they need to run this thing to ground," the general ordered. "This should be a JSOC"—Joint Special Operations Command—"effort with civilian agency involvement too."

"Yes, sir."

"You should add one of our experts from Kirtland," U.S. Air Force General Robert Jeppersons added. "I'll have Colonel Barnes get you some names."

"Yes, sirs. I'll reach across the services." Tonya realized there were politics that had to be played here.

"Tonya, I have a couple of guys from Delta you need," Army general Galveston added.

"Yes sir. Please send the information. I'll be happy to add whoever you want to this task."

"Doesn't matter who you need, Tonya. As Chairman of the Joint Chiefs, I will ask the SecDef to authorize the creation of this Joint Forces and Services Task Force. Should be good to go within the hour. Don't wait on me to get the paperwork started. Get a team together and find those nukes."

"Aye, sir!"

"And make certain I have all this package. This has to get to the Oval Office within the hour."

"Aye."

CHAPTER 8

၅၀

Puerto Limon, Costa Rica
Wednesday
4:20 P.M. Central Time

"WHAT THE FUCK, JOHNNY?" USMC LIEUTENANT COLONEL FRANK Alvarez held an arm out to his right to hold his friend back.

"Sorry, Colonel. I didn't see that." The younger staff sergeant was visibly shaken.

"You *almost* didn't see anything and was *almost* catatonic. Don't move." Frank reached over with his left hand, grabbed a broken mop that was leaning against the rust-orange cargo container, and carefully worked it up into his hand, holding it tightly nearest the mop head. He carefully placed the jagged end of the red wooden handle just inside the door of the container and underneath the belly of the coiled brown-and-black, with lighter diagonal stripes, clearly agitated viper. With a swift sweeping motion, he tossed the snake out of the cargo container doorway. He heard a soft *kathunk* against another container's side and then another as the snake fell to the asphalt pier.

"That's the bad one, ain't it?"

"Fer-de-lance. Fuckers are everywhere down here," Frank said gruffly. "And yes. That's the bad one." Frank paused and looked about the opening for other hazards. No more snakes at least. Carefully, he shined the light from his pistol around the top of

47

the doorway and down each side. He wasn't sure if the locals had put the snake in there as a booby trap or if the damned thing had just crawled in. Since it was a local snake, he was guessing the latter. With a little further thought on the subject, though, he became fairly certain the snake was a booby trap. The dock was a good mile from any vegetation like those things were normally in. He dropped the broken mop softly to the ground and then worked his flashlight back and forth across the cargo container, still searching for any other surprises.

"Just drugs?" USMC Staff Sergeant Johnathon "Johnny" Parvo asked and then he froze as the voice in his ear buzzed.

"Alpha, this is Overwatch, be advised you've got company approaching from the south. Looks like locals, but there are two with them that don't belong...ETA three minutes."

"Copy Overwatch." Frank couldn't hear the drone overhead, but he knew it was up there. "Shit, Johnny, we've got company."

"ETA, sir?"

"Three minutes."

"No way we can go through all this in time," the staff sergeant said.

"I know. But we can't leave here yet." Frank looked at the instrument on his left armband and it was pegged in the red. "Gammas are pegged. There's something dirty in here."

"Yeah, but where, sir?"

"Let's back off and see if our company can lead us to it."

"Right."

Frank eased backward into the container opening with his head on a swivel looking left, then right, then back again. He rolled his view up and over to make certain nobody was getting the drop on them from atop the containers. He did a rough count and estimate and realized there were at least nineteen rows of cargo containers stacked two high and three deep looking westward. It had taken weeks of work to find this one needle in a haystack and he didn't want to lose it now that they had gotten so close.

"Come on. We'll go two rows down and climb up," he told Johnny.

Johnny began closing the cargo door on his side, causing a very loud rusty metal-on-metal screeching sound, and then stopped abruptly.

"Shit, that's loud," he exclaimed quietly.

"All at once and then we go." Frank nodded. The two of them quickly pushed the doors to and closed the latch. Fortunately, the dock had other background noises of ships in the background and moving cranes in the distance running. Maybe, just maybe, they hadn't drawn attention to themselves.

"Come on, Johnny. Let's move!"

The two of them hurried as quietly as they could to the set of containers two rows down, nearest the loading crane that was sitting unattended. Using the crane arm as a ladder they made their way atop one of them. The particular container had been sloppily painted black to cover rust that showed through it. From the stability of the metal container's top, paint flecked off with each step and the rusty metal gave inward. Frank wasn't too certain they weren't going to fall through the damn thing. There were all sorts of foreign letters and words on the side of it that as best he could tell were in Mandarin.

"Alpha, Overwatch has your position. Be advised that your company is about to be in view. Bravo has moved into place to take their egress."

"Copy that, Overwatch." Frank toggled the comms to the team channel. "Bravo, stay ready but do not—repeat, do not—take the egress route until you get a signal from me."

"Copy that, Alpha. We're frozen and waiting your signal." USMC Captain Ellis Jones looked through the scope on his rifle, panning across the three-vehicle convoy that had just arrived. The cars were mostly filled with what appeared to be local drug thugs and muscle for hire. Two of them in the rear car, though, as best Jones could tell, looked like bad news from East Africa. He dropped his rifle to hang from his armored chest and then he turned and looked over his shoulder.

"Gunny!" he whispered.

"Colonel Alvarez?" USMC Gunnery Sergeant Hank Lord appeared from around the corner of a dirty green cargo container. "Clear to the north, sir."

"Great, Gunny. Listen, I'm thinking the colonel is about to go apeshit any minute now. He's got nine locals and two Somalis carrying AKs and who the fuck knows what else almost on top of him. The egress is to the south and we have to keep that cut off from the bad guys, right?"

"Understood, Captain. I can take Tapscott and Rheems and get a drop position on them from the east. You have them here. We could easily put them in a cross-fire killbox," Gunny Lord said.

"Okay, sounds good. But *do not* engage until we get the colonel's sign."

"Did he bother to tell us what that sign would be?" the gunnery sergeant asked, mostly rhetorically.

"You've met the colonel, right?"

"Right." The two men just smiled and nodded. Gunnery Sergeant Lord whispered orders to two of the men in the stack and the three of them moved swiftly toward an eastward position.

"Bravo, Bravo! Overwatch! Be advised three new vehicles approaching from the east. Estimating eleven Somali regulars, well armed."

"Shit. Copy, Overwatch!" Jones looked back through his scope following Gunny, Tapscott, and Rheems. They were still out of view of the roadway between the containers to the east for now. "Gunny, be advised we have more bad guys approaching right at you from the east."

"Copy, Captain."

"Elvis." Captain Jones motioned toward the three men stacked up with him.

"Sir?" Sergeant Leon "Elvis" Anders kept his rifle at the ready but looked over to his squad leader.

"Get the rest of the guys ready to fight. Shit's about to go down."

"Yes, sir!"

✧   ✧   ✧

"They're coming out of the goddamned woodworks, Johnny," Lieutenant Colonel Frank Alvarez whispered. The two of them were lying prone in sniper position with their rifles following the first team of locals and the two Somalis. "Be ready for some kind of shit."

"I'm with you, Colonel. Does it matter what kind of shit?"

"Shit is shit, Johnny."

"Right. I'm ready."

"Good. As soon as they dig out the goods, we drop 'em."

"Yes, sir."

"But not until then! And if you have to shoot the Somalis, shoot them in the leg or something. We need them alive to find out who their buyer is," Frank ordered him.

"Yes, sir."

The entourage stepped around the corner, oblivious to the fact that they were being watched by the marines, a UAV drone above, and from national assets in orbit as they passed overhead. That made them no less dangerous, though. Frank watched them carefully as they cycled open the handle on the container and tugged it open, making a metal screeching sound that could be heard across the dock. Frank looked over at Johnny as if to say *Been there, done that.*

The first man stopped the second before stepping into the container and looked cautiously about. He held them up for bit while he looked around inside for something. Then after a moment he motioned for the other two.

"Well, I guess he couldn't find his slithery friend," Johnny whispered.

"Guess we know now how it got there."

Three of the men with AK-47s stood flank and Frank thought for a brief second that one of them had looked right at him. He breathed and stayed calm until the man's gaze moved slowly about. Frank realized they hadn't been spotted, but the men standing flank were on the lookout.

"Overwatch, can you give me ears?" he whispered into the throat mic commlink.

"Audio coming to you now, Alpha."

"...*esta aqui...esta aqui...*" one of the locals was saying. Frank was guessing it was the guy talking and pointing but the audio was a fraction of a second behind.

"In English..." the Somali with the AK grunted. The other one kept quiet.

"In here...it is in here..."

"You...go in and bring it out to me..."

"*Sí...sí...*"

"Be ready, Johnny, this is it." Frank started slowing his breathing and placed the red dot of the sight clearly on the forehead of the man standing flank nearest their position. "You take the far flank man."

"Yes, sir."

"Overwatch, any change on the Geiger?"

"Not yet."

The three locals who had vanished into the container were

clearly rummaging from the noise. The Somalis were standing patiently and observantly at the ready. Then the men reappeared from within with a wooden crate about one meter wide and deep and about two meters long upright longways on a set of hand trucks. The lead guy dropped the dolly forward and the crate crashed over like a falling domino against the asphalt, almost saturating the eavesdropper mic. Frank flinched from the abrupt spike in the noise amplitude bursting in his ears.

"It is here..."

"Open it..."

"Slight uptick on the Geiger, Alpha."

"Be patient."

The men fumbled with the wooden crate until one of them produced a steel prybar from within the cargo container. Two of the locals worked at the lid until it pried loose and fell to the ground edgewise then teetered over, making a wood-to-metal clank as it impacted against the door of the cargo container. They then began pulling and kicking at the wooden sides until they were knocked loose and fell away revealing another container inside.

"Help?"

"You two..." the more vocal Somali told the two men standing flank. They immediately slung their rifles and rushed to aid the others. A few seconds later four of the men were on either side of the destroyed crate looking at a flat black metal box that was clearly upside down in front of them. After scratching their heads briefly, and some fast chatter in Spanish, the men surrounded the box with the intent of flipping it over.

"Hurry up..."

"Is it locked?"

The men got handholds and flipped the box. By the looks of strain on their faces Frank was pretty sure it was heavy as hell. Finally, after some more Spanish and Somali expletives, the men managed to, very clumsily, set the metal box down right side up. There was some cursing and chatter briefly about being cautious, but Frank couldn't decipher it all.

"Jesus, I hope that thing doesn't have explosives in it," Johnny whispered.

Frank ignored the comment, but was thinking the same thing. Something about the casing looked familiar to Frank, but he wasn't quite sure where he'd seen it just yet. He did a mental exercise to quiet his mind and filter through his memories, but so far, he had nothing.

The men around the box continued fiddling with the hasps for several moments. Finally, one of them gestured at the men on either side of the black metal case to back up as he sprang the final hasp and the top opened. As the lid raised, Overwatch immediately chimed in.

"Geiger counter through the roof, Alpha!"

"Must've been lead lined," Frank whispered to Overwatch.

"That's why it was so damned heavy," Johnny said.

The Somalis both rushed to the open container and lifted a few items from within and put them aside. They appeared to be long Army green tubular items like an old Viet Nam–era bazooka tube and a tripod. Then the leader strained a bit and lifted an oblong oval-shaped black object with a yellow radiation symbol on the front. It was clearly a small bomb. It had a squatty cartoonish bomb teardrop shape about two-thirds of a meter long and about a half meter in diameter at the largest point. The bomb tapered into about sixteen centimeters at the back, with four aerodynamic fins.

"What is that?" Johnny asked. "The 1980s' cartoons called and they want their bomb back."

"Son-of-a-goddamned-bitch. And it would be more like 1960s," Frank whispered.

"Colonel? You know what it is?"

"Yeah. It's a Davy Crockett," Frank said nervously. Suddenly, the pathway to the correct memories in his brain triggered and he knew exactly what they were looking at. He even recalled the technical details from the munitions classes' topic of potential pilfered, lost, or repurposed special weapons threats. "Looks to me like the Somalis have just bought themselves an old M29 with a W-54 warhead and a one-fifty-five-millimeter launcher."

"Seriously . . ." Johnny looked back at him. "Engage? What if we hit the—"

"Overwatch, be advised we have a potentially active nuclear device in play!"

"Colonel, did you say, uh, 'active' nuke?" Johnny gulped quietly.

"Take 'em out, Johnny! Don't hit the bomb!" Frank depressed the trigger of his M27 Infantry Automatic Rifle, releasing the 5.56x45mm NATO round. One of the men still holding his AK-47 at the ready was hit in the head and fell backward. Bright red blood spattered across the man next to him as Staff Sergeant Parvo dropped the hired thug closest to the Somali leader. The two Somalis instantly took cover behind the door of the cargo container, taking the warhead with them. Frank and Johnny continued to shoot at the hired help.

"We can't let them figure out how to activate that thing, Johnny. We need to push." Frank motioned toward the ladder they had climbed up. "When I go, Johnny, you stay here and keep my six clean until I get one container up. Then get there!"

✧   ✧   ✧

"You hear all that gunfire, Gunny?" Captain Jones said into the commlink.

"Yes, sir."

"Well, I guess that's the colonel's signal. Be advised Overwatch has your uninvited company almost on top of you."

"Do we engage them or let them by, Captain?"

"Let them by. Then, we cut 'em down."

"Copy that."

✧   ✧   ✧

"We don't let that bomb out of our site, Overwatch!" Frank fired several more rounds at the men hunkered in behind the cargo container as they peeked around the back side, vying for a better attack position.

"Copy, Alpha. Be advised that Bravo has engaged a second company."

"No shit, I can hear it." Frank looked over at Johnny and grinned. "Staff Sergeant Parvo, it would appear that we are outnumbered."

"Aw shit, Colonel, don't say that." Parvo didn't like the ramifications of that statement. He certainly didn't like what always came next. He knew the colonel was about to go apeshit. And there was always shit when he did that.

"And you know what marines do when they are outnumbered..."

"I had a feeling you were going to say that, sir."

"Attack! Now let's move it."

Frank sprang to his feet like he was doing burpees, leaving a boot-shaped dent in the rickety rusty container top. Quickly, he raced to the edge and leaped outward, grabbing the rails of the crane doing a hand-over-hand walk down the metal lattice of the crane's arm. Once he felt he was close enough to safely drop to the ground with all the weight of his armor and weapons, he did so with a parkour four-handed landing, followed with a less than perfect judo roll. He didn't think twice about if Johnny had his six or not. He trusted the marine would be there when he needed him.

Frank sprang upward and turned, landing with his back against the container on the other side of the crane. He shuffled to the edge and peeked around the corner. Just as his head cleared the corner, metal sprayed and sparks flew in his face as enemy fire skittered off the steel frame of the container. A couple of rounds went right through the metal and out only inches from his head. Frank dropped to a knee and then made a low sprint, almost a bear crawl, across the alleyway between the container rows. Once he made it across the path, he gathered his wits for second, as well as his breath, and looked back to see Parvo leaning around the corner laying down suppression fire.

"Which way, Colonel?!"

"Not straight at 'em! Too thick!" Frank leaned over and fired a few rounds, then pulled back to cover. "Get over here in three!"

Frank held up a two, then a one, then he rolled out, firing down the alleyway again as Parvo darted across to him. The two men fell back against the container wall. Both of them checked their magazines.

"Check that side."

Parvo shuffled to the other edge of the container and quickly ducked back in.

"Shit! Two coming this way."

"Just two?" Frank asked.

"Pretty sure."

"Then they're outnumbered. Come on!"

Frank stood and rushed across all the way to the other side of the opposing alley until he bounced off the container wall. From the moment he stepped into view of the two men pushing toward them he fired his weapon in their general direction. He hadn't expected to hit them, but that wasn't the point. He just needed to distract them. And that is just what he did.

Staff Sergeant Johnny Parvo kneeled around the corner, dropping his rifle in his left palm, his elbow on his kneepad, and fired once. The first local gunman fell. Parvo quickly adjusted to the right and dropped the second just as Colonel Alvarez banged into the container across from them. Parvo was up and moving almost as quickly as he'd dropped to his knee.

"Great shooting, Johnny. Go!" Frank motioned. The two of them ran at top speed down the alleyway, going lengthwise with the containers. Once they reached the end of the cargo container row they stopped and put their backs to the wall on the left side. "I'll take that side. You prepare to cover."

"Yes, sir."

Frank bounced across the alleyway to the right-side landing with his back against the metal wall and his rifle at the ready. Instantly, he expected to be pulling his trigger but there were no targets.

"Alpha, Overwatch! You're being flanked. They are on the opposite side of the container wall you are leaning on and breaching both ends, copy?"

"Copy that!"

Frank made gestures to Johnny telling him that they were about to come at them from each end. He pointed at himself then to the right. Then at Parvo and to the left. Parvo returned a thumbs-up and shifted to a firing position more appropriate.

"Alpha, Overwatch. In four..."

Frank waved at Johnny and held up three fingers on his right hand and counted down with the voice in his ear.

"...three...two..."

He held up one finger and then gripped his rifle.

"...one!"

CHAPTER 9

∾

Puerto Limon, Costa Rica
Wednesday
4:38 P.M. Central Time

"COPY THAT, BRAVO. ELLIS, ONCE THEY'RE ALL TAGGED AND bagged or handed off to Charlie, you and the men clear out to base. Delta has secured our position and we've got a possible hot situation here and no need in all of us sitting on top of it."

"You sure, Colonel?"

"Yeah, we've got this and the NIRT guys will be here within the next few minutes. Once the doc clears our two friends from Africa, we'll have a go at them."

"Copy that. I'll let you know once the doc clears them for a chat. Be advised that the medevac chopper is one minute out."

"Right. Alvarez out." Frank looked over at Parvo, who was bleeding from his left thigh. The once off-white, now bloodred bandage Johnny was pressing against his leg was almost saturated. The tourniquet had stopped him from bleeding out, but he was still bleeding.

"Johnny, you need to get that looked at."

"Yes sir. I think you just said that about a minute ago."

"Well, the situation hasn't changed. Medevac is almost here."

"Just a scratch, Colonel. One of those crazy bastards made the mistake of bringing a knife to a gunfight." Johnny gave a toothy grin.

"I saw that. Good work today." Frank looked at the bomb that he'd placed carefully back in the metal case it had come in. The thing had to be at least sixty years old. It also had to be unstable and dangerous. They had been lucky it didn't go off during all the ruckus. He looked down at his Geiger counter and while there was a very noticeable gamma ray increase, there was no radiation "danger" at the moment. That was, of course, assuming the bomb didn't decide to detonate. Frank had no idea why this thing hadn't been decommissioned, dismantled, and destroyed decades ago. He wondered just how many more like it might be out there. He also was guessing that high explosives surrounding the nuclear core were unstable and might not detonate properly, collapsing the core into a critical mass. Maybe it would go critical. Maybe it wouldn't. But it would still be a dirty fissile mess to clean up one way or the other. The sound of the medevac helicopter caught his attention. There were two of them coming. One of them was a standard, but the other looked like a dual rotor airplane.

"Colonel, a V22-Osprey and it's coming in hot." Johnny pointed.

"I suspect that is our NIRT guys," Frank said.

The two landed just at the edge of the pier about fifty meters away. The rear loading door of the Osprey was open with a gunner standing at the ready in the middle. Several teams jumped out of both aircraft as they sat down. One group had a USMC combat medic, who hit the ground running in a straight line for them.

"Colonel Alvarez?" The combat medic came to a stop and saluted.

"Yes, over here." He pointed to Parvo.

The team piling out of the Osprey all had Nuclear Incident Response Team patches on their jackets. Two of the men from that group approached quickly with Geiger counters at the ready. Two men with Department of Homeland Security armored vests jumped out, too, along with a blond-haired lady in civilian tactical clothes and no armor. From the looks of her, Frank pegged her as CIA. The colonel's Delta team marines fanned out to give them room, but they all were keeping a close eye on the thugs on the ground with zip tied hands behind their backs.

"Bomb's right over here guys." Frank grinned at them. "No signs of other fissile material nearby as best we can tell. But it wouldn't hurt to give the place a thorough sweepin'."

"Colonel Alvarez?" One of the NIRT team approached him. "You've been ordered to come with us, sir."

"Where to?"

"I'm told you'll be briefed on the way."

"Well, I'm not leaving my team or this bomb, this nuclear bomb, without more information than that." Frank grunted. "Did you get that? The *nuclear* bomb part?"

"Yes, sir. I was told you'd respond that way. I was also told to read this to you." The NIRT operative held up a piece of paper, cleared his throat theatrically, and read from it. "Um, sir, the paper says to clear my throat as such first. Then it says, and I quote verbatim, uh, sir, 'Shut up, smart-ass, and get on the god-damned chopper! Alton.' Uh, unquote, sir."

"Jesus Christ!" Frank had only gotten an order like that one other time in his life and had hoped he never would again. "Did they say more?"

"No, sir. I'm told you'll be briefed on the way."

Frank looked down at Staff Sergeant Parvo. The medic had sprayed the cut and sealed it and was already bandaging it with a fresh wrap. They would evac him soon. Johnny was in good hands.

"Johnny, I've gotta go. I'll check in on you when I can."

"Yes sir, Colonel. No worries. I'll be fine."

"Colonel, we need to go," the NIRT operative urged him.

"Understood. Well, let's move."

Frank sat scrunched into the jumpseat in the back of the Osprey, looking out the opened back loading bay at the gunner strapped in and standing to behind the fifty caliber at the ready. He rolled his neck back and forth as he strained his shoulders to pull the seatbelt harness around him and his body armor. The blond CIA lady sat across from him and motioned for him to put his headset on. Frank nodded but took his time. He always liked to watch the ground roll out from underneath as an Osprey rolled gently forward and then suddenly lurched as the twin props engaged, slinging them over a hundred meters in the air almost instantly.

He fiddled with the headset and took a swig from the water bottle one of the NIRT guys had handed him rather than from his own gear. The headset was tuned to the open channel and he could hear other chatter and the pilot and copilot talking to each other about something unrelated to anything important.

"Dr. Ginny Banks, CIA." The blond woman held out a hand. Frank shook it.

"Lieutenant Colonel Francisco Alvarez. Call me Frank." Frank loosened the shoulder harness strap on the left side as it was digging into him a bit much. "Why am I here, Dr. Banks?"

"Please, call me Ginny. And hold one..." Banks unbuckled and approached him. She pulled his headphone cable from its slot and then plugged it into a box she pulled out from a pocket in her black tactical cargo pants. She plugged her headset into it as well, flipped a switch on it, illuminating a green light, and then plopped carefully back into her jumpseat as the helicopter buffeted her slightly off balance. Frank raised an eyebrow at her, concerned she might have hurt something.

"...shit...damnit..." she muttered.

"Dr. Banks, you alright?"

"Fine." She buckled back into the seat. "This is a secure private channel. Once we get on the ground in Corpus I'll give you the full brief. But here is the general situation report. About thirty hours ago a Russian Topol-M missile was hijacked from the missile TEL just north of Oral, Kazakhstan. The crew were all killed with the exception of the commanding officer, a Colonel Vladimir Lytokov, a former MiG pilot and cosmonaut wannabe. We think he is the inside man on this job. The missile was left at the site minus all of the nuclear reentry vehicles within the nose. This was a well-funded operation."

"Jesus, how many warheads?"

"The Russians won't say. The treaty only allows for one. CIA agrees with a Pentagon analyst that there are at most six."

"What Pentagon analyst?" Frank knew most of the active-duty analysts in the nuke-watching business. He'd been part of the response teams for decades.

"Uh, hold one..." She held up a finger and pulled her phone from another pocket. Frank watched as it appeared she was scrolling through emails until she found the right one. "Let's see...aha, here it is. U.S. Navy SEAL Chief Warrant Officer Four Wheeler McKagan."

"What did CW4 McKagan say?"

"He is the one with the six-warhead estimate. CIA analysts agree."

"I've done some time with the warrant. He's a good man.

I'd take his word on this one," Frank said. He was thinking on how truly a small world it was. He recalled being on an inspection team in Iran several years back with McKagan. Goddamned SEALs could hold their liquor. And there was that time the two of them had been put on a Spec Ops joint effort funded through the Defense Research Projects Agency and one of the congressional committees. Now that was a fiasco. The program was still classified to only a handful even though it never got off the ground. "Hot Eagle" was what DARPA had called it. Fun times. A lot of unusual training, brainstorming new and wild techniques, and then there was the evening drinking in the hotel lobby bar. There were a handful of other soldiers on the team but as far as Frank knew they were either killed in Afghanistan or retired out. He and Mac were the only ones from that group still around. He trusted Mac. McKagan was a good soldier.

"So, what's our play?" Frank asked the CIA agent.

"Our play?" Banks shrugged. "Find the goddamned nukes before somebody sets one of them off."

"Sounds about right." Frank agreed with the play, but it was more of an outcome than an actual plan. He needed—well, he at least hoped for—something more. "Any ideas on a starting point?"

"We'll get you briefed in Corpus. Then we'll catch a fast ride to SOCOM, where a joint task force is being assembled. From there, we'll start our engagements."

"Any ideas on if these perps are planning to use the weapons or sell them?"

"Very little I'm afraid. Just, well, Rear Admiral, um, one star, I forget what that's called..."

"Lower Half."

"Right, Rear Admiral Lower Half Tonya Thompson and the SEAL warrant both think they plan to detonate at least one of them."

"Why?"

"With both the Russians and the Americans looking for them, they don't believe they could be fenced or sold without them being caught."

"Sound assessment. Maybe." Frank thought about all the potential dealers, fences, and buyers for WMD-type arms and had to agree. Unless there were new players that were overtly cocksure of themselves.

"We have little more than that right now. All the services and agencies are taxing collection sources and means as we speak."

"Understood, ma'am. So, is that all the info you have for me now?" Frank closed his eyes and leaned his head back to take a deep breath. He realized that he was more tired than he had originally thought. And, as the adrenaline of the fight was wearing off, he realized he had a few bumps and bruises that were starting to ache. As soon as he landed, he intended to take about a bottle full of ibuprofen.

"That's about it. Pictures and such will be available when we land."

"How long till then?"

"About four hours."

"Well then, I suggest we get some rest while we can. Who knows when we'll get another chance?"

CHAPTER 10

⁐

Undisclosed Location
Somewhere off the Coast of Russia in the Black Sea
Wednesday
8:00 P.M. Local Time
1:00 P.M. Eastern Time

IT HAD BEEN A VERY LONG TWO DAYS. MICHAEL WAS TIRED. VERY tired. While, fortunately, the trek south across eastern Kazakhstan and then east across Russian to the Black Sea had been uneventful, unfortunately, it had been very long. Then unloading at night into the "yacht" that was waiting for them had been purely physical labor. He was tired. He'd slept very little in the past thirty hours or so. And to top that off, there had been a bit of weather and the yacht had been rocking terribly, keeping everyone on the edge of motion sickness. Everyone, even the ship's crew, was fighting the urge to be sick—everyone except for Vladimir. Michael had been amazed how the Russian pilot appeared to be completely unfazed by the meters-high waves and the constantly shifting and rocking boat.

"Bah, this is nothing like landing on carriers in the Northern Pacific," he had told him.

Michael watched the liquid pop and fizz as he poured a ginger ale from a can over crushed ice in a whiskey tumbler, sans the whiskey. The effervescence and spicy sweet smell tickled his nose and gave him hope. He hoped the drink would ease his stomach. He had put the fatigue out of his mind for the time being. He had been tired many times and had to work through it. This was no different. Working through being tired was part of the job—but the motion sickness! The motion sickness was a whole other thing entirely.

He looked across the room and out the window on the port side of the common area that he'd appropriated as a work space. He cautiously sipped the soft drink, taking some of the cold ice chips into his mouth too. The flavor, fizziness, and cold were instantly gratifying. The next-to-the-top deck area had light brown leather upholstered executive lounge–style furnishings with several four-to-six-person tables and chairs spread about. The room looked like a swanky cruise ship sports bar, with big-screen television monitors on the walls at various locations for optimal viewing. Who knew what Dorman's motivation was in the décor? Michael had given up trying to understand exactly what went on in Marcus's head. He just assumed it had been thought through for detailed and specific reasons. Everything Marcus did was a calculated move. He suspected that the man even calculated and scheduled bathroom trips for optimal bowel movements and the like.

The ship continued to rock. Michael's stomach continued to sit uneasy.

It was raining hard; so hard that he could barely make out the white-capping waves thirty meters out. The weather was slowing them down some, but the captain had assured them that they were on schedule for their rendezvous. He hoped the captain was right and that the weather eased up soon. If the weather didn't ease up, he thought as he looked forward at the helicopter pad on the yacht, that could really screw things up.

Vladimir's snoring didn't seem to bother Michael as much as the sounds of the rocking boat. Something in a cabinet behind the bar was loose and every time the ship rose to bow it would roll back. Every. Single. Goddamned. Time. Then as the ship fell to bow and rose to stern with the waves, whatever it was would roll forward. Again, every. Single. Goddamned. Time. It was annoying as hell and he'd given up trying to find whatever it was that was doing it.

He looked across at his friend stretched across the couch having zero trouble sleeping. Michael took another larger sip of the soft drink he'd poured and took in a few more pieces of the crushed ice. He still swallowed the liquid cautiously, testing how it felt on his stomach. It was actually soothing, so he threw caution to the wind and took a complete swig, truly hoping it didn't come back up on him soon.

"That's not bad," he said softly. The proximity sensor on his eyeglasses triggered a brief second before he heard footsteps on the stairwell. Someone was coming up from the lower deck. He sat the drink down and turned. An icon in his view identified the glasses and wearer approaching and started shaking hands with the device.

"All six warheads are fully capable, Michael," Xi Singang said through the plastic face shield of his radiation suit. The headgear was fogging over with each of Sing's exhales. He pulled it over his head and tossed it onto an adjacent table, making more noise than Michael wanted to hear at the moment. Michael glanced at the Russian on the couch, but he still hadn't budged.

Sing began to remove the lead-lined apron and gloves, dropping them to the table with another, but less noisy, *thud*. Sweat poured down his face and his dark hair was stuck to his pale forehead. He made a hand gesture at some virtual icon in front of him and then shifted his sunglasses up on his head. Michael made the mental note that the physicist looked like death warmed over. He suspected it was due to motion sickness and being up all night working with the warheads. He hoped that was all it was.

"Have a seat." Michael motioned with his left hand. "You doing alright?"

"Is that ginger ale?" Sing asked.

"Plenty over there in the refrigerator." Michael nodded the direction. "Help yourself."

"Great. I'm hungry, but afraid to eat." He rummaged through the cabinet behind the bar and then returned with a glass of ice and a can of the soft drink. Michael waited for the man to get settled.

"I know what you mean. I'll be glad when we clear this weather. So, how's it going down there?"

"Not bad." Sing took several long drinks from the glass and then set it down, making a sigh of relief. "Ah, that hits the spot, as we Americans say."

"I know, right?" he agreed, trying not to sound impatient.

The physicist didn't even look up from the glass and then pulled his glasses back down and appeared to be reading something. He finally looked up and swiped at a virtual icon.

"This was not as hard as I thought it would be. With the documents Vladimir provided, the help from Keenan, our connected friends, and council from my sister in Malan"—she was at the Northwest Nuclear Technology Institute there—"I've managed to reengineer how the detonation sequence works. Fortunately, I was trained to convert Russian to Mandarin in an earlier life."

"Yes, that is fortunate."

"The circuits we were provided will work adequately. This can be done quickly, I think. Maybe thirty-six hours is possible. I'd rather have seventy-two. And a couple of techs." Sing paused for another drink. Michael assessed the man, briefly wondering how the nuclear engineer would hold up in a firefight. He had investigated him for Marcus a couple years back. He was a Chinese turncoat, a spy. And, from records he could find, he was also a fairly surprisingly lethal individual, trained in Shaolin-style kung fu and tai chi from very early childhood. He was also quite proficient in building and reassembling nuclear warheads.

"Techs are on the way. Damned weather is holding them up." He motioned out the window at the rain. "They're telling me four hours."

"Four hours until they arrive?" Sing asked.

"Yes."

"Oh, well, then I might take a nap."

"Not a bad idea," Michael agreed. "You are serious about the timeline here? What if the techs don't make it for some reason?"

"Seventy-two hours, then. Maybe eighty. Eighty-eight as worst case."

"That soon?" Michael typed the information into an email on a virtual screen in front of him and then he made a similar swiping gesture as Sing just had before. He was keeping actual notes to keep his information straight. This project had a lot of complex moving parts. There were three different countdown clocks in his glasses that continued to tick away.

"I believe so. Like I said, our friends have done most of the heavy work for us. When do we expect to move to our next phase?" Sing asked. "What about the reentry thrusters and heat-shield bodies?"

"Well, that was waiting on you. As soon as you can make

the warheads viable and, more importantly, in our control, we'll move immediately following to the next step of integration. Then, deployment." Michael looked across the swanky decorations of the room to Vladimir, stretched out on the sofa like a frat boy who had landed there after a night of binge drinking and partying. The Russian turncoat was beginning to snore loud enough to become a distraction. Michael looked at Sing as the physicist poured the last bit from the soda can in front of him.

"Give me that." Michael held out his hand. Sing slid the empty can across the table. He then crushed the can with his right hand, grinned devilishly as he took aim, and tossed the crushed can across the room at Vladimir's forehead, hitting him dead center.

"What the hell?!" Vladimir rose up abruptly rubbing at the mark between his eyes, cursing something in Russian that Michael didn't understand. Sing apparently did and started to chuckle.

"Good shot." Sing laughed.

"Hey, V, seventy-two hours."

"*Bozhe moi . . .*" Vladimir muttered while rubbing his eyes with his fists still. "All six warheads?"

"Sing?" Michael looked at the physicist.

"Yes. All six," Sing replied.

"Well, then, Michael, we had best call our friend and start moving on to Phase II." Vladimir straightened himself out and sat up straight. He took a long inhale and then stood, not even wavering in balance as the ship took a deep roll to the starboard side. "You want to call him, or shall I?"

"I'll see if he's available."

"Then, I will have a smoke." Vladimir pulled his cigarettes from a pocket somewhere that Michael hadn't seen. He seemed to just manifest those damned things at will, he thought.

"Not in here, damn it."

Vladimir just mumbled under his breath some Russian curse that Michael still couldn't understand again and then he slowly lumbered toward the door leading to the helicopter deck, lighting the cigarette purposefully before being completely outside.

"What did he just say?" Michael asked Sing.

"Basically, that Americans are pussies." Sing actually laughed out loud.

"That sounds about right." Michael was still annoyed.

✧   ✧   ✧

The avatars of three men—Marcus Dorman, Michael Tarin, and Vladimir Lytokov—all sat at a virtual conference room table. With the active glasses on and in the encrypted channel they might as well have been actually sitting together in a security vault. But in actuality, Dorman was thousands of miles away on the other side of the planet.

"My contact, Georgia, will be joining us any minute now," Marcus Dorman's avatar said. "In the meantime, please, gentlemen, what is the news?"

"Six viable. Seventy-two hours," Vladimir said.

"We're ready to move on Phase II," Michael added. "Are the suits ready?"

Suddenly there was a window that appeared in the middle of the table saying that Georgia was waiting in the lobby. Marcus's avatar tapped the ADMIT button and a fourth avatar appeared in a chair across the table.

"Greetings, gentlemen," Georgia said with a wave of her avatar's hand and a slight flicking of the dark locks out of her face with a shake of her virtual head.

"Ms. Stinson, please advise on the status of the suits and the flight prep," Marcus requested.

"The launch-vehicle tests have all been completed and we can be ready for flight within five days. It looks as if the weather will be good for several days following. The suits are moving more slowly. There was an issue with a seal in the design and they have had to be remanufactured. We are at least three weeks away in that regard," Georgia repeated.

"Shit," Michael said under his breath. "That kills our timetable. The longer we sit on this the more likely we are to be found."

"Can we do it without the suits?" Marcus asked.

"No way in hell," Michael responded. "You can't spend more than thirty seconds in the vacuum without being useless and that would be with lots of practice."

"There is no way to speed up that timeline, Georgia? Money is not a problem if we need more." Dorman held his virtual hands palms up. "You know that our window is very tight here."

"Money would not matter right now. We have all we need. This is a matter of redesign, and remanufacturing, and retesting," she replied. "The pandemics have slowed manufacturing and delivery of many long-lead-time items. In fact, we defaulted to building many of the parts ourselves due to this."

"So, we're screwed by the damned supply chain disruption!" Michael slammed a fist into the table. "Schwab is only there for three more weeks. There just isn't time to wait."

"We all know that, Michael. Please calm down." Dorman gestured with his right hand as if to shush a child who was getting rowdy. Michael didn't appear too happy about that. "Do we have any other options?"

"I'm sorry, Mr. Dorman, none from my end," Georgia said. "I found a couple of old Soviet-era Orlan-D suits for sale by collectors, but I'd be concerned of their viability."

"Vlad, you've been uncharacteristically quiet, my friend." Dorman turned to the Russian.

"Hahaha, 'uncharacteristic,' you say. Maybe. Perhaps at times I'm—how you say . . . boisterous?" Vladimir almost belly laughed. "Ms. Stinson, get the vehicle and my copilot ready. We will bring our own suits."

"Vladimir? What the hell are you talking about?" Michael turned to him.

"Yes, my friend, do tell," Dorman added.

"Michael and I will do what we do." Vladimir smiled. "We'll steal them."

"Steal them?" Dorman exclaimed. "From where? You can't waltz into NASA and steal them. Besides, their suits are custom jobs. And the security on top of that—"

"Dr. Schwab is wearing an unfitted Orlan cosmonaut suit, is he not?" Vladimir asked rhetorically.

"Um, yes, I suppose he is. So?" Georgia answered.

"Ah, Vladimir, you're a freakin' genius!" Michael replied.

"Of course, my friend. That is why you hired me." The Russian's avatar showed a very toothy smile.

"Would one of you two clue me in, please?" Dorman was growing impatient and didn't like being on the outside of information.

"The space tourism company Schwab went through to go to space has them. They use them to train many customers, routinely preparing them for their future space tourism trips. They have many previous-generation Orlan space suits of different varieties on hand they purchased from NPP Zvezda located there in Star City. Schwab had seen to that when he bought the company. We'll steal them from Schwab and he can file it on his insurance." Vladimir rubbed at the ever-present stubble on his chin. "The hardest part will be getting in and out of Star City, but going to a private company makes this easier."

"I'll just buy them," Dorman said, not sure about how much press stolen space suits would cause.

"How would we keep it quiet?" Michael asked. "We don't want to tie you and Schwab together on this either."

"Marcus, my friend, you might could pay off all the various accountants, clerks, security guards, and so on along the way, but sooner or later, probably sooner, some one of them would talk. That implies loose ends that we'd have to deal with. I don't like loose ends. There are already too many engineers involved with the rockets and suits," Vladimir replied.

"We have that contingency planned for." Marcus grunted. "The ones we can't buy, well..."

"Yes, yes. Our problem. And we'll deal with it," Vladimir said. "We don't tell Schwab either."

"But these are just suits." Marcus shrugged. "I could buy them."

"No, buying them is no good. A year ago, sure, you could have bought them. With your recent advertisements about not needing space suits to fly in space, now wouldn't fit. And, after what is about to happen, no. It would be too public. It would implicate you. We need you free to do business. We take them in a way that will never be known they were taken."

"And that is?" Marcus asked.

"Perhaps they have an accident, yes?" Vladimir replied.

"Yes!" Michael agreed. "With lots of fire and maybe even an explosion."

"An accident? What type of accident?"

"One that burns the place to the ground and leaves no evidence of what is missing?" Michael restated more simply. "Schwab will be pissed."

"My thoughts exactly, comrade." Vladimir's avatar turned to Marcus sternly. "Get us a fast chopper here on the ship immediately."

CHAPTER 11

◌

Low Earth Orbit
Somewhere Over the North Pacific Ocean
International Space Station
Thursday
6:15 A.M. Pacific Time

KARL VAN DER SCHWAB HAD BEEN IN AND OUT OF SLEEP MOST
of his sleep cycle due to nausea from microgravity-induced motion
sickness. The drugs his company had made for the very purpose
were only partially helpful. The visually queued app that Marcus
had designed for him only helped while he was awake and wearing
the glasses. At least the drugs had made him drowsy—or maybe
those were the other pills he had taken? He wasn't sure. What he
did know was that he was now floating free of his sleeping bag
and there was a whirling frenzy of activity going on around him.
In fact, there was so much happening he couldn't decipher exactly
what was happening. There were alarms sounding so loud that he
felt his ears would burst. There were violent motions of the space
station tossing him left and right. He flailed about wildly, trying
to grab at some handhold nearby. Anything would do. But he
was helplessly floating about and each time he thought he could
grab something to stabilize himself, it moved away from him.

Bullets had ripped through the bulkhead behind him and he
could hear precious air being evacuated into space. One of the

European Space Agency astronauts was floating and flapping his arms and legs wildly in front of him. Another man floated nearby with blood squirting bright-red jets with each heartbeat between his fingers clasped tightly to his neck. The jet streams of blood sprayed out nearly a meter from him and formed hundreds of red spheres that continued on their vector paths across the compartment only to splatter against the sterile white of the space station interior, making amazing fractal patterns on the wall.

Karl pushed himself to the man and looked down at him. It was Dr. Raheem Fahid.

No! he thought. *I need him!*

"Dr. Fahid! Hold on. I'll get help," van der Schwab told him. The man's eyes only showed fear and the fact that he knew the life was draining from him rapidly with each heartbeat spraying more of his life's blood into the microgravity.

"Damnit! Too soon! I wasn't ready yet!" Karl muttered to himself, only to be startled from a very loud clanging and then a *kathunk!* He finally managed to grasp a handhold and braced for more. He was at one of the computer stations nearest the path of flight direction porthole as what appeared to be the end of a very large spear or harpoon tore through the bulkhead across from him. The barbs of the protrusion extended and then it was pulled back through the hole it had just made until the barbs locked it into place. Karl felt the room shudder as if the entire wall would pull free. He held on for dear life. From somewhere else in the space station, he could hear more gunfire, or at least what he thought was gunfire and then...

"Goood morning, Dr. van der Schwab! It's time to start your day." The high-pitched cartoonish voice of the preset alarm on his data device was just loud enough to break him out of his nightmarish sleep state. It wasn't really that much of a sleep state as it was a choke-back-puke-and-try-to-get-some-rest-between-drug-induced-nightmares state. But sometime about four in the morning either the motion sickness medicine had kicked in or his body finally adapted and he passed out from exhaustion.

Then the nightmares had started. He'd have to report that to his team of doctors, neuroscientists, and pharmacologists. It would be important to see if the motion sickness medicine was interacting with the dendritic protein monoclonal antibodies that he had been taking through a nasal spray. Karl went through the processes in his mind. He had designed the monoclonal antibodies to be wrapped in a dissolving nanosphere so they could penetrate the blood-brain barrier through the olfactory bulb. He had originally gotten the idea from the first-generation pandemic viruses.

Patients had often discussed a loss of taste and smell with COVID-19 and it had often been treated as just olfactory inflammation. But too many of his patients, friends, and colleagues had described an actual "blood and burned metal or plastic" smell in the place of things they used to smell. That had given Karl the idea that the virus was actually penetrating the blood-brain barrier and, in fact, COVID-19 viral particles had been found in spinal fluid and brain tissue. Somehow the virus particles were getting in the brain. Karl had hypothesized that it was through the nose where the olfactory epithelium led into the olfactory bulb. The bulb was in intimate contact with the brain physically, chemically, and biologically.

The motion sickness medicine did have some of the first generation–developed antihistamine diphenhydramine in it, which did penetrate the blood-brain barrier. Perhaps the antihistamine was interacting with the monoclonal antibodies and somehow in return stimulating some response in the brain causing the nightmares. Or, perhaps, it was just coincidence. Karl didn't believe in coincidence.

"Good morning to you, Alvin. Sing me a song, please?" The song "Outlaw" by Alvin and the Chipmunks featuring Waylon Jennings suddenly filled his hotel room. Karl had long since a child been a fan of the animated creation of Ross Bagdasarian and actually had an original copy of the 1958 novelty record "The Chipmunk Song (Christmas Don't Be Late)." The record was priceless now and stored in his vault at his main mansion in an undisclosed location. To Karl the song was beyond priceless the minute he had heard it as young boy. He got a kick out of yelling at his AI device as if he were the fictional David Seville that Bagdasarian played. In his best imitations, which were not good due to his heavy Austrian accent, he would sometimes yell, "Alvin!" Immediately the AI would respond with "Okay!" The little pleasures that wealth afforded him were clearly useless indulgences.

Karl liked those useless indulgences. They separated him from the non-player characters of the rest of the world. He was currently sleeping in what many in the press had considered pretty much the same, an expensive useless indulgence, the ISS. He and Talbot Davidson had followed in the footsteps of Robert Bigelow, but on a much larger scale, spent almost two billion dollars U.S. developing the Davidson-Schwab Inflatable Hotel Module for the ISS. They'd never make their money back via paying customers. But the DSIHM had other purposes that were going to pay off in a very big way someday—someday very soon.

He fumbled clumsily with the sleeping bag system that was attached to the wall, or floor, or bulkhead—he wasn't sure what you called it—of his hotel room suite. He'd seen the brochures and the training manuals and there were fun spacey slash astronaut names for everything that would make the patrons of the future feel like they were getting their money's worth. But Karl had known from the beginning that all of that was a façade for the real purpose of the DSIHM. He'd spent hundreds of hours with Talbot Davidson of Davidson Aerospace discussing the design and true purpose, but he was certain that Davidson never truly believed it would come to pass. But here Karl was in space, in the hotel, attached to the International Space Station.

Karl was in the "Executive Suite," of which there was only one in the DSIHM. There were five other "rooms" but his was the most, well, indulgent. The Executive Suite was about three meters wide by four meters deep by two and a half meters high. The sleeping area had a king-sized sleeping bag that could be zipped into two compartments. At the end of the suite was a curtained-off area for the toilet and hygiene purposes. He reached into a pouch on his bag and pulled out his data glasses and his nasal spray. He took two sprays of the medication in each nostril before putting the white plastic bottle back in the bag. He sniffled briefly and then placed the glasses on. The tabs on the arms of the glasses made magnetic connection with the implants behind his ears and held the glasses firmly in place. The virtual screens lit up as the glasses began handshaking with his audio and neural implants. He started the motion sickness app. "Go ahead and pull up my schedule."

"Yes, sir! Right away," the simulacrum of the cartoon voice replied.

"Thank you, Alvin." Karl fumbled with the motion sickness bags stuck beside his sleep station until he had them sealed properly in the disposal bags and put away in the garbage hamper.

"You are welcome."

"Blech." He turned his nose up at the smell coming from the barf bag as the disposal door *schlurrped* shut with a *whoosh* from the inwardly pulling air flow. He was certain that the odor, what little of it he had anyway, was probably not the actual smell. If he could detect it, he was certain that it must have been bad and probably smelled different to normal people. Ever since his latest round of treatments his senses of taste and smell were only a fraction of what they had been before that infection. And, atop that, the smells he did have for things were different than what he remembered. Bad odors were all now similar, as if the file for vomit, feces, wet dogs, smoke, and many others had been erased from his brain and replaced with the same default smell. He and Alvin had tried to come up with an algorithm to calculate or at least estimate the percentage of smells he'd lost. The best they'd come up with was around eighty percent with a twenty percent error bar. In other words, he estimated that his sense of smell was operating at about twenty percent.

He only wished his immune system was functioning at twenty percent. At least his company had managed to generate his current regimen of treatments based on previous generations of monoclonal antibodies and studies of previous pandemic viruses combined with cancer research he'd funded and HIV therapies that he held patents on. The cocktail of medicines he had required had kept him alive, but he wasn't certain for how much longer that would last. But he had hopes—high hopes.

He pulled his daily pill container, cautiously removed the pack marked THURSDAY, and placed the contents in his mouth. He then chased them down with a swig of water from his squeeze-bulb water bottle. He did his best not to gag when another hint of the barf bag managed to make it to his brain. He continued to make mental notes when he smelled anything.

Actually, the eighty percent of things he used to be able to smell were like that unholy hybrid of blood and burned material, and this problem had erased one of his favorite useless indulgences—tasting wines, beers, and foods. Not only had his brain lost the information about what most things smelled like, it had also lost the ability to taste many things. The default taste was very similar to that default smell. Some things actually had no taste at all. Karl could literally drink from a ghost pepper sauce bottle with no sensation. Before his illness and treatments he could not even stand jalapenos. That was no longer an issue. He'd love to taste the burning sensation of capsaicin once again.

Even with all his money, he'd found no solution to that problem, or the fact that the treatments had basically left him with acquired immunodeficiency syndrome. He took a small plastic atomizer of cinnamon essence and sprayed it in front of his face. Breathing it in gave him very faint hints of cinnamon candies he'd loved as a child—very faint.

Again, if he could smell it, it must have been very strong. He put the atomizer back in his pouch and suddenly realized he had a fairly bad bile taste in his mouth to go along with the "default" smell. Sometimes he wondered if the treatments had made the odor come from within him and he actually did smell that way or if it was, as he currently believed, a neurological disorder—a deletion of some of his source code. The doctors in the general public had no clue what caused the problem or how to solve it. But Karl did know what caused it. He'd been critical in developing it. And he was pretty certain he knew how to cure it. He hoped.

He didn't like the taste he did have currently in his mouth, even though it was an actual taste, so he made his way toward his personal hygiene station and took care of some business there. He brushed his teeth and gargled with an antiseptic mouthwash as he'd trained to do on his previous suborbital flights. In prolonged microgravity it wasn't as easy. But he managed. Besides, the microgravity made other things better, like the continuous pain in all of his major joints. Once he'd hit microgravity almost all of that pain was gone. He suspected a return to gravity would be extremely painful. He wasn't looking forward to that part of the trip.

Alvin scrolled the calendar open in the virtual view display as Karl looked at himself in the tiny round mirror. He wondered briefly if he should worry with shaving. His salt-and-pepper stubble was just barely starting to show through with a day's worth of growth. He decided to wait. He noted that his first order of business for the morning was to do a complete trek from one end of the International Space Station to the other. He had an hour and forty-five minutes set aside for that adventure. It shouldn't take a tenth that, but Karl planned to be thorough and learn every little nook and cranny of the giant low-Earth-orbiting spaceship. Then he had an eating cycle followed by a scheduled appointment with Dr. Raheem Fahid, the noted virologist, astronaut, and creator of the longest self-assembling monoclonal protein crystals humanity had ever created. Had it not been for a previous version of those microgravity-grown miracles, Schwab wasn't certain he'd have survived his last pandemic infection. He honestly wanted to pay the man his compliments for saving his life atop the other reasons he had for being there.

"Sir, you have an incoming encrypted audio message from Mr. Dorman."

"Go ahead and play it."

"Okay," Alvin replied.

The glasses connected on a very close-proximity, low power–proprietary but Bluetooth-like protocol to the tiny implants just behind Karl's ears, stimulating the bone and vibrating the eardrum to reproduce the audio information so that only he could hear it. The glasses did have an external speaker and could also connect to earbuds, but for true privacy Karl preferred the internal connection.

"Greetings, Karl. Hope you are feeling better this morning. Once you are up and about, let me know. We're ready to pull the data feed for the photogrammetry survey of the ISS interior when you are ready to go. Can't wait to compare it to the blueprints and ground model data we have. Also, let us know when you attach the backdoor transmitter to the ISS main systems processor. Our hacker friend is awaiting that signal. And, FYI, our contact at the Huntsville Operations Support Center has applied the software patch to the communications downlink and it is active..."

CHAPTER 12

ᏩᎧ

Near Tampa, Florida
Thursday
6:30 A.M. Eastern Time

"TWO DAYS AGO?" U.S. ARMY MAJOR JAMES "KENNY" THOMPSON leaned back in the beige folding metal chair, balancing it on the back two legs. Frank had to squint to make out features of the man's face and uniform as the large hangar doors behind him, about twenty yards away, were open wide enough for a Cessna 172 to be taxied through, and the Florida sun was causing the major to look mostly like a silhouette. As he rocked back and forth, blocking the light, Frank could observe better detail. He noted both the 1st Special Forces Operational Detachment-Delta (1st SFOD-D) and the Airborne patch on his uniform. He was Delta Force.

Frank decided as the ranking visitor just to sit back and listen for a bit. There was a continuous clamoring and bustling of activity all around them as one team set up barrier walls around them. The walls were soundproofed, about six inches thick, eight feet wide, and Frank was guessing twelve feet high. The crew was pushing them into place and bolting them together to create a large interior room. They maneuvered a panel that blocked out the sunlight from the hangar doors, making visibility better. The panel had a white painted solid core standard door with a push-button cypher lock on it. Frank had a feeling some Special Security officer had required this in order to get Top Secret clearance for the hangar bay area.

Inside the new "room" a second team, an IT team, was working feverishly. They had already connected eight different seventy-two-inch-diagonal, high-resolution monitors on large wheeled stands like rolling whiteboards. There were several printer and scanning stations being set up about the room as well. There were two civilians crawling about the floor and behind the computer stations being assembled, threading cables up pass-through holes in the gray metal computer tables to two Air Force enlisted soldiers who, in turn, were connecting them and powering on the systems.

Frank just watched and continued to listen and wait. He wanted to assess all of his task force teammates and the ancillary workers to determine who he thought would be most useful. After a bit, he was beginning to realize that one young USAF airman first class was the one making the equipment actually come to life and work. She was installing patches to the software and performing whatever computer magic that needed to be done with wizardry expertise. Frank made note of her name, A1C Shannon. Sometimes staying silent and doing some forward recon paid off. Besides, the Navy warrant was doing a great job explaining the situation.

"Yes. Just over two days ago now," Navy CW4 Wheeler McKagan continued. "Dr. Banks and I have gone over and over the intel sources and the best we can figure is they vanished somewhere into the northeastern portion of Kazakhstan near Oral. From there, we have nothing. No intelligence information from any source or method."

"Well, they couldn't have just 'vanished,'" an Army major with Ranger, Airborne, and Sapper patches commented. "No assets overhead, on the ground, or anywhere that has them?"

"Not according to any sources we can find," Dr. Banks said. "Our experts across the intelligence community have nothing. Every resource has been authorized and put to work, but so far, nothing."

"Um, if I may?" A tall skinny civilian in a poorly fitted suit and tie raised his hand.

"Dr. Grayson, no need to raise your hand." Banks turned to the nervous looking thirty-something. "Everyone, this is Dr. Kevin Grayson with NSA."

"Um, yes, okay. Um." Grayson stammered while he tugged at the sleeves of his brown sports coat. He continued to display stammers and tics while fidgeting nonstop and Frank wanted to strangle the man and tell him to spit out whatever the actual fuck he was going to say. "We've run all of our filtering algorithms, even some of my own modified ones, and there are just no hits across any comms traffic. Whoever they are, well, they are using highly encrypted capabilities that we've yet to detect, or they are being so careful about how they communicate that no filters have been tripped and we've yet to spot them. It has only been about thirty-six hours since the HPC facility in Utah has been running on this. Perhaps it is just a matter of time."

"Uh, Professor, excuse me," the Army Ranger interrupted. "HPC?"

"Oh, yes, the High Performance Computing facility. A supercomputer. I suspect, perhaps, the most super-supercomputer ever built," Grayson said proudly. Frank suspected the man wished the HPC facility were a woman, or maybe a man—he wasn't sure. But he was sure the man was in love with his supercomputer. He wanted to chuckle but thought better of it.

McKagan jumped back in. "The only real lead that might be investigated is this Colonel Lytokov. His is the only name we have. Every agency from here to Moscow has pulled everything in every database known looking for leads."

"As you all can see, we currently have very little to go on," Banks said. "We were given this hangar as our tactical operations center with access to whatever we need. The hangar area has been cleared for temporary classified conversations and we have full computer connectivity to the intel networks and databases being set up inside the main offices spaces behind me. Sergeant Robinson here will see to your logistical needs as they arise. Staff Sergeant?"

"Thanks, Dr. Banks." The Air Force noncommissioned officer stood at ease. He started speaking as though he were reading from a to-do list. "There are office spaces down the hallway on each side. If you are lucky, they have a folding chair stored in it. They've been swept and mopped, but, well, these offices have been abandoned for probably a couple years now since the last one hundred percent telework mandate. So, pardon the state of repair. Just pick you a spot for quarters and let me know if you have specific needs. I'm having cots and furniture brought over. IT guys are already connecting classified terminals as well as voice-over IP units in each. As you noted when you entered, we collected all your electronics and cell phones and they have to stay in the lock boxes or outside of the hangar area. Finally, there are bathrooms with showers on either end of the hallway that connects like a T in the middle of the main one. I'm having some general-purpose supplies brought in as well. Again, if you need something, tell me. My job is to make certain you have whatever you need so you can focus on your task at hand. Before you all file out, A1C Shannon here...um, Shannon, raise a hand..."

"Here, Staff Sergeant." A1C Sonya Shannon climbed up from the floor behind one of the computer consoles she was bringing online at one of the tables surrounding them. Her Afro was pulled into a regulation of two braided tails about shoulder length and her nails, while painted blue, were closely trimmed and real. She had the appearance of a soldier hard at work, but one who got personal satisfaction from that work. She plugged a cable into a slot in the KVM switching box on the desk and depressed a power button. Nothing happened. A flash of realization spread across her face and she smiled again and depressed a button on the switch with a red label attached to it.

At that moment one of the big screens lit up with a red image reading TOP SECRET at the top and bottom. She nodded triumphantly and calmly to herself but then abruptly turned stoic as if she were proud of accomplishing one task yet sobered to the fact that there was an undoubtably long list of tasks before her. Frank could tell that the young airman had that quality about her that was a doer, a leader.

"Thanks, Shannon," Robinson continued. "She will get your accounts set up and show you how to work the portal we've set up for all data pertaining to this task force. If you need help, she'll also be here to help you set up your certificates for your other classified email accounts and such. One more note I have is that there are a few more task force team members coming to join us over the next few days. We'll start on their quarters after we get you squared away. My notes show a USAF major, a Space Force lieutenant colonel, and a handful of civilian scientists for various agencies."

"Thanks, Staff Sergeant." Banks nodded. "Any other questions?"

There were a few logistics questions. Frank waited silently

and continued to listen. There was a bit of discussion about getting intel on the Russian colonel, but Frank was sure that was
not going to get them anywhere immediately. If that colonel was
careful enough to pull off stealing six nukes and taking out his
own soldiers then, Frank was pretty certain, any information that
might lead to him was dead, long dead, by now.

They needed a lead. Any lead. Frank wasn't even completely
sure where to start. But like the SEALs say, any hard task is like
eating an elephant. Just take it one bite at a time. The key is just
to start taking manageable bites. Marines, on the other hand,
would tend to just kill that damned elephant and keep moving
forward, but only if the enemy were using them as tanks. And
who wants to eat a tank? Eating it or killing it, one thing was
for certain: at the moment they didn't even have an elephant.

They needed to know where they were taking those damned
warheads. If CIA and NSA hadn't picked up any communications
on the things, then that suggested one of two things. One, they
were not communicating or had very advanced tech. Either suggested a well-thought-out plan and execution thereof. And, two,
there was no intention of trying to sell the warheads, which could
only mean one outcome: They intended to use them.

"Well, can anybody tell me if any of this equipment is actually up and running yet?" Frank asked.

"Sir, this console here and this monitor are up and running.
And they are connected to the Intel network," A1C Shannon
replied, looking up from her present task.

"Okay, then, can somebody bring up the last known location
of the nukes and this Russian colonel on a modern map?" he
ordered more than asking.

"Sure thing, Colonel." CW4 McKagan stepped over to the
console and typed in his username and eighteen-digit password.
"Spy satellite imagery has them just at the border of Russia and
Kazakhstan above Oral. As soon as this damned thing boots up..."

"There are no other data telling us where they might have
gone from there," Dr. Grayson added. Frank repeated that in his
head and wasn't sure if you were supposed to say *is data* or *are
data*. He'd always said *is data*. He thought it sounded pompous
whether it was correct or not.

"...Okay, here we go. Here is the image from the satellite
taken a couple hours before anyone seemed to realize there was

a problem," McKagan continued as the spy satellite imagery video played. He paused it here and there to make points. "Here is the Topol-M TEL right there and everything appears to be intact. You can see the soldiers scurrying about. And if we zoom in here, leaning against the TEL is Lytokov. The resolution isn't enough to determine this from facial features, but from multipoint analysis, gait analysis, and knowing the reported heights of the men in the unit the confidence is pretty high this is him."

"Yeah, yeah. Okay. But I need you to zoom out and show me this place on a map." Frank waved a hand at the screen. "You know, with cities and roads, and rivers, and train tracks and stuff, all of it marked with a legend."

"Well, we can start with Google Earth, I guess," Dr. Banks suggested. "We've been looking through the most recent public map images and data but haven't found anything yet."

"Okay, zooming a bit over Kazakhstan..." McKagan worked the controls until the map zoomed into a region a couple hundred miles wide with the missile's location at the center. "How's that, Colonel?"

"Hit the map layer on."

"Okay, done."

"Hmm, there's a river that leads down through Kazakhstan all the way to the Caspian Sea. Any hits on boats or anything?" the Delta Force major asked.

"Not to my knowledge." Banks shook her head. "The Office of Naval Intelligence has several taskers open and active right now to look for anomalous gamma ray spikes. So far, nothing. And nobody from OSD, the DNI"—the Office of the Secretary of Defense and the Director of National Intelligence, respectively—"or any other groups tasked have found a thing. These guys are like ghosts. We've even tasked HUMINT"—Human Intelligence—"assets in the region. Nothing."

"Zoom out a bit more," Frank requested. There were red lines stretching north and south and in several other directions. "What are those red lines demarking?"

"Hmm, train tracks it looks like," McKagan replied after zooming in some and expanding the legend. "Dr. Banks, could you get any video imagery from assets, street cameras, cell phones, etcetera, along these tracks for the twenty-four-hour period following the satellite imagery?"

"We'll need to task our contacts at NRO"—the National Reconnaissance Office—"the team at Langley—and Dr. Grayson, could you task the computer for that as well?" Banks pushed an unruly lock of blond hair back over her right ear. "Let's get through this exercise, and I'll keep a list. What else, Colonel Alvarez?"

"I don't know. Something about the Caspian Sea doesn't sit right with me."

"Land locked," McKagan agreed. "If I were trying to get out of there and away from prying Russian eyes I'd want to get to sea as soon as I could."

"Why not via air?" A1C Shannon asked from underneath another console. Suddenly, her demeanor turned sheepish as if she had realized she probably shouldn't have been interrupting the senior officers' meeting. "Uh, sirs? I mean."

"Airman," Frank looked expressionlessly at her. In situations like they found themselves currently, he wasn't one to be a stickler about protocol and formalities. Sometimes, damned protocol was useful and necessary, but sometimes it could get you killed. "We've got a rogue Russian colonel with maybe six nuclear warheads planning God only knows what out there somewhere. If you have thoughts about where, don't keep them to yourself. That's an order."

"Uh, yes sir. I was just thinking, why not just fly out of there with the nukes?" Shannon asked sheepishly as she shrugged her shoulders with her palms raised upward.

"Might be too hard to shield the gammas," McKagan said. "They'd have to be in heavy boxes to keep radiation instruments from detecting them. Be a big enough bird that would stand out and we could see easily. Could be hidden in a cargo plane or something similar, but where is the nearest runway for that type of aircraft? Oral is it, most likely. There haven't been any hits on that."

"We're looking, the Russians are looking. Flying isn't the right option," Banks added. "If they're flying, we or somebody else is likely to find them."

"Then trucks?" Shannon asked again.

"Well, we all thought of that, I'm sure, but the problem is, once again, we're looking and the Russians are looking," Banks explained. "There would be street cameras, Wi-Fi hotspots, and plain old traffic cops they would have to deal with."

"I'm thinking the Black Sea," Major Casey Dugan, the Army Ranger, suggested. "Look it, if you want to get to sea, somehow you need to get there first."

"Yeah, but the Russians and NATO are all over the Black Sea," Dr. Grayson said. "And the diplomatic situation there is very dicey at the present."

"Maybe that's not a bad thing." Frank rubbed at the stubble growing on his chin. Time to shave, sleep, and eat in any order, he thought. "For them, I mean."

"How so, Colonel?" Banks asked.

"There are a bunch of nuke ships and subs there in the Black Sea. Plenty of background gammas and stuff. Might be easiest to hide in plain sight. Hell, I know the Russians have nuke subs right there at Novorossiysk, which would be a perfect entry point. But how they would get there from Kazakhstan is another question." Frank looked at the map a bit longer. Nothing was jumping out at him at the moment. "Trains was my first guess, but I'm not really seeing the pathway."

"Any other thoughts, Colonel?" McKagan asked.

"Nah. Hell, I'm grasping for anything here. We need another approach." Frank thought for a moment. "How many physicists and nuclear engineers are there out there that could take MIRVs off an ICBM and reverse engineer them into something useful?"

"Shit, that can't be many." Major Dugan nodded in agreement. "That is a specific skill with specific training requirements. I'm guessing less than a thousand?"

"Alright, I think we start there perhaps. Can we get names of scientists or techs or whatever the hell that could do that and let's start there?" Frank asked. "CIA has to have that kind of stuff? DTRA? Or somebody?"

"Actually, Colonel, that is something I can help with," Banks replied. "I've worked with that group in McLean and the Pentagon. I'll take that action."

"Okay, then. Airman First Class Shannon?"

"Yes, sir?"

"Added to all your other tasks, you keep looking at this map and try to think of how you'd sneak out of there without getting caught. If you think of anything, let me know." Frank held back chuckles. Dr. Banks looked back and forth between them, not sure if he was serious or not. Frank wasn't going to let on which either.

"Yes, sir."

"Staff Sergeant, what about the PX, mess, or a pizza delivery place around here?" Frank asked.

"Colonel?"

"Food. Where do we get food? I'm hungry. You can't fight a war on an empty stomach. No sleep maybe, but an empty stomach, no way."

CHAPTER 13

∾

Low Earth Orbit
International Space Station
Thursday
9:30 A.M. Eastern Time

"LOOKING THROUGH THE MICROSCOPE FEED HERE..." DR. FAHID pointed at the monitor. "You can see the little xenobots working diligently to self-replicate. On Earth, in gravity, they form into shapes like a flattened-out Pacman. I'm sure you've seen the many videos of them. For whatever reason, the stem cell and frog embryo mixture there always reproduces the same shape. This will continue for nearly a dozen generations before they stop reproducing for some unknown reason."

"So, yes, I've seen those on Earth real-time, Raheem," Schwab told the scientist. "These are clearly different."

"Yes, my friend. I can tell you have been paying close attention for the past couple of days. As you notice here, these are more three-dimensional and more like an hourglass than a ball, as one might think."

"Well, actually, if you take the Pacman-shaped ones in two-dimensions with an axis through them along the back of the C, or Pacman's back, and then rotate that C about that axis it makes more of an hourglass shape. Simple rotation of solids-math problem," Karl argued.

"Hahaha! Dr. Schwab, in two days you realized what it took us years to discover. We tried and tried to build the three-dimensional version for a decade and each time the more Pacman xenobot was reproduced by them. Certainly, we have managed to engineer the shape to be circles, triangles, stars, amorphous, but the most fit for survival seems to be the Pacman shape. A Pacman more like a pancake, not a ball." He paused to steady himself with a hand against the console. Dr. Fahid tended to wave his hands about as he spoke and in microgravity this imparted angular momentum.

"Sure, gravity limits their movements. But you'd think being in a mixture and being practically neutrally buoyant might enable three-dimensional growth and replication," Karl said. He had learned to be more still, mainly due to the motion sickness that still hadn't subsided. Any fast movements made his head start spinning, which in turn amplified the nausea. One of Dorman's brilliant coders had also sent him an app that displayed an avatar of him with axes of rotations shown. From the accelerometers and gyros built into the microcircuitry of the glasses and a detailed photogrammetric map of the wearer, which it had, the app would calculate the avatar's rotation and suggest countermovements. Karl had gotten very good at playing the game and keeping his body fairly stationary in the microgravity. Just holding himself still using the feedback of the glasses had an almost meditative effect on the brain. He enjoyed it. Karl made a mental note that some version of that would be a great "spa activity" for the hotel.

"Well, yes and no," Fahid corrected him. "You see, these things are always grown in shallow Petrie dishes whereas there is a flat boundary on bottom and a meniscus on top with only a few millimeters at best of depth."

"Yes, I see." Karl rubbed his chin slowly in thought. "But millimeters of depth is very deep to these micromachines. This is like swimming in an Olympic depth pool for them. My guess is somehow gravity is giving them a restraining direction."

"Hahahaha! Once again, Dr. Schwab you are apparently correct! I see why you funded this research now. You understand it quite well. This experiment proves this." Fahid again sounded impressed by Schwab. Karl couldn't believe the naivete of the man. Did he think an investor would grant millions and not understand to what end? Fahid continued explaining. "It is an effect, but we do not understand the mechanism through which they detect gravity yet. But, that has led us to this next experiment."

Raheem Fahid worked the touch screen through a couple of pull-down menus and then changed the live view on the screen. A new microscope camera view showed a set of the same hour-glass-shaped xenobots self-replicating. But there was something notably different about these microbots. Very notably different.

"Spike proteins!" Schwab exclaimed, pointing so excitedly that it made his freefall unstable. The glasses showed him to move his left hand and right foot simultaneously. He chose to grab a hand-hold to steady himself instead. "Spike proteins and lots of them."

"Yes indeed! Each of these cells carries very large dendritic proteins that seem to be identical in every way on each generation. And, thus far, I have managed to measure nineteen generations with identical proteins and no mutations. These are being built more so than born. Very unique indeed!"

"How many proteins per bot?"

"Interesting question. They are designed from a standard monoclonal antibody or antigen. As you can see here, not all the proteins look the same." He zoomed in on a still shot of the xenobot and rotated it about in all dimensions. "All three proteins for severe acute respiratory syndrome and Middle East respiratory syndrome coronaviruses are here. Others can be added if we like. I made a batch with the p53 and BRCA 1 and 2 breast cancer tumor suppressor proteins. They seemed to be more susceptible to folding that could lead to prions."

"Really? That is very interesting." Karl thought about the applications of that long term. The prion disease diagnostics, treatments, and insurance markets had been a sluggish growth market for the last decade or so. It was a unique place to make a fortune of fortunes. As it stood, only a small percentage of humans got prion-type diseases, which usually ended as brain cancer and death. But if all humans, or just the right percentage, could start getting it, just enough to push the market to trillions, while keeping the growth rate just slow enough to stay under the radar... SARS vaccines and boosters with the spike proteins would be a perfect place to hide such a thing. He made himself some mental notes that his glasses recorded for him.

"The proteins for those still available?" he asked.

"Of course, all of my strange creations are saved and stored."

"And the proteins are longer and more precise than typical monoclonal or chimeric ones grown on Earth?"

"Of these you see now?" He shrugged cautiously as to not whip himself about in the microgravity and then nodded proudly. "Yes."

"Any way to kill these things?"

"Kill them?" Fahid sounded shocked and surprised by the question. "They die out after nineteen or so generations. After six months or so, they simply stop replicating and the population dies like a yeast colony."

Booster shots required, Karl thought but he kept that thought to himself. "So, Dr. Fahid, how many of these things have you made so far?"

"See for yourself." The scientist pointed to the Microgravity Dendritic Growth Experiment module and beside it was a small refrigerator.

Karl pushed off the console to the MDGE and braced his socked feet against the wall to have a means of pulling. The refrigerator didn't open. He stopped rather than pulling harder and looked at the handle of the device. There must be a catch.

"Button on top right," Fahid said.

"Ah, okay, I see." Karl depressed the release button and he could feel the catch let go. The door opened with very little resistance. There was a tray there with a ten-by-ten array of vial holder holes. There were only a handful of empty slots. The rest of the slots contained vials that were filled with a clear liquid. Each had a label with multiple alphanumeric sequences and a date printed on them. A second tray filled with vials marked UNVIABLE sat beside it. "Unviable?"

"Ah, yes, the more experimental ones, like I just mentioned with the p53 and BRCA proteins," Fahid explained.

"I see." Karl shook his head in wonder. He noticed there were also several small rectangular containers with a reddish gelatin substance filling them partially. He assumed those were new samples being grown or in stasis, but didn't ask. Just beside those were several small bags of a clear fluid that could be used for intravenous systems. The bags were marked as trial samples ready for use. Karl decided that the doctor had been busy. Money well spent. He closed the refrigerator door. "Wow. How many viable proteins do you think you have made?"

"A computer algorithm is required to be precise, but the

first xenobot will produce for days before going dormant." Dr. Fahid tapped at the touch screen a few times before pulling up a graph showing population growth versus time. He pointed out various interesting points on the curve and how the experimental measurements of the xenobot population tracked with the mathematical model. "During that time, it will replicate as many as five or six times. And each of those seems to be viable for as many as nineteen generations. Using a Lotka-Voltera–type logistics growth model with no predation leads to something like a hundred billion spike protein xenobots, or SPXs—I call them 'specs' for short—per run. That takes about a month or so, and they stay viable for over six months until they cease functioning."

"And we've no idea why they cease functioning?" Schwab was considering if the things had an off switch. If they had an off switch, they would have an on switch. That could prove useful.

"Not really. Perhaps they just get tired from all that building. Maybe it is a normal lifespan of such a creation. Any answer is truly spec...ulation." Fahid raised an eyebrow at Karl with a smile on his face.

"I see what you did there, Raheem." Karl grinned but not for the same reasons that the scientist did. "Very nice work. I'd like a complete download of all your work by tomorrow night. Design models, failures, tests, processes—everything. Don't worry about nice grammar, typos, and such, just get me the information. I'll throw in another twenty million for the continuation of your research. Just stop what you are doing right now and capture everything and get it to me."

"Another twenty..."

"I want everything...by tomorrow night. That means, even the spec...ulations."

"Haha! I see what you did there, Dr. Schwab. Very nice. I'll get right to work."

CHAPTER 14

∽

Black Sea
Thursday
6:25 P.M. Local Time
10:25 A.M. Eastern Time

"THIS ISN'T LIKE WHEN YOU WERE A PROFESSOR AT MIT AND OAK Ridge, feeding information through the Confucius Institute to the Harbin Deng Fong warhead assembly facility, Singang." Sing's sister, Xi Changying—"Ying"—was very heated with her brother. He didn't really give a shit. He had given his twin sister many opportunities to escape, but she wouldn't take them. Something about her personality would allow her to justify helping her brother, but nothing could overwrite the preconditioning of allegiance to the Party.

And, no matter the conversation topic, she always brought up his time at the Y-12 facility at Oak Ridge where he had worked for several years on the Life Extension Program, or LEP, for the B61-7 and B61-11 ICBM warheads. He had managed to obtain, as an American citizen, the highly coveted Q clearance with the Department of Energy. With that, he became part of the nuclear maintenance program.

He had learned all the details of how the American ICBM warhead systems were upkept, assembled, and disassembled through the LEP maintenance activities. He'd trickled classified information to his sister, who at the time was in the Chinese facility at Harbin, a little at a time in order to keep his Party handlers at the Confucious Institute happy enough to leave him in America. He could have been a Party hero. He had the access to everything they wanted. He could have returned to China and lived there as part of the Party with an upper elitist lifestyle. He could have. But he didn't. He hadn't. Sing didn't want that as his endgame. He had other things in mind. He had kept the majority of the stolen classified information to himself. And, finally, when he'd been recalled to work at Harbin, he didn't return to China. That is when he had to vanish. That was when his father had been arrested and his sister had been moved to the Northeast Nuclear Institute near Malan where a closer eye was kept on her. She had been allowed to continue working for the Party, but on less sensitive things.

"You could not do this without my help," Changying continued. "I was always better than you at reverse design of electronics."

"Yes, Ying, I know. Thank you for the interface device design. Very good work. I'm sure you can use that design to gain social points. And I'm certain the Russian documents I supplied you, and the Party, made you many social points."

"They know I'm in contact with you, Singang, and that is the only reason I'm still alive," she replied sourly. "Do you understand that? The only reason I am still *alive*."

She'd been the smarter of the twins since birth. The two were in constant competition, and since she was female in China, she started off behind even though she came into the world a few minutes before him. Eleven to be precise. Having that initial gender chip against her had driven her to always be better at everything than Sing had been. Sing, himself, was brilliant and accomplished. But Ying...

He had been athletic growing up, playing baseball and mastering Wing Chun and Shaolin styles of martial arts. The mental disciplines of the martial arts also enabled him to master academic subjects such as calculus, chemistry, and nuclear physics at a very early age. Seeing her brother's achievements drove Chingyang to do even more. She had made a point to do the same things as her brother while adding other feats and accomplishments. Her list of skills on top of Singang's included tennis, gymnastics, the piano, chess, software development, and coding electronics.

He was always in Ying's shadow or in the midst of the stress of competing with her.

So, the twins, Sing and Ying, were always at each other's throats. But they were still family. There was still a strange loyalty, if not sibling love, ever-present between them. Perhaps, Sing had often thought, it was an actual physical phenomenon between them. Perhaps there was some sort of quantum bond between twins. He'd read countless scientific and philosophic papers on the topic and was beginning to come to that conclusion.

"They will find you, Singang. When they do, they will kill us both," his sister warned him.

"No, Ying. They will not." Sing leaned back in his desk chair and looked away from the computer screen for a brief moment. Looking out the porthole of his room on the yacht he could see that the waves were subsiding and rays of yellow sunlight were peeking through the clouds. He'd noticed that his nausea was settling as well.

"Singang, I am watched much more closely because of how you left. Mother is in prison now. Do you realize this?" Ying was rightfully angry at him he agreed silently. She had always been much more attached to their mother. Singang was okay with being by himself. He hated life in China. Life in the United States had shown him a sort of freedom he had never thought possible. Then he had met Marcus Dorman and realized there was an entirely different level of freedom he had never considered. Sing longed for that type of freedom. He exhaled softly and turned his view back to the computer screen. His sister stared back at him with what could only be described as pure anger.

"I guess I didn't know that. But it is expected." He was a traitor to the Chinese Communist Party and had a price on his head. His sister had been in a high-level position that required a very high-level skill set and that was one of only two reasons she was still allowed to work at the institute and, for that matter, was still breathing. The other reason, of course, was the hopes of still catching Sing with her as bait. Sing wasn't an idiot. This was why he made contact with her, to make her useful to at least keep her worth something to the CCP until he could figure out how to get her free from their grasp. He had a plan. She, herself, was the biggest obstacle to it being successful.

Their father and mother had worked in a factory near Harbin.

Before the move east just after Sing had refused to return to China, their father had met an unfortunate accident. Ying was transferred to Malan and then their mother had been arrested. Sing and Ying both believed their father had been interrogated to death. That had been almost two years ago.

Now, just to communicate with each other, Sing had onetime-use burner phones with an encryption app installed on them delivered from random sources, at random locations, and random times. Sing made certain that his sister had no idea how he was accomplishing that part. Only when *he* contacted *her* could they talk. Sing, of course, knew how he was doing what he was doing and was getting good at it. He had his wealthier friends help him out with the deliveries. And the mercenaries were very good at doing things without getting caught. Atop that, he had a friend that was really good with computers.

"If they find out what I've done..." Ying said nervously. "Even speaking to you about this technology would get me arrested or worse."

"They will not bother you as long as they think you will get more from me. Ying, don't worry. Just turn on the hotspot for the phone you were just sent, connect to it, and send me that last bit of code through the darkweb link I gave you. Look in the 'Notes' file on the phone and you'll find another set of Russian documents you can pass to your masters to keep them off your back for a while longer. Also, there is a decryption key for an electronic wallet. The wallet can't be traced or hacked and it has crypto coins in it, a million dollars U.S. worth. When the time comes, if you can, use that money and get the hell out of there."

"I am not leaving, Singang."

"If you don't, they will eventually imprison or kill you. You have to be ready to go and cut all ties there. I have a plan to find you once an opportunity for escape arises."

"All you would have to do, Singang, is just tell me who you are working for and you could come home. You don't think only the Russians and the Americans know what has happened, do you?" Ying asked. "Of course not! Our spies are just as good as theirs, or better. The Party knows there are warheads stolen and in play. And they believe you are involved somehow. If you let me tell them, we could say this was part of your deep-cover plan all along, and—"

"That wouldn't work and you know it. I can never come home. And I never want to," he said matter-of-factly. "I wish I could convince you to leave. I have money and resources now that you can't imagine. And an opportune moment is swiftly approaching, Yingang. You must prepare yourself—"

"Not while Mother is still alive. I will not."

"Mother would want you to live."

"They'll not let you use them."

"They will not let me use...them..." He repeated her words, letting what she had said sink in until he comprehended her meaning. "What? The nuclear warheads?" Sing laughed.

"Yes. That is what I mean."

"I don't think that can be stopped at this point, big sister."

"Little brother, you just cannot. You will kill millions!"

"Sister, you are far better at math than that to say such dumb things. I, personally, don't plan to kill anybody. Some might die, but of their own ignorance and stupidity. And I don't plan to use them the way you think either. There is a bigger plan at work here. A plan far bigger than even you have deciphered. You must know that I'll do my part until it is done. Things will change soon."

"It's never that easy, brother."

"Easy? It has never been easy. In fact, it has been extremely difficult. I can save you if you let me. And if you will not allow it, then so be it, sister." Sing shook his head back and forth in disapproval and was slightly distracted by the sound of a helicopter approaching.

"You sound...crazy, Singang! Do you hear yourself?"

"You'll see, Ying. Things will change for better...or worse... but they will change. Very, very, soon. I beg you to take the opportunity when it arises. Until then, goodbye, sister."

CHAPTER 15

〰

Turkey Economic Exclusive Zone, Black Sea
Friday
2:30 P.M. Turkey Time (TRT)
7:30 A.M. Eastern Time

THE VERY LARGE MOBILE OIL PLATFORM WAS AN EXACT REPLICA
of the ones that Dorman's offshore holding shell companies had
gifted the Turkish government. It had been part of the deal. Six
multibillion-dollar rigs with one of them to be left alone for
Dorman's uses. The rig was there "officially" for "experimental
purposes" and under the protection of the Turkish Navy. The
mammoth construction of steel sat on two giant submerged pontoons underneath either side. The gray metallic pontoons rested
mostly beneath the water and were only visible when the water
was smooth and clear underneath. Only when the waves got high
could you actually see them break the surface.

Connected to those submerged pontoons, on each end of
each of them, were giant iron oxide red metal upright cylinders
that led up to the first level square metal deck. From the water
surface upward to the underside of the deck level was a large
construction-grade elevator that also had a ladder running up its
side. The ladder had a yellow metal cylindrical safety gridwork
around it all the way up. Parked at the bottom was a sleek,
black, twenty-meter-long monohull speedboat that was only a
slight exaggeration to describe as no bigger than a flea to a dog.

On one side of the deck was an extension off the main square deck marked with green paint and lights as a helicopter pad. Around the periphery of the first deck were white metal buildings with windows evenly spaced. These buildings had been fashioned from metal cargo shipping containers and were stacked three levels high. The containers were easily brought onboard the rig using cargo ships for delivery and the cranes onboard. The containers were bolted and welded together with metal I-beams for support creating what appeared as a floating cityscape three stories high. They housed crew, equipment, and other interior spaces such as the galley.

Three white-and-red-painted metal crane towers spanned from each of the sides of the platform adjacent and farthest from the side with the helicopter pad. There were numerous yellow and red lights flashing continuously across and around the platform. Blue naval and aviation lights lit each corner, edge, and top of the structure. There was a strange architectural cacophony of gridwork, structure, and containers, with the occasional large window thrown in, making it look more like something from a science fiction thriller movie than an offshore oil rig.

In the very center of the platform stood a singular gantry tower that was different from a typical oil-drilling tower. This tower was slightly off-center and had a metal girder arm that extended about four-fifths the way up from the apex. At the apex sat a white painted room about the size of a single railroad car with large windows on all sides—the command tower. There was a flurry of activity about the upper deck surface of the vessel nearest the large gantry tower. The three cranes each manipulated large metal tubing into place about the tower and connected that to the large tank standing on a tower just behind the main one. The tank had the appearance of a city water tower painted white.

Georgia Stinson stood atop the pinnacle command tower, holding on to a safety hand railing of the opened window, overseeing the work that was currently below her by a good twenty meters. The work was slowing but building closer and closer to her height with a calamitous synchronicity of clanking, banging, welding, and other construction sounds, including workers shouting at one another in various languages. And, of course, there was always the ever-present sound of the sea. In the distance she could see the beige-and-white, one-hundred-meter yacht approaching. It wouldn't be long before it was there and they could move to the next phase of integration.

"Ms. Georgia, the cryo team is reporting a problem with one of the pumps on the LOX—liquid oxygen—flow line. There is a back pressure that is not supposed to be there," reported her chief systems engineer for the rig from a few paces behind. She could sense him moving closer by the shuffling of his work boots across the decking. As he carefully approached, she could tell he wouldn't look outward in the direction of the vast openness and the height of the tower.

"One of these days, Ziheer, I will break you of this silly agoraphobia. A strange place to work for a man with such an affliction. Look out there! Openness as far as the eye can see!" Georgia turned to face him. The ocean breeze fluttered her shoulder-length dark black hair in wild wisps, with several locks of her bangs falling over her virtual glasses. She shook her head and tapped at the window controls, bringing the high-impact-proof glass back down into place. The servos whined against the wind load briefly as they pulled the tinted bulletproof glass down, darkening the sunlight. The room quieted as the window seals *schlurrrpp*ed together. Georgia turned to face the engineer but was distracted by the younger, bearded man to her left. He manned the communications station. She had forgotten his name.

"Ma'am, the yacht has asked for permission to approach and dock."

"Yes, I heard that. Bring them in underneath on the starboard dock. Tell them I'll meet them there. And let me know as soon as the cryo ship approaches. We have to start filling that tank as soon as we possibly can."

"Yes, ma'am."

"ETA till docking?"

"Fifteen minutes or so."

"Alright, that gives us time to get to the cryo level. Lead the way, Ziheer." She held her left hand out toward the elevator doors, the only doors leading to the tower.

✧   ✧   ✧

"Dr. Xi," Georgia greeted the physicist and nuclear missile engineer as he carefully crossed the gangplank. "I hope your voyage wasn't too rough."

"The first couple of days were terrible, just damnable. But sometime last night the weather broke completely and the waves subsided. It was pleasant from there," Sing told her.

"I'm glad you are better. Waves and wind aren't really a problem here due to the size of the platform. So you should feel and be better here," Georgia said. "The payloads are almost ready?"

"Not quite. I need some extra hands, as I was promised."

"The hands are here and ready for your direction. We could not wait for them to ready themselves as our colleagues needed the helicopter abruptly. Sorry you had to wait until you were here." Vladimir and Michael got priority over everything and had taken the only helicopter available to the operation at the moment. She could have sent them on the speedboat, but that was her default escape system. It wasn't going anywhere without her in it.

"Yes, I understand that. Michael and Vlad should have gotten back to Kazakhstan by now. We'll hear about that soon enough." Sing nodded in understanding. "I have one completed warhead ready for integration. With the techs, they should be able to follow my work and we can move much faster."

"The techs will be here any moment now, along with the aerospace chassis."

"Yes, that is the next step. Any word on our window?"

"We are less than ninety hours out. We'll start pumping the LOX up to the holding tank very soon. Once we start that our window has an opening limit. Then, of course, there are orbital mechanics to deal with."

"Any cushion on that?" Sing asked her.

"Not much, so don't waste time talking to me."

"Understood. When will you start actually stacking the rocket?"

"If we follow the launch procedures, we have to start stacking within the next thirty-two hours. At that time, we are possibly vulnerable to overhead eyes. If they have reason to look, which they should not." Georgia turned as the dock elevator clanked down into place and opened. The large metal framework outer gate doors with the black-and-yellow caution paint slid open. The top half moved upward and the bottom downward into the floor. Then the actual elevator doors opened side to side. The very large elevator was filled with a half dozen people, some in lab gear, others dressed normally for an oil rig. They were all standing peripherally around a large pallet jack with several crates stacked on top of one another.

"Not a lot of time," Sing said with a raised eyebrow.

"We've had several years to prepare," Georgia replied.

"Yes, but time seems to crunch in on you as you approach the endgame."

"Endgame? I think your description is flawed. This is merely the beginning, Dr. Xi. Merely the beginning!"

CHAPTER 16

∽

Near Tampa, Florida
Friday
11:30 A.M. Eastern Time

"WHY DID IT TAKE THE DAMNED CIA SO LONG TO GET US THIS?"
Lieutenant Colonel Francisco "Frank" Alvarez was pissed. There
were a half dozen nukes out there somewhere and it had taken
more than twenty-four hours to get a simple analyst report on
scientists and engineers that could, perhaps, with a lot of help,
make a Russian Topol-M warhead a viable single nuclear device.
Why was that such a hard task? Was the CIA slow-rolling them
for some reason? Didn't they have this information collected
already?

"Colonel, it has only been a day." Dr. Ginny Banks sat down
in the chair next to him. "Let's look at what they got and see if
it is useful. I'm certain many people stayed up all night developing this report."

"I'm sure you're right." He still didn't like having to wait
so long for it, though. And conversations he'd had with Mac,
Thompson, and Dugan overnight suggested to him that they
had thought it a bit strange as well. Not strange enough for a
conspiracy, but certainly strange enough for incompetence. There
was plenty of the latter in the federal government.

The two of them sat in front of one of the big screens and

the console table it was connected to. The IT teams and logistics crew had completely built a large high-tech room that had been approved for temporary use as a Top Secret/Sensitive Compartmented Information Facility. That in itself was a fairly amazing effort, but having the weight of the Joint Chiefs behind the task force probably lubricated a lot of sticky wickets in standard procedures, processes, and protocols.

"I spoke with the lead analyst and he assures me that he got no sleep last night."

"Yeah, well, neither did I. And neither did you. And neither did Thompson and Dugan. And neither did McKagan over there. Hell, I bet A1C Shannon sat up all night looking at that damned map." He threw a thumb over his right shoulder, pointing out that the SEAL had been up all night at his console going over every lead he could find. "Dead ends."

Banks pulled the keyboard from in front of Frank and started tapping away at it. She worked the mouse over a few different folders until she had the right file path open.

"Here we go." The top secret file opened with a spreadsheet filled with names, photos, descriptions, and last known locations and contacts.

"How many did it turn out to be?" Frank asked.

"About a thousand." She scrolled down the spreadsheet to the bottom. "One thousand and seventy-one to be exact."

"Damn long list. Hey, Mac!" Frank got the SEAL's attention.

"What's up?" Chief McKagan slid his chair in their direction so he could get a better view of their screen. "What is that? The geek list?"

"Yes."

"Too big?"

"Too big."

"Thirds?"

"Yep."

"Okay, send me my third. You got my JWICS."

"Ginny, you mind taking a third of this and going through it?" Frank asked the CIA operative.

"I planned to go through the entire thing," she replied. "What about Dugan and Thompson?"

"Thompson muttered something about trigger circuits and he

and Dugan went somewhere else. Said they'd be back in an hour or so," McKagan explained. "So, we're it right now."

"Yeah, since we're in a hurry. Dr. Banks, you start with the top third. I'll work the middle." Frank turned back toward McKagan. "Mac, you hit the from the bottom up."

"Copy," McKagan affirmed.

"Anything out of the ordinary—I mean anything," Frank said, "don't just flag it, bring it to everyone's attention."

"This will take some time," Banks said. "Something we don't have much of."

"I know," Frank agreed. "Damn it. I know."

USN Chief Warrant Officer 4 Wheeler "Mac" McKagan had been awake going on two days. He'd made it for triple that during BUD/S but this was different. During Basic Underwater Demolition/SEAL training it was more of a stamina thing. But now, at this moment, he was having to maintain his mental faculties at a level of an intelligence analyst and had to be able to make connections to the most minute of details. At least BUD/S had made his mind and body sharp enough to handle such situations.

He'd started with the scientists on the lists at the very bottom. Number one thousand and seventy-one was a Dr. Rama Zuzarte from New Delhi. Mac laughed at that. He knew Rama fairly well. The two of them had been on one of the Iranian inspection teams for the United Nations. Rama was a good guy. Mac read through the CIA analysts' details in the report.

> *Zuzarte has potentially dangerous extremist political viewpoints involving state department policy with the Muslim tradition in local New Delhi and national politics. His right-wing extremism has been shown through his support of India's long history with the current atmosphere heavily tilted in favor of right-wing extremist politics and lobby groups. His social media interactions have been shut down on all normal sites, though he is still actively posting on the newer right-wing extremist platforms.*

"What is this gobbledygook?" McKagan said under his breath but kept reading.

> *Zuzarte's right-wing extremist leanings are multisource verified and are based on multiple factors including his own personal opportunity editorial publications. Specific agendas include but are not limited to: 1) he has been in continuous opposition of the unchecked Muslim migration into and throughout India with outspoken pleas for closing the border; 2) he is outspoken with the belief that Muslim men are purposefully marrying Hindu women in order to convert them through "love jihad" likely based on his middle daughter of three marrying a Muslim man and converting to Islam; 3) he has been quoted as initially profiling Muslims as terrorists; and 4) he has been placed as a well-known and self-proclaimed Hindu zealot.*

"How in the fuck is this useful?" McKagan whispered aloud. "Zealot? Rama had often said 'praised be God' to everything, but nothing out of the ordinary. This is crazy."

> *Relying on secondary sources, Dr. Zuzarte has been noted as stating the incompetency of other political parties (including left-wing parties). Drawing on several examples, sources cite Zuzarte may be involved with the rise of fringe groups that openly campaign for the eventual turn against the government control of federal socioeconomic and medical systems. The CIA has placed him on a watch list of potential antigovernment religious zealots possibly linked to various insurrection groups.*

The chief continued to read through the data and the mini dossier on his old colleague and wondered what they might write about him. The dossier information was, well, accurate, but completely taken out of context and overblown. He was getting the impression that someone was building a hit-piece on Zuzarte, but to what end he wasn't sure. The one useful bit of information in the report was that Zuzarte had been at the University of New

Delhi now for over a year and was in New Delhi currently with no travel or travel plans noted. Unless the bad guys were bringing nukes to the University of New Delhi, Zuzarte was clean.

"Next." Mac continued up the spreadsheet from the bottom.

> *Tatiana Yorgolvech, currently at Tomsk Physical Institute. Previously employed at the Tomsk-7 Reactor Facility, Seversk, Russia...*

After reading through the Yorgolvech file, he paused and took a breath. This was inefficient. There had to be a quicker way to get through this information. Where was that damned Dr. Grayson's supercomputer? Mac slowly scrolled the spreadsheet list upward and scanned at the names as they passed. There were Yamada, Yazaki, Young, Yates, Yi, three different Yuns and over twenty Yus, there were several names starting with *Y* he'd never heard of, and he was just getting started. He also noted that the list hadn't been alphabetized, but rather the names were grouped by starting letter. He wondered why the analyst hadn't bothered to use the function in the spreadsheet.

He continued to read down the list and then something there nagged at him. He wasn't sure but there was something about one of the names he couldn't put a finger on. Xi Singang. He stopped there and read it again to himself. Xi Singang. He'd heard that somewhere before.

"Xi Singang," he read out loud. "Now why does that sound familiar to me?"

He opened up the dossier on Xi Singang and continued to read.

> *Xi Singang by birth name. Naturalized American Citizen with the name Thomas Sing. No known relatives. He was known as "Sing." Dr. Sing achieved doctoral degrees in General Physics and in Nuclear Science and Engineering from Massachusetts Institute of Technology (MIT). He was the lead scientist with Top Secret/Q caveat clearances among others as well as an active polygraph examination. He worked as a team lead on the Warhead Life Extension Program (LEP) at Oak Ridge National Laboratories. Dr. Sing's whereabouts are unknown. He is suspected of being*

*connected with the ring of spies known as the Chinese
Confucious Institute. There are no open investigative
actions currently as he is assumed dead.*

"Assumed dead? Now that doesn't sound like what I remembered," Mac muttered to himself.

He continued to read through the rest of the information about Xi, but that was about it. There were three other Xis on the list but nothing else other than the name seemed to be correlated. He looked at those files and found nothing useful. The information on those Xis was almost as minimal and cryptic. Something just wasn't sitting well with him on this entry. There was all that nonsense information on Zuzarte, but little on Xi or any of the other Xis for that matter. The Yu and Yun entries were short as well. He made a mental note to mark Xi for the time being and then compare other entries once he had more data.

Mac had been reading for almost an hour when he realized that someone was tapping him on his shoulder and his face was planted firmly against the keyboard. A slight bit of drool pooled at the corner of his mouth and had built up on the space bar. The hand on his shoulder startled him, making him spring awake instantly ready for action.

"Whoa! Easy Chief." Army Major Casey Dugan stepped backward cautiously, giving the SEAL room.

"Uh, yeah, sorry about that, Major. Too many years in the Hindu Kush to be sneaked up on like that." McKagan gathered his composure. "I might need some coffee."

"Yeah, that or some freakin' shut-eye." Dugan laughed. "I know how you feel. They rolled that bed in my quarters but I never got to use it. After years in Iraq and Northern Africa, I'm a little edgy sometimes too."

McKagan nodded in agreement, but decided on the coffee. He rolled his neck left then right and stood with a hybrid mix of sounds crossed between a grunt, a sigh, and a yawn. Then he pulled a Styrofoam cup from the stack by the coffee maker and placed the individual serving cup of dark roast into the device. He depressed the start button and nothing happened. Then there was a beeping sound, a little red light blinked displaying that the unit was out of water.

"Shit," McKagan said. There was a stack of bottled water under the table for just such purposes. He went about tearing some bottles free of the packaging and then refilling the coffee maker. "What's on your mind, Major?"

"So, Major Thompson and I were just talking about what you would actually have to do to reverse engineer a Russian warhead to make it your own personal warhead. We assumed you'd have a Russian instruction manual. We called a mutual UXO"—unexploded ordnance—"buddy of ours and talked that through with him." As he talked, both Lieutenant Colonel Alvarez and Dr. Banks looked from their consoles and started paying attention.

"Yeah, go on." McKagan finally got the coffee brewing. The familiar sounds of brewing and hot coffee streaming into the cup were reassuring.

"Well, there's just no way you could get through the front electronics with keys and passwords and whatnot without, well, keys and passwords and whatnot."

"I can see that," McKagan agreed.

"So, we came to the conclusion that you'd need to strip all that away to the bare bones of the warhead and control the actions of the nuclear explosion process with a new circuit."

Mac stirred a packet of sweetener into his cup and then carefully sipped it. It was hot. He hoped it would wake him up.

"Okay, so you need a new control box," he agreed.

"Yeah, but who could build that? You'd need a new control box to replace the old control box. And you'd have to be able to disconnect the old control box without causing problems. I suspect there is a test unit that can be plugged into these things as they work on them, upgrade, or decommission them, right?" Dugan asked rhetorically. "Ours are, like, in Oak Ridge or the Pantex Plant in Texas or maybe out in Nevada. I'm not sure, but..."

"Wait a minute!" The SEAL set his cup down on the table and went back to the console he'd be using. It had long since locked him out and he had to retype his eighteen-digit password. "There is something to what you're saying. Hold on."

He quickly opened his spreadsheet back up, scrolled to the bottom, and then opened the files on Xi Singang. He scrolled to the main information passage and read it out loud.

He ended with "'Dr. Sing's whereabouts are unknown. He

is suspected of being connected with Chinese Confucious Institute. There are no open investigative actions currently as he is assumed dead.'"

"Whereabouts unknown?" Dugan noted. "And he was at Oak Ridge."

"The big thing is that he worked the nuclear LEP. That's the program for refurbing and maintaining our nuclear arsenal. He would have had access to the test boxes like you are talking about." McKagan had been certain there was something more to this guy than just missing. There was more on this man somewhere in other intelligence he'd seen somewhere else in his life. For the life of him, he still couldn't recall it. "This could be our guy. There's something about him."

"What else does it say about him in the file?" Dr. Banks asked.

"That's just it, there's nothing else," Mac said.

"That's curious." Frank turned to his screen and started scrolling. Mac could tell he was opening the same files on his monitor. "What the hell? Dr. Banks, I think your analysts got tired by the end of this thing."

"What d'ya mean, Colonel?" Banks asked.

"The data files on average seem to be much smaller near the end," Frank said.

"Hmmm. I hadn't noticed that."

"So, where does that leave us with this Sing?" Dugan asked.

"There isn't enough data here to do much with. But I know I've read more on this guy somewhere."

"Hang on a minute," Frank told them. He grabbed the phone and dialed a number from memory. Wheeler and the rest of the team watched the marine curiously. The pause in the conversation gave Mac long enough to pick his coffee cup back up and nurse it some more.

"Who's he calling?" Dugan asked Banks.

"I dunno."

"Toby! Hey, man, it's Frank." Alvarez said cheerfully into the phone. "Can you go secure on your end? Okay...three, two, one, secure. There we go. So, look, I need everything the FBI has on one Xi Singang, aka Thomas Sing. Went to MIT. Worked at Oak Ridge. DOE Q clearance. Whereabouts currently unknown. I need it like five minutes ago... Yeah... Haha... No, it was a

Davy Crockett. You owe me twenty bucks!... Yep. I checked in on him this morning. Just a knife wound. He's gonna be fine... Right... Okay. ASAP, okay?... Alright... Tell Tammy I said hi. Thanks, buddy."

"Friend of yours?" Banks asked.

"You could say that. We were at Parris Island together. Anything the FBI or Interpol has on this guy, we'll know in about an hour or so. Toby is fast," Frank said.

CHAPTER 17

Star City, Russia
Friday
9:30 P.M. Moscow Standard Time
2:30 P.M. Eastern Time

VLADIMIR HAD SPENT THE LAST FEW DAYS GETTING OUT OF RUSSIA, and here he and Michael Tarin were, not on the outskirts or border areas, but in damned Star City in the heart of the country where statues had been erected to honor cosmonauts for their service. They had taken the helicopter from the yacht to Yalta and from there a private jet to an airstrip about fifty kilometers outside the outer ring of the Moscow Oblast region. Simply travelling about the world was only difficult for normal citizens. For people with access to large fortunes, customs typically wasn't even a thing. Dorman's holdings either owned or had access to private airstrips all over the world. Billionaires came and went all the time and nobody was ever curious as to their travel companions or cargo as long as the proper "taxes" were paid. And Dorman had paid all the right "taxes" everywhere . . . on the planet. The rest, the ground game, was going to be the tricky part.

They had alerted the merc team immediately before the helicopter had ever landed on the yacht. The team had been at the airstrip hours before they had arrived preparing. Once the plane taxied into the private hangar, Vladimir and Michael deplaned.

They both reflexively counted heads on the way down the plane's steps. Jamal was missing and so was Sandy.

"Greetings, comrades." Vladimir waved.

"Where're Jamal and Sandy?" Michael asked with a shrug.

"He is getting some last minute, um, supplies. She went with him. They will be here soon," Overtund answered. The thirty-something South African smiled a big toothy grin, revealing the one front gold tooth on the right central incisor. "'I'm certain you will like these supplies,' is what Jamal made me promise to tell you."

"Grenades. It's probably grenades." Arin laughed.

"Look, and here they come now." Overtund pointed as two large four-door, beat-up, white-painted road construction trucks approached. The trucks were Russian-made military Ural flat beds with railings and a tarp covering the bed. The vehicles looked to be a decade or more older and had been repainted and repurposed for farm or construction work. They were the types of vehicles most people wouldn't look twice at. That was the point. The two trucks came to a stop just inside the hangar about five meters away and Michael could make out the rust bubbles and flecks of military green that were making their way through the bad paint jobs on both vehicles. Russians weren't anything if they weren't utilitarian. These vehicles were most certainly that.

A tall, slender, Pakistani man practically fell out of the first truck, almost bouncing with joy like a kid at Christmas, slamming the door loudly. If Michael hadn't known the man didn't drink, he'd have sworn he was drunk. The slightly larger, bulkier redheaded female slowly and deliberately exited her truck adjacently parked and approached. Michael was always impressed by how precise and quiet she was in everything she did. Each step appeared calculated and her eyes were always searching her surroundings—probably for threats or things she could use to kill you with, or both. But her motions were not mechanical or robotic. Sandy moved more like a ballerina or a ballroom dancer or a Shaolin acrobat with fluidity, grace, and purpose—deadly purpose.

"Sandy, Jamal, what'd you bring us besides two ugly piece-of-shit trucks?" Michael asked, drawing chuckles from the rest of the team.

"Pieces of shit!" Jamal feigned at having his feelings hurt. "Maybe they are. But they should blend in without too much concern around here. The party, well now, that's in the back my friend. Have a look see."

Jamal held his hands palms out while slightly bowing and motioning them to the back seat of the truck he'd been driving. He opened the door and pulled out a meter-long pelican-style case. "Sandy, a hand?"

"Of course."

Sandy grabbed the handle on the other end and the two of them placed the case carefully on the hangar floor. The team moved in around them to see what the box contained. There were a few "oohs" and "ahs" and reaffirming head nods as the lid rose.

"This, my friends, is just what the doctor ordered." Jamal pulled a green canister from within and held it up. It was about fifteen centimeters in diameter and about a half meter long. It was covered in yellow Russian Cyrillic letters and numbers. One end of it was pointy like an artillery shell, because, well, that was exactly what it was. Wires extended from the pointy end and led down to a small electronic device taped to the cylindrical midsection. "This little baby here should make quite the bang. I have ten of them."

"One-five-five-millimeter artillery shells?" Vladimir nodded approvingly. "Ten should do nicely."

"What about guns? Standard B and E kit? And maybe some flares and diesel fuel?" Michael asked. "Those were all on the list I sent."

"No worries, man." Jamal made an expression as if his feelings were hurt again. "I wouldn't let you down."

"All is in the second truck." Sandy said in a very monotone voice as if she were bored with the current conversation. "So, what are we doing here?"

"A simple breaking and entering, snatch and grab some fairly heavy gear, then burn the place to the ground so that no evidence we'd been there is left," Michael explained and tapped his glasses, sending them new files. "Here is where we're going. And here is what we are snatching and grabbing. Mostly a piece of cake."

✧　　✧　　✧

"We should have planned for this eventuality two years ago." Vladimir drove the truck down the long straight street that pointed radially outward from the center of Moscow. Currently, they were headed northeast directly toward the city. There were enough side streets, trees, and ancillary buildings alongside the road at this distance out that the area appeared more like a business district with warehouses and shops. They were several kilometers from the gates into the Gagarin Cosmonaut Training Center and only a few blocks from the actual Orlan space-suit manufacturer, NPP Zvezda.

"Dorman insisted that his company would have better, newer, more maneuverable, and more advanced suits ready for us." Michael checked the sideview mirror and made certain the other truck was behind them.

"We could have ordered Orlan-MKs from Zvezda and not be doing this nonsense." Vladimir was clearly unhappy and Michael couldn't really disagree with him. "Dorman owes us for this one. And he's going to owe Schwab, I suspect."

"Yeah, he will. He's good for it. I'm sure after all this he'll be more than good for it a billion times over. But honestly, I bet Schwab wouldn't even know he owned this company if he hadn't bought the damned thing just so he could put himself on top of the flight schedule. He couldn't probably care less about the company in general. It's no cash cow." Michael looked at the map app on his phone and nodded. "Up ahead on the right. Let's put the truck in that alleyway. We'll move around the side alley and into the front door. Arin's earlier recon shows cameras only on the front."

"Just in case the video goes to a web-based server," Vladimir parked the truck and then pulled the black ski mask down over his face. "Don't want to give them any premature information."

"Right." Michael pulled his mask down. "I'll text Keenan and tell him to scrub the area."

"Good idea, M."

CHAPTER 18

Dallas, Texas
Friday
11:30 P.M. Central Time

"I HAVE TO BE SOMEWHERE IN A COUPLE OF HOURS," MARCUS Dorman said. Leaning back in the reclining leather seat, through the window in his private jet he could see planes in the distance taking off and landing. His security staff and his personal assistant, Meena, stood by the open doorway where the stairs led down to the taxiway.

"Then I guess we need to make this short," the man reporting to him said. "There are now four one-hundred-megawatt battery energy storage systems online in Texas. First ever like them in the country."

"Yes, I know this. I paid the Power Construction Group of Greater Dallas to build them over the past two decades. Broad Scope Power is owned by a handful of major shareholders and I happen to be in the majority." Dorman tapped the ends of the fingers on both hands together in front of him. "What I want to know is the status of the five new prototype systems and when they will be online."

"We have crews working all three shifts and we should be ready to roll them out in about a month," the man replied.

"Make it sooner," Dorman said.

"That's probably not possible."

"Okay, then. We will just shut the program down. Starting right now."

"There are thousands of jobs! We can't just shut the projects down now. It would create ghost towns around the areas that—"

"Then do it faster. Hire more people. Two weeks," Dorman said. "And we will need to shut down the batteries that are currently online for a forty-eight-hour inspection on my word."

"That will cause blackouts across Texas."

"Yes. Yes, it will. But you will do it when I contact you. Or I will pull the plug on these projects."

"You just...you...can't—"

"I can. I will. Unless you make happen what you must make happen when I tell you to make it happen." Dorman noted the time in his virtual view. "Now, go. Get it done. I have to be somewhere else very soon."

"I uh..."

"Meena, please show our guest out," Dorman said. "And let's button up and move on to Boca Chica."

CHAPTER 19

⤲

Boca Chica, Texas
Friday
3:30 P.M. Central Time

"...NINE, EIGHT, SEVEN, SIX, FIVE, GO FOR MAIN ENGINES, TWO, ignition..."

Marcus watched eagerly as the new reusable single-stage suborbital rocket lurched upward from the launch complex he had built right next to SpaceX over the past decade. The internal ignition sparkers fired inside the four maneuverable exhaust nozzles, igniting the mixture of Rocket Propellant 1 (RP1) and Liquid Oxygen (LOX) in the modernized reignitable version of the Russian Energia–built RD-171M engine. The rocket flared with bold bright-orange fire and white steam exhaust, blasting sound waves that shook Marcus Dorman's chest even though he was five kilometers away from the launch pad observing from just outside the launch control building. The awesome power of the rocket motors caused his teeth to vibrate against one another almost painfully to the point that he either had to bite down or hold his mouth open.

Dorman Space Unlimited was one of the latest multibillionaire-driven space ventures. Having your own space company and way to space had become a rite of passage for the mega rich. Dorman wasn't going to be left out. His rocket, at least the one anybody knew about, was a single-stage fly-back booster with a smaller six-person reentry vehicle that looked like a miniature space shuttle, though more like a smaller version of the X-37B spaceplane on top. In fact, the design almost appeared as if Dorman had somehow gotten the blueprints of the X-37B and scaled them down to meet his design needs.

The booster was mostly based on the Russian Zenit-3SL first stage with a modified engine so that it could be reignited for booster landing. Marcus had specific reasons for using the Zenit-3SL design that had been used a couple decades prior in the SeaLaunch venture that had gone bankrupt. Marcus had stepped in at just the right moment and bought up as much of the intellectual property as he could get his hands on.

The crew vehicle, called the *Dorman Defender*, used a combination of modern carbon nanotube–reinforced ceramics and a sleek glide-body shape for reentry, much like the X-37 again. The crew cabin was large enough for a pilot and copilot, much like the space shuttle cockpit but more modern with six seats behind them in three rows of two. The crew vehicle itself, once orbital in future flights, would use retro thrusters to slow and deorbit, reenter the atmosphere, then glide to a safe speed to an altitude of about ten kilometers where it would then pop the rear cowling, which covered a pusher propeller. Once the vehicle was slowed to prop speed, the wings extended farther out to make it more like a short takeoff and landing vehicle. The sleek little spaceplane could actually land in less than four hundred meters and could take off under its own power in less than that. While it couldn't return to space without the booster, it could fly as long as it had kerosene or RP1 in the tanks. It also had a ballistic recovery chute system that could be released in the event of catastrophic systems failures.

This was the first horizontal landing spacecraft that actually was powered and had options after reentry about where it would land. The fly-back booster part of the rocket copied the Blue Origin approach and used chutes to slow itself and then it fired the boosters just before landing to bring it down safely. There had long been rumors that there was bad blood between Dorman and Bezos for using very similar software and control system designs. There was even rumor that Dorman had either hacked into the Blue Origin facility, paid off some employees, or did a black bag job and stole them. There was never proof and Dorman didn't care.

Rumors never bothered him and he figured Bezos was too busy to worry with it also. The actual fact was, of course, he'd stolen plans from every single one of his billionaire competitors and even managed to get his hands on classified design information for the X-37. It didn't hurt having the most wanted hacker in the world at his disposal. Again, nobody had ever proven a thing and all the right people had been paid off or dealt with in some manner. Nobody ever would prove a thing. SpaceX was always giving him property boundary hassles and Marcus often had his employees encroach the boundaries just to piss them off. Marcus wasn't thinking about any of those things today.

Today was the first fully manned suborbital flight of the *Defender*. In order to maintain privacy for his crew and passengers, DSU had a strict blackout policy for the occupants. If you wanted to fly in space and let everyone on the internet see it, well, the *Dorman Defender* wasn't your ride. Marcus was looking toward a bigger market than "space tourism." He was looking at using space as a pathway to destinations hard to reach terrestrially.

The *Dorman Defender* was to be the means to other ends. The public and marketing argument was that he'd chosen that name because his main public relations and marketing pitch was that nobody was truly developing a mechanism to save people around the planet during emergencies rapidly—not even the Space Forces of the world could do that. He was taking that mission on himself, hence, the *Dorman Defender*. His publicly defined plan was to build a vehicle that could take off and land on unimproved surfaces such as fields and roads, bringing emergency response supplies to anywhere on the planet in less than an hour. He hoped to push that to thirty minutes or less, like pizza delivery.

"Look at that baby go!" Marcus said excitedly with two big thumbs-up—giving the documentary cameras a quick soundbite for social media advertisements. He shielded the sun with his left hand and pointed to the sky. Of course, his contact lenses would tint and attenuate the sun as much as they needed to but old habits died hard.

"Sir, they have it on the live feed inside if you want to watch it now," Grayson Devaney, the public relations face of Dorman Space Unlimited, told him. She was wearing the space company's uniform: an all-sky-blue, form-fitting jumpsuit with Star Trek-like red-and-gold accent lines across the zipped-up front, cuffs, and waist. The *Defender* patch on the right arm was reminiscent of the space shuttle mission patches of a long-gone era. Dorman had paid top dollar to a designer and a marketing team to pull nostalgic well-known space and science fiction accents into the uniform design. He felt that he'd gotten his money's worth.

"Ms. Devaney, please lead the way," he said.

"Right this way, sir."

Devaney led Marcus into the main Launch and Mission Control Center to a VIP viewing room overlooking the floor. As he entered, several people stood and cleared a path for him to take the front row seat in the center. An elderly man held out a hand as he passed by and Marcus stopped only briefly to shake it.

"Senator Green, nice of you to join us today," Marcus said. "Quite the launch, hey?"

"Nice, Mr. Dorman," Senator Green replied. "Brilliant. And am I to understand it is going to land in Switzerland?"

"Yes, the booster will land here. But we have another one at the spaceport we have assembled near the northeastern border of Switzerland. The ship can be reconditioned and launched from there. It could just fly back under its own power but would have to stop and refuel many, many times, or we could ship it back. I, personally, like the idea of launching it back, which is what we plan to do soon," Dorman replied to the senator.

"How long will it take to replenish it and relaunch it?" another VIP asked. Marcus didn't recognize the woman until his contact lenses did a facial recognition and then a badge barcode scan and told him she was sent from the Texas governor's office.

"Well, we hope to get to days. Right now, probably a month," Dorman said.

"...booster recovery system has been deployed and we are T-minus two minutes from booster reignition..." was announced over the intercom system.

"What a show!" Dorman exclaimed.

✧   ✧   ✧

The launch had been fairly straightforward. The clock hit zero and the RD-171M kicked in, pushing them to about two-and-three-quarters gee. They hit Max-Q about seventy seconds in and there was some shaking and bouncing then. After that it was smooth until main engine cutoff and stage separation. The *Dorman Defender* spaceplane was released and had risen to an apogee of nearly nine hundred and sixty kilometers. There had been almost ten minutes of microgravity before falling back into thick enough atmosphere for deceleration to begin. The command crew and three passengers were all doing fine.

Exactly thirty-three minutes and fifty-one seconds had passed since the ignition clock had hit zero and the mission clock had started counting up. Reentry had gone smoothly and the little spaceplane was performing as planned.

"She's handling magnificently, Control," Captain Jebidiah Reynolds said over the flight channel as he manned the controls of the *Dorman Defender*. At the moment he was thoroughly enjoying how it handled—not unlike the single-engine trainer plane he'd spent hundreds of hours in. "Glide-phase wing extension setting one activated."

Jeb knew that all the telemetry data was getting to the Swiss ground station but he enjoyed following the flight procedures as he had trained. There were manual switches that would enable the wing extensions and flap settings but at the moment the spaceplane was set on software control mode. So, truly, Jeb was only manning the stick and rudder. The spaceplane was fly-by-wire, which meant that he actually could let the software handle the stick and rudder too. But Jebidiah preferred to fly the little spaceplane himself.

"Airspeed dropping through Mach one point zero nine, point zero eight, point zero seven..." he read until the aerodynamics of the spaceplane could no longer push the atmosphere boundary layers out of its way.

BOOM!!

"We are now subsonic and continuing on glidepath," he reported.

Jebidiah continued along flying the prepared flight path as planned and following procedures for the next several minutes. Europe was filling the viewports beneath him as their altitude dropped to that of a typical commercial airliner. A minute or so later the propeller cowling was retracted as they dropped below five kilometers above ground level. The spaceplane was beginning to sound more like a small airplane with the rushing wind against the hull.

"Expanding wings to full." Jebidiah tapped a few controls on the glass cockpit. "Switching over to full manual controls. Pusher-prop startup in three, two, one."

The airplane engine roared to life behind them. Jeb could feel when the blades of the prop caught the air and added thrust. The spaceplane turned glider was now a powered airplane. He adjusted the throttle on the touchpad in front of him and made a note that the temperature, oil pressure, fuel level, and prop speed were all right where they needed be. Flying the little plane was an absolute joy.

"Hey, there are the Alps way off to south!" The flight engineer in the number three seat pointed out the mountains to the passenger beside him and the two behind him.

"How can you tell? It is too dark!" one of the passengers asked.

"Well, if you look closely, you can see the Gornergrat Bahn, the highest open airway train in Europe running along the ridge. See the lights?" the flight engineer continued.

"Aha. I do see," the passenger behind him said.

"Switzerland Dorman Spaceport, this is the *Dorman Defender* vectoring in for a landing, over?" Captain Reynolds radioed to the ground control as they approached.

"Copy you, *Defender*. We show everything is A-okay and your path is spot on. Continue to follow your planned vector path and we'll see you in about five minutes. Be advised that we are having about twelve knot crosswinds from the east and visibility conditions are clear. Over."

"Roger that, SDS. *Dorman Defender* is entering final approach." Jeb watched as the blue runway lights lit up down below and just to the north as he turned from the Base Leg path onto final approach.

✧   ✧   ✧

Landing had been smooth as could be. Jeb was proud of that. He waited for everyone to disembark from the plane before he did his postflight checklist and shut everything down. The flight engineer had already made a once-around the spaceplane twice. The flight had inflicted no apparent exterior damage to the plane. As far as he could tell, if he wanted to, he could get in that plane and take off and fly to wherever his fuel would take him.

Jebidiah casually made his way down the steps of the plane until his feet felt the hangar concrete floor. That was the first time anyone had made a flight like that in history, but there was little fanfare. Anonymity of the flight crew and passengers was something Dorman was pushing. He wasn't interested in the history books. He *was* interested in a capability that had never existed before.

So, there was no press during boarding and deboarding. There were good reasons for this policy, he was sure. Jeb did his best to act as if he were paying little attention to the limousine surrounded by very big men in black suits that awaited one of the passengers. The man had remained completely quiet throughout the flight and walked immediately off the spaceplane to his entourage and then was in the car and gone. Jeb never knew who the man had been and was paid well enough not to ask. He did have some thoughts, though, that whoever that man was, Dorman was going to be asking for a favor from him at some point along the way. Jeb had known Marcus long enough to be aware that every single thing the man did was through intense forethought and calculation.

Thousands of miles away, Marcus Dorman stood at the landing platform, watching the sun starting to sink behind his very successful rocket booster. Marcus found just the right spot to stand so that the reddening sunlight was scattered just across the DSU logo on the rocket body side facing south. The logo was painted on with retroreflective red, white, and blue paint that scattered the sunlight in different ways with even the tiniest movement of one's position. He bobbed his head back and forth sideways subtly and enjoyed the array of colors as he did so.

Looking up at it, he realized that the booster body cylinder was taller than you'd think when you got close enough to it to really tell. He was just outside the radius where the landing thrust exhaust had not burned into the concrete pad and just inside the yellow painted warning circle. The white painted metallic landing struts, three of them, extended out from the base of the rocket and held it firmly in place like the rockets of science fiction from the previous century.

But there was no ladder extending from within from which some swashbuckling hero would emerge. In fact, he thought, with the spaceplane missing from the top, it had a lonely and almost disturbingly incomplete look about it. He turned to the east to look out across the beach at the ocean. Blue and green algae-topped waves gently broke against the shore with almost no spray. There had been no weather and the ocean was fairly calm. It had been a great day to launch a rocket. He turned to look in the distance to what he guessed was in the direction of Switzerland. He allowed himself, for a brief moment only, to revel in his immediate successes. He was proud of his idea. This rocket system could deliver people almost anywhere on the planet in a very short notice. He had all sorts of ideas for it and how it would fit into his larger plans, but there were still a lot of pieces that had to fall into place before those ideas came to fruition. He was confident that they would come to pass, though. He was very confident.

It will be orbital, he thought. But not yet . . . not yet. His moment was interrupted when his contact lenses alerted him that he had an incoming encrypted message. Using his mind-machine interface, he opened the file and read it.

> M,
>
> *Amazing adventure my friend. Safely, here in Switzer-land. My family has arranged further travel modalities. As far as our quid pro quo goes, I have been assured that the concrete has cured, the engine installed, and we will deliver our part of the deal when it is needed. Will be in touch once the other pieces fall into place. Thank you.*
>
> R

Marcus mentally typed out a response.

> R,
>
> *Glad you made it safely. Welcome to Switzerland, the land of no extradition from the United States and the European Union. Enjoy your freedom.*
>
> M

CHAPTER 20

෨

Low Earth Orbit
International Space Station
Friday
6:30 P.M. Eastern Time

"WELL, NATALIE, I HOPE YOU HAVE A VERY HAPPY BIRTHDAY!"
Major Allison Simms told her niece through the video link to
Earth. The little girl was turning six and sat excitedly in her
father's lap and beside her mother, Abigail, Allison's sister. From
the noise and activity in the background, it was clear there was
a party happening. There was the noise, sure. But there was also
the fact that the little girl was wearing a party hat, a princess
dress, and a ribbon across her chest that said BIRTHDAY GIRL.
"Did you get the present I sent you?"

"Yes, Aunt Allie, I love it!" Natalie exclaimed while holding
up the little astronaut-suited stuffed tiger. "Did you really take
him to space with you?"

"Yes, I did! In fact, I kept him with me the entire time I
stayed on the International Space Station on my last mission. He
floated about all over. I've had a really difficult time getting to
sleep up here this time without him to take care of me." Allison
acted tired and faked a yawn.

"I promise to keep him with me all the time!" Natalie could
barely contain herself. "Can I go show the others, Mommy?"
she asked.

"Sure, and don't give him any cake." The little girl jumped out of her father's lap energetically with the little stuffed astronaut tiger clutched in her left hand.

"Hey guys...look what my Aunt Allie sent me from space!"

"Haha! Reminds me of you," Allison told her sister, Abigail. "All that energy."

"Thanks for calling her, Allie. I think it made her day. Especially with her grandpa not being able to keep his promise that he'd be here," her sister's husband, Daniel, added with a solemn look on his face. He exhaled slowly and started to rise out of the chair hesitantly. Then he put on a smile that was both a façade from sadness and real from joy at the same time. "I'd better go and keep an eye on them or they'll tear down the house. Stay safe up there."

"Thank you, Daniel. You stay safe in there with those screaming girls!" Allison laughed. "I'm much more afraid for you than me!"

"Big Sis, when are you going to be home?" Abigail turned serious now that her daughter was in the other room playing with her friends. Allison could tell by how somber Daniel had looked and now Abigail's abrupt facial expression change that the news coming was not going to be happy news.

"Right now, Abby, if things stay the way they are, I'll be back on the next resupply. That is in three weeks," Allison told her sister. "So...the elephant in the room?"

"Dad isn't getting any better. And the prognosis...well... they don't give him three weeks. His lungs have filled up again and the pneumonia from the inflammation has returned." Abby looked as if she were holding back tears. "Mom is a basket case."

"The chemo didn't work, then," Allison said. She was disappointed. They'd all had high hopes that the new chemotherapy treatment could stop the cancer in her dad's lungs from getting worse, but that appeared not to have been the case. "What do they plan to do next?"

"Not sure. There was talk of monoclonal antibody treatment, but I dunno if insurance will cover it and...it's very expensive." Abigail shrugged and nodded her head left and right with a frown on her face. "They said, um, let me think, it was something like soo-gee-molley-mub or something. I have trouble understanding the doctor's Pakistani accent."

"Okay, if you have any details, email them to me. I'll try to get time to research it sometime later today." Allison looked at the timer on the screen for her call. She was approaching her bandwidth limit for the call.

"I don't think he's—" her sister started but Allison wouldn't let her finish.

"We've been this close before. Tell Dad I said to fight!" Allison blinked tears back. "I'll tell him myself in three weeks!"

"I'll see him in the morning. I'll tell him."

"I'll make a video and email it to you tonight," Allison said.

"I'll play it for him." The two of them fell silent for a brief second or two. Both of them aware that their father could pass before Allison could return home to see him. Allison couldn't handle being overwhelmed by negative emotions. She fought them back and focused on something positive. That's how she'd always been. Stay positive, she thought.

"Abby, smile, your little girl is six!" she said.

"I know, she's growing so fast," her sister agreed while wiping the tears away. A thin smile made its way across her face. "She's growing up fast..."

"It will be..." Allison couldn't finish the sentiment and had to choke back the tears herself.

"She wanted Dad to be here so badly." Abby sobbed softly and then sniffled and wiped at her eyes.

"I have to go now. You tell everyone I'll be home as soon as I can be. Give my niece a big hug for me. And tell everyone..." Allison paused to regain her composure. "And tell them I love them."

"Be safe up there, sis."

"Always. Love you, little sister."

"Love you."

Allison closed the window and terminated the connection. She felt large singular tears building at the corners of both eyes. With no gravity to pull them down her cheeks the tears continued to grow into balls that washed over her eyes, blurring her vision to the point that she couldn't see. She blinked and wiped her eyes with her thumb and forefinger of her right hand and then wiped the moisture away into her jumpsuit. The tears were accompanied by several slight sniffles and unstoppable sobs. She took in a couple of deep breaths doing her best to regain control.

"Everything...uh...okay, comrade?" Dr. Solmonov stuck his

head around the corner of her private area. "I thought I heard someone being sad over here."

"Eavesdropping, cowboy?" Allison straightened herself and made certain her eyes were wiped clear. Then she wasn't sure if her eavesdropping insinuation was hurtful or not. She hadn't meant it to be. She decided to soften it with a more back to business comment. "I'm fine. What's up?"

"Up? Down? Left? Right? Which way is that here?" He raised an eyebrow at her, trying to lighten her mood. "Space confuses me."

"Perhaps I should have asked, what's happening, then?"

"Aha! Happening. Lots of things and lots of nothing. There are checklists and schedules and timelines and on and on."

"Life in space...lots of everything and lots of nothing." She wiped her eyes again.

"I'm about to grab something to eat from the galley and wondered if you cared to join me?" Solmonov asked. The two of them had spent a lot of time together over the last couple of years training and flying and being in space. They had become very close friends. Solmonov was about the age of her father. Allison wasn't certain if she was looking at him that way or if there was something else happening between them. Training had made them so busy neither of them had been able to make the time to find out.

"Sure. I could eat."

"Allison, you know Raheem." Solmonov floated next to the European astronaut. "I asked him to join us for a moment or two."

"Dr. Fahid," Allison greeted him, wondering what the Russian cowboy was up to. "Nice to meet you...for the millionth time."

"Yes, indeed, Major Simms," Dr. Fahid replied. He was drinking some bright red fluid from a squeeze bottle and nibbling at something that was a freeze-dried chunk of brown stuff. Allison had no idea what he was eating.

"You two are so formal!" Solmonov slapped Allison on the shoulder, causing himself to spin slight. He grabbed a handhold to stabilize his motion. "Relax. Raheem, tell her what you told me."

"Ah, yes, about the protein dendrites?"

"Yes, that, my friend."

"Dr. Solmonov—" He was interrupted by a grunt from the Russian. "Eh, Peter, said that your father was battling stage four lung cancer?"

"Yes, he's in pretty bad shape." Allison glared at Solmonov, not certain why he would be talking about that with the crew. Just the thought of it forced her to hold back the sobs and tears.

"Do you know what type of lung cancer?"

"Uh, what do you mean?" Allison wasn't sure she understood. It was "lung cancer."

"Is it small cell or non-small cell?"

"Oh, yeah. I know that. It is non-small-cell carcinoma."

"What treatments have they done?" Fahid asked.

"Radiation, didn't work." She ticked off on her fingers. "Surgery, didn't work. And they just did a round of chemo that didn't seem to help."

"Pneumonia?"

"Yes. The inflammation and fluid in his lungs are apparently very bad." Allison did her best not to cry again. She was distracted by Solmonov handing her a squeeze bottle. She accepted it and took a swig. It was sweet, like some fruit-based syrup with a strong taste of ethanol. She shot a quick glance at the Russian to acknowledge he wasn't supposed to have that up there. She took another squeeze before handing it back.

"You keep it. I have my own." Solmonov manifested another squeeze bottle from within a pocket somewhere on his jumpsuit. "Cheers, comrade."

"What's the next treatment planned?" Dr. Fahid made no expression to indicate whether or not he had seen the surprise on her face from the contraband. Allison recalled what her sister had told her earlier on the video chat.

"There is some monoclonal antibody thing, but I don't know if our insurance will cover it."

"Which one?"

"Which one what?" Allison asked.

"Which monoclonal antibody?" Fahid asked in return.

"Oh, um, I haven't looked it up or even have the right pronunciation. My sister said it sounded like soo-gee-molley-mub maybe?"

"Sugemalimab. Yes. That was just approved for use recently and is an anti-PD1-L1 inhibitor." Fahid nodded knowingly. "That just means the antibody is designed to attach to the Programmed Cell Death-1 Ligand-1 checkpoint of the cancer cell."

"Not sure what all that means, Doc," Allison said.

"Cancer cells are mean and sneaky. If your father's doctor is using this, and he knows why he is using it, and he is using it correctly, it suggests to me that your father's cancer cells are growing unchecked. You see, the PD1-L1 turns off your immune system to these cells. It's like a cloaking system to keep it hidden and growing unchecked. The anti-PD1-L1 inhibitors are designed to attach to the bad cells and send out a signal saying 'here is the bad cell, come and get it.'"

"A target designator," Solmonov added.

"Yes, Peter. Of sorts."

"But will it work, my friend?" Peter asked.

"Well, there has been success with it. I'd honestly suggest combining it with brentuximab vedotin and pembrolizumab, but insurance will only let them do one at a time," Fahid said. "This is one of the reasons I left being a clinician and went to pure research. The damned treatment protocols are dictated by the insurance companies not the physicians."

"So, um, what are you saying, Dr. Fahid?" Allison wasn't certain what exactly the point of this conversation was turning out to be. On the other hand, she knew her friend. She trusted that he had some intention behind all this. "It isn't the right medicine?"

"Oh no, my dear Major. It might be just enough." Allison could hear an unsaid "but" in the end of that sentence.

"But...?" she asked.

"But, this being stage four and the patient being hospitalized, I'd prefer much more aggressive. Time is critical here." Fahid paused, realizing that he might have been insensitive. "I'm sorry, Major. I don't mean to suggest there isn't hope, nor to discourage."

"No, no. If you have data, or a suggestion, I want it. I agree. Time is extremely short," she said, fighting the tear buildup again. She wiped at her eyes and then took another squeeze from the bottle Solmonov had given her.

"Well, if you are amenable to it, I am running a current trial as we speak for Schwab Medical Industries. There is, actually, highly likely, the best treatment for your father here in the refrigerator. I would be more than happy to have your father brought into the trial," Fahid told her.

"Thank you very much, Dr. Fahid, but I fear that might be too late. I couldn't get him anything from up here for almost a month from now."

"Yes, I realize this." Fahid waved a hand at her as if he were annoyed by the interruption. "I will have my team go tomorrow morning and start him on an aggressive treatment to help him until we can get to him. The first thing is to get the cytokine storm in his lungs under control."

"You would do that?" Allison asked. "How expensive would that be?"

"I would do that. And there is no expense. This is a trial, you see. It is part of my research and I need volunteers."

"What would you need from me?"

"Just terrestrial points of contact information and I can have them make calls first thing tomorrow," he said. "And drift through the protein growth experiment in the morning and I will prepare a sample for you to take to your father on your return."

"That is amazing. Thank you."

"You are quite welcome. But really, thank you. I honestly need more candidates for my research. And, of course, while I've had great success thus far with this particular protein, you must realize there are no certainties, yes?"

"Yes. I understand. At this point, I would try anything."

"I'm certain you would," Dr. Fahid said softly. "I did the same when my daughter passed. But that is another story for a different time."

"Thank you," Allison told him.

"Major, you are very welcome even though you are doing me a favor too."

"Thank you, Raheem." Solmonov turned to Allison and tossed her a pouch filled with what appeared to be freeze-dried chili. She reached out and grabbed it before it floated past. Then he held the squeeze bottle up in front of his face. "Sometimes, comrades, it pays to have dinner."

CHAPTER 21

~∞~

Houston, Texas
Friday
5:17 P.M. Central Time

"SO LET ME GET THIS STRAIGHT, MARCUS," TALBOT DAVIDSON
asked. "You have a completely reusable launch vehicle, but you
will not allow the press to know who is flying on it?"

"That is the plan, Talbot." Marcus swirled his wineglass a
couple of times and selected to set it back down and stick to the
water. He was bored with the meal and had other things that he
needed to be doing. But he was in town and needed to stoke the
fires with his fellow billionaire and competitor Talbot Davidson
of Davidson Multinational and Davidson Aerospace. Davidson
owed him a favor. It was time to call in that favor.

"You're missing out on a lot of promotion," Davidson replied.

"Not my thing." He shrugged it off. "The time is coming
when the market for the *Dorman Defender* will be sorely needed."

"The world has already been reset, man. We made out like
bandits." Talbot grinned knowingly. Marcus just sat stoically and
didn't respond. "The incursions into Ukraine and Taiwan and ten-
sions between North and South Korea will last forever. Davidson
Multinational has rolled in billions in support contracts."

"To forever wars." Marcus sarcastically raised his wineglass.

"I'll drink to that!" Talbot followed suit and gestured the toast
with his already raised glass. "And more to follow."

"Talbot, aren't you worried about the wars going on and on and on?"

"I'm worried about them *not* going on and on." Talbot seemed stunned by the question. "There will always be wars, Marcus. Somebody has to see to it that the wars don't get out of hand. I see it like being firefighters battling a forest fire. Forest fires happen. They're Mother Nature's way of clearing out the old and bring in new. But humans, well, we fight the new and cling to the old. Too much new all at once, well, is just too much for society to handle. So, we fight its growth rate not its growth. We are 'flattening the curve,' to borrow a slogan."

"It's more like a euphemism at this point—but I seem to recall this speech from a TedTalk, Talbot." Marcus wasn't impressed. "And I quote...'It is our job as freedom-seeking humanity to seek to the new but at a rate which doesn't destroy us'...unquote."

"Hahaha! Did I actually say that? Sounds like me."

"Yes, it was you. Eight years ago, in Paris," Marcus said. "And then again at Davos."

"I recall that. I think Gates went on after and talked about depopulation or some such nonsense." Talbot screwed up his face. "Now *that* guy—"

"I think you're both over the precipice. Well, or at least standing on the edge looking over the chasm." Marcus let himself laugh to lighten the conversation's edge. "If you asked me, and you didn't, I'd say there's more to exploit and maneuver through than these little skirmishes."

"Do tell. There might be another couple billion in it somewhere."

"Look, you know me. I stay out of global affairs except when it enables opportunity." Marcus leaned back and pushed his plate away. He wasn't interested in food at the moment. "And, honestly, I don't really care what one country does to another, unless there is opportunity there for me. I guess that's where you and Multinational come in. But there's one thing that these damned pandemics and skirmishes and uprisings have shown me and that is it is too chaotic to make predictable outcomes. Predictable outcomes are what create incomes."

"Man, you sound just like you did at Stanford, back in the day." Talbot looked back at him with a reminiscent smile on his face. "So, what do you propose we do about this chaos?"

"'Too many chiefs and too many Indians,' is what Gates would say." Marcus circled the conversation back. "But I don't agree. The world is like a combination of *Minecraft* and *The Sims 2*, really. Probably why Musk is convinced we live in a simulation. Honestly, I couldn't care less. A simulation or real world—what does that even mean? Nah, you see, in *Minecraft* you can build stuff, you can go to the Nether or the End, you can meet something akin to God if you beat the Ender Dragon, or you can just hang out in there and player-versus-player to your heart's content. Hell, there are entire servers where all the kids do is PvP one fight after the next across the World Map, in *Sky Wars*, in *Bed Wars*, and other such scenarios endlessly. Sounds a lot like our forever wars here. *The Sims 2* is about the same, but more like the modern world of building and interacting in neighborhood environments and not all pixelated as hell. But the coders that made these games, Notch and whoever the hell did *The Sims 2*, they are the real winners."

"Damn right. Gates bought *Minecraft* from Notch for like two billion U.S. dollars. And there was Baszucki whose part of Roblox is worth over four billion."

"Yes, but not my point." Marcus glanced at the timer in his contacts virtual display and decided to get to the point. He had a lot to do and he didn't want to spend all night with Davidson. "Who can we sell our world to?"

"I don't get it."

"We are inside *Minecraft* or *The Sims 2* or pick your world-building game, doesn't matter which. All we can do is manipulate this world from *within*." Marcus breathed a sigh of frustration. "We can PvP and build and craft until our hearts are content and then some. Even if we found a portal to the End and defeated the Ender Dragon and met God, we'd get dropped into the world back at the start or something as equally frustrating. It's an endless trap. We can't get out of it. The UFO conspiracy nuts call it a 'soul trap' that we are in. *We* can't be Notch and sell the world to somebody else for two billion dollars."

"Jesus, man, I don't think I've heard you talk like this since that time we dropped acid in college," Talbot said. "So, if we're in this trap and can't sell our world and move on to the next project, like Notch for example, then what do we do? What would you propose?"

"Take the trap."

"Take the trap?"

"Yes. Forget the Ender Dragon and meeting God. We take the world. All of the world. We stop the world from the endless single-player adventures and give it purpose. Purpose to become so big and ominous and in a different direction than the programmers planned for it. Then and only then will we be able to see if there is anybody that shows up from elsewhere interested in negotiating for it or to set it back on the intended path," Marcus said.

"Wait, you mean take over all the world?"

"Yes. Take the world."

"Take the world. Now *that* I'll drink to, for sure."

"I need Davidson Aerospace to deliver on the order I requested a few years back," Marcus said abruptly.

"What? What order? You mean..."

"I mean."

"When?" Talbot looked surprised.

"About ninety hours from now." Marcus checked the countdown in his virtual view. The most recent update from Georgia and Singang had the clock showing ninety-two hours, seventeen minutes and counting down. His tracking data for Vladimir and Michael showed them inbound to the rig and soon to be there. They were on schedule.

"Seriously?"

"Seriously."

"Holy shit," Talbot whispered and looked about the restaurant, as if they were being watched or spied on.

"Holy shit indeed. Can you make delivery, Talbot?"

"Jesus Christ."

"Talbot. Can you deliver?"

"What? Uh, yes. It was done. I'll deliver."

Marcus then picked up his wineglass. He preferred to think of it as half full. He swirled it twice and then held it up. "To Notch."

"To Notch," Talbot said reluctantly and finished his glass nervously. "Jesus, Marcus. You're really doing this?"

"Yes. Yes, we are."

CHAPTER 22

∞

Reston, Virginia
Friday
10:30 P.M. Eastern Time

"OVERWATCH, ALPHA, COPY?" LIEUTENANT COLONEL ALVAREZ spoke quietly into his radio throat mic. There was typical big city noise in the background, but the cul-de-sac they were on was fairly quiet. There was a faint yipping from a small-breed dog coming from somewhere a few houses down and there was music coming from that same general direction. But that typical suburban noise was mostly drowned out by the heavy traffic noise coming from the multi-laned and always busy Dulles Access Road less than a kilometer away. The large noise barricades that had been erected along the highway to shield the neighborhoods from the noise pollution were barely effective.

"Copy Alpha. There are three—repeat, three—heat signatures. Two on the first floor and one on the second. Perimeter is secured to three blocks. Fairfax County PD is in place outside of that and the roads are blocked. All teams moving into place now. You are good to go."

Federal Bureau of Investigations Special Agent Tobias "Toby" Matthew Montgomery III heard the report the same as everyone else on the team. He gave his longtime cohort and former commanding officer, Frank, a nod, checked that his earpiece and

143

mic were secure, pulled the black ski mask over his face, and reflexively felt his belt for extra pistol magazines. He felt inside the waistband holster at his back for the backup Glock 43 to make certain it was there too. The magazines and the backup were there. He felt again—just in case—to appease his obsessive-compulsive disorder habit. Reassured he had backup mags, he pulled his backup gun and chambered a round. He put it back in his holster. He pulled his primary weapon and chambered a round from the magazine currently loaded in the nine-millimeter Glock-17 Generation 5. He felt the familiar custom polymer grip he had built himself, checked to see that the green dot Modular Optical System was functioning properly, and then he raised it to ready. He sighted the green dot on a spot on the ground. He took a deep breath, held it for a moment longer than normal, and then slowly let it out through pursed lips, calming his mind and body. He was ready. He turned to Frank, and tapped his fist on the FBI letters displayed across his body armor.

"You breach, and I'll go," he told the big marine quietly. "You heard the drone report. My men are already on the rear perimeter. Check your guys."

"Hang on." Frank paused and keyed the radio again. "Mac? Kenny? Case? You good?"

"Mac's good," CW4 McKagan replied.

"Thompson is good," Major Kenny Thompson replied.

"Dugan is good. Have your entrance in the crosshairs," Major Casey Dugan reported in. Frank looked behind him and could see the Army Ranger in prone position, peering through his scope on top of the house and giving them a thumbs-up.

"Dr. Banks? Your team good to go?"

"Copy that, Colonel. And note that there are no hot readings."

"Copy, that." Frank gave Toby a thumbs-up. Then he adjusted his earbud and pulled down his mask. "Mac. You and Kenny keep your eyes peeled. We're going in in ten seconds starting now, now, now, ten...nine..."

Frank did the rest of the countdown in his head then held up three fingers for Toby to see. Then two. Then one. Toby banged a fist against the blue front door of the modest two-story vinyl siding middle-class home. It was a typical cul-de-sac suburban house of a typical GS-14 federal employee just like the majority of the houses down the street, across the street, and in most of the neighborhoods in the area. This part of Virginia was either unmarked office complexes—which meant CIA, DIA, or some other intelligence-based agency or office—or cul-de-sac neighborhoods of middle-class houses, which also mostly meant employees of said agencies and offices. If they lived around the area and weren't part of the intelligence community, they were most likely other federal workers of some sort.

Knock, knock, knock.

"Open up. FBI!" Toby shouted. "You have ten seconds to open or we will enter with authority of a federal search warrant. Open up!"

Frank held his M4 barrel down but ready and facing the door. Toby had slid beside the door with his back against the wall and his pistol at waist height pointed down. "...five, four, three, two, one..."

Knock, knock, knock!

"Open up! FBI! Last warning!" Toby looked up at Frank, who was already nodding at him.

"I don't think they're letting us in," Frank said.

"Do it!" Toby told him.

Frank raised his right knee almost all the way to his chestplate armor and then stomped right where the doorknob's bolt met the strike plate. The door gave but didn't go all the way through. The recoil back up through Frank's leg sent him staggering off-balance slightly.

"Shit." Frank grabbed at the side of the house to stabilize his balance.

"Losing your touch, big guy?" Toby grinned at Frank and restrained a chuckle. "I can have my guys bringing up the battering ram."

"Fuck that." Frank slung the M4 to his chest armor and rolled the twelve-gauge pump from his right hip. He chambered a shell, fired, pumped and fired again. The two rounds of double-ought buckshot tore into the door, spraying splinters from the wooden door and doorjamb. With a final kick the door flung wide, slamming against the doorstop. He dropped back a step with the shotgun at his shoulder, scanning the room to cover Toby's entrance.

Bang! Bang!

Two rounds hit him in the chest plate just above the stock of his rifle hanging there. The force from the rounds knocked him backward flailing against a shrub in the flower bed behind him. Toby could see Frank reflexively grabbing his chest and checking for holes.

"Shit! Fuckin' Hell!" Frank cursed pulling himself up from within the unkempt crepe myrtle tree. He checked his chest plate for holes. "Forty-five cal."

He'd been stupid and—thank God—lucky. The pistol rounds had hit him dead center on his chest and the ceramic armor stopped them cold. Had they been a couple inches higher or armor piercing he'd be dead right now.

"Frank?"

"I'm good, go. Go!" Frank used his voice of command. Either that or he was just pissed.

Toby dropped low, sweeping the green dot of his pistol sight that only he could see back and forth across the room. Frank had chosen to just stick with the shotgun and stacked in behind his friend. There were several other crashing noises in the back and there was a flicker of motion and some light flickering across the room toward a door at the end of the main hallway and out the back. The room lights were off, but light from the streetlamps outside that filtered through the windows was more than enough for the dark-adapted eye to see inside. Toby could make out the two men as they moved quickly and in cover fashion. They were pros.

"Freeze or I'll shoot!" Toby shouted.

"Fuck that." Frank let two bursts from the shotgun spray across the darkened living room. There was a faint scream and more ruckus through the kitchen and the screened-in back porch.

Toby did his best to get a dot on a figure diving through the doorway at the end of the room, but the men were moving too fast and the hall was too narrow. He didn't want to fire random shots at an ambiguous target either, because he knew his guys were out back somewhere in the general direction he'd have to fire his weapon. He could tell Frank wasn't as worried about that with the shotgun. Toby nodded to Frank to follow and the two pushed faster through the house.

"Frank!" Toby whispered at him and tapped his nose with his forefinger. "You smell that?"

"Yep." Frank took a whiff and responded, "Diesel."

"Shit!"

"Overwatch, Alpha. We have an arson situation here. Get firefighting teams here immediately," Frank said.

Bang! Bang! Bang!

They both dropped as several more shots were fired at what seemed to be their general direction, but likely not at them precisely. A window behind and between them made a crashing sound as one of the bullets hit.

"Cover fire," Frank whispered. "They're running scared."

"Several shots fired! Repeat, several shots fired!" Toby shouted into the comm as if they didn't hear them. With a quick movement he slid into the doorway, opening firing at one of the men in cover position behind the island bar in the middle of the modestly furnished kitchen. He pulled back down to cover as bullets slapped against the drywall and past him. "Bring it in and surround the house. Nobody gets away! I repeat: Nobody gets away!"

Bang! Bang! Bang! Bang!

Suddenly the kitchen lit up bright red and the sound of a flare burning hissed loudly. Then the flickering orange of quickly growing flames washed the room in front of them. Toby could hear sirens in the distance.

"They better hurry!" Frank said.

"Damned right!"

"Overwatch, this is Alpha. We've got multiple shots and at least one, maybe two runners," Frank said into his mic. "Fire in the north rooms spreading quickly! We need that firefighting team!"

"Copy that, Alpha." There was a brief pause. The radio clicked to static briefly and then back on. "Thermal showing two signatures moving north to the rear of the house, barely detectable from the large thermal signature growing and the third signature is still stationary upstairs."

"We're cut off from them, Frank!" Toby shouted. "Any evidence will be destroyed!"

"I know," Frank said. "We can't get them."

"Fight the fire, then!" Toby responded.

"Mac! Kenny! Headed your way!" Frank said on the comm channel.

✧　　✧　　✧

USN CW4 Wheeler "Mac" McKagan lay in prone position behind the small white latticework that hid an in-ground swimming pool pump, pipes, and filter from view of the main backyard.

The yard was small. In fact, it was just barely large enough to hold the swimming pool, its surrounding concrete walkway, and a small metal shed on the end opposite the diving board. Mac adjusted the optical sight on his M4 to a low light setting and carefully scanned the house. He stayed very still and calmly listened in to the radio during the break.

Mac was beginning to get a bit of an itchy trigger finger. Then a slight breeze picked up and he got a strong whiff of kerosene. Then he could see fire throwing light through the windows. The back door to the house flung open and two men exploded out at a full sprint. Mac could see the first one as clear as if it were daytime in the night-vision setting of his sight. He tracked the man running point, finding a soft spot to put the dot on, and he gently squeezed the trigger. There was a brief suppressed muzzle flash and the muted sound of a silenced rifle accompanied by the sound of a bullet hitting the man dead center of his right thigh, dropping him instantly. He began screaming in pain.

Before Mac could target the other man, Thompson had dropped him with a double tap—one to the right shoulder, then one to the left leg. He fell only inches from his cohort, also screaming in pain, just as loud if not louder. Mac and Thompson charged before the men could gather their wits and grasp at their firearms. The one in the lead was just about to grab his as Mac placed a size-eleven boot on his hand.

"I'd stop about there unless you want another one," Mac said, looking down at him. Thompson gave him a thumbs-up and dropped to zip-tie their hands and feet. Mac keyed the radio. "Rear of the house is secured. Runners apprehended."

CHAPTER 23

〜

Reston, Virginia
Friday
10:41 P.M. Eastern Time

SEVERAL SILENCED SHOTS FIRED AND THEN THERE WAS SILENCE
for a few seconds. Toby looked up at Frank, who was swinging a
window curtain furiously at the blazing kitchen table about the
time he heard Mac's call.

"Rear of the house is secured. Runners apprehended."

Toby had quit wondering if they were in the clear after he'd
heard the back door and the shots. Even though they knew
there was another person upstairs, that person hadn't moved
since they'd arrived. He or she was either tied up or recently
dead. Either way, they couldn't get up there if this fire burned
the place down. And, more importantly to possibly millions of
lives, they absolutely had to preserve the evidence in this house.
It was their only lead. The couch cushion he was using to swing
at the flames ignited as some of the diesel fuel adhered to it.
He continued to fight as the flames grew. Swinging the cushion
only added more air to the fuel and made the flames grow more
quickly. He tossed the cushion to the floor and started looking
for something else to fight the fire with. Frank had slung the
curtain across the island sink just enough to lower the flames
by the faucet. Toby pulled the water on full and grabbed the

dish sprayer. The water went about a half a meter to a meter at best. The flames were too hot to even reach with it, but it might create a fire break in the floor.

The two of them had easily overpowered the two men they were previously fighting, but fire was a force multiplier that rapidly advanced. They were losing ground and starting to lose the fight. Seeing the water being useless, Frank kicked at one of the cabinet doors under the kitchen sink, knocking it open. There was a tiny home fire extinguisher underneath.

"Toby! Extinguisher!"

"Got it!"

Toby quickly grabbed the fire extinguisher, pulled the pin, and started spraying. The monoammonium phosphate dry chemical sucked the oxygen from the base of the flame against the kitchen wall and started to reduce the heat on his face. But almost as soon as he'd depressed the squeeze handle of the tiny kitchen extinguisher it was empty. The fire continued to build just a little more slowly in that one spot. There was too much diesel splashed about and they were standing in the middle of a fueled hotbox that was rapidly engulfing them. The kitchen had reached a point with bright orange flames surrounding them and black smoke filling the room that they could no longer safely stay and fight.

"Frank! We gotta get out here!" Toby said, coughing from his burning lungs.

"Out the front!" Frank shouted over the flames. "Goddamnit!"

Suddenly, several men in firefighting gear burst in with a large hoseline and started spraying. Two more men flanked them with large extinguisher packs clearing a path for them to evacuate.

"Get out of here, guys!" one of them shouted at Toby and Frank. "This way!"

"Got it!" Toby said. He turned back over his shoulder on the way out and yelled as loudly as he could. "We have to stop this fire!"

"Understood! Now clear so we can do our job!"

"Come on, T." Frank grabbed Toby by the buddy collar and yanked him backward toward the clear exit.

"There's still someone upstairs," Frank told him as he motioned with a hand toward the stairwell. There was the possibility they were tied and gagged, but neither of them was expecting that to be the case. They had to also keep in mind that there was always the possibility that the first two men were the distraction and delay to give a third time to do something else—steal files, erase files, cover tracks, escape out a window. The simple fact was, they had no idea what was going on upstairs with the other person, so they had to be cautious and prepared for anything.

"Let's get up there and see what is what just in case the fire gets out of hand. We can always bail out a window." Toby popped in a fresh magazine and brought his pistol back to the ready. Frank nodded in agreement and shoved a few more shells into the shotgun. The racking of the pump was barely audible over the noise from the firefighting.

"Two down in the backyard," Chief McKagan's voice came over the channel. "Need medics. Noncritical."

"Copy that, Mac," Frank replied. "Casey, we're going upstairs. Keep an eye out for second-floor egresses."

"Copy that. I still have you on thermal and in the crosshairs," Dugan confirmed.

"Mac, Kenny, keep an eye on the other first-floor exits and windows."

"Copy that, Frank. The major and I have our eyes peeled."

"Your dance, want to lead?" Frank asked Toby.

"Sure," Montgomery replied. Then he keyed the mic open. "Get some guys in here now to cover the fire team's rear and protect evidence!"

"Copy that. On our way now."

Toby started up the stairs facing forward with his back hugging the wall. While it appeared that the firefighters had the blaze mostly knocked down, the smoke was brutal even through his ski mask. Frank stayed a couple steps behind him, looking backward to cover their rear, just in case they had missed something. There were no lights on in the house other than their flashlights, the lights the firefighters were carrying, and the light from what flames were left. There were no radios, televisions, or computers making any noise but there was plenty of noise from downstairs. The sounds from the smoke alarms and the high-pressure hose spraying water against the walls were almost deafening. Toby noted that even with all that background noise, the only sounds he was truly hearing at the moment were his footsteps and his heart pounding in his chest from the adrenaline.

The stairs were hardwood and made it difficult to quietly step up them. He hoped that all the ruckus and background noise drowned their approach up the stairs. The hardwood stairs led to a carpeted hallway. Toby noted that once they stepped off the stairs and onto the carpet their steps were practically undetectable. The smoke alarm in the hallway suddenly went off, startling him to the point that he spun toward it raising his handgun. He almost put a round through the thing. Frank placed a hand on his shoulder.

"Easy, T."

"Right," Toby whispered. "Goddamned adrenaline."

At the end of the hallway was a door about three-quarters of the way open. There was a source of light—slowly flickering mauves and some deeper purples with a brighter flicker here and there—but still no sound. There was just enough light that Toby could see the knee-high cloud of smoke wafting through the hallway ahead of them and rising slowly toward the ceiling return vent of the central air unit. The odd air currents at the end of the hallway underneath the return vent had created a swirl of smoke that was forming a vortex. He thought it resembled the skinny twister in *The Wizard of Oz* that had carried Dorothy away.

"We're not in Kansas anymore," Toby muttered quietly. "Sorry, I couldn't resist."

Frank smiled but didn't respond. He pointed with a nod of his head at the cracked-open door at the end of the hall. There was a flickering of light shining through that suggested a computer monitor or a television screen was on.

They quietly and cautiously took one step at a time on the carpet. It seemed like it was taking them forever to cover the three-meter distance. Once at the end of the hallway, Toby made a few hand gestures to Frank, telling him that he was going in on a count of three. Three finger ticks later, he burst through with Frank behind him. His pistol out in front and ready to fire, he came to an abrupt halt.

"Freeze! Don't move!" Toby said to the man slumped in the computer chair, placing the green dot of his sight on his desk chair about vital organ high. The screensaver from the computer monitor on the desk continued changing what looked like vacation pictures of various scenes and locations, changing the lighting in the room. He moved closer and spun the chair with his boot, weapon at the ready.

"Shit!"

Toby pulled the black tactical armored glove from his right hand and dropped it to the floor. He placed two fingers at the man's throat, trying to find an artery beating somewhere, anywhere, but there was nothing. He squinted briefly as the lights in the room flicked on and then turned to see Frank by the light switch looking down at them.

"Dead?"

"Yep," Toby said. "Shit."

"Overwatch, Alpha," Frank said. "Any other signatures?"

"Negative, Alpha. Area is secure. Fire team reports the blaze is out."

"Copy. Thanks, fellas."

"Case, you got anything?" Frank asked.

"Nothing, and the FBI guys have surrounded and entered the house. The flames appear to be out, Frank," Dugan reported. "If you can spare me, I want to go check something out nearby."

"Clear to go, Casey. Anything we should know about?" Frank asked.

"Not sure."

"Overwatch, Alpha."

"Go, Alpha."

"Clear from me and give Major Dugan the bird's-eye," Frank said.

"Copy, Alpha... transferring to Beta track."

"Be careful, Case," Frank said.

"Copy that."

"Alright, Toby. Looks like we're good to get your forensics guys up here," Frank said. "In the meantime, let's have a look around."

"Frank." Toby looked at the dead man. "How did... whoever they are know we were coming here in time to beat us and to tie up this loose end?"

"Good question." Frank pulled his mask off and rubbed at the stubble growing on his chin. It was at that point where it was starting to itch. Toby slid his own mask up to his forehead. "Did you tip them off by making inquiries, or did I, or did somebody else on the Task Force do it? Either way, it means we're being watched."

"Or it means you can't trust somebody on your team," Toby warned. "How well do you know them? You got a mole?"

"I don't know any of them except for the SEAL, really. I met him a few years back on a mission. He's a good Squid. Not a marine, mind you, but a good Squid. I asked about the others in the usual places. The guys in-service, well, they check out with some damn fine service records. I trust them. The CIA lady, I just met her. But she checks out as far as I can tell. Same for the NSA expert. Honestly, maybe you should do your thing. For now, we trust, but verify. So, do some verifying for me if you don't mind?"

"Don't mind at all. Got it," Toby agreed. "I'll get the team on it as soon as we tag and bag this place." Toby made a mental note to get backgrounds and tracks on all the members of the Task Force. He thought it might be a good idea to get one on everyone, including Frank, so it wouldn't look suspicious. He'd make it look like a typical background check. He'd even put in a request for any new members coming onboard to have their information sent through the usual FBI background check process. That would be a good cover.

"If you find anything, come to me with it first. The Joint Chiefs will need to know," Frank said.

"Our guy here, quite the rabble rouser." Toby pointed at the book titles spread about on his bookshelf. There were many of the books you'd expect an engineer or analyst to have, with tabs marking pages and such, but there were also many political and philosophical books that gave insight to his personality profile.

"Saul Alinsky's greatest hits, it appears." Frank nodded that he understood and looked closer at the books, titles, and authors. "Marx, Engels, World Economic Forum Report, climate change stuff—we've got a true believer here."

"Look at this one." Toby pointed at a book on the side of his desk. Frank leaned in and read it.

"*Nuclear War Survival Skills: A Civil Defense Manual.*" Frank exhaled nervously. "Think he knew something we don't?"

"Look at these prepper books." Toby tapped a stack of various survival skills and prepping books stacked on the floor with his boot, being careful not to knock them over. "Dude was preparing for an apocalypse. I bet if we looked around, we could find directions to a prepper shelter somewhere."

"Coming up!" a female voice from below shouted. It was Dr. Banks. They could hear her footsteps as they stepped off the stairwell and onto the carpet. Toby reflexively pulled the mask back down over his face. He'd been undercover so long it was just a habit.

"Frank, check this out." Toby used the barrel of his pistol to pull a stack of papers to the left of the keyboard on the desk more open so he could read them. There were missile design drawings of American, Chinese, and Russian ICBMs of the nuclear variety stacked there. There was a detailed drawing of a Russian launch vehicle printed out with numbers that had been highlighted in pink. Several of the printed papers had sticky notes jutting out from within, marking specific pages and passages. There was a notepad of green-lined engineering paper with multiple pages flipped over the top and tucked under the back. The page facing upward had a maroon-colored Skilcraft mechanical pencil of the government variety sitting on top of it. The page was filled with drawings of ellipses with intercepting curves and lots of math scribbled about. Toby bumped the mouse to clear the screensaver and luckily for them it hadn't locked itself out yet. On the screen was some sort of simulation running, showing a big blue slightly squished circle with a red arc intercepting it. There were numbers changing and an equation at the top with the words, "goodness of fit = 0.99724322."

"What is it?"

"Our guy here. He was reading up on ICBMs," Toby said. "And doing some sort of rocket science or something."

"Wasn't that his day job?" Frank asked.

"Whose day job . . . ?" Ginny paused, seeing the dead man slumped in the chair. He had a single bullet hole in his forehead and there was red and gray splatter over the high-backed black-and-blue gamer's chair he was in. Blood pooled in the floor underneath him, saturating the carpet. "Oh shit."

"Yeah, 'oh shit' is right," Toby agreed. "He's your man, right?"

"Phillip Watkins?" Ginny asked. "Well, let's see."

She took out her cell phone and snapped a picture of the man's face and then texted it to someone. Then she gingerly took his right hand and placed his fingertips on the screen and pressed the side button. The screen flickered a couple of times. She sent another text or email or whatever. Her phone buzzed a couple of times and then she looked up at the two of them.

"It matches. This is Phillip Joseph Watkins, the analyst that put the nuclear scientist dossier together for us."

"The question is..." Toby paused, knowing they could finish his thought for him.

"Right. Why is he dead now?" Ginny asked.

"My thoughts exactly," Frank agreed.

"We need to get a complete inventory and workup of everything on this desk, in this computer, and in this house," Toby said. "Dr. Banks, we need every personnel file CIA has on this man. This is now a murder and an FBI investigation."

"Don't forget the bigger picture, Toby," Frank said.

"All part of it," Toby said. "Anything I can do to help, I'm all in."

CHAPTER 24

ᕕᕗ

Reston, Virginia
Friday
10:41 P.M. Eastern Time

"COPY, ALPHA . . . TRANSFERRING TO BETA TRACK."

"Be careful, Case," Frank told him.

"Copy that," U.S. Army Major Casey Dugan acknowledged. "Alright, Overwatch, I've got a vehicle approximately two hundred meters due west of my location. I'm going to designate it. Give me a thermal on it."

"Copy that, Beta. Go for designator."

Casey pulled the infrared laser designator from his pack and splashed the car with it. From the rooftop he had a clear line of sight to the front end of the car, but the back half was blocked by a tree and a hedgerow. As far as he could tell it was a newer model electric car. If it was a getaway car, that made sense. Electric cars were quiet.

"Designator detected. Vehicle is occupied. There is one signature in the driver's seat." Overwatch alerted him.

"Copy that, Overwatch."

Dugan rolled over onto his back, pulling the sniper rifle around to his chest and folded the bipod down. Quickly, he slid down the steep angle of the roof to where it flattened out over the back patio area and slung the weapon on his back. He climbed over the edge until he hung from his fingertips and dropped to ground, landing parkour style to catch his balance.

"Follow me, Overwatch, and guide me in. Keep an eye out for signatures that ain't ours," he said into the throat mic.

"Roger that, Beta. We have you closing at one hundred seventy meters. Clearest path is between the house to your left and the one in front of you. We have dispatched a support team to surround the area and give you backup."

Casey paused for a step to get his bearings on what Overwatch had just told him, but only for a brief step. He crossed the street to the sidewalk, avoiding the fire truck by turning left to the west past one house. He cut between the two houses into the drainage cut, splashing in the mud that covered the concrete ditch. He broke through to the cul-de-sac on the backside behind the Watkins residence and through the yard across that street there.

"You are on the side yard of the house behind the house where the vehicle is parked. The backup team has moved into place and awaiting your action."

"Copy that, Overwatch. Bring them in." Dugan crouched and slipped past the hedgerow and out onto the street behind the target vehicle.

"Out of the car—now!" Dugan shouted, startling the driver.

Instantly, the car silently shot backward with the silent deadly acceleration of an electric sportscar. Casey barely had enough time to react, jumping up and forward as the car slammed into him, sprawling him across the hatch. He grabbed at the luggage rack for a handhold and managed to wrap his left hand around it.

"Stop the goddamned car!" he shouted.

The tires skidded as the reverse motion stopped instantaneously. The force of it slinging him back felt like it would rip his arm out of the socket. Casey managed to roll his body over and fire his handgun through the rear hatchback window as the car started accelerating forward. The rear glass broke and the thrust of the car forward once again almost threw him off the vehicle. He managed to get a foothold on the bumper just enough to push himself upward and fire two more rounds into the car. The window gave, bringing Casey crashing through it into the back of the vehicle.

The driver swerved the car hard to the left, throwing him into the right side of the cargo area. Casey had had just about enough of that. He flipped the rear seat release and folded it over, sliding forward with a kick of his boot against the broken windowpane of the hatch. This gave him enough stability that he rolled forward, placing the handgun against the driver's head.

"Stop now, slowly, or I pull the trigger."

The driver slammed on the breaks, slinging them both forward. Casey pulled the trigger but he was already out of position and he caught an elbow to the side of his jaw. He did his best to block it and grapple as the man continued to swerve the vehicle wildly. With a swerve, they power-slid into the curb and up onto the sidewalk. Casey lost his grip on his pistol. There was a flash of metal that glinted with the passing streetlights that caught his eye. The driver had a gun in his left hand and was trying to bring it around to fire at him over his right shoulder.

Casey tried to roll to the left but his rifle barrel caught on the seatbelt strap. So, instead of rolling to the left he dropped to his back and popped the sling release. Then he rolled just in time as the driver fired two shots where his head had been a second before.

He grabbed the driver's side rear passenger seat seatbelt and stretched it over the front bucket seat and around the man's head and left arm. The driver slammed on the brakes again, let go of the wheel with his right hand, and slung his free elbow around at Casey. But this time, Casey was prepared for it and blocked it with a right outer block and then punched the man in the side of the head repeatedly. The armored knuckles of his glove tore the skin with each blow, turning the driver's face nearest his temple and right ear into a bloody mess.

"I SAID ... STOP ... THE ... GODDAMNED ... CAR!" Casey continued to pummel into the man. When it looked to Casey like he had the upper hand he grabbed the pistol, switched it to his right hand, and then hit the driver in the face with the butt of it. The polymer hilt of the weapon tore a gash in his forehead. "Stop!"

The car slammed into a parked pickup truck, causing the airbag to deploy into the driver, knocking him unconscious. Casey was slung forward but he managed to tuck his head and let his body armor take most of the crash. Stunned for a brief moment, he lay sprawled across the middle console, staring up at the bloody pulp of a man in front of him. It took him several seconds before his mind cleared enough to realize he was still in the car with a potential killer. Then the beam from a powerful flashlight hit his face, blinding him, and the driver's door was slung open.

"Don't move! FBI!"

CHAPTER 25

ᢙ

Washington, D.C.
The Pentagon
Saturday
8:30 A.M. Eastern Time

"MAC, I'M NOT SURE I'M FOLLOWING THIS." RDML TONYA DENISE Thompson was going to have to update the J2 and the Chiefs soon and she needed to fully understand the status of the investigation. Why was there a dead man in Reston, and why was there no sign of the nuclear warheads as of yet? Simply put, it was a shit show and she hated starring in it.

"Yes, Admiral, pretty much all of our sentiments exactly," CW4 McKagan agreed. "Let me try again."

"Feel free," Admiral Thompson told him. "This time maybe I'll get it."

"Okay, starting from the top. We had zero leads from anywhere. This in itself is a lead, I think. It means whoever did this are so connected that they could avoid law enforcement, intelligence organizations, and private and public cameras and sensors. Damned smart. Well funded. Highly connected. So, with no real leads, we started with asking CIA to make us a list of scientists and/or nuke specialists that could reverse engineer the Russian warheads into a viable weapon," Mac started, again.

"Logical."

"The list took longer to get than we expected to start with. I found that curious." Mac waited for that to sink in. "Then once we got it, there were over a thousand names on it. We split it up into pieces and started in on it. What we found was a very unusual list showing a very strong bias toward, and I quote, 'right-wing extremists,' unquote."

"And?"

"Well, we soon noticed there was never anything listed about 'left leaning' or other types of politics. It was odd that politics would be a data trend in such an analysis, so we double-checked that and looked for omissions," McKagan explained. "But there still wasn't enough data to base any conclusions on. And people are free to have whatever political beliefs they want. However, at first, we were concerned there was some sort of politically motivated connection. But—"

"Is this going to take long, Mac?" RDML Thompson tapped her foot against the floor impatiently. Mac realized he'd better cut to the chase.

"Well, ma'am, Lieutenant Colonel Alvarez had a contact at the FBI that he trusted to get us a similar list. When the FBI contact got back to us, there was a clear discrepancy in the known data."

"How so?"

"Firstly, the political bias stuff seemed to be a personal thing from this particular analyst's background. He was quite the political activist in undergraduate school, which carried forward in his online activities. Secondly, there were serious detail omissions in only one scientist on the list—the same scientist that had stood out to me from my analysis: Xi Singang, a naturalized American citizen who changed his name to Thomas Sing. The data from CIA had him with no known relatives. Multiple PhDs from MIT, Top Secret/Q clearance with DOE. And, he was a team lead on the Warhead Life Extension Program—LEP—at Oak Ridge National Laboratories. The file said he was believed to be connected with Chinese Confucious Institute and his whereabouts were unknown."

"Okay, and the discrepancy?"

"The file from the FBI was far different." Mac handed her the file and flipped it open to a specific page. "He has a sister still actively in the CCP nuclear programs. Here's her picture here. This is him. They are twins. There was also a file from his clearance investigation showing known acquaintances of the time. One of the acquaintances interviewed was a Phillip Joseph Watkins with a master's degree from MIT in aerospace engineering and another from the University of the CIA in Intel Analysis. The man was *roommates* with Sing for two years in Boston while they were at MIT. They actually had a third roommate who is currently on the FBI and Interpol Most Wanted lists. Keenan James Ingersol. A hacker that stole something like six hundred million in cryptocurrency from one of the big banking networks."

"Jesus, sounds like a den of thieves."

"Maybe. Certainly more than serendipity enough for a closer look. So, we looked closer."

"Watkins is our dead man, right?" she asked, not looking up from the file.

"Yes, ma'am."

"What about this Ingersol person? Any leads on him?"

"Sorry, ma'am. The last he was seen was over two years ago. Nobody knows where he is now. And according to what I can find on him, the FBI, Interpol, the CIA, and many of the banking private security networks have huge rewards out for him. Whereabouts are unknown, no leads."

"Any leads from the raid?"

"Well, Dr. Banks and Lieutenant Colonel Alvarez have been with the FBI questioning the two assumed assailants and their driver all night. Not sure what they have gotten yet." Mac handed her another folder. "But these were found as files on Watkins's computer and hardcopies on his desk."

He waited for Admiral Thompson to flip through the pages.

"What is all this?"

"Not sure, ma'am. But there are clearly detailed schematics of the Russian glide body from the Satan-2, and these other pages are ICBM trajectories, rocket mathematics of some sort, and what might be fuel burn rates for low-Earth-orbiting rockets. Outside of my expertise."

"Have you found somebody to look at these yet?"

"Dr. Banks is passing it along to CIA analysts, but..." He paused to see if she would come to the same conclusion.

"...but you don't trust the CIA now." Thompson nodded in agreement.

"Yes, ma'am."

"Well, then, we're in a pickle, huh?" Thompson continued to

flip through the drawings and calculations. "Anyone in the J2, DTRA, or maybe over at ONI?"

"I'm sure there are, ma'am, but I haven't identified them yet. It being a Saturday and all, nobody is in the office."

"What about the rest of the Task Force?"

"The Army Ranger, Major Dugan, he thinks he might have a contact in Huntsville, Alabama, at the Missile and Space Intelligence Center that might can help. He's headed there now. Hopefully, he'll come through with something there. Or Colonel Alvarez will get something out of our assassins."

"I wouldn't bet on that."

"Me either."

"Any ID on the assassins or this driver yet?"

"Up until I came in the secure area, no, ma'am. Alvarez said they won't talk. I'll check my cell as soon as I'm back out by the phone lockers and will send you an email when I can. But they appear to be very tight-lipped."

"Okay, then. We have a dead body, three live bodies, some data, and the name of a potential Chinese spy whereabouts unknown. No Russian colonel tie-ins as of yet?"

"No, ma'am."

"Keep digging, Mac. Keep digging! And find those goddamned nukes!"

CHAPTER 26

❦

Turkey Economic Exclusive Zone, Black Sea
Sunday
10:00 P.M. Turkey Economic Exclusive Time
3:00 A.M. Eastern Time

"YOU MEAN WE COULD HAVE JUST STOLEN THE GAUNTLETS?"
Michael was frustrated with the launch segment part of the plan.
Over the past six years there had been one delay after another.
The chief engineer, Georgia Stinson, had made delivery promises
again and again that had been delayed, reimagined, and completely thrown out the window. Michael wasn't a rocket scientist
but he got that it was difficult. But it made planning operations
damned difficult when there was a major key component to the
plan that kept shifting about ambiguously. He and Vladimir had
managed to keep the plan fluid enough to be malleable based on
the evolving situations. But the changes never seemed to stop.

Just like with the suits. Stinson had promised better, more
modern and maneuverable space suits several years back. Then
at almost the last minute, they were told the suits wouldn't be
ready. So, Vladimir and Michael solved that problem by taking
the risk of going back into Russia and stealing suits and commit-
ting arson along the way. Then, *at* the very last last minute there
was a change. Now Stinson was telling them that the new suits
from Dorman's suit-building effort could be mated to the gloves

165

from the Orlan space suits they had stolen from Schwab's place near Moscow. That would have been some very useful information a few hours prior.

"I'm sorry, Michael, but my suit design and test team didn't think of this earlier until they actually started conditioning the suits you brought from Russia. We just simply didn't know that they would fit to the Dorman suits with a simple CNC adaptor ring," Georgia said.

"Can we trust the integration?" Vladimir asked. "If so, the Dorman suits are far more maneuverable. I would prefer them to the Orlan."

"Yes. They were a simple alteration and integration. Had we bought Orlan suits to reverse engineer rather than starting from scratch, I think we'd have ended on this design anyway. It actually will be a better design. The Orlan gauntlets are well tested and very functional." Georgia turned from the large window overlooking the cleanroom where the suits were being prepped.

Behind her were four engineers or scientists or technicians—Michael wasn't certain—feverishly assembling the new Dorman suits. The suits had a hard torso with compression sleeves and pants that led to more boot-looking foot coverings than the Orlan space suit's boots. Michael knew that, from design, the torso would also function as Level IV body armor, meaning that it would stop most modern rifle rounds below sniper caliber. There were multiple cables plugged into the suit leading to a computer panel displaying all sorts of data and graphs that were changing with each adjustment the team made. It was clear that this was indeed a very high-tech operation. Michael did understand and respect that.

"And you're certain these will be ready in time?" Michael asked.

"Oh, they will be ready within the next eighteen hours or so." She looked at the two men with a very sincere frown on her face. "I am sorry that you went to the trouble of bringing all the suits here. I realize they are cumbersome and heavy. And that you put yourselves at risk to accomplish this. But now, we have spares."

"The plan doesn't require spares," Michael said gruffly.

"Maybe not. But it doesn't hurt to have them," Georgia said.

"Michael, it doesn't matter." Vladimir put a hand on his shoulder to reassure him even though Michael shrugged the hand off, annoyed. "Let her get back to work. She has lots to do and very little time. Besides, Sing could probably use some extra muscle. We're all on the clock."

Vladimir tapped at his glasses to make the point. Michael currently had several clocks running in his virtual view. One of them was getting very close compared to what it had been over the past few years. They were all getting a bit anxious as to what was about to come to pass for them. They were nervous about what they were going to bring to pass for the world. It was going to happen soon. And it was going to change the world in ways Michael was not even sure he believed. It *was* going to happen. It *was* going to happen very damned soon.

"Okay, then. I get it. You didn't know. I guess you couldn't know. Georgia, keep me posted if there are any more, um, unforeseen hiccups." Michael placed a hand on Vladimir's shoulder, tugging him toward the exit letting him know that he was ready to go. Then over his shoulder he added, "And update the clocks as often as you can."

"Certainly, Michael," Georgia Stinson replied, unfazed by his gruffness.

✧　　✧　　✧

"Most certainly, Michael," Sing said. He looked completely exhausted. Michael understood that. They all were exhausted. But they had to get everything across the finish line in time for him and Vladimir to get another full sleep cycle in before the countdown clock in his virtual view hit T-minus zero. "We're ready to integrate the first one into the capsule. This will be a great time to go over the modifications we had to make from the training setup."

"Modifications? I hope they were minor?" Vladimir asked the physicist. "Do we have time to learn a complicated new procedure?"

"No, you don't. And yes, it is simple. But you'll need to learn a new checklist. I've sent them to your secure emails." Sing tapped his glasses knowingly. "Come on."

Sing looked over his shoulder at the crew of techs prepping the other five warhead glide bodies and boosters. Michael could tell they had things under control for the moment and he surmised that was Sing's impression as well. "Once they are completely ready, at the last moment, before you board, we'll fuel the thrusters on the reentry vehicles. The fuel is nasty stuff."

"Hydrazine?" Vladimir asked.

"Yes. Will kill you if you get too much exposure." Sing grinned. "And by too much, I mean any."

"What will it do?" Michael asked.

"Well, besides being, uh, rocket fuel and highly combustible? Let me see . . ." Sing ticked off on his fingers with each deadly effect the chemical had. "One, it is extremely toxic. Two, it causes cancer."

"That's probably only in the state of California," Michael joked. Sing ignored it and kept ticking off the list of deadly things.

"Three, it's caustic, and just coming into contact with it will burn the living shit out of you. That means it'll burn your eyes out, your nose, mouth, skin, lungs, esophagus. All those things the human body needs to not die. Oh, and four, the stuff is a neurotoxin to boot. So, it will kill your brain or make you so fucked up that you won't understand that the exposure is killing you."

"Um, and we're putting this shit in the capsule with us?" Michael asked rhetorically. He knew that had been the plan all along.

"Fortune favors the bold, comrade!" Vladimir slapped him on the back and laughed.

"You've been waiting for, like . . ." Michael tried to remember how long it had been since they had had that conversation. It had been in the truck on the pipeline road, he thought, but wasn't certain. "Like *days* for the right time to say that, haven't you?"

Vladimir only grinned back at him.

"I would recommend that you keep your faceplates down and only breathe suit oxygen once these things are fueled." Sing said it nonchalantly, like it was no big deal.

"Important safety tip. Thanks, Sing," Michael said dryly.

"This way. The capsule was assembled in the hangar container nearest the western crane." Sing led them through a metal hatch with a large wheel latch. He turned the metal wheel in the middle of the door a couple of spins and the hatch hissed loose from the overpressure in the corridor. "Come with me. We keep this area at a constant overpressure to the exhaust scrubbers on the aft side of the deck in case there is a leak during the fueling process. Georgia's design. She really is a very good engineer."

They followed Sing down two corridors and out onto the main level platform in the open for a few meters and then into another larger container or makeshift hangar area. Sing continued to explain about the overpressure and the exhaust scrubbers and how safe it was, or wasn't, but Michael was only half listening to the scientist. He was tired. He had a million things on his mind. And he was, at the moment, contemplating climbing into a rocket with six nuclear warheads loaded with a chemical rocket fuel that would vaporize his lungs and kill his brain if he breathed it. Fortune truly did favor the bold. Michael almost laughed out loud when that thought crossed his mind.

The hangar container had been built up from several single units with the ceiling and floors removed to make a double-stacked-container high bay. There were several raw oxidized steel I-beams welded up the side walls and across the top of the high ceiling supporting the structure. There was a roll-off door at the end of the high bay opposite of them. Michael approximated the room to be forty meters deep, over thirty meters wide, and at least eight meters high. And there it was.

There was their means to an end, or beginning as Dorman continued to remind them. In the middle of the room sat a white and shiny new space capsule that looked almost identical to the Bezos *New Shepard* space capsule but not quite as cosmetically appealing. There were several windows about the circumference of the capsule about, Michael was guessing, one meter by one meter on a side, about waist high up the capsule. He'd been in the virtual capsule to practice and become familiar with the systems, but that was nothing like seeing the real thing. Michael paused and stood in awe. Vladimir was doing the same. He could tell by the look on his Russian friend's face that the man was immediately in love. Michael could tell that he was particularly fond of the fact that over the entry hatch was painted a word in Russian.

"Very nice, Comrade Sing," Vladimir said overdoing his Russian a bit. Then he read the word aloud. "*Vyrezka?*"

"V, does that mean what I think it means?" Michael asked. His Russian wasn't perfect. And, like English, there were many Russian words that had multiple meanings based on their context of use.

"It means 'cut ditch' or 'groove' or 'slot,' perhaps," Vladimir said. "Or maybe 'notch.'"

"Sing, did Dorman order that?" Michael asked.

"Yes, Michael. And he specifically wanted it spelled as a proper noun."

"Of course, he did." Michael shook his head and almost laughed, but he was too tired for that at the moment. "It means Notch, then."

"Why notch?" Vladimir asked.

"It's a proper noun, not just a groove. It's a name. Notch is the video game programmer who created the world of *Minecraft*, then sold it to Bill Gates for billions. Dorman sees this as creating a new world and himself being Notch. I don't know who he thinks we're gonna sell it to." Michael shrugged. "You know Dorman."

"My friend, Marcus has his reasons and goals. I don't care if he calls it Shit if it gets us where we need to go," Vladimir said. "I have my own personal reasons and goals. Besides, I like it!"

"Agreed." Michael nodded. "It's a nice-looking spaceship."

"Whatever it means, there's a lot to do in the next twenty-four hours to get it ready," Sing said pessimistically. "That's how much time we have before Georgia needs to start stacking the rocket. I'm sure the two of you can see that on the countdown clock and schedule."

"Yeah, sure we can, Sing. I get it. Vladimir gets it. Not much time and we have to get to work. So, V and I can follow your email instructions. We'll figure the changes out. You get back to work."

"Yes, but first, I want to show you this." Sing led them to the entry hatch and into the capsule.

The interior looked very similar to the interior of the Blue Origin *New Shepard* crew capsule and Michael was familiar with the interior from the virtual training. There was a central cylindrical console in the middle with flight couches dispersed about it circumferentially. There were the six large windows evenly spaced around the capsule at just the right height to enable viewing from the couches. Unlike the Bezos capsule, however, there was a panel at seat number three that looked more like a gunner's station than something that belonged in a space capsule for tourists. Michael noted that was his seat. He briefly eyed the console through the window as they rounded to the boarding ramp and ducked in.

"I have a surprise for you." There were several technicians working inside the capsule and there was a man they all recognized sitting in the pilot's seat. "Jeb got here just before you two did."

"Michael, Vlad." Jebidiah Reynolds nodded at them as they entered. "She's looking good."

"Jeb!" Vladimir shook his copilot's hand and then grunted at him in Russian something only the two of them understood. They both laughed. "My friend, I suspect that is my seat you are in."

"Right you are. Even if I have more hours in space than you." Jebidiah raised from the flight couch and offered it to Vladimir. "All yours, Colonel. Or should I say, Captain?"

"So, you made the flight, then?" Vladimir asked. "We have been busy and have paid no attention to things."

"Yes. Flawlessly. We made it to just under ten kilometers apogee."

"Very good! Impressive little plane. I'd love to fly it again, but in space next time."

"Yes, great plane," Jeb agreed.

"Michael." Jeb shook his hand. "Good to see you. I heard about the debacle with the suits."

"Taken care of. Sing. What do you need to show us?"

"Ah, yes, sorry. Here it is." Sing stepped behind the central panel and pointed to the space where the Bezos ship contained three other flight couches. In their places were six mating rings for mounting the glide bodies. "Here at the bottom of the mating rings. Georgia's new booster design for Munition Number One will not fit the standard ring we'd originally designed. We are building the adaptors as we speak. The first one is complete and the training glide-body shell is outside. You should practice mating the munition with the adapter."

"I see," Vladimir said. "Good thing you are here to practice with us Jeb."

"How long do we have, Sing?" Michael asked.

"We need to start integrating the actual munitions in the next five or six hours from now," Sing said. "So, you need to get started."

"Which is it, Sing? Five or six hours?" Michael opened up another counter in his virtual view. "I'm going to start a clock."

"Say five and a half, then," Sing answered.

"Starting now," Michael told him. "I'll send you the link."

"Jeb, let's go get the munition surrogate," Vlad said.

"Let's get to work, gentlemen," Michael said.

"We should practice in the suits," Jeb noted.

"Not sure Georgia has them ready yet." Michael said. "But in a perfect world . . ."

CHAPTER 27

〇〇

Huntsville, Alabama
Sunday
10:00 A.M. Central Time

U.S. ARMY RANGER MAJOR CASEY DUGAN WAITED IN HIS CAR
outside the coffee shop that was just outside the gates to the U.S.
Army Redstone Arsenal in North Alabama. He could see the gates
about a kilometer down the long multilane road. All the gates
had a red *X* lit up over the top of them except for one that was
green. *Not a lot of traffic on Sundays*, he thought.

The coffee shop was mostly empty as it was Sunday morning. Most people in Huntsville, Alabama, were either still in bed,
just getting up, or were sitting in church somewhere. Casey had
flown in first thing and had already reached out to the contact
he had in the area. She should be meeting him at any moment.
He leaned over to turn the radio of the rental car down and
grimaced slightly. His ribs ached some from the car crash the
night before. He pulled the visor down and looked at the swollen red-and-blue spot just below his right eye where he'd caught
an elbow, and exhaled.

"Should've ducked, I guess," he said to himself. He turned his
head to get more of a profile view of his face. It wasn't that bad.
In a day or two the bruise would probably turn brown or yellow,
maybe some purple thrown in, and it would be sore to the touch.

But it wasn't too bad. He just hated that he'd have to miss out on the fun of trying to get useful information out of that asshole. Casey was betting that they would get nothing. Those guys had "pro mercs" written all over them. They knew if they talked, there would be another team of pros coming to shut them up.

He checked his wristwatch again but disregarded the time as he recognized the woman driving the green Tesla sportscar pulling in next to him. It was an old friend he'd worked with years ago on a program to stop al-Qaeda rocket-propelled grenades. He'd been a Sapper at the Army Corps of Engineers in Vicksburg, Mississippi, doing his best to find an armor system to protect convoys from Russian pilfered and/or supplied—nobody knew which—RPG-22s and RPG-18s. The engineers had tested everything from battleship-hull plating steel to concrete with very little luck. Somehow, and he wasn't even sure he recalled how, he was put into touch with a team of scientists and engineers from the Redstone Arsenal in Alabama. And that is where he had met Dr. Amy Castlebaum. She was brilliant, funny, and mostly a lot of fun. He recalled the evenings after work hanging out a local bar near the university with her and the rest of the team. It had been fun. While there had never been anything romantic between them, there had always been something friendly and flirtatious.

The sportscar silently pulled up beside him and a tinted window rolled down. Castlebaum smiled at Casey and waved.

"Well, I'll be damned," she said. "It is you, after all."

"Long time no see, huh?" Dugan replied.

"About nine years or so." She smiled at him. "And you never called or wrote or emailed. Nuthin'."

"Hey, I could say the same about you, Dr. Castlebaum."

"Oh, are we being official this morning, Lieutenant Dugan? Oh wait, it's Major now, isn't it?" For the first time Dugan was turned toward her enough that she noticed his face. "Jesus! Casey, what happened to you?"

"Long story. Tell you later. And, Amy, while I'd love to spend a lot of time playing catch-up drinking coffee with you, there just isn't time for that right now. As I told you on the phone, I'm here because of a matter of utmost urgency and national security. And the clock is ticking away on us very swiftly." Dugan talked to her through the car window. "We need to go to your secure facility as soon as possible so I can brief you."

"Yeah, okay. You're so all-business now that you're a major and all. I can't imagine what you'll be like when you're a colonel. Follow me and be prepared to show your Common Access Card." She waved her hand with a "come here" motion for him to follow.

"Got it." Casey held up his badge. "After you."

Casey followed her car through the main security gate to the Army base and then continued behind her down several main roads. There were several NASA buildings on either side of the road. One of the buildings had a huge engine out in front of it—space shuttle, he thought. He wasn't sure if it was a mockup or the real deal. There were several other spots along the way where rocket engines or actual rockets were stood up. There were large satellite dishes strewn about the landscape between buildings and the occasional missile launcher here and there.

At times when the trees were separated or when he was in the right spot, he could see the large Saturn V moon rocket that stood over Huntsville at the U.S. Space and Rocket Center a few kilometers to his west. He was surprised at how much the Arsenal had changed since he'd been there almost a decade prior. Many of the places that he recalled to be pastures were huge, recently built multistory buildings. While there were still some large green pastures filled with cows grazing along the way, there were also shiny new brick-and-mortar complexes with very large parking lots. Dugan noted that it was quite the dichotomy of scenery. It being a Sunday, there were almost no cars in any of the lots.

A few more turns and they came to a new security gate. A guard at the shack came out and spoke to Amy for a second and he could see her motioning toward the car behind her—in other words, at him. Casey pulled his badge out and handed it over as the guard waved him up.

"Good morning, sir."

"Working on Sunday, huh?" Dugan said.

"Pays the bills." He scanned Dugan's badge with a laser scanner without ever touching it. Then he depressed a button and the red-and-white-striped rail started to raise. "Have a good day."

It had taken them a few minutes to get parked, badge into the front door, have Amy escort him up to her floor level, wait on him at the men's room for a bit, open the SCIF, and then get settled in. She powered on the computer system in her office and offered Dugan a chair next to her desk after she turned on her personal coffeepot.

"Alright, Casey, we can talk at any level of classification you are cleared for in here, so what's this all about?"

"I sent you a file through JWICS late last night. Bring that up first."

"Okay, that'll take a second." Amy toggled her screen to the secure side and typed in her very long password. The screen lit up with the words TOP SECRET/SCI in a banner at the top and bottom of her screen. She waited for the system to spin up and then clicked open her email application. "Here it is."

"Okay, open it, and I'll start."

"Done." Amy opened the PDF file that was attached to the email. A spinning icon appeared on the screen saying that the file was being scanned for malware and then it finally opened. Amy scrolled past the classification cover page and started reading the first page with information on it. It was a compressed version of a PowerPoint slideshow. The first slide was a typical intelligence briefing explaining the classification, date, time, and originator of the data.

"Go ahead and flip to the next slide," Dugan told her.

"A Topol-M?" she asked rhetorically. "I've seen jillions of them."

"Well, five days ago, this particular Topol-M TEL was attacked by a highly skilled team of mercenaries or some similar group who killed all of the Russian soldiers—except for their commander, a Colonel Vladimir Lytokov, who was in on the attack it now appears. They then made off with some plural number—as of yet unknown, estimated max of six—nuclear warheads each possibly up to one hundred and fifty kilotons," Dugan explained. "As far as we know, neither us nor the Russians have any idea where the nukes are now."

"Holy shit! Seriously?" Amy gasped.

"Seriously."

"What are we doing about it?" Suddenly, Casey figured, Amy's thoughts had gone from wondering what the major was doing for dinner to fear—the type of fear that some asshole was about to set off a nuclear weapon and kill millions of people. Casey could tell she was looking at his face differently now.

"A task force was stood up by the Joint Chiefs almost immediately following. We started chasing any leads we could find.

That investigation has now led us to a former Oak Ridge nuclear physicist and likely Chinese spy who, while in college at MIT, had two roommates. One has turned out to be the wanted fugitive computer hacker Keenan James Ingersol, whereabouts unknown, and a Phillip Joseph Watkins, aerospace engineer and missile systems analyst for CIA, now deceased."

"Jesus H. Christ!" Amy said so reflexively loud that she looked about to make sure nobody was disturbed by it. She then realized it was Sunday, and nobody else was there. "Shit, Casey! This is crazy. Deceased?"

"Yeah, he lived in Reston, Virginia. We captured three men who were sent there to kill him—how I got this bruise on my face last night—but we were too late. Watkins had already been shot in the head at point-blank range in his study. We did get a lot of information from his house, desk, bookbag, and his computer. That is why I'm here."

"Damn."

"Yeah. Damn at the least. Look at the next slide."

"Okay." Amy scrolled her mouse to bring up the next slide. It was an image of paper with handwritten notes and calculations on it. Amy quickly recognized the *vis viva* equation and the Tsiolkovsky rocket equation. There were some others that looked like orbital calculations from Kepler's Laws and so on. "Basic rocket science stuff here, it looks like."

"Well, if you keep scrolling through the next several pages, you'll see lots of such calculations. They were beyond most of the analysts on the team. And that's the reason I'm here."

"You mean you're not here because of my big brown eyes and wonderful personality? You certainly know how to woo a girl." Amy laughed.

"Well, sorry. Maybe next time." Dugan smiled at her and thought briefly that perhaps he wished she had pushed the boundaries of their relationship a bit back then. He could tell that she shrugged it off and was becoming hooked by the detailed rocketry in front of her. There were more important things to deal with presently than to be worrying about an ancient relationship that might have been.

"Okay, this is like..." She looked at the total page number on the slideshow. There were over one hundred and thirty slides. "This is, um, gonna take some time to go through."

"How much time?"

"Uh, I don't know. Hours? Days? I won't know until I get into it." Amy turned and looked a bit sheepishly at the Army Ranger. "What do you need from me?"

"I need to know what this is about, Amy. The Secretary of Defense has authorized this task force to do what it takes to find and stop this threat. Whatever this threat turns out to be. If you need approval to work overtime, you'll get it retroactively." Dugan paused for a breath as if giving her a chance to say something. But she, likely, simply didn't know what to say. Dugan continued.

"Amy, I need this done as fast as it can be done. If you can start on it now, that is what I was hoping for."

"Uh, Jesus, yeah. Okay." Amy looked at the slide on her computer screen and then back and forth a couple times at Dugan. "I'm not exactly sure how long this will take, but I know it is gonna take some time. Look, I get it. I realize that every second wasted is another second closer to one of the nukes going off... maybe. Um, Casey, how do we know that these mercenaries aren't just going to sell the nukes?"

"Nobody to sell them to." Dugan could tell by the look on Amy's face that she didn't understand that comment, so he added, "We've chased that down a few rabbit holes, but our conclusion is that they plan to use them because the nukes are so hot right now. The Russians, we think now the Chinese, and the U.S. are all looking for them. The U.N. and NATO will be briefed on this tomorrow. There's no way they could sell them to anyone without getting caught."

"Hmmm." Amy just nodded as if she understood. Casey wasn't certain that she did. But that didn't matter. There were over a hundred pages of rocket science in front of her that she needed to figure out. "Okay, then, this is going to take hours at least. You want me to escort you back out so you don't have to just sit here waiting?"

"I was up all night," he said. "Maybe I could go check into a hotel and get a nap."

"Okay, good idea. Do you have reservations anywhere?"

"No. Just jumped on a plane and got here." He shrugged. "Grabbed a rental car at the airport, and, well, here I am."

"There are several hotels outside the gate that still run government per diem rates," she said. "I'd take Martin Road east and then take the Parkway north and there will be several hotels on your right down there. I have your cell number. I'll call when I get something."

"Okay, maybe that's what I'll do. You mind walking me out?"

"Not at all, handsome." She was still flirty, but he could tell she was anxious to get those numbers back on her desk.

CHAPTER 28

᠙

Saratoga Springs, Utah
National Security Agency
Utah Data Center, Code Name "Bumblehive"
Sunday
10:00 A.M. Mountain Time

DR. KEVIN GRAYSON HAD BEEN UP ALL DAMNED NIGHT RUNNING algorithms on the massively parallel Cray XC30 supercomputer, code name "Cascade." Kevin had the system currently optimized and overclocking at a bit over one hundred petaflops, over one hundred thousand trillion calculations per second. The actual speed it was running was above Top Secret. There were rumors in the public that the system had reached an "exaflop," or over a quintillion instructions per second, but Dr. Grayson could neither confirm nor deny such claims. At least he couldn't if he planned on staying out of jail for violating national security secrets and wanted to keep getting paid to do the thing he loved most—solving computational problems.

He had been looking for anything useful about the missing Topol-M warheads. He'd tried the names that Colonel Alvarez and Ginny had sent him via JWICS and had crossed correlated and cross-referenced every piece of information that they had dug up with each other in every possible combination imaginable. So far, he'd come up with nothing. He'd tried running lists of names, keywords and phrases, locations, times, dates, anything pertinent to the event but still the computer had yet to spit out anything new. He'd made the algorithm start sending web crawlers and agents out through every internet protocol hub in existence looking for a match on any of the data keywords and phrases, images, sounds, and concepts. So far, not a single superbot had brought a thing back into the fold. The might of the National Security Agency's most advanced computer was still coming up with nothing. Whoever had been behind the warhead theft and whoever had funded it were a mystery. They were good at covering their tracks or erasing them altogether.

Grayson had racked his brain to the point of having nothing else he could contribute. He had reached a complete fugue state of hopelessness, helplessness, and was at a total loss as of what to do next. There just wasn't enough data yet to figure out who, what, when, or where. He leaned back in his desk chair and rolled his neck left then right to remove the cramping in his shoulders from the bad ergonomics and posture of hovering over a keyboard and staring deeply into a monitor for hours. He was tired. The bags under his eyes and the bloodshot whites of his eyeballs were testament to that fact. He also needed to shave and probably shower on top of that. He had existed on coffee, soft drinks, then energy drinks, and junk food out of the vending machine in the break area for double-digit hours.

Perhaps that was the problem. Kevin decided that he was just too tired and burned out at the moment to think straight. So, he made the concerted effort to force himself up from his desk chair, stretch his body, put on his jacket, and go for a damned walk around the Bumblehive complex. He hit go on the latest search algorithm, waited for it to signal that there were no errors, and then left Cascade to do her thing. He had no idea how long the latest iteration on the cross-correlation search would last, but he had time for at the very least a ten-minute walk. And, maybe, he had time for another cup of coffee.

"Who, what, when, or where," he muttered to himself. "Hell, any single one of those would be something we don't know right now."

He passed out his office and down the hallway and badged out into the common area. The building was usually a busy beehive—that part of the facility's code name had always been apropos, although Kevin had always wondered why "Bumblehive" as opposed to other more industrious bees like honeybees. But today, the Bumblehive was pretty much a ghost town. It was Sunday morning, in Utah. Most people were at church. Other than security teams, he'd only seen a single-digit number of people so far. He figured they were wrapped around some conundrum of national security like him, but he didn't take the time to stop and chat with them to find out.

A short flight of stairs down—he often decided against the elevator, not really for the exercise but more because he didn't trust computer-driven machines—and another badge-through and he was outside standing on the sidewalk with the Bumblehive standing tall behind him. It was a brisk morning in Utah, almost forty-five degrees. He zipped his jacket up, put his hands in his pockets, and started walking. The employees there often walked, jogged, ran, biked, rollerbladed, and other forms of outdoor exercise around the periphery of the building. He decided he had time for about two to three kilometers' worth of walking before he needed to get back and check on Cascade.

The Utah sky was perfectly clear. There wasn't a cloud as far as he could see and from there, that was likely seventy kilometers or more. Kevin often made the walk and watched the skies as he did. The rumors of unknown aerial phenomena flying over the state had been around for maybe thousands of years. He'd been working there nearly a decade now and had yet to see a damned thing with his own eyes. But many of his colleagues had video on their phones of UFOs they'd seen. He had never really been certain what to think of it. He'd used Cascade several times to search through the classified databases on the topic but usually came away with more questions than answers.

That had always bothered him. How was it that with all that classified information he'd never been able to find the who, what, where, when, or how of the UFO story? Oh, he'd found plenty of credible videos, sensor data, photos, and eyewitness accounts from trained military officers, but none of it proved what the damned things were. Why hadn't he found the "program" that really knew what they were? Was it because it wasn't there? Was it covered up better than even the NSA could uncover? And more importantly, why? It had always truly boggled his mind as to why anyone would cover up just the knowledge of existence.

He could understand keeping ways and means and technological breakthroughs a secret, but why just the general knowledge of existence? Why?

"Why?" he actually said aloud. He stopped dead in his tracks and said it again. "Why?"

The thought rang a bell in his mind about something. Why was the question that needed to be answered, but he had to ask the right "why." They had exhausted themselves trying to determine the existential motivation, politically and philosophically, as to "Why" somebody would steal nukes that could be so devastating. But that was the wrong question.

"Wait a minute..." he said with the realization that the right "Why" was a much more pragmatic one and was maybe even not a "Why" with a capital *W.* It was a smaller, more applied "why." Or maybe it was a small-case "what," as well.

"Why!" He smacked his right palm against his forehead. "Why? Why do they need the nukes? What are they going to use them for?"

He immediately decided that his walk was over and now walking was the action needed to get him back in front of Cascade. He did a full 360-degree turn and looked at his progress, trying to determine if he should push forward or turn back for the fastest path back to the office. He realized he was just about at the halfway distance, so it would make no difference. He started back walking and seriously picked up the pace and pushed forward.

"What could you do with six nukes?" he asked himself. "That's the parameter..."

CHAPTER 29

〜

Huntsville, Alabama
Sunday
3:00 P.M. Central Time

DR. AMY CASTLEBAUM HAD BEEN PORING OVER THE DOCUMENTS
that Major Dugan had given her for several hours now. She had
put together a few simulations on her computer using Python
code and some Matlab, using some programs she'd written over
the years. A few modifications here and there and she could
simulate rockets, satellites, missiles, suborbital flights, orbital
flights, and just about anything that had to do with putting an
object of a given mass at any altitude, location, or orbit about
the planet. She had programs running that could tell her the
maximum "throw weight" of a missile and then convert that into
a similar maximum "orbital payload mass" for the same missile
being used as a launch vehicle.

She had hand calculations, notes, printouts, and wadded-up
pages of scribbled-on engineering paper all around her garbage
can where she'd missed it but was too busy to worry with pick-
ing them up. She adjusted a plot that was currently on her main
computer screen showing two particular trajectories she had
managed to reverse engineer from the notes Dugan had sent her.
One was an orbit. It was not a very specific orbit as far as she
could tell. It was in low Earth orbit (LEO). The calculations were

for a perfectly circular four hundred kilometers above sea level orbit at no specific inclination. In other words, it could have been anything in space orbiting the Earth at four hundred kilometers' altitude. The orbit could be at the equator's inclination of zero degrees, over Huntsville at about thirty-four degrees, or over the North Pole at ninety. With no data given on the inclination there was no telling what orbit it was. There were LEO satellites in orbits ranging from about three hundred kilometers above sea level all the way out to geosynchronous orbits at thirty-five thousand kilometers, and at just about every single inclination between the poles.

The second plot was a rendezvous trajectory, not an orbit. It originated from sea level. Amy noted that it was from no particular place or inclination either, which meant it assumed equatorial. So, as far as she could tell, this was a launch of a rocket of some sort climbing upward and intersecting with the circular orbit there. The rocket calculations showed a three-stage rocket.

The first-stage burn numbers showed a burn time of two and a half minutes at eight meganewtons of thrust. Those numbers had jumped off the page at her. She'd studied enough Russian launch vehicles in her day to guess that was a Russian-built RD-171 LOX/kerosene rocket engine from Energia. The second-stage burn was just under a meganewton of thrust with a burn time of five minutes and fifteen seconds. That one smelled like a Russian RD-120 to her. Again, another Russian LOX/kerosene engine. The two stages of the rocket supplied enough thrust to take a payload mass of over six thousand kilograms to a four hundred kilometer LEO.

The third burn was sort of a residual calculation. It simply matched the trajectory altitude of the launch vehicle to the circular LEO orbit and showed the burn needed to put the launch vehicle's payload mass into a circular orbit that matched the spacecraft already in orbit at four hundred kilometers. Amy noted that there was no accounting for inclination cranking and orbit phasing—at least not in the fifty or so pages she'd already made it through. She also noted that there appeared to still be plenty of propellant mass in the third stage for orbit cranking and such shown in the calculations even though Watkins hadn't done that.

What was clear to her was that this wasn't an intercept— meaning, the launch vehicle wasn't making an attempt to shoot down the orbiting vehicle. Instead, this was a rendezvous. The launch vehicle was meeting the already orbiting vehicle, matching its speed, and then mating or docking with it. That was her current working assumption. She had made a significant amount of progress here. But there was a lot still unknown. And she still had about eight pages to go.

She restarted the model to watch it once more just to make certain she hadn't missed anything. The computer screen showed an image of a generic Earth in the animation window with a red circle above it. The Earth and the orbits were not to scale. She made a mental note that she'd have to explain that to Dugan when she showed it to him. A blue curve started building from the equator at sea level until it matched with the red circle. At three different points on the blue trajectory curve there were asterisks with notes showing "Main Engine Cut-Off," "Second Engine Start," "Second Engine Cut-Off," "Circularization Burn," and "Rendezvous." She added a callout block with an arrow pointing at the spot before "Rendezvous": "Inclination Cranking, Orbit Phasing, and Speed Matching Burns Here."

As far as she could tell, her graphic matched a napkin drawing and some notes drawn on engineering paper that were part of the images in the PDF file that the dead guy, Watkins, had on his desk.

Amy was pretty certain that this was the intent of the first fifty or so pages of the man's notes. Now that she had gotten that far, it was time to push on through the next fifty or so pages. Maybe they would help her make sense out of what was going on. At this point, as far as she could tell, there were no calculations for ICBMs or nuclear detonations. But there were many pages left. And Dugan had told her that there were encrypted files on his computer that they had yet to crack. Who knew what was in those?

CHAPTER 30

֍

Washington, D.C.
The Pentagon
Sunday
8:00 P.M. Eastern Time

"SO, WAIT A MINUTE. YOU MEAN THAT SIX NUKES COULD BE enough to shut down the planet?" Lieutenant Colonel Frank Alvarez said it as if he didn't believe the words coming out of his own mouth. "Is that what you are saying, Dr. Grayson?"

"No, that *isn't* what I'm saying." Frank watched as the man spoke to them through the secure video system connecting the Pentagon, the NSA in Utah, the Missile and Space Intelligence Center in Alabama, and A1C Shannon and two new Space Force officers from Tampa. The original team members had all been on the move and had yet to have time to get back to the Task Force headquarters in Tampa to meet the new players. Other than the brief introductions in the beginning of the secure video conference, Tampa had stayed on mute.

"That is not what I said at all, Colonel Alvarez," Grayson insisted.

"Okay then, I'm confused. Please, rephrase what you just told us from the top, if you don't mind." Frank looked around the conference table at Mac and Kenny and could tell they were somewhat bewildered, but they managed to maintain decent poker faces.

"Well, six nukes, even if these were of the megaton class—and they aren't—wouldn't do much damage from a global perspective if they were detonated from the ground. People always think nukes will blow up the planet—based on Hollywood movies, I suspect. They always get it wrong. Oh, please don't get me wrong here— from a city-sized perspective, yes, absolutely millions could die if they are detonated in a metropolis like New York City, Paris, London, Tokyo, and so forth. That would be very bad." Grayson continued to explain as he turned a monitor on his desk so the classified VTC camera could pick it up. "You can see the damage areas marked here if all six were detonated on the North American continent."

The monitor had a slide of North America with six red dots spread across it; from the continent level, they were barely perceptible. Grayson zoomed in on the screen to the city level, where a centimeter represented about five kilometers. From that perspective, the damage would be significant and the red dots became large red circles.

"New York City, for example, would be gone," Dr. Grayson explained. "But only that."

"A nuke that size would destroy a city. That's bad enough," Frank said. He'd been working proliferation of weapons of mass destruction for most of his career and he had been trained on what size bombs could do what damage. But he'd never really focused on a global perspective. He'd always assumed that if somebody stole a nuke, they would use it for terrorism and blow up a city for show and posturing or to just be an asshole of epic proportion. That's just how terrorists and warlords worked—assholes. They wanted to punch the big bully, the "great Satan," or whatever other evil king of the hill right in the nose and they didn't give a shit about all the moms, dads, sons, and daughters that got killed in the process. Assholes. Of epic proportion.

"Yes, major damage citywide, many deaths, but—and here is the catch—in only six cities or so. That is a very small-minded, yesterday type of thinking. The global pandemic invasions and rampant cyberattacks show us that there is a new breed of evil mind out there. There are bad guys thinking in terms of global manipulation, stock market collapses, national currency devaluations, election outcome management, population control, and yes, maybe even global domination. Sounds like a spy movie, but it has become reality. Just what if *that* is the kind of mindset we are dealing with here?"

"What if?" Thompson shrugged. "He's wearing an eyepatch and petting his cat somewhere."

"Where's Mike Myers when we need him?" Mac added. Frank did his best not to glare at the two of them. He did think the comments were funny, even though he was pretty sure Major Thompson wasn't old enough to know who Austin Powers or Ernst Blofeld were.

"Mike Myers—ha! I get that reference. And, unfortunately, what if you are *not* that far from wrong, Chief? You see, well, I was considering what six nuclear warheads could really do if they were put to an optimally devastating use on as large a scale as possible. That is when I realized these might not be old-school terrorists we're dealing with here. No, not at all. These might be the global currency devaluation, election-rigging, pandemic-invading nut jobs of conspiracy theory websites. But not conspiracy and practically doable. By thinking along those lines, well, that is when I started really focusing on what they would do with six nukes rather than who or where they are or what. The current evidence we have tells us they aren't typical terrorists."

"How so, Doc?" Alvarez asked, although he was beginning to come to similar conclusions himself based on how the operation had gone. Somebody had really thought this through. Somebody had really covered his or her or their tracks. Somebody out there was really smart, well funded, and surrounded by very very competent and loyal people. Frank was thinking much more loyal than the type that would dump a backpack full of ballots into a ballot box while the cameras were watching, smiling all the while and waving to fans. No, this was the type of loyalty that would take a bullet in the head for a cause. A very bad and dangerous cause. These weren't dumb kids doing stupid things and thinking they were changing the world. These were people planning to do something horrific and dangerous and would change the world in a very bad, bad way. This shit scared the hell out of Frank and he knew it had to be stopped. Somehow.

"Well, if they are typical, why did they only grab the warheads and go? Why was there no message or anyone claiming credit? Because I think these guys are smarter and better prepared than that. They have a plan."

"What plan, Doc?" Mac asked.

"To blackout most of the world."

"What?"

"What if the nukes were detonated at altitude—let's say an altitude of thirty kilometers or so, could be higher—and what if they were strategically placed around the globe before detonation at said altitude? One model I have run suggests a detonation in the U.S., somewhere over Kentucky, perhaps, one over Moscow, one over Beijing, one over maybe Paris, maybe New Delhi, and maybe somewhere in the Middle East or on the west coast of the U.S. The electromagnetic pulse, or EMP, impact on the power grids and communication networks would be devastating. Probably far, far more people would die from the long-term infrastructure impact than would from detonations in cities on the ground. Also, the radiation problem wouldn't be as bad either. There would be very little fallout and it would be widely dispersed in the upper atmosphere fairly quickly."

"That makes perfect sense, Kevin." Frank didn't recognize the female voice. But from Grayson's reaction on the video screen, he did. As the secure video conferencing software put the speaker's video up, he could see Major Dugan and a woman looking to be somewhere in her late forties with long, straight black hair, wearing black-rimmed glasses, a black Mötley Crüe T-shirt, and a light green cardigan. The video system labeled her as MSIC: DR. CASTLEBAUM. "They'd need a way to get them all airborne, though."

"Yes, Amy, that is the one thing I have yet to figure out. Airplanes wouldn't get them high enough. They'd need to get them on rockets or missiles to get them up there."

"They're not going to put them up on rockets or missiles, as you say. That would be too costly," Dr. Castlebaum said. "Besides, you'd have to launch six different rockets from six different locations to do that. What you could do is just drop them from space."

"Say again? Drop them from space?" Chief McKagan said from across the table from Frank.

"Seriously?" Thompson muttered under his breath.

"How would they get them there? They should have just kept them on the missile and launched that thing if that was what they wanted to do," Mac added.

"Well, not really, Mac. Listen to what the doc has to say. She's got this figured out, I think," Dugan said and nodded back to Amy.

Frank watched and noted there was a bit of familiarity between them. He'd have to get the backstory from the Sapper later. But Frank had checked the in-service guys out and they all were good men. He either had served with them or served with someone who had. He trusted them. He trusted Mac, Kenny, and Casey. And Major Casey Dugan seemed to trust this Dr. Castlebaum, so he would give her the benefit of the doubt for the time being.

"Yes, right." Castlebaum took her glasses off with her right hand and pointed with them as she started again. "If they had launched the Topol-M it would have required major reprogramming, and even then, I don't think they could have gotten the kind of coverage that Kevin is talking about. At least from a rocket science perspective it would be difficult, if not impossible, for that one missile without serious modifications and testing. With hypersonic glide bodies you could spread them apart, but not globally. At least I don't think you could. Kevin?"

"Correct." Grayson nodded. "While one Topol-M with multiple reentry vehicles could cover several areas, it would only be on a single continent, according to all the data we have available on those systems. But, Amy, we got that data from MSIC, so I trust your assessment."

"Right. Uh, yes, that's what my assessment suggests anyway. Plus, as good as these bad guys might be, hacking and launching a stolen Topol-M would still be quite a feat. I think it would be easier to steal the warheads and use them," Amy said. She put her glasses back on and tapped at a computer keyboard briefly and then looked back toward the screen or wherever the camera was located. "If you could get the nukes into orbit to about four hundred kilometers' altitude, then you could deorbit them to wherever you wanted to put them on the globe as you passed by. It's a little more complicated than that, but not significantly so. I was thinking of hitting targets and the accuracy needed confused me because that would be harder to pull off. But hearing what Dr. Grayson is telling us about using the bombs for EMP and just getting them to hit targets of sort of state-sized locations at thirty kilometers' altitude or higher, well now, that is very, very doable. It absolutely could be done."

"Alright, so they blast out the lights and some radios and stuff. How bad could it really be?" Thompson asked.

"Kevin, you want to answer that one?" Amy asked.

"I'll take it," he said. "So, we actually ran a study on this a few years back. We used the supercomputer here to run a simulation of such a global scale event. At the time we simulated solar flares and even some nuclear detonations. I also have read one JASON study where they looked at this. All of it so classified nobody ever read it, really."

"Sounds useful." Amy laughed.

"I have to agree," Mac said. "If you have access to that study, please send it to us. My CO probably would like to see it."

"These simulations and studies took into account as many variables as possible to make them as accurate as possible. The study cost over sixteen million dollars and took about sixteen months to complete. The results were fairly clear. A well-placed single EMP event over North America from either a nuclear airburst or a CME would blow out a large portion of our power grid. There would be blackouts for weeks, months, and maybe even years because of the loss of power transformers, switches, and other susceptible items that are replaceable but with limited reserves. Think about the transformers alone. There would be many tens of millions of those potentially damaged by one EMP blast. At any given time, the U.S. has about fifty to one hundred thousand replacement parts."

"Can't we make new ones?" Frank asked.

"Yes, but, the backorder times on them is something like six months. It could be years before they were all replaced. It was suggested in the report that leaving parts of the old grid derelict and standing up a new one might be easier," Grayson said. "These six well-placed nukes could put large parts of the world back in the dark for a long time to come. Maybe even indefinitely."

"Not to mention all the dead internet systems, cars, and other infrastructure items." McKagan shook his head knowingly. "Jesus, could this really be what they are planning?"

"I don't know the exact hows, or for that matter even the exact whats, this 'they' of yours is planning," Amy said, "but a very general 'what' was drawn out and worked out in some fairly good detail on the notes from Phillip Watkins that Major Dugan sent me. There is a detailed analysis of using a rocket launch vehicle that I'll bet a dime to a donut is a Russian rocket that's meeting up with a vehicle already in orbit at about four hundred kilometers. Then, later on in those notes are calculations for deorbit burns of much smaller payloads. This fits our scenario perfectly."

"A Russian rocket?" Frank asked.

"Yeah, the burn times and thrust requirements for the launch calculations you found suggests specific Russian-made rocket motors for both the first and second stages. The numbers used are pretty much a fingerprint for exact rocket motors. The problem is, several rockets around the world use those motors," Amy explained.

"Yeah, but are the Russians the only ones that make them?" Frank asked.

"Not even that generic," she replied. "They are made by a specific Russian rocket company... let's see," she said, checking her notes. "Energomash made them for the Energia Zenit rocket family. Variations of that motor are used for other rockets including the Atlas V, which uses the RD-180."

"Wait a minute," Mac interrupted. "The Atlas V is an American rocket made down there in Decatur, Alabama, by you, right? It uses a Russian engine?"

"Don't get me started on that fiasco," Amy commented.

"Where in Russia are these things made, Dr. Castlebaum?" Frank asked.

"Call me Amy. They come from Ukraine... um, let me see, I wrote it down in case I forgot it. Yuzhnoye Design Bureau, in Dnipro."

"How many of these can there be?" Major Thompson asked.

"And how many are unaccounted for?" Mac added.

"That's not my realm of expertise," Amy replied. "I'm the reverse engineer rocket person, not the current inventories person. But there has to be plenty of them still around."

"I'll start a search on that now," Grayson said.

"As soon as Dr. Banks checks in, I'll ask her to look into it as well," Frank said. Ginny had stayed awake about as long as humanly possible. She had been going in and out on Frank earlier during a conversation. He told her to get some rest. They were in D.C. near her actual home, so he told her that he thought she should go home while she had the chance and get some rest in her actual bed and not a cot or hotel room.

"I can ping my colleagues at DTRA," Mac said. "Somebody there might have some insight."

"Great, Mac. Let me know if you find out anything. You, too, Dr. Grayson." Frank waited to see if anybody else had anything new. They didn't. "Dr. Castlebaum, this is great work. Can you and Major Dugan get that summarized for me in a briefable package ASAP?"

"We'll do it, Colonel." Dugan replied. "And you never told us what you got out of the two assailants and the driver up there."

"Not a peep, Casey. Not a damned word," Frank replied. "Completely tight lipped. You probably beat more noise out of the driver than we've managed to get from him since the doctor cleared him for questioning."

"Unfortunate."

"Maybe you should've hit him harder, Case," Thompson suggested.

"Next time." Dugan smiled.

"Toby is at FBI HQ across the river running their fingerprints and facial patterns through all the known criminal and terror and international law enforcement networks. Hopefully, he'll get something. Anybody have anything else?"

"No, sir."

"Nope."

"Negative."

"Alright then, stay in touch. If anybody comes up with something new, call immediately."

CHAPTER 31

∽

Washington, D.C.
FBI Headquarters
Sunday
9:00 P.M. Eastern Time

SPECIAL AGENT TOBIAS "TOBY" MATTHEW MONTGOMERY III HAD
been frustrated by bad guys before. Frustration was good. It meant
that there was something that somebody didn't want him to
uncover. He was good at overcoming that frustration and uncovering the details of whatever the situation at hand might be. He was
very good at uncovering the uncoverable. He'd worked every type
of bad guy from drug lords to gunrunners, from terrorist assassins
to organized crime bosses. For the past ten years or so he'd been
working weapons proliferation into the U.S. from terror-based
sources. He knew what seemed like everyone in law enforcement
around the world working similar efforts. And nobody—not a
single one of his contacts in the U.K, Australia, South Africa,
Japan, New Zealand, Interpol, the NATO teams, or even some of
the privately funded organizations—had anything about the stolen
Russian nukes. So, there was no need to keep beating that dead
horse any further. No, Toby knew that he would have to take a
different path that might take him the long way around, but just
might in the end lead him to them. Whover that "them" was.

The three men they had captured and the dead body was

a path. A very fresh and new path with new clues. Why was Watkins killed? He seemed to be part of the effort—whatever the "effort" was. Killing off your experts suggested that said experts either were no longer needed, or they had turned on you and were going to blow the whistle, or they were stupid and about to get themselves caught, or they weren't part of the effort and were trying to leverage their way in. And there was also the possibility of any combination of those options.

Which of those choices was Watkins? Toby knew that Watkins was dead for a simple and clear reason. No matter which one of the motivations, or combinations thereof, he matched, there was somebody out there that thought he was going to talk or reveal something they didn't want revealed. There was absolutely a bigger bad guy out there somewhere who wanted to keep Watkins from talking. And dead men could tell no tales. Maybe.

That brought up a couple more questions as Toby stared blankly at the wall of data he had accumulated. He liked to work old school. There was a whiteboard in his office with sticky notes, taped-up photos, and lines of different colors connecting people and events. It had taken him a couple of hours to put it all there in front of him. He figured that he would snap an image of it with his secure phone and send it to Frank once he had it all there. But there was still a lot to decipher and he was guessing they were running against an already ticking-down clock. And they had gotten to the starting line late.

One thing was for certain: Watkins wouldn't be talking to anyone. Who didn't want him talking? And what didn't they want him talking about? The fact that the assassins were sent to not only kill Watkins but to burn his house and whatever evidence was in it—well, that meant that he had data in his house somewhere that could incriminate someone somewhere.

And as far as the identity of these three men they had apprehended went, well, as far as Toby could determine, they were ghosts. The data that had come back from fingerprints and facial recognition showed that these men were dead defense contractors, each from unrelated small businesses and having supported different overseas defense or intelligence operations within the last decade. The information on the deceased contractors showed that they had been killed in combat support. But here they were in Virginia, killing a CIA analyst. Not bad work for three dead guys.

Fingerprints and facial imagery matched with ninety-seven percent correlation. Therefore, these three men hadn't died when their records showed. They were alive and in a holding cell in a private facility outside the Beltway. He tracked their economic and tax records, showing that none of them had much of anything before death and they had no families of record still alive. They were individuals who could "die" and then vanish with no loved ones around to ask questions. Toby had seen this before. It was a standard modus operandi for recruiting terrorists and spies. Which category were these men in?

Toby looked at the whiteboard closely. He stared at the printout pictures of the two assailants and their driver. He looked at the picture of Watkins. He looked at pictures of Watkins's college roommates, Thomas Sing and Keenan Ingersol. He looked at the picture he had of Colonel Lytokov. The only connection was hypothetical. He had nothing tangible. Whoever the big bad was had covered his or her tracks well.

Who or what was tying these people together? Toby looked up because his computer dinged at him with an email alert. He had a new email from forensics. He wasn't surprised. There was always some overzealous forensics scientist down in the labs that had no life other than the job—the stereotypical nerdy geeky type they always showed in the movies or television shows that practically lived at work in the lab with the dead bodies and such. Well, in this case it would be dead computers and electronics, but Toby laughed at the stereotype. Then it dawned on him that it was sort of like the stereotypical special agent undercover that was always on the job and never had time for a personal life. Those guys were always on those types of shows as well. He actually laughed out loud halfheartedly at that thought. He was just another character in another silly movie or television drama. Or worse yet, he thought, what if he were a nonplayer character in a video game? He laughed again and decided he needed a damned nap.

He swiveled in his chair and opened the email. The content was minimal. It merely requested he come downstairs to the computer lab immediately to see what had been uncovered. That was cryptic enough.

"Okay, I'll bite," he said.

✧   ✧   ✧

"I didn't want to say this through email, secure or not." Vineet Mathur, an FBI computer and electronics forensics engineer, showed Toby to a metal folding chair next to his desk. The desk was covered with a laptop spread open in pieces but wired together with new cables. There were red and blue logic probe wires connected throughout the circuit points on the motherboard, most of them leading into a flat ribbon cable that was in turn connected to a logic analyzer, which in turn was connected to three separate computers that appeared to be randomly located about it. There were several small external boxes that were clearly customized components that looked as if Vineet had put them together from Arduinos, Raspberry Pis, and even IOS- and Android-based tablet devices, each of which appeared to be running and connected directly or wirelessly to something. There was a big red placard above his desk on the wall with a form bearing multiple signatures from various directors stating that THIS AREA IS AUTHORIZED FOR WIRELESS ACTIVITY.

"Why?"

"Even bad guys can use the Freedom of Information Act. I don't even want my name connected to this," Vineet said nervously. "At least yours isn't real and is classified. I'm hoping that will keep it out of FOIA."

"Okay, I say again"—Toby shrugged—"why?"

"We'd gotten most of the basic files—Matlab, Open Rocket, a paid subscription to RockSim—and there were some Python programs and the like, a few things in Java and CC++ that were all unencrypted and being used by your dead perp. Really, normal engineer kind of stuff," Vineet explained. "But once I started digging into the machine, I found a hard drive partition. It was hidden and encrypted."

"Really?"

"Yes, really. And hidden under that partition—hidden from Watkins, mind you—was a keylogging malware. And it was also sending the keystroke log—meaning every single key or button Watkins depressed on his computer—to somewhere. I'll get to that in a minute," Vineet said nervously and looked over his shoulder and around the room before he continued. He opened up a file and put it on his biggest monitor for Toby to see. There were rows and rows of letters and symbols together in one big run-on sentence. Toby realized it would be the way any keylogger data file must look without punctuation auto-returns, tabs, and spacing of standard text.

"What are these odd symbols here?" Toby pointed.

"Oh, those represent a mouse right button, that one a left button, scroll wheel and so on. These here are representing his touchscreen. There's a code for every single pixel," Vineet explained. "Hang on, I can filter all that and just give you the text. For now, that's what I need you to see."

He tapped at his keyboard a few times and then hit the enter key. A busy circle spun on the screen for a moment and then another window opened with a much more readable set of keylogger data. Toby noted how it had better spacing, tabs, paragraph spacing, and separations from one app or email to another.

"Yeah, that is much better." Toby nodded. "So, what is it that you don't want to talk about on email?"

"This here." Vineet typed in something in the FIND command function window and the text scrolled to a yellow highlighted word. The word was "nuke." The paragraph was dated almost six years prior and read as:

Sing,

It would take at least a Zenit or maybe an Atlas V to do what you are talking about. The orbital mass is much higher than just throw weight of a missile. You can't just launch a nuke to the orbital height and think you're gonna dock with an orbital platform there already. The velocity differentials would be like 7km/s. You'd destroy everything. Gotta have a second or third stage to circularize the orbit some, crank the inclination, and then phase to catch the orbital platform. Not as simple as all that.

Phil

"Holy shit! They've been planning this for a long time!" Toby exclaimed. "What else is in here?"

"That is just the start of it. Read this one like a year later." Vineet hit the NEXT button on the screen.

Sing,

*It would take burns to deorbit the payload, but aero-
dynamic bodies with control surfaces could give a lot
of control. You could use something like what is on
the Satan-2 for reentry vehicles.*

Phil

"Then here's one about two years ago."

Sing,

*You are a crazy sonofabitch! I had no idea you were
seriously acting on these crazy notions. I thought
you were writing a science fiction book or a theory
white paper for DOE or something. This is treason!
We could go jail for the rest of our lives if we were
caught. I want nothing more of this.*

Phil

"So, our guy here wasn't a willing part of it?" Toby asked
rhetorically. "That explains some of it. Do they ever say anything
about the details? Like what orbital platform or how many nukes
or for what purpose?"

"Never. It is always very vague and generic like a homework
problem for a graduate student or something. I did a search
through the DOE databases and found no reports ever submitted
by these two as official reports. My thoughts were unless they are
SAPed and unacknowledged reports, they don't exist. This wasn't
official government work as far as I can tell without approval to
get into the DOE SAP information." Vineet was talking about
the Department of Energy's Special Access Program.

"Wait, you looked at standard sensitive compartmented information caveats, right?" Toby asked.

"Yes. All of the known and acknowledged SCI caveats have
no such study I can find. I did see some similar concept type
studies for solar flares and a few nukes detonated by terrorists by
the JASONs and one by NSA, but nothing about orbital intercepts
and such," Vineet explained.

"We need access to the DOE SAP databases," Toby said.

"Above my pay grade." Vineet shrugged.

"Okay, I'll work that. What else you got?"

"There must have been some sort of encrypted chat app that he used a lot but I can't find it. That said, this keylogger malware was top notch and still caught the chat stream from his keyboard. Here, look at this. It looks like keylogs of a live conversation." Vineet pulled out another set of paragraphs from the large file and highlighted it for Toby to see.

... What do you mean I'm in it? You can have the money back. I didn't know this was a real plan!

... More money? No, but how is that changing the world for better?

... Same thing. Small group of elites running things.

... I have to admit I could run that better than it has been.

... No way in Hell! That is insane.

... Or else? No choice? What the hell does that mean? No choice?!

... Okay, maybe I did really know all along. But millions of lives?

... The long run? That's not building back better, that's destroying and starting over!

... To your point. They do mean the same thing. I guess I never thought of it that way. But I will not do this!

... Georgia guide stones? What the hell does that have to do with anything?

... I know they're nuts! You're nuts!

... You can trust me, Sing! We've known each other for years!

... Okay, okay. I'll help.

"And here's the last one he was typing before he was killed. I get the impression he knew he was in trouble."

"I think that last couple of exchanges tells us that Watkins knew he was a dead man if he didn't cooperate with them. All his political stuff was just him and not part of this, I guess?"

"Oh, yeah. He was a total eco-Marxist nut job. There are posts and posts in all this about extreme left-leaning politics and changing the world and stuff. But I don't get the impression they are directly connected to the nukes," Vineet said. "I do have to admit I haven't read all the logs yet, though. Would take days or weeks or more."

"Okay, show me the last conversation with Sing."

"Here."

> *Sing,*
>
> *I know how you are going to do it. I may not be able to stop you but I can tell some people that can! You can't do it this way. Too many peophholhpjjjjjjjjjjjjjjjjjjjj-jjjjjjjjjjjjjjjjjjjjjjjjjjjjjjjjjjjjjjjjjjjjjjjjjjjjjjjjjjjjjjjjjjjjjjjjjjjjjjjjjjjjj-jjjjjjjjjjjjjjjjjjjjjjjjjjjjjjjjjjjjjjjjjjjjjjjjjjjjjjjjjjjjjjjjjjjjjjjjjjjjjjjjjjjjjj-jjjjjjjjjjjjjjjjjjjjjjjjjjjjjjjjjjjjjjjjjjjjjjjjjjjjjjjjjjjjjjjjjjjjjjjjjjjjjjjjjjjjjj-jjjjjjjjjjjjj*

"The 'j' is the last key he ever typed. Was he found on his keyboard?" Vineet asked.

"No. But there was blood on the keys. He probably fell over on it or something and the assassins moved him upright. Not sure on that. The timestamp here, though, was only minutes before we got there." Toby nodded his head knowingly. "Maybe his hand was on the keys. I don't recall exactly. There was a lot of shit going on."

"Right. The forensics team must have cleaned the blood after they recorded all the evidence. It was clean when I got it."

"Uh, you said something about who was doing the keylogging?" Toby reminded him.

"Oh, yes." Vineet feverishly tapped keys and dragged his mouse about through various menus until he appeared to have gotten what he was looking for. "I did a search through all of the data, looking for any types of internet protocol addresses, and there was nothing. I scrubbed the entire computer hard drive, all the temp files, the registry, the damaged partitions of the drive, even replicated the malware on another computer to see if there was anything there that would lead me to its point of origin. Nothing."

"And?"

"Well, while I was setting up my probes, I did an 'IPconfig' and found something interesting."

"Ipconfig?"

"Just tells the IP address of every port connected on the computer."

"Okay. And?"

"There were more ports there than on the exterior of the computer." Vineet paused for Toby to understand. Toby didn't. "Okay, I can tell by the look on your face... Let me see... Okay, you know how a computer has USB ports, Wi-Fi connections, Bluetooth sometimes, and other ports you can connect stuff to right?"

"Yes."

"Well, this computer had six total ports including the built-in Wi-Fi and Bluetooth. But there was an extra 'COM' port I couldn't identify until I cracked the case open. Look here at the motherboard of this thing. You see this cable leading to the USB port on the exterior case?" Vineet pointed at the motherboard where a cable was pinned in and then traced the cable with his finger to the computer case where it connected to the outside USB connection port. Just on the inside of the case before the cable reached there it formed a Y.

"Yes. I see the split of the cable there. What's on the end of it?" Toby asked.

"Simplest hack ever." Vineet pulled at the cable and flipped the dangling other Y end over to reveal a small USB dongle attached. "This is a wireless keyboard dongle. The thing adds a wireless keyboard and/or a mouse to the computer. But there was only one set of such things that came in with this so I'm assuming the user didn't know this was there."

"How can a wireless keyboard dongle hack the computer?"

"It's a transmitter same as Bluetooth and Wi-Fi. There just needs to be a receiver somewhere, probably within fifty meters or less to communicate with it. That could have been done from a car, the local router on the cable internet box, or damned near anywhere. You should get a warrant and a team to search the internet boxes nearest his house. But I bet your guys took them."

"So, somebody put this in his computer, right?"

"Correct."

"Then they collected the information from his computer and sent it somewhere, right?"

"Correct."

"Okay, so where did they send it?"

"Good question. And, at first, I thought I wasn't going to be able to find that information without finding the receiver. But, after connecting to the dongle myself, well, there it was plain as day. An IP address."

"An IP address to where?"

"I followed it through multiple ghost channels, bad paths, and blind alleys. The only path that was actually somewhere, well, that went directly though to an IP address in Pentagon City. From there, I hit a firewall at a DoD address."

"Wait, the Pentagon?" Toby started to look over his shoulder now. "You mean whoever was watching our dead guy was from the Pentagon?"

"Somebody at the Pentagon has known about this, whatever it is, for years now. This computer is at least seven years old. From the dust in here and on this dongle, the thing has been going for more than year."

"How did he not notice it?"

"My guess is that our guy here had so much on this computer and it worked for him that he didn't want to alter or upgrade. He probably had a newer laptop he used for day-to-day stuff, but this was the one he worked on. Unless he looked in here, I doubt he would have known it was there. Maybe, over time, he might have noticed his hard drive was reducing in size, but these text files, while it is a lot of text, are just text. The file isn't that big compared to the hard drive size. It would have been years before he caught it. I'm surprised whoever put it there didn't just send a reformat command in to wipe it clean. Maybe they were planning to, but just didn't get around to it yet."

"Maybe we got there before they could."

"Maybe."

"Jesus! The Pentagon? Who?"

"Again, above my pay grade. That sounds like special-agent shit to me."

"Yeah. I guess it does."

CHAPTER 32

❧

McClean, Virginia
CIA Annex Building, Undisclosed Address
Sunday
10:31 P.M. Eastern Time

DR. GINNY BANKS SAT IN *HER* OFFICE WITH HER FEET PROPPED up on *her* desk. She was leaning back in her ergonomic leather desk chair with her shoes off and taking a moment to close her eyes. For the last hour or more she had been scrambling to gather as much information together as she could. Everything she had tried up to this point to figure out what was going on with the stolen nukes had led her to nowhere. Ginny had a doctorate in Data Science and Mathematics from the University of the CIA and she had a Masters in Computer Science from Georgetown. She was good at taking large chunks of seemingly disconnected data and finding what actually connected them. But at the moment, she didn't have a freaking clue.

The bad guys, whoever they were, had truly covered their tracks. Ginny was at the point where she had one more ace card to play, but it was a sensitive one. It was an ace card she could only ever call on if things got dire and she knew of no other way to turn. As things stood at the moment, she knew of no other way to turn or which direction to go.

She was dead tired and about to call it a night and she had

207

to catch a very early military flight with Frank back to Tampa first thing. She wanted to have this done before she headed to her town-house apartment just down Highway 123 near Tyson's Corner. Since what she was doing required classified printing, she didn't want to wait until she got back to Tampa to finish it. She sat quietly, resting and listening to the paper feeding in the printer and spooling out once it was printed on. As far as she could tell, she was the only one other than the security guard at the front desk in the building, so it was quiet. The printer continued to whir along.

This time of night the drive home would only take ten minutes so she had no worries of falling asleep at the wheel. And it would only take her just a few minutes more over the drive time until she was parked, in her apartment, packed, and turned it. The classified laser printer continued spitting out the documents one after the other. It stopped, causing her to look over at it and then at her screen, which had locked her out already. She wiggled the mouse a bit and then typed her password into the system. Before the screen opened, she noticed the alert on the printer digital display. She needed to add more paper.

"Well, damn." She willed her tired body to move. She rocked the chair forward and proceeded to reload the paper tray. "Might as well go ahead and write this up while it finishes."

She pushed the tray closed and hit the RESUME button. Then she sat back down at her desk, but this time took out a pen and a few sheets of the blank printer paper. She shuffled the papers against her desk to even them and then sat them down with the intent to put her pen to the page. But what was she going to write there? It needed to be precise.

She was printing every picture, file, and report, along with everything the Task Force had uncovered about the missing nukes, Colonel Lytokov, Phillip Watkins, Thomas Sing, Keenan Ingersol, and the information and drawings that Dr. Grayson and Dr. Castelbaum had sent her over JWICS. The printer continued to churn out pages. She thought about the process she was about to undertake and knew from previous exercises that it had to be exact and clear. She started to write.

Case #: CIA2211AzF1024-TF-1

She looked at the last case number to make certain she had used the right algorithm and then copied the number on a separate very large empty file folder with a TOP SECRET/SCI cover on it as well as on a sticky note by her keyboard. She then returned to the original page and continued. The first thing she wrote beneath the case study number was a date—the date and time that the warheads were stolen. Then she added precise detail.

> Where are these items currently located? Who took them? What are they doing with them?

She sat the pen down and thought about it for a moment. She decided that the questions were precise enough yet vague enough to get her what she wanted out of the exercise. But with this method, one was never certain. The printer finally stopped.

Ginny stood and gathered the empty classified file folder and took it with her the four steps across her office to the printer. She sat the folder on top of the printer while she collected and tapped the pages square with one another. She then placed them in the file folder and walked over to the very heavy-looking gray metal safe standing in the corner of her office. The drawer one from the bottom displayed a red magnet with the word OPEN in white letters written on it. She pulled the heavy drawer open and slid the file into the folder holders.

"Shit! Nearly forgot." She snapped her fingers and turned to her desk to collect the page she had just written. She placed the page into the file folder and closed the safe cabinet drawer until it clicked. She spun the combination dial a few turns and then flipped the magnet over to the green side displaying the white letters CLOSED. She initialed the form on top of the safe before sitting back down at her desk.

Ginny opened her unclassified email and typed.

> Paul,
>
> Hope you are doing well. I would like this done with top priority and three sources repeated. Usual billing method. Here it is:
>
> Case #: CIA2211AzF1024-TF-1

This is top priority and I need this by lunchtime tomorrow, if possible, COB at the latest. Standard analysis and include dowsing.

Regards,

Ginny

CHAPTER 33

∞

Near Tampa, Florida
Task Force HQ
Monday
2:51 P.M. Eastern Time

"NO, I CAN'T REVEAL THE SOURCE OF THIS INFORMATION, BUT I can tell you it is from three separate sources, each completely unaware of the others," Dr. Banks explained. "It just came through to me and I haven't been able to verify it yet either."

The entire Task Force from enlisted up, all the civilians, the two new Space Force guardians, and a new U.S. Air Force captain had joined them. The FBI special agent, Montgomery, had just landed in a small plane and had literally taxied just outside the hangar, tied down his plane, and badged in to the secure area.

"Glad you could join us, Special Agent Montgomery," she told him as he found a seat at the large conference table that had been set up for them.

Ginny didn't know the undercover agent very well, but she could tell that Frank did and that was good enough for her. There was something about Lieutenant Colonel Alvarez that she liked and trusted. It wasn't the fact that she had read his personnel file and looked at his background investigations. And it wasn't the fact that she had seen him in action, which was impressive. There was just something about him that said *Trust me*.

211

"I printed out copies for everyone and I'll not tell you any of my interpretations until I hear yours," she started. "I will answer questions about what you might be seeing and how to interpret the...no, that's not right...how to understand the nomenclature. I want your interpretations."

"Very cryptic, Ginny," Dr. Grayson said as he accepted the three printed and stapled together packets from her.

"Don't say anything about your interpretations out loud, please," she instructed them. "Just write down what you think and ask questions. But we'll hold off on sharing our thoughts until everyone has an opportunity to look at these. Note that I've only scanned them so far and haven't really looked at them either. Let's take, say, the next ten minutes and look and take notes. At the end of the ten minutes we'll compare and go from there. Good?"

"Suits me," Alvarez said.

"Sure thing," Mac added. There were various head nods and grunts of agreement around the table.

"Okay, we'll start now. And no cheating." Ginny grinned at Frank as if scolding him.

She sat down and looked at the first page of the first packet. There was a date, time, and location stating when and where the analysis was conducted in the upper right-hand corner, with the name "Paul" above that. A few lines of space were skipped and then on the left-hand side the case number was handwritten. To the right of that was the letter A.

> *CIA2211AzF1024-TF-1*   *A. branches, dendritic, dim,*
> *AOL. Tree limbs at sunup*

She considered the training she'd had on the intelligence sources and she understood that *A* was just a list that the analyst discovered. "AOL" meant "analytical overlay," which was the analyst giving his or her own interpretation of what the list meant. Ginny continued studying the page. There were some scribbled drawings that looked like a long truck with many wheels or maybe a tube on a trailer. Ginny got that part right away. There were more *A*s and AOLs and here and there were some *B*s that followed the *A*s that suggested a second feature.

CIA2211AzF1024-TF-1   A. *loud, fear, unassembled*
                          B. *new people, determined*

There were more drawings and scribbles. There were some words that were almost unintelligible, as if written by someone with their eyes closed. She flipped the page. At the top right corner was the number 2 and in the middle at the top was written "S2," followed by a long list of words. The words included: time or haste, movement, black, large body of water, six. There was no AOL by this list until nearly at the bottom of the page, where there was a drawing of a large box with structures jutting out from it upward in multiple directions. The box sat on four legs and there was a wavy line at the bottom covering them. On top of the box near the center was a tall structure standing upright. The analytical overlay read "CRANE OR TOWER." The words listed by it included: ORANGE, BLACK, WHITE, WATER, MANY PEOPLE, METAL.

Ginny wasn't certain what to make of that page yet, though she had some thoughts. She flipped to what was labeled as page 3 in the upper right-hand corner and again had an "S2" in the middle of the page. There was a drawing that started with a single amorphous blob. The number "239" was written beside it. There were dotted lines and then a second blob with a "235" by it. There were arrows drawn around the second blob pointing inwardly at it. There was a large circle drawn around it with a large sloppy "X6" by it. Ginny got that drawing very quickly. The AOL beside it said "NUCLEAR BOMB? HOLY SHIT!"

The line from the "Holy shit!" drawing had an arrow from the "X6" to a blank spot on the left of the page where a quicker, smaller, sloppier version of the box-tower-on-legs thing from the previous page. Written beside that was the sentence "HERE FOR NOW."

Next page.

Page 4 was just as interesting and useful and useless at the same time. There was a scribbled drawing of an arc intercepting an ellipse. Then the list of words that followed read as: loud, bright, 3 men or knights, loud, beginning. There was an analytical overlay describing possibly men in body armor but more people not wearing the armor. Then there was an odd list of numbers written on the page that Ginny didn't understand.

1 25544U 98067A 2974.31742528 -.00002182 00000-0

The numbers continued underneath as if the analyst had run out of room on the page.

-11606-4 0 1027

A second line of numbers began.

2 25544 51.6416 247.4627 0006703 130.5360
325.02881002537

There was a drawing of a blob or stick figure–type thing on the ellipse drawing with another thing near it attached by a wavy line. Then the list of words read: bright or flash, dark or darkness or quiet, nothing or no communication...

There was a final page with a row of letters and numbers across the top, and beneath each one of those a summary list of what the analyst seemed to think was most important to go under whatever each of the letters meant. Ginny always had to look at her cheat sheet to recall what each column of data was. She sat the first one aside and let out a long sigh. She realized it had only taken her about two minutes and that everyone else was waiting for her to look up.

"So, what is an AOL?"

"Who's Paul?"

"What the hell is this scribbled stuff?"

Ginny spent the next minute or so explaining that an analyst received this information based on a means to be discussed later and that the AOL was his or her interpretation of whatever that data from the source was and could be a bias to be ignored but was important enough to the analyst that they felt they needed to mention it. Once she felt that she had the team calmed down and educated just enough to read the documents and make up their own minds, she looked at the second packet. This one was done by "Sarah" and her penmanship and drawing skills were either better or done more slowly and concisely. But other than those differences and the occasionally different adjective, the two packets were almost identical. But on the "Sarah" pages the two words "Door" and "man" was repeated. Each time the word "Door" was written, the letter *D* was capitalized.

The third packet was only slightly different in that the only numbers written in sequence were "25544" and the letters *T*, *L*, and *E* appeared. There was also the word "doorman" on the last page at the bottom. Ginny didn't know what to think of the latter parts of all three analyses nor did she understand the similarities. She had a few ideas, but she waited for the team to finish before she spent too much effort thinking it through.

CHAPTER 34

Near Tampa, Florida
Task Force HQ
Monday
3:05 P.M. Eastern Time

"REMOTE VIEWING HAS BEEN USED BY THE CIA SINCE THE 1970S to varying degrees of success," Banks explained, trying not to get heated. "Hey, none of this is admissible in court, but it is data!"

"I can't make heads or tails out of any of this gobbledygook." Dr. Grayson smirked as if the concept were too fringe and not real science for such a serious individual as himself. "Have you actually gotten actionable intelligence from this in the past, Ginny?"

"Many times," Ginny said softly as she sank back into her chair.

"I've seen stranger shit," Mac added. "But I'm not sure where, Dr. Banks."

"But do the words or drawings mean anything to any of you?" she asked. "Some of it does to me."

"Yeah, but they had all the information about the missing nukes so that part was easy." Grayson laughed. "Fortune-tellers."

"Not at all! I neglected to explain this to you. No. No, they didn't. Each of the three viewers is trained through the CIA school, but live in locations in different states. They couldn't have cheated because the only information they were given was the case number. All other data pertaining to this case number is in a file folder locked away in my safe in my office with this case number written on it. They don't even know it came from me—well, except for Paul. I sent the number to him. But he is bound by contract not to reveal any information but the case number to the other analysts. And—I repeat: and—the viewers encrypt the packages and send them to a certain shared drive. That is all the common knowledge they have."

"How in the fuck could that even work?" Major Thompson was sincerely amazed, by the look on his face. "Look, I'm not a nuclear physics guy, but I know the drawing of a fission-fusion-fission bomb when I see one and all three of these people drew it! And all three of them said there were six of them in some form or fashion."

"I agree with you, Major. And nobody has developed a test-able theory, yet, as to why this works. But we're desperate. And it won't hurt to take a look and see if these efforts help us." Ginny nodded. "Anybody have ideas on the rest?"

"Uh, sirs, ma'am?" A1C Shannon raised her hand.

"What you got, Sonya?" Frank asked loudly, trying to get some order back to the table.

"Uh, well, um, Colonel, I was watching this old video the other night. *Man of Steel*. Ever seen it? Was the old Superman movie made back, forever ago," Shannon started explaining. Her description was clearly showing her disparate age in comparison to the others' as there was a mutual groan about the table.

"Seen it, airman. Keep going." Frank motioned his hand in a circuitous motion.

"Well, there's a very short scene in there where Clark Kent rescues people on an offshore oil well out at sea, and..."

"Son of a bitch!" Mac shouted while slapping the table with his right hand. "Oh, sorry. Airman, you're right. I've done enough practice raids on offshore rigs to know this is exactly what is drawn here. Look here, we have the four pillars each standing on a wavy line. Water. All these rigs have cranes on them and the oil tower in the middle and so on."

"Okay, that narrows it down to like a billion oil wells." Grayson was beginning to sound more interested but from the tone of his voice he still wasn't ready to buy in to the whole remote-viewing thing. "But I'll start a search. Any parameters to narrow that down would be good."

"Look at this list," Dugan added. "Black, water. Black Sea, maybe?"

"There are many offshore rigs in the Black Sea," Frank noted. "Why not start there? It *is* close to the last known location of the nukes. Mac, you might have been right about getting to the Black Sea rather than the Caspian."

"Pretty sure that was your assessment, Colonel," Mac said humbly.

"Anything else?" Ginny asked the group.

"Well, I'm still getting up to speed on everything," Captain Shelly Ames of the U.S. Space Force interrupted. She was new to the team but seemed highly skilled and knowledgeable about missile and space systems. Frank noticed she was adorned with a patch of some sort of wings like pilot's wings but he'd never seen that particular patch before. He made a mental note to ask some day. "But I'm pretty sure these curves here are the same launch and orbit trajectories in the notes from Watkins. Dr. Castlebaum, wouldn't you agree?"

Everyone turned to look at Amy, who had been completely quiet and totally absorbed in the reports, scribbling notes and doing math on the page. She flipped to another page, comparing the drawings and numbers by pointing to one with her left pointer finger and the other with the pencil in her right hand as she turned her head back and forth between them. Dugan elbowed her lightly.

"Amy?" he whispered.

"Oh, I'm sorry. Give me a minute." Amy got up from the table and ran over to one of the terminal systems that had been set up in the room. "Oh, shit, I don't have an account on any of these. Could one of you log in for me?"

"Yes, ma'am." Airman Shannon stood up and tapped in her information, opening a screen for her. "I'll get you an account today. Sorry, ma'am. What do you want to do here?"

"Type into your favorite search engine 'International Space Station CO SPAR ID.' Just like that. C-O spacebar S-P-A-R spacebar I-D."

"Okay." A1C Shannon entered the data, then read the return from the search engine. "Says here, '1998067A.'"

"Right. Thought so. Now this: ISS Satellite Catalog Number," Amy said.

"Yes, ma'am. Um, it says, '25544.' Wow!" Shannon replied. "I get it!"

"'Wow' is right." Amy said and she walked back to the table and plopped down in her chair. "I was pretty sure when I saw this second string of numbers here—the 51.6416. Anybody that lives in Huntsville, Alabama, and is a rocket scientist knows that is the inclination angle of the ISS. But double-checking the ID numbers, well, I'm certain."

"Amy?" Dugan looked at her wide-eyed. "Care to clue the rest of us in?"

"Yeah. Sorry, oh, shit, wait! Shannon, right?" She turned to the airman.

"Yes, ma'am, you can call me Sonya if you prefer."

"Oh, yeah, sorry, Sonya. Search this for me. Just like this: 'current two-line element for ISS.'"

"Yes, ma'am." Sonya started tapping away at the keys. "Okay, here is a bunch of numbers and stuff. It starts like these other numbers with the number 1 and then 25544U, just like those." Sonya turned and looked back at Amy.

"Copy them onto a doc and print them out for me," Amy said. "We'll need to get somebody from Space Command in Colorado to give us the real up-to-date classified data. The *U* is the 'unclassified' version."

"Of course!" Captain Ames apparently realized what the rocket scientist was talking about. "These numbers are TLEs! I'll be damned. Ma'am, I can get that from here."

Ames jumped up and logged into an adjacent terminal and did some searching and typing and dragging the mouse around until she apparently had hit pay dirt. Dugan still looked at Amy wide-eyed and clueless. He wasn't alone.

"Here is the unclass one, ma'am." Sonya handed her the printout.

"Okay, great. This is the TLE, the two-line element data that we use to tell us where any orbiting spacecraft is located at any given time. We can project them forward with some accuracy based on the NORAD radar data. You see this first number '1' just means line number one. The second set of numbers is the ISS ID. Every bird up there has its own identification number. All these other numbers in the first row just tell us the orbital parameters of the particular spacecraft that we use to put into our Simplified General Perturbations prediction model. There are a few other models that work better but this one gets you within a kilometer or so of the actual location. You get that close to the space station and you can't miss it. Hell, it's damned near as big as Bryant Denny Stadium."

"So, these numbers tell us its general orbit?" Ginny asked.

"Yes, and between the first and the second lines we can determine where it is now," Amy said.

"Alright, here are the classified numbers, Dr. Castlebaum. Should get you even closer." Captain Ames handed her a printout with the word SECRET printed at top and bottom.

"Okay, so here is the thing, it's this number here in the first line that tells you what year. Okay, that's us. Then this long number here with the decimal point is the day of the year and fraction thereof. In other words, the date and time," Amy said. She started looking at the numbers just handed to her and comparing them to the numbers in the remote viewing package. But there was a discrepancy. "Look here. The numbers for now today are 2973.21742528. First two numbers are the year. Next set of numbers is the day of the year and then the fraction. Today is the seventy-third day of the year."

"Amy, the number in this packet says the seventy-fourth day," Dugan pointed out to her.

"I will note that sometimes the analysts get the numbers and finite details very wrong," Ginny added.

"Ha! I can't believe that," Dr. Grayson said.

"Hey, wait a minute," Frank added. "I'm looking at the two that had numbers and they are exactly the same numbers, 2974.31742528."

"That would be some time tomorrow," Amy said. "I mean, if this is real stuff. And honestly, I've been thinking on what platform these guys were planning on launching to. There aren't many up there. I was assuming they were going to launch a satellite into orbit. This makes much more sense!"

"Wait!" Frank held up a hand, quieting people down. "Dr. Castlebaum, what makes sense to you?"

"These guys are going to use a Russian rocket. Probably a Zenit variant using LOX/kerosene propellants. They are going to launch from, I don't know, maybe an oil... Holy shit! Sea Launch! They're copying Sea Launch. Back in the nineties, a private company tried to get started up but failed in the end. They were called Sea Launch. They launched over two or maybe three dozen times using a—wait for it—Russian Zenit-3SL rocket using LOX/kerosene. And they launched from a modified oil rig. They put a bunch of satellites into orbit—even all the way to geosynchronous orbit. A Zenit-3SL could easily do what the Watkins drawings and calculations suggest. Once at the ISS, they could easily do the reentries with the nukes on glide bodies like Dr. Grayson has suggested." Amy sat up in her seat and crossed her right leg over her left triumphantly swinging her foot back and forth underneath the table. "I think they are going to launch a Zenit-3SL with six nukes onboard, and probably people, from a modified oil rig, maybe in the Black Sea, maybe some other body of water, to the ISS sometime tomorrow."

"We need eyes on the Black Sea right now!" Frank said.

"I'm on it, Frank. I'll get with my guys at NRO now." Mac stood and hurried to a secure phone.

"The Black Sea is damned big," Ginny said.

"I can start running parameters on imagery of oil rigs through Cascade," Dr. Grayson said. "Maybe we can narrow it down some. Amy, are there any other telltale signs that might help us discriminate this oil rig from a standard one?"

"Hmmm, let me think. They'd probably have to evacuate the rig before launch so there would be a command or launch control ship nearby. Since the Zenit uses liquid oxygen, it is cryogenic, meaning very cold. So, I bet, like most other land launch facilities using cryo propellants there will be a tower near the launch tower with a cryo-tank on it. How many oil rigs have two towers on them? I dunno?" Amy said.

"I need to call the Joint Chiefs," Frank said. "Ginny, somebody needs to reach out to the Director of National Intelligence. That's up your bailiwick."

"Agreed."

"Mac, you might reach out to your one-star when you get off that call," Frank said loud enough for him to hear.

"Copy that." Mac nodded as he cupped the receiver with his hand.

"Frank." Toby caught his attention. "Before you call your bosses, I need a minute."

"Do we even have enough diplomatic relations that we could do a strike in the Black Sea?" Major Thompson asked. "I mean, isn't part of it owned by Turkey too? This shit might start a war. Maybe someone should tell the Russians?"

"Above our pay grades," Frank said. "But somebody needs to stop this launch."

"I doubt we'd have time to get anybody there," Captain Ames said. "If Dr. Castlebaum is correct, these people plan to launch tomorrow midday."

"Holy shit!" A1C Shannon said almost simultaneously, covering her mouth as she did.

"Holy *fucking* shit, Airman," Major Thompson corrected her. "Yes, sir."

"We have to report this up." Ginny turned to Castlebaum. "Great work."

"You're the one with the freaky analysts." Amy laughed. "How in the hell this works is beyond me."

"I would say luck, but now I'm concerned my take on the universe is, um, limited," Grayson said. "This is beyond fascinating and, frankly, very terrifying."

"I have heard of RV, but never been part of it. Damned hard to comprehend," Captain Ames agreed. "I'll get on the horn with Space Command right now and have them start watching for radar tracks. We should contact the high and low infrared asset units and put them on high alert for launch detections. I need to contact my CO also."

"Please go pass that along to Chief McKagan when he gets off the phone, if you will?" Banks told her.

"Copy that, ma'am."

"I have calls to make." Dr. Banks was already folding her things together and was rising to move out on whatever action plan she could manage to put together in the next few minutes. "We have more to go on now. And we'll take it. Everyone, please keep moving forward on this assessment as it appears we may have little time until something else happens."

"Toby, with me." Frank stood and started out the SCIF door with the FBI man in tow.

"Amy, you did it." Dugan smiled at her. He didn't budge when Castelbaum turned just enough so that her swinging toe slid behind his right calf muscle and stayed there gently rubbing up and down. There was so much excitement in the room a man in a gorilla suit playing basketball could have walked through and nobody would have noticed it.

CHAPTER 35

ⵗ

Washington, D.C.
The Pentagon
Monday
6:55 P.M. Eastern Time

"SO, LET US MAKE CERTAIN THAT WE HAVE THIS ENTIRELY CLEAR. What you are telling us is that you now believe that there indeed are six stolen nuclear warheads. These six nukes are being put on a Russian rocket, this Zenit-3SL or variant thereof, that will be launched from an oil rig somewhere in the Black Sea tomorrow?" the Chairman of the Joint Chiefs, Army General Harold "Harry" Galveston, summarized. "Is that correct, Lieutenant Colonel Alvarez?"

"Yes, sir!" The marine lieutenant colonel on the other end of the VTC responded from a full-attention posture even though he'd been told to at ease. The CIA senior analyst sat next to him almost as stiffly. The two of them had been tag-teaming the briefing in rapid-fire style. There had been a lot of information briefed in the past thirty minutes. It had been like trying to drink from a firehose. Army Colonel Allan Vinderman sat quietly drinking from that hose, listening, and refilling the coffee cups for the Chiefs. All the while, he continued to make mental note of the unbelievable events that were being predicted by this Task Force. How they had managed to reach the conclusions they had seemed almost impossible to Vinderman.

225

"And you believe they will launch tomorrow with an astronaut or cosmonaut crew to the International Space Station?" the Chairman continued. "Sounds like goddamned science fiction."

"Yes, sir." The CIA analyst nodded but then defended their position. "It is the best intelligence from multiple sources and means that we have, sir. It matches the records from the dead, likely unwitting, complicit CIA analyst Phillip Watkins. It matches the location and most likely scenario for moving the nukes out of Russia into the Black Sea. And this matches rocketry that has been accomplished in the past by private endeavors."

"To what end?" USSF General Kimberly Hastings asked. "Why do they need the ISS again?"

"Well, General, we believe they have either gained access to a highly classified study, or figured it out on their own—maybe a bit of both, no matter which. The concept is to detonate the six nukes at altitudes of over thirty kilometers at strategic locations around the globe. The resulting EMP will devastate the power and communications grids of the civilized world."

"The ISS, Dr. Banks?"

"Yes, ma'am, that is the best LEO platform to set up basecamp and launch the reentry vehicles from. It could have been done through automation but that would require much higher fidelity and complicated systems. This is simpler, cheaper, and faster to have dumb reentry rockets pointed in the right direction by hand and fired at the right times by hand. The target error and timing are easy enough for that. They only need to hit a spot somewhere within the size of, say, Texas, between twenty and eighty kilometers above the surface. No extreme high tech needed for that. But they do need an orbital platform to do that from."

"I see."

"Frank, what does your gut tell you?" US Marine Corps General Alton Cole asked the marine lieutenant colonel. It was clear that there was history between the two men.

"Sir, the Task Force is full of very smart and good people. I trust them. This is the assessment across every service member on the team, the CIA, the Missile and Space Intelligence Center, the NSA, and the FBI. I am behind our assessments a hundred percent," Lieutenant Colonel Alvarez replied. "Sir, there's little time. We need to determine a rapid response plan."

"Thank you, Frank. That's good enough for me. We'll get back to you on the plan once we brief the president. And somebody needs to get in touch with the NASA administrator ASAP."

"We need to get the SecDef and the DNI over here. Then we'll need to brief the White House. The Secret Service will want to move the president immediately. All of this has to happen simultaneously, and yesterday." Galveston turned and looked over behind him. "Colonel Vinderman."

"Sir!" Vinderman responded immediately, stepping from the shadows.

"Colonel! We need to contact the right people as fast as possible, understood?" Galveston ordered.

"Yes, sir."

"Good. Get the National Security Advisor on the horn ASAP."

"Yes, sir."

✧   ✧   ✧

It had taken Vinderman about ten minutes to get through the switchboard and reach the White House National Security Advisor's liaison. Apparently, the NSA was in a meeting and had asked not to be disturbed. Her assistant took the information and promised to get her in touch with the Joint Chiefs immediately. This emergency took precedence.

That had taken another seven minutes before the call had been patched through securely and between the White House and the Joint Chiefs. It would have taken longer to actually travel across the river and meet in person, so it was still the most efficient means to get the information in the right hands. Vinderman handed off the NSA to the Chiefs and from there he had his orders. He had to notify the "right people." Those had been the Chairman's orders.

Once he was certain that the White House call was put into place and the Chiefs would take it from there, Army Colonel Vinderman had a few minutes to himself to make good on the rest of his orders. He didn't need a break. He had work to do. Very important work to do. He rushed across the open court and to his office and grabbed his coat. He made his way out the security gate to the outside lockers and pulled his cell phone and his sunglasses from it and then put the key back in the lock and left the door to the little gray metal box open. He passed through the turnstiles and stepped out into the open air outside the security perimeter of the Pentagon by a matter of meters. He walked to the end of the covered walkway and then across to the parking lot as if he were just taking a stroll.

Once he stepped off the sidewalk curb onto the parking lot, he was clear of any spoofing systems looking for spurious electromagnetic emissions. Vinderman placed his sunglasses on. They adhered to the magnetic implants behind his ears and he could hear the *ding-dong* of them making contact. The virtual screen opened and he could see his desktop. He quickly used the mental mouse and keyboard interface to open the instant message application, found the right contact, and then began to type out an encrypted message.

> *M,*
>
> *They know! I don't know how, but they know all of it. Response will be coming soon somehow. Unclear yet on that. The politics and poor diplomacy of your location is your best shield at the moment, but you have to go now. Better rush the timetable as fast as possible. They know about Sing and Ingersol, but still have no idea who is really behind it. Or why. Good luck. Reset the Reset!*
>
> *A*

CHAPTER 36

ᕲᕽ

Las Vegas, Nevada
Monday
4:25 P.M. Pacific Time

FORBES MAGAZINE HAD RECENTLY ESTIMATED THAT TALBOT Davidson had a net worth of somewhere between seven and ten billion dollars U.S. and likely had other offshore holdings that had not been reported. *Forbes* had no idea about the money in Cayman and Swiss banks that he'd acquired through supporting data theft operations, drug running, piracy in the Indian Ocean, and trafficking everything from counterfeit toys and clothing to guns and humans. And *Forbes* had no idea about the crypto mining farms he had set up all around the globe having yet to reveal the total number of crypto currencies he had amassed. No, *Forbes* had no clue. In reality, Talbot was worth more like ten times what Forbes had estimated. He knew all the right people, had large legitimate operations to launder his clandestine funds through, and had paid off or gotten leverage on enough congressmen and senators in the U.S. to overturn a veto or impeach a president. Talbot was untouchable, almost. There were only a handful of people who had managed to gain leverage on him, and by a handful, Talbot knew that really meant one.

He swerved his Lamborghini through the traffic at breakneck pace, weaving in and out between the sluggish drive time middle class Luddites. Those sheeple had no idea. They truly were nonplayer characters—NPCs, as Marcus called them—and their lives were inconsequential. A majority of them were inconsequential. In fact, he and Ingersol had run a simulation based on Marcus's version of the Simulation Hypothesis and found that the amount of suggested power for maintaining connectivity between real players and a worldmap as complex as our reality would have an asymptotic limit on the number of real players. The power and computation requirements would tend to infinity as the numbers grew larger. The inflexion point on that curve was somewhere around five hundred million people. That had proven to be an interesting number and turned up in many conspiracy theories. Talbot did have to confess that the model he and Ingersol had developed had a shit-ton of assumptions and wild-assed guesses, so they could have been very wrong. What he did know, though, was that there were a lot of lives in this world that seemed to have zero impact on humanity and weren't important—maybe even detrimental.

His life, on the other hand, was extremely important, at least to himself, but he was also certain it also was to the actual real human players in the Simulation or whatever the Hell Reality turned out to be and that he had to survive and thrive in order for humanity to do the same. He had done his best to thrive and to avoid being compromised or to allow someone, anyone, to get leverage on him. But he had loved Marcus too much through college. The man was nothing but brilliant and exciting to be around. At one point earlier in life he'd allowed himself to become compromised in a way he couldn't get out of. But Marcus had saved the day for him when nobody else could. And now he was the one person who still had leverage on him. And the one Real Player, the one Superuser, Marcus Dorman, had called in a favor on that leverage. It was time to make good on a promise he'd made years prior. He knew it had been on the horizon since he and Marcus had dinner just days before, but once the order came through his universe, his role in the Simulation had been activated.

It couldn't have come at the most inopportune moment either. Talbot had been in his penthouse overlooking the action of the Strip from his all-glass exterior bedroom suite wall. In the middle of the afternoon, he had managed to clear his schedule long enough to order his two favorite NPCs up to his suite for some fun. Power and money afforded any indulgence and Talbot enjoyed indulgences from both persuasions, usually at the same time. He was in the middle of the throes of those indulgences when his virtual glasses went into alarm mode.

The glasses had been sitting on his nightstand by his double California king-sized bed when the buzzing in his ears went off. At first he was certain that he hadn't reached some new level of pleasure, but the buzzing soon turned into an alarm that squelched desire. It was a feature of the glasses. If they were within Bluetooth range, they could send alerts to the implants and that was exactly how it happened. The buzzing had quickly escalated from a "you've got mail" level to a blaring klaxon alarm suggesting that the world was on fire. It wasn't, yet.

"You two, don't stop what you're doing," he had told his indulgences as he untangled himself from them and crawled off the bed. Taking his glasses from the nightstand and stepping to the glass wall, he felt and heard the handshaking of the glasses with his implants. With hindsight he realized how iconic of a moment that had been as he stood naked, his tight perfect billionaire's body sweaty from sex and glistening in the sun as it filtered over him. Wearing nothing but the sunglasses, looking out over Las Vegas like the god he was, he stood straight and still while he read the incoming message.

"So, what's all the ruckus, M," he whispered under his breath.

T,

NOW! NOW! NOW!

M.

That was all the message said. It didn't need to say more. Talbot completely understood what had to happen next. He hadn't hesitated. His mind completely ignored the rest of the world and set forth on what had to be done in the next few moments, the next hour, the next few days, and so on. He immediately turned to his walk-in closet, one that was larger than most of the penthouses in the building, and began throwing on clothes as fast as possible, all the while ignoring his indulgences, who were theatrically overdoing the sounds of passion as if they were making cheap internet porn. There was no time to worry with them. If Marcus needed him "NOW! NOW! NOW!" then that meant NOW! NOW! NOW! And he wasn't about to let Marcus down.

Talbot tucked in his T-shirt, buckled his belt, and zipped the Armani trousers. Quickly, he then pulled on a golf-style technical material shirt that he could leave untucked. Once he'd slipped it on, he grabbed his nine-millimeter Sig Sauer P226 Emperor Scorpion in the carbon composite inside-the-waistband holster and slipped it inside his pants at his back, clipping it to the belt. He adjusted the fit and how the grip rubbed at his lower back until it was comfortable and then threw on his Level III armored dark gray sports coat and didn't look back. If he never made it back to that penthouse, it would be of little loss or consequence to him. He gave his indulgences no further thought.

It had taken him less than ten minutes to get dressed, five to get down the private elevator to the parking garage, and then another couple to make it to the freeway. The bright red sportscar was likely nothing but a flash to the NPCs driving—if that's what you called it—along his way. He zigged and zagged through and around them and pushed up Interstate 15 past North Las Vegas at over one hundred and eighty kilometers per hour. He could see the Bigelow building off to his west. His plans to one day steal all of the UFO secrets from Bob would have to wait. Besides, Talbot had plenty of his own secret weird things to sort through.

He had built the U.S. offices of Davidson Aerospace just outside of Nellis Air Force Base properties so he could overwhelm the other support contractors with presence. It had worked. Davidson owned most of the business in and out of Nellis, which included the highly classified stuff over the mountain near Groom Lake. Davidson Aerospace was connected to every aspect of highly classified space efforts, missions, equipment, and technologies, including the things that people didn't want to believe in—other than the true believers and conspiracy nuts.

The tires squealed as he pulled off the exit to his complex. The building was a testament to all of the research and work that had gone on in the high-tech military space arena for the past twenty years. The large, high bay at the center of the campus stood taller and spread out farther than Madison Square Garden. The ancillary buildings spread about it filled an area as large as a division one college. Talbot employed almost three thousand people at those locations. Between there and the other campuses around the world, the Davidson-Schwab campus in Austria, and his clandestine locations, he likely had over twenty thousand people working for him around the globe. Most of them, he was certain, were all non-player characters and unimportant.

Finally, he made it through the campus traffic to his parking spot. Talbot didn't badge through security like everyone else. He was waved through. The doors and gates all opened for him as he approached. He'd added software to the security systems he could control through the implants in his head a long time ago. There were no metal detectors for him—if there were, he'd simply overwrite the software for them. He had sent orders before his arrival to have all the hallways cleared and people removed from the path he was planning to take. He had no time for chitchat with a security guard or any of his engineers and scientists or any of the many office assistants needing his signature on this or that. There was no time. Marcus needed him NOW! NOW! NOW!

Through several doors and to the main office he rarely frequented he continued. There was a biometric lock he pressed his palm against for show. The screen scanned his palm with a red fanned-out beam and then it turned green with the words ACCESS GRANTED in white letters across the middle of it. The real lock he controlled with his implants. The door opened and he rushed in to his desk. The door closed automatically behind him. He sat in his desk chair and sent several wireless mental commands to activate the command center. Multiple monitors rose from mahogany cabinets around the room. A projector screen slid down from the ceiling and the whirring of the fan in the projection system filled the room as it warmed up.

Talbot pulled the top left desk drawer open, revealing another biometric panel. He pressed his thumb against it and thought in his password sequence at the same time. The top of the desk slid back about fifty centimeters, giving him a full desktop area with no clutter in his way. Through his virtual view there were multiple machines, keyboards, touchpads and screens sitting on the clear desktop. There was nothing there in the real world but his virtual worldview was a smorgasbord of data overload.

Talbot activated several of the touchpads and began typing in commands at a furious pace on the virtual computer systems. Finally, he had made it to the main menu for the Davidson-Schwab Inflatable Hotel Module control system. The system connected through various backdoor pathways into the Huntsville Operations Support Center in Alabama. The pathway was a completely new technology for transmitting and encrypting data. Once it had been invented, he and Dorman had bought every piece of knowledge of its existence and had everyone involved either paid off or taken care of. He had friends who were good at doing either of those when needed.

He started up the operating system commands for the DSIHM and could see a virtual three-dimensional wireframe model of the module as connected to the ISS in front of him. The three-dimensional data that Karl had transmitted to them a few days prior had updated all of the connection points, electrical systems changes, and additions to the ISS as the model continued to build itself. The data connection that the Huntsville contact and Ingersol had been able to create added real-time ISS data through the NASA Near Space Network system. There before him was the entirety of the International Space Station. As long as there was data flowing between the network of communication systems around the globe and the space station, Talbot could see real-time whatever NASA would see, plus a more detailed set of data coming from the instruments built into the DSIHM.

He pulled down the file menu and opened a folder marked as RESET. He waited for the program to activate and then there were suddenly red and blue lines that appeared in the DSIHM and throughout the ISS. Now was the time for boots on the ground. He opened the messenger application and virtually typed out a message.

K,

How are you, my man?

T

Talbot waited for a bit longer than he'd expected. He was starting to grow impatient when his implants buzzed at him to let him know there was a response. He opened it and read.

T,

Better. Took a new injection today that is helping. How can I help you?

K

K,

It is time. Throw the switches as planned.

T.

T,

Understood. Five to ten minutes depending on traffic.

K

Talbot exhaled for what seemed like the first time since he'd gotten the "NOW!" orders from Marcus. He had nothing else to do until Schwab came through on his end. Talbot had spent over two years trying to figure out how to make things happen in a fully automated way, but in the end, there had to be somebody there in space to perform certain aspects of the procedure. While he waited, he logged into the autopilot of his two-man hexacopter and had the preflight warm-up sequences begin. He wanted it to be ready when it was time to go.

CHAPTER 37

༄

Turkey Economic Exclusive Zone, Black Sea
Tuesday
2:30 A.M. Turkey Time (TRT)
Monday
7:30 P.M. Eastern Time

"THAT ALARM IS TOO GODDAMNED EARLY!" MICHAEL STRUGGLED to make himself slap the alarm on his phone. But once he managed to grab his phone and flip the silent switch and look for a snooze icon, he realized that it wasn't his phone making all the ruckus. The noise was coming from inside his head. "Oh shit."

Michael scrambled for the glasses at the edge of his bed, knocking them off accidentally to the floor. He threw the blanket back and rolled over to fish around on the metal deck plating that was cold to the touch and a bit dirty. He continued to feel around until he bumped the glasses. He grabbed them cautiously and then rolled back over onto his back, putting them on. The glasses made the handshaking sounds with his implants and then the virtual screens lit up. The full field of view was red and flashing and had a message from Marcus.

> M,
>
> *We have to go now! U.S. officials are on to our plan and are starting action now.*
>
> M

Michael thought about that. His first thought was to wonder just how in the hell they had figured out what they were doing. They had been very, very careful to cover all of their tracks as they made them. Then he switched his train of thought to a more pragmatic one, along the lines of what needed to be done and how much time there was to do it. If the Pentagon or the intelligence community had figured it all out, even if they figured out exactly where they were, it would take hours for them to get a force to them. Even if there were diplomatic ways to convince Russia to move in, the best sonar and radar in the world, which the launch rig had, showed no seagoing vessels within a thousand kilometers except for one, and it was expected. There was nobody currently near them that they didn't know about. Then atop that, they were in Turkish controlled waters. The Turks didn't allow incursions into their water or air spaces lightly. They had time. But not much of it.

Knock, knock, knock!

"Comrade! Get up!" Vlad's voice was coming from outside his quarters. "It is time to go!"

Michael forced himself out of bed and winced just a bit from the cold metal against his bare feet. He slipped on his moccasins and shuffled to the door, releasing the hatch. There was his Russian friend, standing shirtless and only in underwear, socks, and slippers, smoking a cigarette.

"Wait a minute, V." Michael scratched at his head to stimulate some brain cells. "Socks and slippers?"

"My feet get cold at night."

"And nothing else, I see." Michael motioned to Vladimir's mostly naked body in front of him with a sleepy and grumpy chuckle.

"Georgia has skipped some steps," Vladimir told him, puffing out his chest as if to show he was proud of his body carrying the joke forward a bit longer than needed. But the expression on his face was more of excitement and focus. "Jebidiah is up. We must go to the preflight room and start taking the intravenous fluids and then suit up. The general quarters evacuation has already started."

"Yeah, yeah." Michael waved him off. He had been in the middle of the best sleep he'd had in over a week, or longer. And it had just been cut short by about two and half hours. "I'll see you there after I brush my teeth and stuff."

"Stuff? What stuff, comrade?" Vladimir took a last drag on the cigarette and dropped it to the floor and twisting it into the metal hallway deck plating with his house slipper. "We're going to space, my friend, and you are doing 'stuff'?"

"I have to pee, V!" Michael laughed and grunted sort of at the same time. He was both joking and annoyed.

"You can pee in the suit!" Vladimir grinned.

"Yeah, okay, five minutes. Meet you down there." Michael flipped the light to his quarters on and closed the door. He wasn't going to pee in the suit until he had to.

"We are less than T-2 hours and fifteen minutes!" Georgia was shouting at somebody. "There are still almost two hundred and ninety-six metric tons of LOX that have to flow into the oxidizer tank, and then once it is to the right temp and shake we move the one hundred thirteen tons of kerosene into the fuel tank. We have to keep teams on that cryo pump there and this line here to make certain we don't ice up! Is that understood?"

"Yes, ma'am!" The technician in the bright orange fire suit rushed away as the three men approached.

"Are we going to make it?" Michael asked her. He looked up at the now completely stacked rocket towering a bit over fifty-four meters above them connected to the gantry tower. The Vyrezka was resting in place at top of the rocket. Someone had spray painted "Demokles Kilici." Michael snapped a pic of it for his virtual glasses to translate. The response was that it was in Turkish and it meant "Sword of Damocles." He agreed.

"We will make it barring supersonic jet attack," Georgia said. "Don't think they could get permission for that, though."

"Russians would not have MiGs close enough. Even at Mach two they would be at least two hours out, and that's assuming there were MiGs available near the Russian border. With the skirmishes in Ukraine, not likely," Vladimir said. "We have time. Are your crews evacuated yet?"

"Only any superfluous ones, which aren't many. No. We'll work up until the T-15 mark. The command center ship is already spun up, but for now I'm running things from the tower." Georgia looked at the three of them. "The warheads are stored. Sing is up top waiting for you and so is the doc. It's time to suit up, gentlemen."

"Been waiting all my life for this!" Vladimir said eagerly.

"You've been waiting all your life to take over the space station and drop nukes on the world, V?" Jebidiah asked halfheartedly.

"He probably has, J," Michael responded. They had started using their initials already to get into the forced habit of no names. "He probably has."

CHAPTER 38

❧

Low Earth Orbit
International Space Station
Tuesday
2:30 A.M. Turkey Time (TRT)
Monday
7:30 P.M. Eastern Time

KARL HAD BEEN IN THE DSIHM, LOOKING OUT THE PORTAL AND meditating on the world, when the message had come. The nausea from microgravity had gone and the only nausea he had currently was likely from the intravenous bag of nanobot spike proteins he'd given himself an hour earlier. There were plenty of them in the MDGE cooler. They were his. He had paid for them. He had no qualms taking them as he needed. So, with that in mind, he had started a treatment sequence on himself the day before. He'd just taken his second dose. He had calculated that he might need another dose in six months, maybe, but if the medicine worked, the viral infection in his brain would be cured. He just hoped he didn't get prions as a side effect. Hell, he hoped he didn't have the beginning of prions from the virus infection he had already. The spike proteins on that damned virus variant were long enough that they could fold and wrap up other brain cells, causing the dreaded "wasting disease" prions.

The view from the large viewport in the DSIHM was nothing short of breathtaking. They were about to roll over Egypt any minute. He was waiting to see if there were noticeable cityscapes in the lights that he would recognize. If they ever really were to put hotels in LEO, he hoped they had a big window just like this one. Then there was the message from Marcus. A few seconds later was the message from Talbot.

"Uh-oh, Karl, it's time for some trouble!" his AI, Alvin, told him in the high cartoonish voice.

"Alvin, it's not nice to eavesdrop on people's emails, chats, or conversations," he scolded his AI pet.

"Sorry, Karl."

"Forget it. And you are right. It is time to get to work," he said. "Open up the internal map file called 'Easy Button.'"

"Very well. Here is the map."

A wireframe three-dimensional map appeared in his virtual view. It had red dots representing work he'd already been up to. And there were green dots showing what was left for him to do. There were just a few important and very key bus breakers and software toggles he needed to see to. Then there was the all-important final blow. But he had to follow the steps laid out or the plan wouldn't work as it was supposed to.

For the past few days Karl had been placing small magnetic dongles in unlikely-to-be-discovered places. The ISS was big. There were lots of nooks and crannies about and Karl had lidar and Wi-Fi mapped them all. Many of those spaces were very near key communications lines, telemetry systems, power conduits, and various other systems. Each of the small dongles contained a piece of malware code that could be initiated wirelessly through induction onto the internal wiring of any system. Ingersol and Talbot had designed the things and used them to slowly steal billions from various banks, businesses, governments, individuals, and organizations around the world for over a decade. In places where they could get a direct USB connection it was even easier. But everything nowadays was spoofable and had a big, wide-open front door with the wiring leading into it, the central processing units and graphical processing units, and most of the mother-board and daughterboard components and chips, broadcasting microwave digital leakage that could be connected to from many tens of meters away. More than half of the systems in the world weren't properly shielded from direct motherboard or ancillary processing hacks from wireless broadcasts. If a person was smart enough, that weakness could be exploited. Ingersol and Talbot, well, they were more than smart enough.

The wireless systems would work on most of the weaker disconnected systems within the ISS such as the amateur radio system the astronauts would use to sometimes communicate with civilians around the world. There was the station's Wi-Fi system and a few others. But the main secure systems of the ISS required a direct assault. All Karl needed to do was make certain he had a beacon dongle plugged into the right places. Between Ingersol, Talbot, and their contacts at NASA and DoD they had every wiring diagram and every line of code used on the ISS before they had gotten there. They knew exactly where to hit it. They knew exactly how to hit it. And they were winding up and getting ready to punch with everything they had.

Karl pushed through to the Columbus Module and back through Node 2. There were the all-important ISS DC/DC Converter Units, DDCUs. Those systems were the key power buses providing the one hundred twenty volts direct current secondary power to the Japanese Experiment Module (JEM) Electric Power Distribution Units—PDUs. After the PDUs were the Power Distribution Boxes—PDBs. The main power from the large solar panel array outside the space station came into the JEM DDCUs, through the PDUs, on through the PDBs, and from there to the rest of the ISS. The JEM was the main line of defense from power anomalies. It prevented any spikes in current or overvoltages from making it through to the rest of the systems on the ISS. The only systems having their own distribution network were the legacy Nodes there before the JEM was put into place. The NASA/US Lab Module and the ESA Module each had their own DDCUs. Karl would need to get there as well.

Karl pulled the tiny sugar-cube-sized metal box from his waist-pouch and activated it. Then he reached in behind one of the main panels on the DDCU junction box and let it go. The magnetic base on the device quickly pulled it to the panel and stuck it into place. It immediately started handshaking with the processors inside the DDCU looking for a weakness to exploit. Nobody had expected simple on-site hacks for the ISS so they hadn't been firewalled for such. Oh, all the electronics were ruggedized for erroneous space radiation surges from solar flares and such, but not for a direct coupling attack on the motherboards. The little device worked its magic and soon Karl saw the green dot turn red. When they needed it, he and his friends would have complete control of that system.

While the primary power systems ran through these modules and nodes, the secondary power did as well. There was a redundancy in system to the design but not a redundancy in path or location. Taking out one system could be piggybacked with taking out the other if the attack were physical in nature. And the planned attack, well, it would be very physical in nature.

Karl quickly placed the next box and pushed himself forward into the U.S. Lab Module. From there he hit the ESA module and had then made his way back to the DSIHM. He had worked up quite a sweat in the process from all of the moving about and from the stress of maintaining the appearance of a tourist in everybody else's way. He looked at the wireframe model of the ISS in his virtual view and saw but one green dot left and it was in the DSIHM itself.

"Last thing before suiting up, Alvin. Play me a song."

"Okay!" The background suddenly filled with the Chipmunks' version of Stray Cats' song "Rock This Town."

"Interesting choice, Alvin," Karl said. Looking at the map in his virtual view he pushed and swam himself through the microgravity to a panel on the wall just outside the door to his suite in the DSIHM. He slid the cordless socket driver from the pouch around his waist and fit it on the bolt head at the upper right corner. He backed the bolt out and placed it in his pouch. He followed the procedure three more times and then tugged the panel free from the wall. It had magnetic seals on it, so he stuck to the panel on the wall adjacent to him to keep it from floating about and bumping into things it shouldn't be bumping into. Then he turned his attention back to the opening in the wall he'd just created. There in the wall was the main circuit bus bar keeping the DSIHM from doing what it had been designed for. He traced his finger down the long cold metal crowbar looking for a switch until he found the safety interlock pins keeping it from being thrown into the on position. He smiled as he gripped the bar in his right hand and pulled the three safety interlock pull-pins until they locked into the open position one after the other. As Alvin had said, it was indeed time for some trouble.

He used the mental mouse and keyboard and opened the encrypted messenger application.

T,

All systems are in place. Throwing the bus bar on DSIHM now.

K

CHAPTER 39

⤫

Near Nellis AFB, Nevada
Davidson Aerospace
Tuesday
2:38 A.M. Turkey Time (TRT)
Monday
7:38 P.M. Eastern Time

THE DSIHM WAS MORE THAN JUST A HOTEL FOR FUTURE SPACE tourist idiots. Talbot, Schwab, Dorman, Ingersol, Sing, and Stinson had designed it with excruciating detail and had taken years of modeling and simulation, scaled model designing, building and testing, and then testing a full-sized working model in a secret lab in order to perfect its exact design and purpose. Just like their overall plan for the world, the DSIHM served multiple purposes, but with one sinister one most specifically.

The large cylindrical hull of the hotel consisted of an exterior conductive mix of an epoxy and various metal compounds. There was then an internal layer of purely nonconductive epoxy followed by another layer of the conductive epoxy system. This process was repeated over a mandrel in a geometry that had allowed the module to be folded into a smaller cylinder of only about a meter in height. Once it was deployed and attached to the ISS the year prior, it was brought to full ISS pressure, which inflated and expanded it to full size. Once the DSIHM reached full stable inflation, a curing agent was injected into the layers. That agent was sunlight. After a year in orbit the epoxies and compounds had solidified, creating the now very large and solidified cylindrical hotel module. But the key to its true purpose was in the layers and how they were constructed and connected.

The multilayers of conductor then insulator then conductor and so on made for a very good high-voltage storage capacitor. Davidson Aerospace had taken major painstaking efforts to isolate the DSIHM from the rest of the ISS power systems, clandestinely, so that NASA wouldn't be able to tell that the DSIHM had been slowly building up a high voltage charge over several months. And once the hidden "bus bar" was thrown—basically a very large switch—all of that electrical charge that had been stored there would go rushing backward into the ISS power grid, blowing out junctions, boxes, and wires like power lines during an electric storm. The current indicators showed Talbot that there were over three million volts stored in the DSIHM module currently. Once released, there would be thousands of amps bursting through the circuits throughout the ISS.

The magnetic induction boxes Karl had put in place would be the icing on the cake. While there were breakers and filters along the path to prevent just such an electrical discharging accident, the ISS grid design wasn't designed to prevent an actual high voltage attack from within, specifically designed to burn through those preventative measures.

Talbot watched as the power system lines from the Main Bus Switching Units started showing a ripple on top of the voltage waveforms feeding back through to the DDCUs. There was also a slight ripple beginning to appear on top of the power systems on the other side of the PDBs feeding through to the entire ISS. The magnetic induction systems Karl had placed strategically were creating a positive feedback of overvoltage on both sides of the protection system and confusing them as to what actions to take. Soon they would be chaotic enough that the system would lose its mind. Once that happened, the system's filters most certainly couldn't manage the three-megavolt overvoltage spike that was coming.

The red lines on the virtual wireframe ISS floating in front of him were showing surges and alerts being triggered. That's where the wireless dongles came in. It was a three-pronged attack. Prong one consisted of the magnetic induction attack on the voltage and power conditioning system filters. Prong two was a computer attack.

The code that he and Ingersol had uploaded into the ISS main computers through the Huntsville contact was now taking all of its information from the dongles Schwab had placed in strategic locations. Those dongles were telling the computers on the ISS and on the ground in Huntsville that everything was "A-okay" to use the astronaut lingo. Talbot watched as the power unit in the DSIHM began to overload and then the message from Karl came.

> T,
>
> *All systems are in place. Throwing the bus bar on DSIHM now.*
>
> K

Prong three of the attack would be the knockout blow. Prong three was the giant voltage and current spike released by the DSIHM. And Karl Schwab had just thrown the final knockout punch. Before any of the filtering units and safety systems of the ISS had a chance to do a thing, a major spike of over three million volts with over several thousand amps of current poured through the power grid all within a tiny fraction of a second. Within seconds, every single system onboard the International Space Station had been burned out aggressively. Talbot imagined there were showers of sparks and some flames starting up in places. Whether that was the case or not, most certainly all the lights, computers, and communications equipment on the ISS had just been shut off.

"Score!" Talbot shouted. He reached over to the desk drawer and placed his thumb on the scanner. The main desk cover moved back into place. In his virtual view he pulled down a menu marked DUMPSTER FIRE and activated it. A ten-minute countdown clock appeared in his view and started. He walked over to his liquor cabinet and grabbed the $250,000 fifth of Macallan Anniversary 1928 Single Vintage Malt he'd been keeping for this moment and cracked the top. He took a long draw from the bottle and waved goodbye to the office space as he walked out the door.

> M,
>
> *It is done!*
>
> T

CHAPTER 40

~∽

Near Tampa, Florida
Task Force Headquarters
Monday
7:45 P.M. Eastern Time

"I REALIZE THAT!" FRANK SAID. HE WAS FRUSTRATED WITH HOW slowly the Pentagon and the White House were responding to the pending nuclear attack that was coming. He was certain it was coming. And there seemed to be little, if anything, he could do about it. "But if we don't stop them on the ground, what can we do? I mean, doesn't it take months to get a rocket ready?"

"That's what I'm getting at, Colonel," Captain Ames continued aggressively. Frank could tell that the younger Space Force Captain wanted to tell him something important, but for whatever reason wouldn't or couldn't. "If it were any other day, I'd say we could do nothing. But we're lucky. We are lucky today, I mean!"

"*How* do you mean, Captain?" Dr. Banks asked.

"There's a launch planned in two days out of Vandenberg Space Launch Complex 3E. We could take it," Ames said. "The next one will be another two weeks from that."

"What launch?" Frank asked.

"Launch? Of what?" Banks asked. "Who is launching?"

"I'm not authorized to tell you, but it is goddamned fortuitous! But if we want to divert the launch, we need to act like right now!" Ames said.

"Captain, from the authority given to this Task Force by the Joint Chiefs and the SecDef I'm telling you, ordering you, that you have authority to brief us on anything that is pertinent to stopping a nuclear attack on the world!" Frank barked at the Space Force captain.

"I'm sorry, sir. But you and Dr. Banks both must know that ain't how this works," Ames said sheepishly. "You can't use rank to compel me to violate national security. I don't have the authority to read you into a program without permission."

"What the—" Frank started but was interrupted by Ginny.

"She's right, Frank. And we both know that," Ginny said.

"Shit. Yes, Captain Ames you are following OPSEC appropriately."

"Thank you, Colonel Alvarez." Captain Ames hesitated. "But..."

"Alright, Captain Ames, I get it." Ginny nodded. "I'll ask. If you think there is a program we need to know about, then who can brief us and how do we get them on the line right now?"

"That, I can manage. But we need to clear out anyone from this room that won't have a need to know," Ames explained. "Who stays?"

"Banks and the active service officers, and Mac," Frank said.

"And Dr. Castlebaum," Ginny added. "We might need a rocket scientist."

"Okay, then. We'll try that," Ames said. "Get the room cleared and I'll start the TSVOIP call."

Frank clapped his hands together several times getting everyone's attention. Once he was pretty certain they were all looking his way, he started barking orders. He had no idea what Ames was about to tell him, but he wanted to be ready.

"Everybody but all active-duty officers or warrants and Dr. Castlebaum needs to clear this room double time!" Frank said. "Except for you, A1C Shannon. I need to see you for a moment."

"Sir?" A1C Shannon turned toward him and stood at attention.

"Airman, at ease, for God's sake. I need you to do me a favor." Frank grabbed a sticky note and a pen and started scribbling on it. "I want you to contact Captain Ellis Jones. If you don't get him, call Staff Sergeant Johnny Parvo. If you don't get him, then call Gunny Sergeant Hank Lord. Any of them can get this done for you. But it must—I repeat: must—get done. You tell them that I need a full kit for a small team of about six ready to be loaded within two hours. They'll know what that means. Oh, and tell them location and transport information coming."

"Yes, sir."

"Now, skedaddle." Frank waved her on. "And thanks."

"Yes sir."

✧   ✧   ✧

"The what?" Mac looked perplexed. Frank agreed with the SEAL. He simply had no idea. Frank figured that had been the point.

"X-37D," the U.S. Space Force brigadier general on the other end of the Top Secret Special Access video conversation said. "Our current mission is to launch every fourteen days, alternating between eight vehicles. We can pretty much hit any orbit with enough time."

"Jesus! That must be expensive," Banks gasped.

"The budget is black and need to know," the one-star general replied. "But it is piggy-backed on the X-37B program as our cover."

"I thought that was all conspiracy theory nonsense?" Major Dugan asked. "I mean, we have never seen a manned X-37 variant launch, to my knowledge. You mean it's real? Next you'll be telling us that the TR-3B is real too!"

"I know nothing about any TR-3B, Major. But the X-37 variants may or may not have flown many times, manned, without public knowledge," the general said. "What are you proposing, Dr. Banks?"

"I'm not exactly sure just yet, sir—" she started, but Frank cut her off.

"Has Captain Ames briefed you on the current situation, General?" Frank asked.

"Yes, Colonel, but there is truly nothing we can do. While we have a manned capability, presumedly, there is no super-secret group of space soldiers. We have requested budget for that through several of the budget cycles, but it hasn't even made it through to the NDAA much less being appropriated by the Senate Appropriations Defense subcommittee. What we do have are pilots and engineers trained to do space missions with satellites and to do reconnaissance missions. We do have a core group of trained astronauts whose existence is above Top Secret. Ninety-nine percent of the Space Force soldiers are trained for satellite control missions sitting at a desk in Colorado, California, or Alabama.

Nobody has truly trained to fight in space," the general told them. "Let me guess, you want to fly up there to the space station and take those nukes back before these bad guys use them?"

"I hadn't thought it through that far, but yes sir. And sir, you should pull my training record along with CW4 McKagan's and look up the program 'Hot Eagle' from about ten years ago," Frank said. "I might add that that program was above Top Secret as well, even though some mention of it was leaked by a congressional staffer to the press. Probably why it didn't make it any further than it did. Which I regret to say, well, wasn't very far."

"Hot Eagle?" the general repeated.

"Oh shit, Colonel, you're not bringing that up?" Mac whispered. "That was years ago."

"Yes sir. Hot Eagle. It was a DARPA, Navy, Marine Corps, and congressional intelligence committee project about a decade ago. While we might have never fought or been in space, General"—Frank turned and looked at McKagan—"Chief McKagan and myself *have* trained to do so."

"No shit?" The Space Force general was surprised.

"No shit, sir."

CHAPTER 41

∽

Low Earth Orbit
International Space Station
Monday
7:55 P.M. Eastern Time

ALLISON REMEMBERED AN ALARM GOING OFF AND THEN SHE HAD heard a loud *pop* in one of the modules distant from her. She felt the hair on her head stand straight out and that was it. Well, she did recall feeling like somebody had suddenly hit her with a truck. And *that* was it. There was nothing but blackness after that. Then she could suddenly feel her entire body as if it were a cracked tooth with aluminum foil and ice touching the raw nerve. She tried to move her body, but there was only the pain. Then she heard another sound. This time instead of the popping sound it was more of a sizzle like bacon frying in a pan. But the smell wasn't bacon. A strong, pungent, toxic chemical odor burned her nostrils and she could feel searing heat on one side of her face. The smell forced its way down her throat into her lungs, forcing her to gag and cough.

Allison forced herself to open her eyes. When she did, she almost panicked. Almost. There was a monster only a couple of meters from her, flailing about. It was blue and spheroidal at the central body, radiating immense heat. It had one long more orange tentacle *swoosh*ing away from her as if it hadn't seen her. Again, Allison almost panicked.

"What the f—" She stopped midsentence from the knock against the back of her head as she floated into an equipment rack nearest the viewing port. A smoldering laptop there dug into the side of her neck. "Ouch! Shit!"

Allison squinted and tried to clear her mind as she grabbed for a handhold. Whatever it was she had grabbed was so hot it seared to her hand. She quickly jerked away, shouting in pain. Then suddenly, maybe because of the pain, or direness of her situation, or her training, or the fact that she had finally become fully conscious again, suddenly, for whatever reason, she regained her wits and realized what was going on.

"I was unconscious," she said out loud. "The station is on fire!"

The large blue flame floating above the main control panel in the U.S. Lab Module was growing and looming closer to her—or she was floating closer to it. She wasn't certain. There was airflow coming from somewhere. That airflow was something Allison couldn't understand at the moment. The power was out. There were only the backup battery–powered emergency lights making light other than the fire. None of the systems in sight showed any signs of functionality. As far as she knew, there wasn't a single system functioning currently anywhere on the ISS and that included the air handling system. But there was light right in front of her. There was the nearly two-meter-diameter blue ball with the orange dendritic-looking extension jutting out across the room in front of her, burning away at anything it touched. One of the main things she recalled from fire training was that in microgravity fire doesn't spread about like on Earth because there is no buoyancy to make the hot air rise upward and spread. With no "up" direction in space, fire typically had to stay put and burn in an oxygen-sucking blue ball of flame. But past experiments and fires on the Russian Mir Space Station had shown that airflow into and around the fireball would extend the flames in the direction of flow, enabling it to spread. And currently, this fire had a spreading tentacle of orange flickering flame following some air flowing from somewhere or maybe to somewhere.

It was difficult seeing through the smoke that just sort of hung around with a vortex whirling slowly with the orange tentacle. The light in the room was a confusing mess now almost like a dance club was the hovering blue ball of flame pulsed slowly, consuming the air within it, the flickering tendril of orange whipping about, and the battery-powered safety light flickering through the smoke. The blue fireball with the single tentacle wavered abruptly and turned almost violently making it appear as if it were an odd-looking space unipus from an old science fiction movie from the previous millennium that was coming to eat her.

Crackle, crackle. Pop!

The flame tendril engulfed one of the experiment racks and the battery-powered safety light nearest it. That hadn't been good. The battery deflagrated, throwing shrapnel into the bulkhead and kept bouncing about until something stopped it. One such something had been Allison's left calf muscle. The shrapnel hit her with so much force that she spun wildly, arms and legs akimbo, head over heels. She did as best she could to spread her arms and legs wide to reduce her angular momentum until she slammed against the opposite bulkhead into another smoldering equipment rack. Fortunately, it wasn't searing hot. She grabbed and steadied herself. Then she looked at her leg where the pain was. She wasn't certain, because of the odd lighting in the room now only from the fire, but she thought she could see a red blotch forming on her pants. To top that off, the burning battery, plastics, and other materials were throwing off putrid and suffocating fumes throughout the room. Allison coughed and wheezed, doing her best to keep clear of the flames and cover her mouth with her T-shirt at the same time.

"Anybody on the other side of that thing?!" she shouted.

"I'm here, comrade! Nolvany!" the major shouted over the battery-backed-up fire alarms. "Are you okay?"

"Uh, I think so. A little shaken up," Allison said.

"I can't see you through this!"

There were flickering lights behind her and then there was another muted explosion, perhaps just a deflagration, of another safety light battery system. She could hear someone shouting "Fire! Fire! We've got casualties! Can anybody hear me?" behind her from one of the other modules. It was Commander Yancy's voice.

"Nolvany! Do you have eyes on the fire extinguisher?" she asked. "And the safety breathing equipment?"

"Have the extinguisher in hand!" he said and then Allison could hear hissing as he sprayed it.

"Great! I'm backing as far across as I can and to the RAM direction side of the module! Hit the flame!" she shouted. "It's growing fast!"

Allison heard the hissing and spraying sound again. There was water-based foam suddenly hitting the center of the blue ball of flame. It was an extinguisher from the Russian module. The ones from the other modules were carbon dioxide based.

"Stay back, Major Simms!" Vasiliy Nolvany continued to spray and approach closer as the fire was suppressed to something less monsterlike. The orange tentacle from the fiery unipus shrunk as it whipped back and forth with whatever air current was still flowing until it shrank to a tiny string and then it withered and died.

"What has happened?" Nolvany used a short jet of the distorted beach ball–sized orange stretched spherical or ellipsoidal solid–shaped extinguisher. "All of the systems are out and there are fires on almost all the modules, I think. The Russian modules are all out of power completely but with less damage, I think. It looks the same here, just more fire and damage."

"I don't know. Must have been some sort of catastrophic failure somewhere. But first things first!" Allison said. "How do you know there are fires in most modules?"

"From the shouts, Major Simms." He shone his flashlight up and down her body, stopping at her leg. "You are hurt, Major. Do you know how badly?"

"No, it just happened when the damned battery pack exploded. Or, well, I'm more worried about the concussion I think I have from whatever knocked me out. I came to just in time for that damned battery pack to blow," she said. Allison raised her leg closer toward her and inspected the tear in her pants. She pulled her pants open, making the rip large enough to see a long sliver of something metallic sticking out. "Shit."

"Yes, Major," Nolvany agreed with her assessment. "Do not remove it, unless it is too painful."

"No, you're right. Let's fight these fires first. I'm not bleeding out, it doesn't appear. And I don't think it is by any major arteries. I'll get it out and bandaged later. We need to figure out where this air is flowing from. Or to. That isn't a good sign."

"I was thinking the same thing. The air handlers are down, so why is there flow that is fast enough to cause a flame like that? I can feel it on my face." He touched his face and held up his hand trying to follow the air current.

"Okay, you go *against* the flow," Allison said, pointing back in the opposite direction than she was facing. Her nostrils, mouth, throat, and lungs burned from the fumes and smoke. "I'll go *with* the flow. We'll see if something is *blowing* or if something is *sucking.*"

"Very good, Major," Nolvany agreed. "But be careful."

"Right. Careful."

Allison gently kicked off the wall with her right leg, being *careful* not to aggravate the metal sliver sticking out of her left one. She stopped at an equipment rack and found a flashlight that was magnetically stuck to the edge of it. She tugged it free and flipped it on. It worked. Using the flashlight, she searched the rack for the emergency Portable Breathing Apparatus. She found a couple PBAs, flipped one on, and slipped it over her face. She placed an extra one on her hip just in case she came across someone in need. There were others still in the rack in case somebody came along looking for one.

She flipped the system on and started breathing. The cool, fresh air flowed onto her face and some of the burning in her lungs subsided. She then rolled over with her back now facing the Earth side and looked at the wall of the module where the air seemed to be pulling or pushing the smoke. She followed along with it into the connector to Node 2 and could feel tremendous heat. She grabbed at a handhold along one of the bulkheads to stop her motion. And did her best to contort her neck about so she could see in the direction she was floating.

"Oh, hell," she said and then she scrambled for the fire extinguisher in that module. She finally found it and released it from its mount and pulled the pin. She kicked instinctively off the wall realizing that she had used her left leg once a shooting pain jetted up her body. She also thought she could feel more wetness around the wound, suggesting that the blood was seeping out worse now. Had it been a serious artery she'd have seen blood squirting out, most likely, because there was no gravity to pull it down her leg and the pants surrounding it had been torn free. The only thing holding it to her body was viscosity, polar liquid sticking to her, her tattered pants material absorbing some of it, and the fact that it wasn't a gushing wound. But if she kept moving that piece of shrapnel about it might tear a larger hole in something more important.

"Damn it!" She grimaced in pain briefly and then did her

best to recompose herself. She tore a bit from her T-shirt and gently wrapped the wound, trying to stabilize the shrapnel. She took a deep breath and then focused on the problem at hand as best she could. The ISS was on fire in multiple locations and there was air flowing to or from somewhere, which meant there was a leak. Something was either leaking into the cabin or out of the cabin. Neither one of those would be good scenarios. If it was leaking out, they were losing air. If it was leaking in, that meant a propellant, fumes from a fire elsewhere, or who knew? It would just be bad and must be stopped.

She managed to get her right hand on a bulkhead between two racks and gripped it. She then pushed hard enough to sling herself in the direction of the immense heat. Allison worked her body upright in the direction of travel using her abdominal muscles to crunch her feet in and then to stretch orthogonally to her direction of flight. She hugged the fire extinguisher against her chest at the ready.

As she entered through Node 2 and into the interface of the Japanese Experiment Module, she felt such intense heat that she feared she had burns on her body. Instantly she fired the extinguisher. The spray acted as a rocket pack and stopped her forward motion slowly and then began pushing her backward. She managed to stop herself with both feet against an equipment rack, again throwing sharp shooting pains up her left leg. Allison ignored the pain and braced herself to fire the extinguisher again.

Just inside the hatchway to the JEM she could see a large blue ball of flame with multiple tentacles of multicolored fire slinging about and burning into the cabinets, equipment, wiring, and pretty much everything there. She sprayed the carbon dioxide liquid into the blue and orange beast, doing her best to fight against the thrust created as she did. The white icy spray particles spread about barely caused the fiery monster to flicker, but the thrust twisted her about in the microgravity randomly like she was trying to hold onto a greased hairless pig.

She didn't stop spraying until the heat on her bare skin backed off enough that she could move closer to the door. Once she was close enough to the module's hatchway, she sprayed a panel to the right of it to cool it some. The white icy spray sizzled as it stuck to the gray metal panel and melted, sublimating instantly to carbon dioxide vapors. Then she removed what was left of her torn, sweaty, and soot-covered T-shirt and wrapped it around her hands, letting the extinguisher float next her freely. As she tied the shirt to her right hand, she could feel a sting from the burns on her palm and fingers. She had to ignore that for now and push on.

Allison stabilized her motion against the entryway by holding on with both hands to the opening, which from her reference frame was just above her head. Once she was sure she wasn't going to spin free into the multi-tentacled monster in the JEM, she let go of the hatchway and grabbed at the hatch itself. Making certain she had a good purchase on the hatch she then pulled at it, using the mass of the door to alter her body position, swinging her legs inward against the bulkhead to give her leverage until she had something to push and pull against. The door slid into place. Allison worked the manual hatch locks and then pulled the lever inside the panel that then revealed the completely manual system that could open just that specific module to the vacuum of space through a small exhaust path.

While she didn't really have time to think about it, she did notice that the smoke flow had stopped once she had closed the hatch. That meant there was a leak in the JEM that was venting precious air into space already. Eventually, the JEM fire would lose air and burn itself out as the air pressure leaked down. She didn't want to wait that long, so, she worked the manual controls and interlocks until she could pull the right sequence of levers. The controls were built into each of the modules as part of the fire safety procedures and had been part of all of their training before leaving Earth. The sequence of interlocks was pulled and then she released the lever. She could feel the mechanical release through it. The air and smoke and fire in the room quickly dissipated and was out.

"Whew!" She wiped the sweat on her forehead and suddenly felt very tired. Shouts from somewhere else down the line of nodes brought her attention back to the current problem. As Nolvany had told her, he believed that most of the modules were on fire.

"One down." Allison pulled the extinguisher back to her body and rolled it about until she could see the gauge on top. It was still half full. "Good enough for now."

Allison turned with the intent to start from that end of the ISS and work her way to the other. She kicked against the hatch door instinctively without thinking, using both legs. A sharp pain fired up her left leg.

"Son of a bitch! That hurts!" she said through gritted teeth.

"Son of a bitch! That hurts!"

"I know. I can see it must. Hold still and I'll see if we can find something to splint it." U.S. Space Force Captain Tom Alexander scanned the Cupola for something, anything to splint Dr. Denton's compound-fractured arm. But the Cupola module was small, designed for viewing nadir at the Earth and seeing outside to control the large robotic arm. It wasn't a hospital or a storage compartment. There was little available other than camera lenses, a laptop, about a fifteen-centimeter-long flashlight, a few ink pens, various battery supplies for several cameras, cameras, and a shit-ton of Velcro stuck to every damned thing. But little that a person could use for a splint.

"My head really hurts, Tom." NASA astronaut Dr. Lawrence Denton was beginning to tremble. Tom knew it wasn't cold in there. Hell, it was probably thirty degrees Celsius or hotter. Had he not closed the door to the Cupola Module when he had, it would have been a lot hotter than it was currently. He could still see the flame flickering through the window in the hatch. There was a fire on the other side of that door.

"Look at me, Larry." Tom pulled the little flashlight from where it was stuck to the bulkhead and moved the light back and forth over his pupils. There was almost no response. Denton was going into shock. He needed medical attention now, but that wasn't coming anytime soon. He sort of jerked suddenly and Tom was afraid he was going to go into convulsions. But both fortunately and unfortunately, he moved his broken arm, sending pain through him that focused his mind on that. He screamed in pain.

"Jesus Christ, my arm!"

Tom did his best to hold him steady and looked at his arm more closely. It was turning reds, blues, and purples. There was plenty of light in the Cupola for now as they were currently on the dayside of the planet. Just outside the window, it seemed like only meters away, he could see the Soyuz capsule docked in place with the black multilayer insulation blankets diffusing the sunlight and Earthlight back at him. The spacecraft seemed no worse for the wear. Whatever had happened didn't appear to have damaged it. He hoped. The Soyuz capsules were their lifeboats. There were only three attached to the ISS currently, which meant they had lifeboats for nine. There were seven total humans onboard presently. That was the good news.

"Okay, we have to splint this to keep you from moving it," Tom said to Denton, but wasn't certain he was coherent enough to understand him.

Tom looked about the Cupola for more things he might use as he grabbed one of the blue handhold bars placed all around the periphery of the windows, hatches, and racks throughout the ISS. One of the blue metal bars only had two socket-head cap bolts holding it in place, one at either end. There was nothing attached to the bar other than a quick-release camera mount. Tom rummaged through the brown canvas camera pouch just beside the intercom unit. There wasn't an Allen wrench there but there was a shiny metal multitool. He quickly extended the pliers attachment and went to work on the bolts. He managed to break the first one loose and then worked it the rest of the way out with his fingers, placing the bolt back in the hole it had come from. He worked the second one until he had the blue metal bar free. He disconnected the camera mount and secured it to one of the other blue bars.

He looked around some more and found the light blue hand cloth stuffed inside a cubby just above the robot arm controls that they often used to clean the windows with. Tom unfolded the blue cloth and then used the multitool knife blade to cut it into strips. He managed to get several strips about three centimeters or so wide and about a half meter long each out of the cloth. That would do.

"Hold still and let me put this on you," he said, looking Dr. Denton in the eyes. Denton seemed to calm slightly but the trembling continued. Tom could see the man's lips quivering as if he'd been out in the cold for too long.

Tom gently held the bar up next to the broken arm and let it float next to it. He quickly wrapped above the break with one of the strips of cloth. He looped it around the arm several times and then tied it like a shoelace to itself. Carefully, he repeated the process with the other two strips of cloth until the arm was immobilized. At least for the time being. He had no idea what to do for the shock the man was suffering.

"That has to be good enough for now." He pulled the bandage tight around the makeshift splint, sliding a finger underneath it to make sure it wasn't so tight that it cut off Denton's circulation. The left arm below the elbow was clearly fractured, very badly. "I know it's easier said than done, but try not to bang that into anything."

"Thanks, Tom," Lawrence said through gritted and chattering teeth. "If we can get to the medical bay, we can do this better."

"Yeah, and take some pain meds. Maybe Dr. Fahid can take a look at it." Tom was doing his best to be reassuring.

"Maybe. But I'm certain it is broken. What about you?" Lawrence asked him. Tom could tell the man clearly wasn't thinking straight. Yes, his arm was very broken. That part was obvious from simple visual inspection.

"Me? It's just a bump on the head." Tom replied with a quick smile. It was *just* a bump on the head. At least that was what he was planning on. Tom could barely see out of his left eye as it was swollen shut. He didn't think it was a concussion more than it was a black eye, or going to be. "Just where the camera got me when you slammed into me from whatever tossed you across the Cupola Module. I was looking through it closely and *bam*! The lens hit the window and I hit the camera. It hurt."

"Sorry," the trembling astronaut replied. "I think I was electrocuted."

"Hey, I knew you didn't throw yourself across the room on purpose. Something pretty serious has just happened. I think the power is out everywhere. Maybe it was a grounding problem or something, but there was a serious electrical malfunction. We need to get in touch with Huntsville." Tom could now see orange along with the blue light coming through the tiny round window in the hatch door, but the door was so hot, getting close enough to look through the viewport was out of the question. He reached his hand up closer to the ISS Cupola Module hatch door. It was blistering hot. He pulled it back, shaking it to cool it off. "Shit, that's hot."

"Had you not had the presence of mind to close it quickly we might be burned alive right now," Lawrence Denton said grimly. His body and teeth still trembling and chattering. "Now, we'll either just die of carbon dioxide poisoning or be dry roasted like peanuts. At least we'll die with the best view from the station."

The Cupola Module was like a large bay window looking out from Node 3, also known as the Tranquility Node, in the nadir direction, toward Earth, with a view never before rivaled unless you were on an EVA. Well, that is, it was never rivaled until the DSIHM had been installed. Tom had to admit, it was an amazing view, but he sure as hell didn't plan on dying looking out that damned window. But again, it was getting very hot in there and if the power was out, he wasn't sure what that meant about the carbon dioxide scrubbers. He started doing math in his head on how long before two men created enough carbon dioxide in a given volume before it was dangerous. Since the first symptom of carbon dioxide exposure was a headache, neither of them was in a good position to test that as both of them had fairly severe head injuries at the moment.

"Die in here? No, we're not dying in here. Okay, sure, the Tranquility Node is on fire and blocking our way out, for now. Soon, and I mean soon, somebody out there will be along to put out the fire and get us out of here," Tom said. "Or, we'll be clever and figure something out."

Denton just nodded, teeth still chattering.

When whatever had happened, happened moments earlier, Royal Canadian Navy captain and ISS Mission Commander Teri Yancy had seen cosmonaut Dr. Peter Solmonov thrown hard across the room and completely out of the Tranquility Module. He banged the back of his head against the hatch into the entrance orthogonal to the main habitat module direction. She had gone to Dr. Solmonov and given him a shove forward to keep him moving away from the fire.

"We have fire! And we have casualties here!" she shouted. Then she had dove headfirst into that compartment, the Quest Airlock Module, while throwing him in front of her. Tumbling along behind him, she managed to somehow get tangled up with him and the ISS peripheral fixtures. There were cables, boxes, racks, computers, and other miscellaneous equipment jutting out from every surface on the ISS and in this case, all of that scientific space stuff hadn't been particularly helpful.

Teri's right hand had gotten caught in a bind between him and the square cutouts of the matte bronze colored metal ring encircling the rounded corner rectangular hatch. Her momentum had carried her forward, twisting her wrist in a direction it didn't want to go and, she was fairly certain, the impact into the cutout had snapped several of the bones in her hand. She had actually heard the *crack* when she hit. Adrenaline had allowed her to overcome her mad spinning, the pain, and confusion in order to perform the lifesaving task of sliding the door closed and sealing it behind them with her remaining functional hand. The problem now was that Solmonov wasn't breathing. That had to be corrected before she could do anything else.

"Dr. Solmonov! Can you hear me?" She breathed into his mouth, counted to three, and repeated the process as per her training. While she counted and got her breath, Teri then lightly slapped the Russian scientist across the face. She shook him with her left hand. The right one was just completely useless with the bad wrist. "Peter! Peter! Can you hear me?!"

Teri leaned in as closely as possible to the man to listen for breathing, a heartbeat, anything. There was nothing. She breathed into his mouth again. With her good hand she made a fist and slammed it against his chest, tossing her off balance spinning away.

"Damn it all to Hell!" she shouted as the added angular momentum pushed both of them in opposite directions randomly and closer to the very hot door leading back through the kitchen in Node 1 and toward the Tranquility Module. There was a bad fire in there and at the moment there was nothing she could do about it. She hoped someone else was working it.

Teri used her socked feet to hook under one of the blue metal balance bars and then she grabbed another one with her left hand to stabilize her spin. She pushed off the bulkhead and rolled in a forward tuck toward Peter's lifelessly floating body. She opened her legs just as she approached and then locked them around his midsection, making the motion an inelastic collision transfer of momentum. They bounced into the wall. It hurt. But the end result was that Teri had Peter's motion stabilized and they were connected, giving her a platform to work on him with.

She leaned closer to his face, listening for breathing while searching his neck with her left hand for a pulse. She couldn't find one. She breathed into his mouth again and then banged on his chest with her left fist three times. She breathed. She used her fist again.

"Come on, Peter!" she shouted, hitting him in the chest again. "Come on! Breathe, damn it!"

Solmonov made a deep gasping for air and suddenly began to react to her. He was breathing. His heart was beating again. She sighed with relief.

"Peter, can you hear me?" He didn't respond. "Peter?"

"Dr. Itokawa! Please listen to me!" Dr. Raheem Fahid shouted as he banged on the door for Docking Compartment 1, which was just beneath the Russian Service Module. A Progress Module was attached to Docking Compartment 1 and the Japanese astronaut had disconnected the air duct that had been stretched in there and closed the door. Raheem wasn't sure what the man was planning, but he could tell by his voice that he was panicked and not thinking clearly. He needed to get him out of the Progress Module before he did something under duress that might have bad results.

"There's a fire! We have to keep the compartments closed from each other!" Itokawa shouted.

"Satoshi! The fire is out here. It was only a small one and is under control," Raheem told him. "Please open the door. There are likely others that need our help elsewhere on the station."

"There's no fire out there?" Itokawa asked. "Are you sure you got it? Space fires are unusual and hard to spot."

"No. There is no fire out here now. I wouldn't be here so calmly if it were," Raheem said. He could suddenly feel the vibrations on the door and it pulled open. "Nice to see you are in one piece, Satoshi. Are you sure that you are alright otherwise?"

"Yes. I was not touching anything at the time it happened. I think that saved me. I was eating and then suddenly *bang*! There was a major electrical discharge throughout the module and everything was blown. Then there was a fire near Node 1. I moved away as quickly as possible and ended up here."

"Looks like this was a safe spot. I don't see as much damage here. I was in the Progress at the end of the Service Module, retrieving something for Dr. Schwab when it happened. The Russian systems seemed to have managed this event better than the rest of the station," Raheem said. "Come on. Let us go see if we can help."

Raheem reached in through the hatch to the Progress and gave Itokawa a hand out. He noticed three large, bright orange canvas bags fastened to the wall just inside the module. One of those was marked FIRE EXTINGUISHER in Russian. Raheem stopped and studied briefly how to unfasten it.

"This might come in handy," he said. "We should head back the other way. The Russian modules all the way out to the Soyuz on the air lock and the Progress at the end of the Service Module things seem to be okay. There's no power, but okay."

"I heard a lot of shouting earlier," Itokawa said.

"Me too," Raheem agreed. "And it was that way. Come on. Let's go."

CHAPTER 42

⚬⚬

Turkey Economic Exclusive Zone, Black Sea
Tuesday
4:47 A.M. Turkey Time (TRT)
Monday
9:47 P.M. Eastern Time

MICHAEL FELT THE MODIFIED NINE-MILLIMETER WEAPON MAGNETI-cally stuck to his chest armor. It was big and clunky and had very large mechanisms so it could be manipulated while wearing a space suit and looked like nothing that resembled either a pistol or a rifle. But it was a firearm designed to use in space while wearing a space suit and he had practiced with it over the past few years. It gave him comfort. At the moment, he reveled in that comfort. While he was excited about moving forward with the plan and finally see-ing it come to fruition, the thought of being on top of a new and untested version of a thirty-year-old rocket with a rushed launch schedule made him a bit apprehensive. Jebidiah and Vladimir, on the other hand, seemed as happy as kids at Christmas. Or maybe this was just more of their element. Michael was certainly not in his.

"Control, we had the slosh baffle indicator on stage 1 flash red for a second then went back to green," Jebidiah said over the comm channel. "Is that a problem?"

"Copy, Vyrezka. That was a circuit breaker reset causing that light to blink. We saw that in the dress rehearsal. Stage One

269

Slosh Baffle telemetry shows green here. No problems. T-minus ninety seconds and counting."

"Ms. Stinson, I hope you did your job well!" Vladimir said.

"Colonel, I hope you do yours well. Good luck gentlemen."

"Be advised that rendezvous will be sooner than expected as we are on a launch window putting us three orbits early. We have updated the guidance burn package," Stinson said. "This puts us nearly three hours ahead of schedule in all regards."

"Understood, Control," Vladimir said. "Main power to igniters is green."

"Copy Vyrezka, igniters showing green. T-minus fifty-seven seconds."

"You are being very quiet, Comrade M!" Vladimir said. "Be happy, my friend! We are going to space today or will die trying. Either way is great with me. This is our fortune and time to be bold, my friend!"

"I'll prefer the first one, V. I've never been a big fan of the whole 'die trying' thing," Michael said. He looked through the virtual display at the little stuffed animal hanging from a string tied to the ceiling of the capsule. The plush stuffed black, brown, and beige animal's eyes stared back at him. Vladimir had called it a Cheburashka when he had hung it up. Michael had no idea what that was. Or for that matter, why it was there.

"I'm with you on that one, M," Jebidiah agreed. "I'll forego the die trying part."

"Control, we show all tanks at full pressure!" Jebidiah announced. "Propellant feed umbilical detach sequence start. Power umbilicals detach sequence start."

"Copy, Vyrezka." There was a slight pause. "We are showing Prop and Power umbilicals detached. T-minus twenty-nine seconds."

"Hydraulic generator startup has been initiated," Vladimir said. "Showing full power on main engine gimbals. Thrust vector control and inertial guidance mode is active."

"Copy, Vyrezka. Lock-down clamps detach."

"Detach light is green. Tower is down."

"Ten, nine, eight..."

"Ignition startup sequence on!" Jebidiah said.

Michael gripped his armrests tightly as he felt the rocket beneath starting to vibrate to life. He took a deep breath and tried to relax his mind. He watched in his virtual view built into the helmet visor an outside camera view of the platform that Control was feeding them. The Dorman space-suit helmet visors had the same functionality as the Dorman virtual display sunglasses. The video was perfectly clear in ultra-resolution. Michael assumed it was from cameras on the command center on the yacht.

"... three, two, one!" Stinson's voice was suddenly drowned out by the sound of a million rivers rushing by during a freight train convention during a tornado. "Ignition! We have ignition!"

The liquid oxygen mixed with the kerosene rocket fuel and ignited, throwing green flames out the base of the RD-171 engines that roiled into an expanding pillar of white exhaust all around the base of the rocket and across the modified oil platform. Michael watched his virtual view in awe but at the same time gritted his teeth. He'd been in very heated firefights before and in knife and gun battles to the death, but he'd always been in control in those situations. At the moment, the rocket could explode and there was absolutely nothing he could do about it. Needless to say, he was nervous. He was nervous as hell.

"Vyrezka, you have cleared the launchpad."

Vladimir shouted something in Russian that was unintelligible as far as Michael was concerned. He suspected it was along the lines of a cowboy whoop. The whooping was drowned out by the ever-increasing noise of the rocket engines and the capsule shaking.

"TVC powering up! Big current draw!" Jebidiah said excitedly. The Thrust Vector Control system, which consisted of the powered gimbals used to steer the four separate RD-171 nozzles in order to control the rocket's trajectory, was making corrections and in turn was showing up on Jeb's panel as electrical current being drawn from the Hydraulic Generator Power Supply System.

"Roll maneuver initiated!" Vladimir shouted over the noise. "HGPSS is in the green."

"Copy Vyrezka, roll maneuver package is active. HGPSS telemetry looks good," Stinson told them. "Pitch angle adjusted for inclination insertion. You are looking good, Vyrezka! You are looking good!"

"Clock shows launch plus a minute twenty-three, twenty-four," Jeb announced. "Approaching Max-Q."

"Throttle at eighty-two percent," Vladimir said.

Michael watched as the Cheburashka, a stuffed Russian bear—or whatever the damned thing was—spun and bounced wildly at the bottom of the string above the center console. His own body felt like it weighed over three or maybe four hundred kilograms. He made no effort to move. Even blinking was difficult. He was amazed that the stuffed bear didn't have an effective weight large enough to break the string holding it to the ceiling of the capsule. Then there was a loud violent-sounding explosion that rattled throughout the rocket capsule that startled him.

"Mach one!" Vladimir shouted.

"Jesus, that was loud," Michael muttered but then suddenly some of the vibrations diminished and the ride smoothed out. There was still extreme force pressing him into his seat but it wasn't as violent.

"Going for throttle up!" Vladimir shouted.

"Roger, Vyrezka, you are go for throttle up."

A brief moment passed and then Vladimir said, "Mach two."

Michael was forced into his seat even harder as the modernized new version of the Zenit-3SL with a manned capsule on top pushed past the speed of sound by a factor of more than two and raced toward orbital altitudes, continuing to increase speed. The force against him continued to increase to nearly bone-crushing weights. Michael was glad he had strong bones.

"Vyrezka, initiate throttle-back sequence."

"Copy, Control. Initiating throttle-back sequence." Vladimir replied.

As the rocket climbed higher and higher the atmosphere became less dense, creating less dynamic pressure against the hull. With less pressure against the rocket the thrust increased, adding more gee loading to the occupants. If the rocket were allowed to accelerate unchecked it would attain gee loads of five to six times Earth's gravity. While the astronauts could survive such a trip, prolonged exposure to such high loads could cause injuries that they didn't need. It would also totally exhaust them. Hence, there was the "throttle-back sequence." The flight computer would start throttling back the RD-171, keeping the acceleration at a steady four gees. That was going to last for another minute or so and would be taxing enough on the crew.

"Hang on! Staging in fifteen seconds!" Vladimir said. Michael could do nothing but hang on. "...Three! Two! One!"

Bang! Bang!

The Zenit pyrotechnic charges blew the stage faring as the

small RD-8 second-stage vernier rocket fired, pulling them away from the still hot, burning but now separated first stage. Then a few seconds later another force thrust Michael back into his seat as the second-stage main engine, an RD-120, ignited and continued to accelerate them higher and faster to space. The Cheburashka swung erratically back and forth and bounced up and down so violently Michael wondered just how heavy the thing would feel if he tried to hold it. And he still wasn't certain that the thing wasn't some joke or version of fuzzy dice hanging from the rear-view mirror of a hot rod car that cosmonauts used as a show of their prowess. He then wondered why they *hadn't* used fuzzy dice. Vladimir had assured him that the stuffed animal was a necessity that Americans never understood. It had a purpose. All the Soyuz capsules had them. Michael just gritted his teeth and watched. And watched. And watched. The Cheburashka watched back, not blinking a stuffed eyelid.

"Launch plus seven minutes!" Jebidiah said. "SECO coming up in thirty."

"Copy, Vyrezka, Second Stage Engine Cut-Off in twenty-four, twenty-three..."

Michael watched the clock in his virtual view as it ticked down to SECO. Suddenly, the capsule was very quiet. The little stuffed bear above his head floated about almost motionlessly. And then Michael completely understood why it was there. He got it. The thing was an accelerometer. The bear would tell them if they were in microgravity or if they were being accelerated. It did have a purpose.

There was a moment of microgravity while the computers updated the capsule's whereabouts and generated Kalman filters to predict the right sequence of burns to raise and circularize their orbit. The onboard systems connected to as many of the American Global Positioning Satellites and as many Russian Global Navigation Satellite System satellites as they could detect. From each of those detections the flight computer used timing delays and signal multipath calculations to create a precise two-line-element sequence to feed back into the state vector of the spacecraft. Once the computer knew where they were, how fast they were going, and where they had been most recently, it could determine where it needed to go and what it would take to get it there in the way of rocket burns.

"Vyrezka, we show you at an inclination of fifty-one point six degrees, an elliptical orbit with apogee predicted to be two hundred and ninety-two kilometers. Be prepared for Hohmann Transfer burn on perigee. Phasing burns currently being calculated. We are handing off all flight control to you now, now, now. You have the ship."

"Copy that, Control. Vyrezka is autonomous," Vladimir said. "Onboard flight computer has us under control. Great work Control."

"Vyrezka, be advised that all comms will now be cut and you are on your own. We have initiated Sink and Swim here. Do you copy?"

"Good Copy, Control. Thanks for your help and good luck down there. I hope your boat is fast enough," Vladimir said and then flipped the comm to the internal channel only. "You heard her, comrades! Vyrezka has control. Welcome to space, gentlemen. Welcome. To. Space."

CHAPTER 43

∽

Near Tampa, Florida
Task Force Headquarters
Monday
10:37 P.M. Eastern Time

"UNDERSTOOD, SIR!" FRANK SHUT THE CLASSIFIED VIDEO CONFERENCE off and looked about the headquarters briefing table. The White House had been briefed and they had been authorized to do whatever in the hell they could to stop a nuclear disaster. Word from the Russians was that they had no rockets ready to go. The State Department was considering reaching out to the Chinese but that was likely not to generate help either. What they did know was that there had been no communications with the ISS for over an hour. And it had gone out before anyone told them there were six nuclear warheads headed their way. Basically, the shit was hitting the fan at hypervelocity. The video system showed that the connection had been cut and Frank relaxed back into his seat and exhaled through pursed lips. "Jesus H. Christ."

"Got the data from Space Command coming in now, Colonel," Captain Ames said. "Looks like they launched out of Turkish waters in the Black Sea into an inclination of—wait for it—fifty-one point six degrees. There is no doubt about it. You were right, Dr. Castlebaum."

"I wish I hadn't been. And there is no way that complete

275

loss of communications with the International Space Station is a coincidence. But how in the hell did they manage that?" Amy replied.

"Captain Ames, what is their expected time to rendezvous?" Dr. Banks asked.

"About six hours from now."

"Captain, you just heard generals Hastings and Cole give us authority to move ahead with your plan. How soon before the X-37D can go?" Frank was scribbling notes down as fast as he could think of them. There were so many things that would have to happen before they could even consider what he was considering. They would need EVA suits. Modified weapons. Rapid training on the ride and the ISS.

"General Cates assured me that if authorization was given, we could be ready to launch as early as thirty-six hours," Ames said.

"How many passengers and how much cargo?" Mac asked.

"The X-37D has six seats in the cargo bay. Or they can be removed for cargo or payloads," Captain Ames explained. "There are two seats in the front for the pilot and copilot. The flight engineer typically sits in the first seat on the left behind them. So, assume a team of five."

"Well, the Chiefs have just authorized it so start us a countdown clock. Make sure he gets it." Frank hesitated briefly. "Alright, I need special combat volunteers. Combat experience, any type of aerospace or special training is a bonus. I've briefed you on Hot Eagle. Mac, myself, and a few others went through training for similar contingencies about a decade ago. According to all the records, Mac and I are the only members of that exercise still active. But I have to warn you, the training was short and not very extensive. In fact, it was more of a fact-finding exercise than actual training. I'd say it was more like Space Camp for adults with guns. I likely won't have any more of an idea of what to do than anybody else. And we won't have time for much more training than briefings. But there are nukes out there and somebody has to do something."

"I don't understand why we can't just shoot them down with missiles." Toby shrugged from across the table.

"Typical misunderstanding," Amy Castlebaum said.

"How do you mean?" Toby asked.

"While we have been experimenting with ballistic missile defense systems for decades and decades, they are designed to shoot at missiles either as they are boosting up, theater-sized rockets, artillery, and mortars, or to possibly hit reentry vehicles. But the modern-day reentry vehicles are hypersonic and maneuverable and damned near unstoppable. We really don't have a way to just 'shoot them down,' no matter what you saw at the movies," Amy explained.

"Well, Frank, I'd love to go, but I'm working that other assignment you gave me. And I might be onto something," Toby said.

"Understood. Stay with it, Toby." Frank nodded. "Volunteers?"

"I'm the only other one trained." Mac held up a hand. "I'm in."

"I'm in," Major Thompson said. "As long as I don't have to wear a red shirt."

"Me too," Dugan added.

"I'm in," Captain Ames said. "I have some training on this system."

"That's our five," Frank said just as Dr. Banks started to protest.

"I'm going, Frank," Ginny said. "The DNI will want representation. I'm a pilot. And I've seen plenty of combat."

"Not enough room, Dr. Banks. Sorry."

"Wait a minute, Colonel," Captain Ames interrupted him. "When I said I was going, I didn't mean as one of your five. I'll be in the pilot's seat. So you will have one more. I will point out, though, that all crew will be tested by medical and with flight before anything is one hundred percent."

"Okay, then, Banks. Looks like you're in." Frank looked at Ames curiously, realizing now what the patch with the strange wings represented. "We need to be on a plane to Vandenberg ten minutes ago."

CHAPTER 44

 ∾

Low Earth Orbit
International Space Station
Monday
11:21 P.M. Eastern Time

"CAN YOU HEAR ME? HELLO?" TOM SHOUTED TOWARD THE CUPOLA hatch door. There was something going on out there. He could hear voices shouting but couldn't make out what they were saying. He tried placing his ear to something structural but there was just too much stuff attached everywhere for that. He checked Dr. Denton's pulse to make certain he was still okay. The man had finally succumbed to his pain and was unconscious. "We need help in here!"

There was a sound of spraying and a continuous sizzle against the other side of the door and then several minutes had passed. There was no light at all in the Cupola other than some flashlights that seemed to flicker past the window in the hatch. The ISS had passed to the night side of Earth and it was much darker. Then after what seemed like forever there was a banging on the door.

"Yes! We're in here!"

The hatch seal broke free and then slowly and in an uneven motion was forced up. Tom could see two sets of hands, one in gloves, the other with cloth wrapping them, pushing up the hatch door. Then a light shined in at them, moving from him to

279

Dr. Denton and then back again. Then one of the lights pointed away at a bulkhead and Tom could see Major Simms looking back at him.

"Tom! Are you alright?" Allison asked him.

"Yes, ma'am. Dr. Denton, though, well, I think he's in shock. He has a compound fracture in his arm and maybe a concussion. He said he had been electrocuted," Tom answered. "Damn, it's good to see you, Major Simms."

"You, too, Captain. Now let's get you both out of here and to our medical area."

"Good to see you are okay, Captain." Major Nolvany stuck his head in. "Major, take the Captain Alexander and I will manage with Dr. Denton."

"Right," Simms replied. "Come on, Tom. Let's get you checked out."

✧   ✧   ✧

Allison's left leg was strapped down to the top of the multi-functional tabletop in the Zvezda or Russian Service module. The hatches were all opened and Nolvany was in the Soyuz capsule just outside, attached to the docking module just meters away. The entire crew was in voice range of one another. Dr. Fahid hovered about Allison's leg, debating with himself about what treatment she was about to receive. Dr. Denton, Solmonov, and Commander Yancy were on the other side of the Forward Docking Port of the Service Module just inside the FGB Module. Solmonov was still unconscious but stable for the moment. Denton wasn't better and was in and out of consciousness. Dr. Fahid was concerned he had a more severe head trauma than could be determined on the ISS. Itokawa stood beside her in case Dr. Fahid needed assistance. Dr. Schwab had returned to the DSIHM to assess any damages there. Tom had gone with him as Commander Yancy had ordered for nobody to be anywhere alone until they got power back and assessed the situation.

"Just get the damned thing out of there," Allison grunted. "Any luck, Vasiliy?"

"Patience, Major!" Nolvany shouted back to her.

"I agree with our cosmonaut friend, Major." Fahid grasped the metal sliver with a pair of forceps and locked them into place. "I am going to have to make a slight incision here to reduce tearing as I remove this."

"Just do it."

Suddenly, lights seemed to flicker from the docking module and there was power there. Vasiliy had the Soyuz capsule powered up. Allison breathed a sigh of relief once she heard Vasiliy speaking in Russian, trying to reach the ground stations.

"There, that got it." Dr. Fahid held up a long white and metallic gray sliver of metal about ten centimeters long. "Now, a few staples and you'll be fine."

"Wasn't as big as it felt," Allison said.

"Yes. Now hold still." Fahid swabbed a gelled clear antibacterial disinfectant all about the wound and then snapped a staple into her leg. Allison hadn't felt a thing since he had applied a local anesthetic there. She watched as Dr. Fahid snapped seven more staples.

"That should do it. Let's get a bandage there," he said. A few seconds later Allison was bandaged and good to go.

"Thanks, Doc." She started unstrapping her leg before he could protest. She pushed off the table toward the entrance to the Soyuz capsule. The sound of communication in Russian filled the space. She was glad of that. "Any luck?"

"Shh. Shh." Nolvany waved at her to be quiet. Then he turned the volume up and handed her a headset. She worked her way into the seat next to him and put it on. The conversation was in Russian.

Allison cut her mic and quietly asked Vasiliy if he could reach U.S. Mission Control.

"Major Simms has requested we connect her to her command," he said.

"Yes. Stand by."

Vasiliy cut both mics and spoke to her in English. "Somebody has stolen nuclear weapons and launched a rocket. They are coming here, Major."

"What? That sounds crazy," Allison said wide-eyed. "How is that even possible?"

"I do not know." Vasiliy shrugged. Then the radio buzzed and he reconnected their microphones.

"ISS, this is Mission Control. Do you copy?"

"Major Simms here."

"Major, where is Commander Yancy?"

"Major Yancy is in the FGB tending to wounded. We've had

a complete power failure, multiple fires, and loss of systems. All are accounted for and alive, but we have two with serious injuries. Dr. Fahid is unconscious and Dr. Denton is severely concussed with a broken arm. Commander Yancy also has a broken hand."

"I see. Major, we have become more of an incident of global proportions and unfortunately you seem to be right in the middle of it. A few days ago, a Russian missile was raided and six nuclear warheads were stolen. A few hours ago, a rocket was launched from an oil platform in the Black Sea on what appears to be a direct trajectory to the ISS. Current radar data and trajectory prediction algorithms show them reaching the ISS in less than three hours."

"Why are they bringing nukes *here*?" Nolvany asked.

"Our team on the ground believes that they intend to fire them off and detonate them over certain locations at high altitudes to create a global EMP blackout."

"What can we do to help?" Allison asked.

"You have been ordered to evacuate the ISS immediately before they can get there. There are plans being put into place. But you must evacuate as soon as possible. Especially with the status of the ISS currently unknown, there would be no time to repair systems. Evacuate immediately. That is the order directly from the White House."

"Understood. We will start evacuation procedures immediately." Allison nodded to Vasiliy. "ISS out."

"Major?"

"Well, first things first. We have to get Solmonov and Denton into suits," she said.

"Yes. That will take time," Vasiliy agreed. They both checked their watches. "Less than three hours."

"I'll go with Tom and start powering up Soyuz capsule two. If you get done soon, you might prep the other one."

"Yes. Good idea. Follow the checklists."

"Of course."

"No, goddamnit, Peter!" Yancy's voice shouted from the FGB. "Dr. Fahid! I need you. Solmonov is crashing!"

Allison and Vasiliy quickly climbed through the Orbital Module of the Soyuz capsule to see Dr. Fahid passing by swiftly overhead with a defib device in his hands. He had so much momentum he would have crashed right into them had they not ducked back down quickly. Once he flew by, they pulled themselves into the Zarya, FGB, module. Commander Yancy was giving mouth-to-mouth to Solmonov.

Dr. Raheem Fahid calmly but quickly worked the hasps on the defibrillator container and pulled the pads from within. The monitor beeped, showing a full charge. Raheem pulled up Solmonov's T-shirt and placed the pads on his chest. He checked the device controls one last time.

"Clear, Teri. Clear!" he shouted and then depressed the discharge button.

Solmonov's body curved upward as the pads released the high-voltage surge into him. Fahid checked him for a pulse and listened for breathing. He recycled the defib device while Teri continued to breathe for him. The device beeped it was ready.

"Clear!" Fahid waited for Yancy to back away, then depressed the discharge button again.

Again, Solmonov's body convulsed in with his chest making an arc toward the bulkhead above and then relaxed. Fahid felt for a pulse frantically. He checked several times. It was clear from the expression of terror on his face he wasn't finding one.

"Clear!" he shouted again and depressed the button, again draining the device completely of power. He put his ear to Peter's chest. He felt for a pulse. Then he balled his right fist and swung it down hard against Peter's chest. There was nothing.

"No!" He rummaged through the med kit and pulled out an epinephrine pen and jabbed it into Solmonov's chest, injecting him with pure adrenaline. He continued to beat on his chest with his fist, trying to stabilize his movement. "Breathe for him, Teri!"

"Breathe, two, three, four, clear," Fahid said and then pounded three times. Then repeated. "Breathe, two, three, four, clear."

Fahid and Yancy continued to repeat the process for what seemed like an eternity as all of the ISS astronauts and cosmonauts floated, helplessly watching. It was becoming more and more clear that there was little anyone could do.

"Breathe, two, three, four, clear." As Fahid raised his fist to strike, Vasiliy Nolvany caught the man's wrist.

"It is okay, Dr. Fahid," Nolvany said somberly. "He's gone. He's gone."

"What?" Fahid turned and looked back at everyone in the room watching.

"You have done what you can," Nolvany said. "You as well, Commander Yancy."

Tears built up at the corners of Allison's eyes. There was nothing she could do. Her friend was dead.

"How did this happen?" she asked.

"We may not ever have time to figure that out, Major," Itokawa said.

"What now?" Tom asked.

"We evacuate. Those are our orders. We must evacuate in less than three hours," Nolvany said. "We do not have time for mourning and philosophy right now."

"Major Nolvany is right." Allison dried her eyes with her fingers. She had yet to put on a new shirt. "Our orders are to evacuate. Go get what you want to take home. We're leaving now."

"Major Simms, a word with you, please?" Nolvany said, motioning her to follow him to the Service Module end of the station. "We need to discuss priority evacuation."

"Yes, of course."

❖   ❖   ❖

"What exactly is it you wish to check on, Dr. Schwab?" Tom asked the billionaire scientist. "Didn't the DSIHM get fried like everything else?"

"It would appear so, Captain Alexander. But with the current state of the ISS, it is design procedure for the DSIHM to be closed off and depressurized. I don't want to take a chance that it could destroy itself by an overpressure from the Bigelow Expandable Airlock Module it is connected to," Schwab explained.

The interior of Node 3 just over the Cupola seemed to have been one of the most highly damaged parts of the station other than the JEM area. From the damage Tom could see in the dim lighting from his flashlight, it looked like there was a wave of fire and destruction that had torn through that area just as bad as near the power conditioning area in the JEM.

"Jesus, look at that laptop, Doc. It absolutely exploded. There's no telling how much debris is floating about in here. It'll take years to repair all of this," Tom said.

"I'm afraid so," Schwab agreed. "Might be cheaper to build a new one."

"Wouldn't that be a shame. All this history."

"Maybe. Not a big fan of history," Schwab said.

The two of them floated through the Bigelow Expandable Airlock Module—the BEAM—into the DSIHM. Sometimes it was also referred to as the "Activity" module rather than "Airlock" module. As the two of them surveyed the damage along the way it was clear that there was almost no damage in the hotel module. Tom had only been in that module a couple of times but had never taken time to sightsee from it. He floated over to the giant circular bay window. It was larger than the Cupola. At first it gave him bad memories of being trapped in the Cupola with Denton while a fire raged just outside the door, but he shook that off and whistled in amazement as the Sun began to rise ahead of them.

"Damn nice view here."

"That was the point," Schwab replied from over his shoulder back to him. He was busy pulling away a panel and working manual hatch systems. "That should do it. We can egress into the BEAM now."

As they egressed through the hatch between the BEAM and the DSIHM, Schwab pulled the Russian-style hatch door to behind them and turned the handle, sealing it in place. He turned and looked at Tom, who was still surveying damage everywhere when more shouting started just a module away.

"What's going on?" Tom said. "You done here, Doc?"

"Yes, let us go see what is happening."

CHAPTER 45

ᘛᘚ

Low Earth Orbit
International Space Station
Tuesday
1:01 A.M. Eastern Time

"IS HE IN?" ALLISON DOUBLE-CHECKED DR. DENTON'S SAFETY harness. It had been tough going but they had managed to get him in a suit and loaded all while he was unconscious. His condition had gone from bad to worse. Allison and Tom were working him into position from within the Orbital Module, loading him into place feet first through the hatch into the Descent Module. At one point Allison had accidentally grabbed the man by the broken arm and was glad that he was unconscious because she was certain that would have generated enough pain to make him pass out. Dr. Fahid had removed Tom's splint, set the bone as best he could, and then rewrapped it so it could fit in the suit. That had been the part taking the most of their precious time.

"I have him!" Vasiliy exclaimed. "Hold him there one moment."

Allison and Tom did their best to hold the man into place as the cosmonaut pilot strapped him in. There were a couple of clicks and then he felt snug into place.

"Got it."

"Great. Now let's get Dr. Schwab in here."

"I'm here," Schwab said from just outside the Orbital Module in the Transfer Module outside. "Okay to enter?"

"Yes, Dr. Schwab, please make way to your seat and strap in," Tom told him.

"Very good, then." Schwab swam by and then rolled over feetfirst. He carefully eased himself into his seat.

"Okay, Comrade Alexander. You now," Vasiliy told Tom as he climbed out of the Descent Module. "You are now commander of this Soyuz flight. Congratulations."

"Short trip to space," Tom told him. Then he turned to both of them and saluted. "Majors. We'll see you back on Earth."

"Good luck, Commander Tom." Nolvany returned his salute.

"Godspeed, Captain." Allison saluted and then the two of them waited for the hatch to close, double-checked the seals, and then departed the Orbital Module and repeated the process. They banged hard on the hatch three times and then moved away and sealed the Docking Module hatch. Allison could hear the docking clamps release. She wished she were in the Cupola so she could watch the release and descent. Tom was a good pilot. He had trained with the Soyuz, as they all had. He could handle it.

"Alright, next one." Vasiliy pushed out of the Docking Compartment 1 across the Service Module Transfer Compartment to the MRM-2 module. There the second Soyuz was being manned by Commander Yancy, Itokawa, and Dr. Fahid, who were all getting into place. Commander Yancy only had a broken hand. She could manage the flight, especially with Dr. Itokawa's help.

"Are you ready, Dr. Fahid?" Vasiliy asked.

"Yes."

"Dr. Fahid. Just in case. Would you take this to my father?" Allison handed him a small cooler pack holding what was left of the nanobot spike proteins. "I'm not certain I will be out of debriefing in time to get it to him quickly."

"Of course, Major. Why do I get the feeling that isn't the entire story?" Fahid asked.

"I have no idea what you mean," Allison replied pushing backwards from the hatch. "Okay, Commander Yancy. Time to go. See you on Earth."

"Godspeed, Allison."

"Godspeed, Teri."

"Good luck, Commander," Nolvany said.

The two of them went through the process to close them up

and seal the hatch to the MRM-2 Module. Vasiliy looked at his watch. "Cutting it close."

"Yeah. Let's get Peter," Allison said. "We can go ahead and load him first. Did you retrieve the packages from the other Soyuz capsules?"

"Yes."

"After we load, Peter, we load all of the extinguishers."

"Yes. There should be plenty of room to store them in the Orbital Module."

"Good. Let's get to work, then." Allison looked at her watch. "It'll take some time donning the suits. We better hurry."

"Agreed, Major."

CHAPTER 46

᳅

Low Earth Orbit
Orbital Two-Line Element:
1 25544U 98067A 2974.31742528 -.00002182 00000-0-
**   11606-4 0 1027**
2 25544 51.6416 247.4627 0006703 130.5360
**   325.02881002537**
Tuesday
2:34 A.M. Eastern Time

> *V, M, J,*
>
> *ISS is evacuated.*
>
> *S*

"I've got the ISS on radar and on the telescope," Jebidiah announced as the Vyrezka continued to close the gap between them. They were almost in range. "Fifty thousand meters and closing fast. The ISS is locked in the crosshairs."

"Copy that, J. If you look out my side you can actually see it shining in the sunlight ahead of us and slightly above." Vladimir pointed out the window to his right. "M, prepare the capture mechanisms."

"On it, V." Michael unsnapped his harness and floated his way to the central console. Unlike the Blue Origin version of the space capsule, the Vyrezka had a cylinder measuring about twenty centimeters in diameter that was located precisely in the center running from floor to ceiling. Michael opened a panel and toggled a large red-covered rocker switch and then pushed in a manual circuit breaker switch. He closed the panel and then grasped the large space-suit-glove-sized pull lever on the side of the cylinder.

"Power switch in the on position. Circuit breaker in. Main panel power relay is on," Michael reported. He kicked back to his seat just as the retro thrusters did an automated course correction burn, causing him to miss his mark. He grabbed at the seat with his left hand and frantically pulled himself into it. The sudden strange acceleration of the ship caused his inner ear to spin him a bit, reminding him of the seasickness he had suffered only a few days prior while on the yacht in the Black Sea. "Whoa, damn!"

"Did that make you dizzy, M?" V asked him with a raised eyebrow. He seemed more concerned than goading.

"I'm fine, V."

"Yes, I'm sure you are. But if you do get dizzy, violently shake your head like saying 'no.' It will reset your inner ear," Vladimir explained. "Cosmonaut secret learned from watching cats fall out of trees."

"I thought American astronauts came up with that," Jebidiah said.

"*Nyet!* Cosmonauts," Vladimir retorted. "M, give me status of capture system?"

"Uh, yeah, right." Michael strapped himself back in. He couldn't help but look up at the little stuffed bear to see if it was floating or accelerating. "Bringing the virtual controls up... I am sighting in on the target now. Still forty-five thousand meters out of targeting range but closing fast."

"Good, keep me posted when we get in range," Vladimir said. "J, link us the view through the telescope. I want to see how many Soyuz spacecraft are still docked."

"Right. Linking now," Jebidiah said after tapping his virtual touch screen. "You both should have it."

"Yes." Vladimir replied. He reached out in front of him and grabbed a spot in the air with his thumb and forefinger. Then he expanded them. He then used both hands to explode the virtual view. "Are you two seeing this?"

"Yes."

"I got it."

"I see a Progress here, but no Soyuz spacecraft. All three of them have gone. S's message was right." Vladimir looked at his connectivity bar for his suit's visor—he had a strong connection to the Dorman satellite network. He thought about sending a message to Dorman but decided to wait until they had taken the station and activated the first launch. "Amazing, gentlemen. Had we attempted to take our payload here around the world in aircraft, trains, rockets, or boats we would have been caught. The only way to do this was to do it quickly, abruptly, and from on high where they could not touch us."

"While I agree this is the best approach I can think of, V, we're not across the goal line just yet," Michael responded. "There's still a lot of work to be done."

"Americans and your football references," Vladimir said. "To use the same. I see no goal-line defense before us."

"Let's hope not," Jeb added. "Twenty-five thousand meters and closing."

Michael sat prepared but waiting. He watched the crosshairs of the sighting system for the capture mechanism and the range-to-target number continuously. The numbers dropped rapidly from twenty-five thousand meters to twenty, then fifteen, then ten. Finally, they were in sighting range.

"Five thousand meters to target! Capture system acquisition sensors activated," Michael said.

"Prepare for braking burn," Jeb said. "In five, four, three, two, one, burn!"

The retro thrusters on the nose of the rocket fired in unison to reduce the relative velocity between the two spacecraft. They continued for a little more than ten seconds. The continuous burn stopped, leading to short correction burns from each of the thrusters about the ship. Each new correction took feedback from the optical sensor on the telescope to keep the ISS in the central pixel of the camera's crosshairs.

"One thousand meters to target closing at fifty meters per second," Jebidiah said.

"Too fast," Vladimir said. "There will be another burn soon."

Just as Vladimir had said that, the computer popped up a warning message for all of them in their virtual views that a braking burn was firing in ten seconds. There was a countdown. Jeb counted out loud with it.

"...three, two, one, burn."

This burn was much shorter and there were fewer retro thruster correction burns to follow. The three of them sat anxiously as the much larger space station loomed over them. Then the large window of the DSIHM glinted at them in the sunlight. The crosshairs locked onto the image and several short burns from the retro-rocket thrusters fired.

"Target point acquired!" Michael said excitedly.

"Range to target three hundred meters and closing at ten meters per second," Jebidiah said. "Two ninety, two eighty, two seventy..."

"Prepare for full stop burn at fifty," Vladimir reminded them. "Ms. Stinson really did her homework."

"So far," Michael added.

"Two hundred, one ninety..."

"M, target lock yet?"

"Negative, V. Still too much position jitter."

"One thirty, one twenty, one ten..."

Another alert message appeared in their visors flashing red, telling them to prepare for a braking burn. Then at one hundred meters to target the software fired the retro thrusters for a seven-second burn, completely stopping the Vyrezka from closing the gap between them and the ISS.

"Showing fifty meters to target. Relative velocity negligible," Jebidiah announced.

"Target point acquired and locked, V. Sending the activation signal to the receiver mechanism now." Michael activated a transmit icon that would send a ping to the DSIHM. Inside the exterior hull of the hotel was a battery powered electromagnet and a wireless receiver. Once the receiver detected the transmit signal from the Vyrezka, it powered up the electromagnet.

"Magnet capture armed. Preparing to fire harpoon," Michael said. "In three, two, one, firing."

Michael depressed the trigger of the armed capture system. When he did, the interior of the Vyrezka capsule vibrated enough that he could feel it through his chair, through his suit, and to his teeth. There was a very loud *whoosh* that sounded like a rocket launching right next to them. That was because it was a missile of sorts that had been launched.

Beneath the cylinder was a pressurized air tank. Within the cylinder was a harpoon system. The overpressure of the tank was released into the cylinder, propelling the harpoon out of the cylinder through the plastic diaphragm at the apex of the Vyrezka capsule. The harpoon flew across the fifty meters between them in seconds, spooling out polymer cable behind it as it closed the distance. The cable had been tested to withstand thousands of metric tons worth of force. The harpoon was rapidly pulled to the electromagnet behind the bulkhead point just above the bay window of the hotel module until the barbed arrowhead pierced the outer layer and then was stopped by a solid plate of high-density polyethylene and Kevlar between the magnet and the harpoon's tip.

The impact of the harpoon deployed barbs to extend forward and lock into place behind the exterior composite bulkhead. That spot had been designed to accept the harpoon. Once the harpoon barbs extended, the battery-powered microcontroller triggered a release valve on the end of a small container. Once the end of the container was exposed to the vacuum of space, the contents were literally sucked from within it. The adhesive mixture in the container immediately expanded rapidly filling the gaps and holes around the harpoon and then started to cure. Within minutes the expanded gel epoxy would harden, sealing any leaks that might have been formed on impact.

"It's a hit!" Michael cheered. "Harpoon is locked in place!"

"Great shot!" Vladimir cheered with him. "Start the reel-in sequence."

"Reeling us in." Michael initiated the sequence and the soft whine and vibration from an electric motor slowly starting to turn began. The cable pulled taught and then there was a slight acceleration Michael noticed as the stuffed animal on the string stretched toward him and held tight.

"Okay, gentlemen, it is time to get to work." Vladimir unstrapped his harness and rose from his seat. "You all know what to do. Just like we practiced."

CHAPTER 47

〰

Low Earth Orbit
International Space Station
Tuesday
2:48 A.M. Eastern Time

IT HAD TAKEN THE HARPOON REEL ABOUT TEN MINUTES TO close the fifty-meter gap between the ISS and the Vyrezka. Once they closed to within ten meters the motor was stopped and the three of them were ready to open the Vyrezka to space. Jebidiah immediately set forth connecting backup safety lines from hardpoints on the capsule to hardpoints on the hotel module that had been designed for just such an occasion. The ISS was dynamic and the entire structure wiggled and wobbled and moved like a porpoise through space. Rather than building, designing, testing, and flying an expensive docking rig they had decided long ago just to tether down like a boat on a dock. And there they were. The Vyrezka was tied down just so.

Jebidiah's next job was to start placing explosive charges at specific points about the DSIHM's airlock door. He gathered his pack and was ready to move on to his next task while Michael and Vladimir would start on the release mechanism.

"The tether is secure. We're clear to egress to the entrance."

"Copy, J." Michael slid slowly across the tether under the power of the suit jets. The suits had cold gas thrusters built in that were controlled via the virtual view in the visors. An icon of the astronaut showing pitch, roll, and yaw angles as well as velocity and range to objects was displayed in the lower right-hand corner of their view. Using the mental mouse they could control their trajectory and position orientation.

He landed against the hull with a muted thud as his boots made contact with the ceramic composite hull just above the large three-meter-diameter hotel window. He quickly attached another tether to a handhold to keep him in place. Michael had the cold realization that his maneuvering in space was indeed much more uncontrollable as there was no water viscosity to slow his movements and reaction forces. But the suit's software helped with that. "Removing outer casing cover and setting the hull-clamp."

"Good, M." Jebidiah said while doing his best not to be distracted by the incredible view of the Earth as they passed over the Pacific Ocean. It was dark, but there were still lights to be seen. "We have to be careful here, just like in the training, or we can explosively decompress the chamber."

"Doesn't matter, other than debris hitting the Vyrezka. We don't need that really," Michael said. "Looks like the ISS is completely abandoned anyway."

"Is that a good thing or a bad thing?" Vladimir sounded sincere as he tethered himself beside his companions. "It is boring, comrade."

"I like boring," Michael said.

"Yes, we've had this conversation," Vladimir replied. "You like boring."

"Initiating impact driver now," Michael said, ignoring the comment. After removing several socket head cap bolts around a rectangular composite panel covered in multilayered insulation material, he handed it to Vladimir. Looking under that panel revealed an internal aluminum panel cover. Two more bolts and it was removed. This time instead of handing it off he simply chucked it overboard.

"How long you think that'll orbit till it burns up on reentry?" Michael asked.

"My guess would be months, maybe a couple of years?"

The opening in the interior of the hull revealed a sliding panel over a metallic box. It had been heavy on Earth and underwater, but in space that wasn't an issue. In fact, the device was actually bolted and epoxied in place and it would take a significant amount of effort to remove it. Fortunately, removing it wasn't part of the plan. Michael slid the cover back revealing two toggles and one red light pushbutton, like an old-school video game cabinet. The device was approximately eight centimeters thick and twenty centimeters on a side. There was also a metal tubular U-shaped handle that protruded from the middle of it large enough to get a space-suit gauntlet around. It was painted black and yellow and had a spring-loaded space-rated safety pin in it. He didn't recall the pin from the training. He inspected it more closely and realized that it must have been added as a man-rating process for the aerospace structure. Michael thought that was funny considering that somebody during the process was certainly paid to look the other way on the DSIHM but this safety procedure made it through the design. Michael twisted the pin to break the tie-down, or stake as it was called in aerospace jargon, and then pulled the pin.

"V, this is a three-handed job unlike the training," he said.

"Let me...ah, yes. I got it. Hold the pin." Vladimir pulled the lever.

"Firing." Michael flipped both toggles and then hit the red pushbutton. Four spring-loaded pitons fired simultaneously inward into the handle mechanism, releasing the box from the ceramic and aluminum layers of the DSIHM's airlock door, generating a slight vibration in the structure he could feel through his tether. "J, ready to blow the hatch mechanisms."

"Copy," Jeb replied. He'd already placed the charges in the predetermined critical points along the periphery of the DSIHM airlock door and was ready. The door was almost two meters in diameter and had been designed for egress and ingress of Orlan space suits. While it had never been tested by astronauts yet, it had been designed to be a functioning airlock. If it explosively decompressed it could kill them instantly from impact. If it missed them and hit the capsule it could still be bad for them. "Stand clear. Three, two, one."

There was no noise like on Earth. There were no air bubbles under the water racing to the surface. It was quiet. There was only a short, bright, red flash and then a shudder through the DSIHM structure they could feel through their handholds.

The large circular airlock door wasn't flung away at dangerous decompressive explosive velocities. Instead, the door floated gently out of position and looked like a can of soup with the lid pulled up and still attached to a sliver of the can on one side.

"It didn't clear it completely," Vladimir said.

"I'll take care of it. You go help J," Michael told him.

"Affirmative." Vladimir pushed away toward the Vyrezka as Michael jetted his suit toward the now loosely connected window.

Michael inspected the exterior airlock door and noted that what was keeping it connected was electrical wiring. He carefully removed the oversized snips from his left sleeve and cut the wires one after the other until the door was free. He gave it a shove away from the module and it drifted slowly away from them.

"That one is bigger. I doubt it stays in orbit as long," he joked.

"Did you get it, comrade?"

"Exterior door is detached and gone."

"Okay, then, the next step, pull the interior hatch to the DSIHM airlock and enter the DSIHM," Jeb said.

"I hope S depressurized the hotel like he was supposed to," Vladimir added.

Michael made his way into the airlock to the interior door that would lead into the hotel interior. If it was pressurized it would be stuck and they wouldn't be able to open it simply due to overpressure against it. It would be like trying to open a car door under water.

"Okay in three, two, one!" Michael gave the handle on the interior door a twist and then pushed against it with his jets in the forward position. M pushed until he felt it give and then the hatch let loose, releasing the door. Once the hatch was pushed clear he hit his thrusters and entered feetfirst, waiting for his boots to make contact with the bulkhead nearest him. He looked about quickly, making certain that nobody was hiding there waiting to jump on him. There wasn't. He tethered off to the main entrance hatch.

"Interior breached. Feel free to enter and then we can seal off the outer hatch and use this room as our airlock," Michael said.

"Got it." Vladimir thrusted into the hotel near him slowly. "Let's seal it off and power it up. Then it's through the BEAM to Node 3."

"Yes, and then let's sweep the ISS to make sure there are no surprises. I don't want any surprises," Michael said. "J, while we secure the platform, you start installing the launcher and secure the warheads to the DSIHM bulkheads."

"Copy that," Jeb replied. "Time to message K to hit the restart sequences from the ground."

> K,
>
> *Start the startup sequences for the launcher and begin the restart of the platform systems.*
>
> *J*

> J,
>
> *Roger that, J. Starting the launcher startup sequences. Let me know once they are installed on the DSIHM exterior.*
>
> *K*

"As soon as we get pressure in here, we can take the hill," Michael said.

CHAPTER 48

〜

Low Earth Orbit
10,000 Kilometers Ahead of the International Space Station
Tuesday
3:48 A.M. Eastern Time

"SOYUZ MS-51 HAS COMPLETED BRAKING BURN PACKAGE AND HAS begun to deorbit. Reentry blackout projected in two hours and thirteen minutes. Soyuz MS-52 has completed braking burn and has begun to deorbit. Reentry calculations underway." The Russian Roscosmos version of the NASA CAPCOM—Capsule Communicator—spoke with Commander Vasiliy Nolvany. Allison sat quietly and listened, doing her best not to think about the body of her dead friend in the seat on the other side of Nolvany. "Preparing burn numbers for you now, MS-53."

Nolvany muted the communications channel to Earth and did his best to turn his head toward Major Simms. Allison was waiting for this moment and had already prepared what she would say. Had Nolvany been American she'd have said something about wild horses.

"Are you sure you are up for this, Major?" Nolvany asked her. "Once we make the choice, we must commit to our actions. We are likely to be arrested if we make home."

"Goddamned right I am, Vasiliy. We might be the only thing standing between the Earth and a nuclear war," Allison assured him. "I am up for this."

"Very good. I, too, am up for this." Nolvany held up the small pistol-gripped metal rod that the commander of Soyuz capsules used to touch controls out of reach and then depressed a sequence of circuit breakers. "There. Mission Control cannot fly us from the ground now. We are in complete control of the spacecraft."

"I see." Allison nodded her approval as Vasiliy toggled the microphone back to the open communication channel.

"Mission Control, this is Soyuz MS-53. Belay the deorbit burn calculations and please prepare a package for returning to the ISS."

"Uh, could you repeat that, 53? It sounded like you said you were going to return to the ISS."

"Affirmative, Control. MS-53 is returning to the ISS either with or without your help. We would prefer to do so with help," Nolvany said. "Standby, Commander."

There had been several minutes of heated conversation in Russian, but finally Nolvany had told them he would simply shut off the radio if they were not going to be of any help. Several minutes after that, a new voice had taken over as their CAP-COM—General of the Army Pyotr Ustimenko.

"Major Nolvany, Major Simms, I am General Pyotr Ustimenko. I will be directing you from now on. I want you to know that while you are in a direct violation of orders to return home, what you are doing is damned courageous. I have instructed Roscosmos to cooperate with your plans whatever they might be. Maybe we can help to minimize what is about to follow." When the new CAPCOM spoke, Vasiliy seemed to stiffen to an attention posture. He muted the internal mics and turned with a very serious and all-business look on his face.

"Army General Ustimenko. Would be equivalent of your Joint Chiefs," he explained.

"I understand," Allison replied. Vasiliy unmuted the internal microphones.

"It is unclear how many of them there are," the general continued. "They seem very adept and clever. They are well connected. It is likely that Colonel Lytokov will be with them. He and his cohort criminals have already killed an entire squad of Russian National Space Force soldiers when they attacked and stole these warheads. They are deadly killers—make no mistake about what you are volunteering to do. Do the two of you understand this?"

"Yes, sir!" Nolvany almost shouted.

"Major Simms... we have a communication channel open to your superior. I will wait a moment for them. General Hastings, are you there?"

"Yes, General Ustimenko. Thank you," the Chief of the United States Space Force replied. This time it was Allison who stiffened in her seat. "Major Simms, do you hear me?"

"Yes, ma'am!" Allison wasn't certain if she had responded more loudly than Vasiliy.

"Major Simms, as General Ustimenko has just briefed you, whoever these criminals are along with Colonel Lytokov, they are deadly, vicious, and have no concern for life, it appears. If you make this decision, you will be going into this with no hope of backup and it is likely a one-way trip. Do you understand this?"

"Yes, ma'am."

"Then why would you do this?"

"Because it is my job, ma'am," Allison said. There wasn't even a pause long enough to take a breath before the general responded.

"Your job, soldier, was to follow orders and return home."

"With all due respect, General, I have family, friends, and billions of people I don't know down there that are helpless to do anything to stop this. Major Nolvany and I might be able to do something. Anything. We have both sworn oaths to protect our country and we think this is what we must do to uphold those oaths." Allison wasn't certain how her speech would go over. History was filled with officers who thought they were doing right by disobeying orders but who finally ended up in prison or on the firing squad. Allison didn't like either of those options.

"Since we realize there is nothing we can do to turn you around, both General Ustimenko and I agree. If you are going to do this, then we want you to have the best opportunity to succeed. So inventory your assets for us as well as give us a rundown of your current plan."

"Well, ma'am, we have three short-barrel triple-barrel shotguns that we took from each of the Soyuz capsules. We have three Russian sidearms with three full magazines each. Nolvany and I are trying to figure out how to fire them in our suits, but have had no luck as of yet. Any help on that from the engineers down there would be helpful. And, ma'am, it would be helpful to know more about their plans."

"We are reaching out to Roscosmos, NASA, and Space Force engineers now. Hopefully, we will hear from them soon."

"Allow me a moment, General Hastings..."

"By all means..."

"As the Americans have worked out what they believe is the plan of these criminals, we think we might add some insight here. We think this is based on an old Soviet-era study of using an orbital platform for nuclear weapons. The platform would implement Fractional Orbital Bombardments. The idea is simply as stated. Use an orbital platform like the old Almatz systems with reentry vehicles aboard. When the platform is in the right location in orbit above a target, the reentry vehicle is deorbited to target. Colonel Lytokov most certainly has studied this report. It is historical and long been discarded for treaty purposes. That said, the ISS could function as such a launch platform for the RVs. The American analyst team believes this is their plan based on intelligence gathered so far. Our intelligence agrees. These enemies of the state, of the world, plan to detonate the warheads over multiple locations to create a global EMP blackout. To what purposes we do not know."

"Are they religious or political extremists? Or is this something else, sirs?" Nolvany asked. "Have they attempted to make any contact?"

"There has been no attempt of any contact or negotiations," General Hastings added.

"Honestly, Major Nolvany, we simply do not know their motivation," Ustimenko said.

"Sir, is there any estimate on how long it will take them to launch from the ISS?" Allison asked.

"No, Major Simms. Everything we have are guesses only. A week ago, nobody would have even thought this possible."

"Our team does have some thoughts on that," General Hastings added. "One of our rocket scientists has drawn up a rough sketch of what such a system would look like and she believes that, if it is prebuilt, they might be able to install it in less than a day. NASA EVA timeline planners agree with this. It might take longer. This has been such a surprise so far, we put nothing past them and their capabilities."

"Then we must hurry!" Nolvany said.

"Yes. We will be listening, majors, but we will hand you back to CAPCOM so you can speak with engineers."

"Understood, sir."

"Good luck."

CHAPTER 49

༺༻

Low Earth Orbit
International Space Station
Tuesday
6:55 A.M. Eastern Time

"MAJOR SIMMS? ALLISON? ARE YOU AWAKE?" NOLVANY YAWNED as his watch beeped. He stopped the alarm and then checked their orbit status. They had completed a Hohmann transfer to a slightly higher orbit than the ISS and had rephased back almost directly over them. All of that had taken several hours. Since the computer could handle it, the two of them had decided to get some sleep.

"Are we there yet?" Allison groaned awake.

"Yes. See for yourself."

Allison squinted and blinked a few times to clear her vision from the sleep, and then focused on the monitor Vasiliy was pointing to. The Earth was bright beneath them.

"Do you think they have seen us, Major?" Nolvany pointed at the ISS beneath them several kilometers through the periscope view. "Perhaps they have not looked up?"

"I hope they believe we have left them alone and are not coming back. Maybe they're on a sleep cycle," Allison said. She reached into a pouch on her left arm and withdrew an energy bar. "We should probably eat."

"Yes, we probably should," Nolvany agreed and did the same. "Did we do a braking burn?"

"According to the computer we have. The lidar shows us at three thousand four hundred thirty-one meters from the ISS with negligible relative velocity."

"Three and a half kilometers is a long way to go," Allison said more as a thought than a negative view of their plan.

"Yes. Nobody has ever done an EVA that far away from a platform. We will break the records by a very long way."

They watched through the periscope view quietly for a few moments as they finished eating, both of them considering what they had to do next. The plan was mostly suicidal and reminded Allison of those movies where people were offered a chance to get out of prison to go on extremely dangerous and low probability of success missions in order to achieve a pardon. "Suicide mission" was always the term used to describe them. Allison took a final swig of water and then pulled out the pack of zip ties from a stowage bin. She took the odd-looking shotgun she had placed beside her and started working the largest zip tie through the trigger guard and then connected the tie to itself. She practiced holding the short triple-barrel pistol-looking weapon with her right hand and making the motion of pulling the zip-tie loop around the trigger of the shotgun with her left. "This will be tricky."

"Yes. But doable," Nolvany agreed. "If we survive this, I will design a weapon for space suits."

"I hear you." Allison looked out the window down at Earth. The ISS was glinting brightly beneath them. "While I know the 'official' word is there are no more weapons in space, I'm glad the Russians still have these survival kits."

"Me too." Nolvany taped another one of the triple barrels to his left forearm. "These are newer versions. You should see the older ones."

"Will the gun blast toss us on unwanted angular spins?" she thought out loud. "Hmm."

"Let's do the math then, Major. Let's assume that the weapon has a muzzle velocity of say five hundred meters per second, the gun weighs about four kilograms and if it were a bullet, we could guess a standard bullet weighs about five to twenty grams. The space suit weighs about a hundred kilograms and let's assume the astronaut weighs seventy kilograms. Then the weight of the gun, astronaut, and space suit is about a hundred seventy-three kilograms. Let's say one-seventy for ease of math. Given the muzzle velocity of five hundred meters per second, the bullet will have a momentum of, let's say, twenty grams times five hundred meters per second, which is 0.02 kilograms times five hundred meters per second, which is exactly one Newton second."

"So not much thrust," Allison said. "You're pretty good at math. Okay, I see where you are going with this. So, in order to determine the velocity imparted to the astronaut plus suit plus gun mass, we just simply can assume all the momentum is transferred. So, we divide that momentum of one Newton second by the total astronaut mass, which is one Newton per second divided by a hundred and seventy kilograms. That gives us, um, about 0.006 meters per second or six millimeters per second. Sound right to you?" Allison asked.

"Yes. That is, let me think a moment, two hundred twenty-thousandths of a kilometer per hour. You won't even notice it when you fire the weapon unless you are really extended and there is an angular momentum imparted, but I suspect that is extremely small."

"Yeah. I get it," she said. "Never really thought about before, but movies get it so wrong."

"Yes. Even Russian movies get it wrong." He started attaching the triple barrel to his arm with tape.

Allison watched how Nolvany attached the weapon and then did the same to her right arm with the barrels sticking out just beyond her glove fingertips. She taped it in a way that she could get to the safety mechanism and the zip tie. Then he handed her another weapon.

"Here, put one of these in your pouch. Zip-tie the trigger."

"Thanks." She took the smaller Makarov semiautomatic pistol and thought about how she could use it. First, she zip tied the trigger. Following that, she wasn't sure what to do.

"Put that in your pouch. Use it second." Then he handed her one of the survival knives from the one of the survival kits. "Use this third."

"Hope we don't get to that point."

"Major, have you ever been in combat?" Nolvany asked solemnly.

"No." Allison almost sounded sheepish. "I have been through training, though."

"Not the same. But I'm glad you have training." Nolvany frowned. Allison realized it wasn't a frown at her, but rather at what was to come. "Combat is not a place for philosophy or ideals. We are not police. These people, these criminals, they plan to kill us and maybe millions of people. We mean nothing to them and they will kill us instantly. Our only hope is to kill them as soon as we see them. Can you do this?"

Allison looked at her dead friend lying beside them and then back to Vasiliy. She thought about her father dying of lung cancer. She thought of her sister and her niece. Allison thought of all the people down there who might die. She could do this. She *could* and *would* do this.

"Like I said before, I'm good, Vasiliy." Allison placed the handgun in her pouch and unsnapped her restraints. "Now, let's get the fire extinguishers and do this shit."

CHAPTER 50

ରୁ

Low Earth Orbit
International Space Station
Tuesday
7:49 A.M. Eastern Time

VLADIMIR AND MICHAEL HAD WORKED ON THE INTERIOR OF THE
ISS for most of the night, getting power to the systems they needed
power to. The DSIHM came on line very quickly. With a few modifications to the door they had pulled, they managed to keep the
hotel pressurized. They had gotten power to the main Quest Airlock
module and could use it to lock in and out through the station as
they needed. Jebidiah had continued working in connection with
Keenan on Earth to set the launcher systems in place. Around five
in the morning he had locked through to take a nap. The three of
them had taken a three-hour sleep cycle and were starting to get
their day back on schedule. They had no idea how the Americans
or the Russians would respond, but one thing they did know is
that they would respond in some form. It might take them a day
or two or more, but they would respond. There was a race against
the clock right now and the three of them knew that.

"We have the life support systems now functioning and the
main airlock. Lighting works in Node 3 and in the Russian wing."
Vladimir ticked through his list of things to do. "J, you should
have full power to the interfaces on the DSIHM exterior."

"Yeah, I saw that come on in the virtual dashboard. I had hooked the command line in before the sleep cycle." Jebidiah pulled the space suit in place and then adjusted the gloves. The Dorman suits were so much easier to get in and out of than the Orlan suits that hung in his way. He did a pressure check and his suit read that it was sealed. The three-dimensional icon in his virtual view showed the suit was fully functional and ready to go.

"You good?" Vladimir tapped at his helmet visor and looked in at him.

"Good." Jeb gave him a thumbs-up and proceeded through the airlock door into the outer lock. "Time to go to work."

"Good. Let me know if you need help," Vladimir said. "But I have to calculate and adjust our orbit for the first target. Michael will be ready to help you soon once we finish pulling the power line from the Service Module to the DSIHM."

"Is the propulsion module running yet?"

"Fortunately for us, they are Russian made." Vladimir grinned. "They still work."

"Right."

✧   ✧   ✧

"V, that's two of the warheads bolted into place. Four to go. The other four are free-floating in the capsule waiting to be connected. I'm going to take a break from loading the warheads and check in with K on the communications and software uplink," Jebidiah said on their open channel. He looked at the clock in his head. He'd been at it for almost two hours nonstop. At this rate it would take a full day to get all of the warheads in place. He hoped it would go faster once Michael and Vladimir came out to help.

"Copy that, J. We are almost in control of the Service Module systems and will be getting that wired to the DSIHM for uplink soon."

"How soon do you think you'll have that up?"

"Five minutes, so smoke 'em if you've got 'em, as the Americans say."

"Nobody says that," Michael added.

"Okay, I'll wait five and then I'll connect with K." Jebidiah looked down at the Earth underneath him. "I haven't had a chance to enjoy the view yet anyway."

Jebidiah found a spot on the nadir-facing side of the DSIHM

and relaxed for a moment. He tethered to a handhold only a meter or so from where the next warhead would be mounted. Davidson and Schwab and the rest of the team had done an amazing job designing and developing the hotel slash EMP storage capacitor slash nuclear reentry vehicle launch pad. There were panels on the nadir side of it that, once pulled, were a perfect match interface for the glide-body structure Sing and Stinson had designed. Each one snapped into place with six breakaway bolts and two umbilicals. The two wired connections were for power for the ignition sequence and for computer connectivity up until launch. The target location for each glide body could be updated right up until ignition of the deorbit rocket motors.

"What a view," Jeb said out loud. "You guys really should get out here and see this."

✧   ✧   ✧

"Michael, my friend, how is the nausea?" Vladimir asked as he pulled himself into the Russian Service Module. Michael had started getting sick and was forced to use the motion sickness app in the Dorman glasses to overcome it.

"V, you know better than to use names."

"Who will hear us up here?" Vladimir laughed. "We are quite alone, comrade!"

"The walls might have ears."

"Very well, then. But I say it doesn't matter. They know who I am by now," Vladimir said. "I might even be the world's most wanted."

"You can be certain of that," Michael said. "But I prefer anonymity."

"Yes, and boring, as I recall." Vladimir laughed. Then he gave him the large umbilical they had hardwired into the Service Module dashboard panel and wrapped a service loop of the three-centimeter-thick cable around one of the handhold bars. "Can you spool this to the hotel main power block panel?"

"Got it." Michael gathered the cable in front of him and started rolling out line and pushing the spool forward as it floated in front of him. "Once you get it there you know what to do. Then we need to give J a third hand."

"Got it, V." Michael pushed at the wire spool and it unwound into the FGB.

✧   ✧   ✧

"K, do you have the command data feed showing active?" Jebidiah asked over the encrypted audio line he had connected through the ISS satellite uplink. Keenan answered directly from his computer desk in his island refuge.

"Yeah, J. I have it. If you'll plug one of the specials in, I should be able to shake hands with it."

"We're probably still a couple hours away from that. M and V have some more work to do inside before they can get out here with me. How are we looking on our timeline?" Jebidiah did a hand-over-hand walk using the exterior handholds on the DSIHM. Once he reached the umbilical command line plugged into the panel built into the hotel structure, he looked at the readout panel. "K, the panel is showing you are still routing through the Vyrezka. Are you ready to shift to the ISS feed yet?"

"I am, but what I'm showing is that you are not," Keenan replied.

"Hold on a minute," Jebidiah said and toggled the channel over to the Vyrezka team channel. "M, I need that power bus line from the Service Module connected before K and I can move forward. You have an ETA on that?"

"Uh, yeah, I just pulled the line through the BEAM and entering the DSIHM now. Give me a minute and I'll get you the power feed."

"Okay. Thanks." Jebidiah toggled the channel back to Keenan. "M is doing that now. Any minute now."

Suddenly the readout panel showed data traffic and there was a high-bandwidth connection. The computers of the Russian Service Module were now being routed through the DSIHM system and it wouldn't take Keenan even seconds to overwrite and control them. Especially since he had already uploaded hidden code in the flight software through their Huntsville connection months prior.

"Got it, J! Hold on...and...BINGO! The ISS is online and ours." Keenan cheered. "V should be able to control the propulsion modules now."

"Good news. I'll pass that a—" Jebidiah stopped midsentence as a strange shiny field of what looked like fireflies sparkled around him in the glinting sunlight. He waved his right glove through the cloud of particles but wasn't sure what to make of them.

"J, what's going on?"

"Hold on...there's something we...son of a bitch!" The panel next to him suddenly had several holes appear in it and some of the MLI blanket material sprayed upward as if it had been hit by a micrometeorite. Something hit the torso of his suit hard but didn't penetrate the armor. Jeb turned to look behind him.

✧   ✧   ✧

"Shit! I think I missed!" Allison said over the radio link between her and Nolvany's suits.

She reacquired her handhold on the fire extinguisher and adjusted her course. Then she let a long spray from one of them go directly at the man in the space suit on the back of the hotel module. The cloud dispersed around him in a shiny spray of ice particles and skittered about like fireflies until they boiled away to nothing. Nolvany fired his extinguisher, speeding him in the direction of the man even faster. Just as he hit feetfirst, he fired the shotgun taped to his wrist, hitting the man square in the chest. The shotgun pellets ricocheted off of the tan-colored breastplate in all directions.

"Their suits are bulletproof armor!" Nolvany shouted. "You must shoot at soft spots, Major! Maybe the legs!"

Allison had slowed her descent to the ISS to a near stop and tried to take aim. Nolvany had become entangled and twisted up with the other astronaut and they were spiraling in a whirling ball of arms and legs and helmets across the top of the DSIHM until they broke free from the module, drifted a few tens of meters of open space, and then slammed hard into one of the Russian solar panel arrays. Vasiliy didn't bother to scramble for a handhold. Instead, he fired the extinguisher, pushing him away from the other astronaut, hoping to given him room to target the man again. He fired one of his arm guns but must have missed or hit the man's armored sections. Allison wasn't sure where the shot went. She did her best to aim for a clear shot at the enemy astronaut, but they were moving too erratically relative to her motion for her to target him. Once it looked like Vasiliy was free and clear, unexpectedly, the other man's suit fired multiple jets, stabilizing him almost instantly. That was something that neither the NASA nor the Russian suits couldn't do. He reached to his chest and pulled a device that appeared to be magnetically stuck there. The device looked almost like a giant water pistol with a steel barrel, and it could only be one thing—a firearm designed for space combat in a space suit.

"Vasiliy, look out! He's got a gun!" Allison aimed for his head and let the trigger to her shotgun go. She hit the man with multiple pellets and some solar panel surface material shattered and scattered behind him. The motion the gun imparted to her was minimal and as their calculations had suggested were basically undetectable. But the flailing about, trying to get a shot, imparted unusual angular rotations to her that she had to dampen out with the fire extinguisher. While her shot had hit home, they had yet to penetrate the man's space suit and he continued to draw his bead on Major Vasiliy Nolvany. Nolvany fired his left gun again as he jetted sideways with respect to the man. Then a bright green laser dot hit dead center of Nolvany's chest and the man fired his odd-looking weapon. Suddenly, Vasiliy's suit decompressed and bright red spheroids of blood boiled out from holes in the front and back of his suit, almost fluorescing as the sunlight hit them. The air from within the suit sprayed out from both holes until his oxygen supply was drained.

"No!" Allison shouted. "Nolvany!"

"Ugh...flare..." were his last words.

Allison knew exactly what he was telling her. She fired her extinguisher, putting her on a path toward the astronaut assailant, and took aim with the third barrel of the shotgun. The man turned to face her, bringing his laser sight toward her. It panned across her helmet briefly but not before she had taken aim and pulled the trigger of the shotgun.

The third barrel had been loaded with a potassium perchlorate flare just in case they were going to have to burn through something on the station. They had been in the survival kit because, well, flares are in survival kits. There had been many cases in the past where Soyuz crews had landed in the wilderness and had to be found. Back then, flares came in handy. Then there had been those few years where the politicians had managed to keep even the Russians from bringing the weapons to space. But a few years following that decision there was a Soyuz mission that had been lost for days and the Russians had rethought the silly American politics and put the weapons back in the capsules. At the moment, Allison was very glad they had and was rethinking her politics on the subject as well.

Bright white and slightly red potassium perchlorate fire stuck to the faceplate of the man's helmet when it hit. The stellar-hot fire melted through it and straight into the man's face as his suit ruptured and decompressed. Bright orange flames briefly flared within the suit as the oxygen was burned up. If the flare hadn't killed him, and the exploding oxygen-rich fire inside the suit hadn't killed him, then he would most certainly be dead from exposure to space vacuum before long. The man was dead. Nolvany was dead.

They were both dead. There was nothing she could do for either of them. And Allison suspected the assailant had somehow communicated with his friends that she was out there. She quickly fired her extinguisher toward Nolvany and grabbed his fire extinguishers. She snapped them to her torso harness and let them go. Then she dug through his pouch and grabbed the pistol he had placed there. She didn't have time to untape the shotguns on his arms. She hated leaving him, but she also knew she didn't have much time. She started to jet away but then had a thought.

She let a spray go on her extinguisher to push her toward the assailant. There he was, floating dead. More than half of his face was gone. It was a gruesome, sickening, smoldering sight. Combat was dreadful, as Nolvany had warned her. The flare was still giving off a faint glow deep inside the boiling and freezing blood inside his helmet and inside his skull. She had to look away, it was so grotesque. She did her best not to let herself gag in the suit. That would be bad. She traced her hands over him to his hand and looked at the weapon that he still clutched tightly. She examined how it worked and decided she could use it.

Allison pried the space-suit combat gun from his grip, realizing it was magnetically held there. When it was free of the magnetic attraction it was easy to manage and clearly the trigger mechanism had been designed for space-suit gloves. She wondered if this was what Nolvany might have come up with had he been the designer. With a quick kick off of the solar panel nearest her and a few short blasts from her last full extinguisher, she jetted for the far end of the truss structure near the P6 Integrated Truss Structure on the port side, uncertain of what she should do next. But she needed a moment to gather her wits and develop a plan. She checked the suit vital sign monitor, which told her that her heart rate was at 170 beats per minute and her blood pressure was high.

"No shit." She whispered to herself as if someone might overhear her. She tried to slow her breathing and calm herself. "Damn it! Nolvany. What do I need to do?"

She first mentally checked her inventory. Her last remaining extinguisher was probably three quarters full at this point. She had Nolvany's two extinguishers. She had two pistols and the new gun she had taken. Her triple barrel was empty and she didn't think she could untape it, reload it, and tape it back during the EVA. She had enough air to stay in the suit for days, but that would truly suck. She really really needed a plan.

Allison looked around the ISS from her vantage point, trying to get an idea as to what she could do. She had taken out one of the assailants, but at the huge cost of Nolvany. She could always tuck her tail and run back to the Soyuz that was parked three and half kilometers away. She still had enough extinguisher to make the nearly thirty-minute trip.

Suddenly, one of the propulsion thrusters on the Russian segment fired and that made her decision for her. If she stayed on the ISS now, and they continued to fire off the thrusters adjusting the orbit, she likely wouldn't be able to make it back to the Soyuz depending on what type of orbit correction burns they were making. She also knew that she couldn't just let them fire off those nukes. Then a glint of light off the tethered space capsule flashed across her line of sight, flash-blinding her briefly. That gave her an idea. She probably had minutes at best before it would be too late, assuming they were planning other burns. And she probably had less than ten minutes before some of the assailant astronaut's pals could cycle through the airlock to come out to her. If she hurried, she might get lucky.

Allison aimed herself at the capsule and fired one of the fire extinguishers in the opposite direction and held on for a bit longer than she probably should have. She gained in speed, zooming quickly toward the end of the BEAM and DSIHM and the tethered vessel. She hit a braking thrust in front of her, saturating her vision briefly from the glare off the ice particles like bright headlights in a fog bank, as she passed through the cloud. Then the capsule rushed up at her. She hit feetfirst and then sprawled belly forward into a face-plant. Her suit skittered and scraped across the surface until one of the tethered extinguishers became entangled and jerked the cable taut, yanking her to an abrupt stop.

Allison caught her breath for a brief moment and then set about untangling the extinguisher tether. She ended up having to disconnect the carabiner and feed it through a knot and then she was free. She reconnected it and worked her way around the capsule to the open hatch. Above the opening she could see a name painted in black that looked Russian.

"Vye-rezzzz-ka," she enunciated. "Hmm. Sounds Russian."

Once she popped her head in it was pretty obvious that the capsule design had been stolen from the Blue Origin spacecraft design, though with some unusual modifications. And floating there in front of her were four tethered charcoal gray, carbon-spun-fiber-composite reentry vehicle glide bodies.

"Jackpot!"

Allison examined them closer and knew they could only be one thing—nuclear warhead reentry vehicles. She quickly traced the lead to where it was connected and popped the release mechanism. It was a simple spring-loaded metal carabiner. She snapped that to her torso and then began feeding the mass of entangled cables and tethers snapped about her waist and torso through the hatch. As soon as she was clear of any structures that could ensnare her, she fired her extinguisher in a direction that would push her toward the Soyuz. She thought about the extra mass of the four reentry glide bodies and how much that would slow her down. She just had to overcome the inertia and get moving. It would be a longer trip back than it had been on the way here, but she would make it.

CHAPTER 51

૭૭

Low Earth Orbit
International Space Station
Tuesday
9:10 A.M. Eastern Time

"ASTRONAUTS!" VLADIMIR SHOUTED. "THEY DIDN'T ALL LEAVE!"

"I'm going, V." Michael dropped the faceshield on his helmet and pushed himself from the middle of the BEAM and DSIHM interface through Node 3 and across. "Meet me at the Quest Airlock to cycle me out."

"See you there!"

Michael turned himself feetfirst and floated through the hatch across Node 1 and into the Quest Airlock. He could see Vladimir coming toward him to his right. He reached down to his chest and pulled the firearm free of the magnetic holster and checked to make certain there was a round in the chamber. Then he flipped the safety off and stuck it back in its place.

"J, come in," Vladimir said over the comm channel. "J, do you copy?"

"Shit! J, do you copy?" Michael added. "They must've got him."

"The nukes!" Vladimir said.

"I'm going. Cycle this damned thing." Michael sealed the hatch behind him and waited for the pressure to release. They had been keeping the pressure at about a third of an atmosphere just

323

in case they needed to cycle through the lock quickly. Michael floated impatiently, changing the view on his screen to a wire-frame three-dimensional map with signal ping dots for all of their locations. Jebidiah was out there by the Russian solar panel array nearest the P1-ITS. He wasn't really moving.

"Clear," Vladimir said as the light went from red to green.

Michael opened the hatch and worked his way out, not worrying with a tether. Using the mental mouse, he drew a path directly to Jebidiah and hit the go button. The jets of his suit fired and took him in that direction. He then toggled on an overlay of the map that showed any other movement. The computer in the visors used the digital radio signals between their suits and the Vyrezka as a passive multipath radar and would detect motion. He didn't see anything but he did his best to keep his head on a swivel inside the suit. He put the rear-facing camera view in a small window on the upper left of his virtual view just in case somebody tried to get the drop on him.

The suit came to a stop right beside Jebidiah. It was a fairly gruesome sight. A couple of meters to his right and below there was a man in an Orlan space suit spinning slowly. Michael checked him out.

"J is dead, V. Looks like he took a flare to the face." Michael studied the other astronaut. "He got one of them before they got him, though. I'm synching my view. You got it?"

"Yes. Look closer at the man," Vladimir instructed him. Michael leaned in.

"D'you see?"

"Cosmonaut. Not astronaut," Vladimir said.

"You know him?"

"No, but I just did a facial recognition with the ISS crew. He is Major Vasiliy Nolvany. Cosmonaut," Vladimir said. "Check the Vyrezka."

"On it." Michael adjusted his course and jetted toward the space capsule. It still floated freely and tethered to the ISS from the original harpoon system and now multiple umbilicals that Jeb had connected over the last several hours. Michael shined his light through the open hatch of the Vyrezka and his heart sank along with his blood starting to boil. "Fuck!"

"What?"

"Nukes are gone."

"Check on the DSIHM launch plates."

Michael turned and looked back out the hatch across the ten meters are so to the DSIHM and there were two glide bodies attached and for all intents and purposes ready to be fired away at some target.

"Two nukes in place and they appear ready. Hold on, I'm punching in K on this." Michael worked through a couple of virtual menus and then brought Keenan into the loop. "K, are we ready on one and two?"

"What happened to J?" Keenan asked.

"He's dead. Are one and two ready?"

"They will be as soon as I finish the target location data. You need to give me that," K replied.

"In a minute." Michael thought. "Where did they come from?"

Michael pushed himself out of the hatch and floated out into the free space between the Vyrezka and the DSIHM. He looked down at the now night side of Earth and realized they would likely have seen them from that direction. He adjusted his position, doing a 180-degree roll, and stopped, looking straight up and away from the Earth and the ISS.

"What are you doing, M?"

"Wait."

"For what?"

"Just wait." Michael sat patiently as the Earth turned beneath him. A few minutes passed as they were approaching the morning side of the orbit. He continued to wait.

"What are we waiting for, M?"

"How long until daylight?"

"Seven more minutes."

"Then we wait seven more minutes," Michael told them. He continued to run through scenarios in his mind and had really only come up with one. If he were going to launch a raiding party on the ISS with little time to plan or few assets, he would come from a blind spot. He had a hunch about just where that might be. The sunlight peeked over the horizon and there it was.

"There!" he said excitedly. "There's a bright spot about three to five clicks straight up."

"Hold on, I will look," Vladimir said. A couple minutes went by before he responded again. "I see them. Probably a Soyuz."

"Well, that has to be where our nukes are," Michael said. "Do we get in the Vyrezka and go?"

"Not yet," Vladimir said. "I'm sending a note to M. We need some information. Come back inside. We will call their capsule."

✧   ✧   ✧

M,

We need information now. There are cosmonauts still up here. They have 4 of the specials. We have two ready to go. We need to get them back. Whatever data you can get for us on who is doing this will be helpful.

V

V,

Fuck. I'm on it. Fire one of them now if they are ready. As soon as you pass the primary target. Do not hesitate. Make that your first priority. Then make your second priority target number two. Then focus on getting the others back.

M

A,

Some cosmonauts have fucked up our plans! Tell me who it is now.

M

Ten minutes later...

M,

There were two. A cosmonaut, Major Vasiliy Nolvany. Your men got him. The other is astronaut USSF Major Allison Simms. She is from Melbourne, Florida. Her parents, sister Abigail, brother in-law Daniel, and a niece, Natalie, live there. I'm sending you her file now.

A.

V,

USSF Major Allison Simms. She is from Melbourne, Florida. Her parents, sister Abigail, brother in-law Daniel, and a niece, Natalie, live there. Her file is attached. Does M want his team sent to take them?

M

M,

No, I have a better idea. Thanks.

V

K,

I want a warning that a nuke is going to go off in Melbourne, Florida, to go viral across the internet. I want the highways completely jammed.

V

V,

Understood. Done.

K

CHAPTER 52

⁓

Low Earth Orbit
Approximately 3.5 Kilometers Above the International
  Space Station
Soyuz MS-53
Tuesday
9:58 A.M. Eastern Time

"YES GENERAL. FOUR OF THEM."

"That's great news Major. Sorry to hear about Major Nolvany," General Ustimenko replied. "That is a terrible loss."

"He died fighting and his last words saved my life, sir. He was a hero." Allison did her best to keep tears from forming at the corners of her eyes. There was already one dead friend in the spacecraft with her. And now she had to leave another behind. "I'm sorry I could not retrieve his body, General."

"You did what had to be done, Major Simms. Now we need to get you out of there."

"There are still two more nukes in play, sir. I saw them attached to the base of the Davidson-Schwab Inflatable Hotel Module," Allison said. "They looked like they were almost functional."

"You have done what you can do, Major. It is time to get you out of there." That time it was General Hastings. "Major, it is time to come home. That is an order. Roscosmos is working the deorbit burn package now. Stand by for further instructions."

"Yes, ma'am."

"Freedom Platform calling United States Space Force Major Allison Simms. Do you copy?" Allison was startled as the unexpected Russian voice broke over an open channel.

"Soyuz MS-53, Major Simms, this is the team currently in control of the spacecraft formerly known as the International Space Station. Do you copy?"

"Who is this?" General Ustimenko interjected. "Lytokov? Is that you?"

"Ah, General Ustimenko. I'd know that voice anywhere." Allison didn't respond. She wasn't certain what she should do.

"General. This call is not for you. I am calling for Major Allison Simms of the United States Space Force who is currently in the Soyuz capsule above us with four of our nuclear warheads."

"Those are property of the People of Russia," General Ustimenko said.

"Finder's keepers. General, stop wasting my time. Major Simms, I guess you are asking how we know who you are?" the voice said. "Well, we know a lot of things about you. Like, for example, the street address of your little niece, Natalie, the hospital your father is currently undergoing treatment, and we even have pictures of you and your high school sweetheart from your yearbook."

"What do you want?" Allison toggled her mic to the open channel.

"Ah! Major Simms. So nice to meet you at last. I suspect you met our comrade. It appears you must be the one who killed him. I don't hold that against you. You were just doing your job, as are we. Part of that job is unpleasant sometimes. And I hate the killing of a Russian hero cosmonaut like Major Nolvany. I regret that had to happen. I truly do. And Major, I do not wish to kill such an American hero either. But make no mistake, I will."

"What...do...you...WANT?!" Allison almost shouted this time.

"I think that should be obvious," the Russian replied. "You must bring us back the warheads."

"Why would I do that?"

"Because, Major Simms, if you do not, we will be forced to do something I do not wish to do."

"You monster!" Allison toggled the mic open. "You better not lay a hand on my family!"

"Major, Major, you misunderstand me. I will not 'lay a hand' on your family, as you say." The Russian paused dramatically. Allison was certain he was doing it purposefully, as if he were enjoying it in some sick twisted way. Allison was certain that the man was bat-shit crazy. "I will destroy all of that part of Florida if you do not comply. I am certain you noted that we had two warheads ready to go."

"Why?"

"Why? Because I need all six of my warheads in place now!" The Russian was agitated now. "You will comply or in seven orbits when we pass the appropriate launch window a major portion of Florida will be destroyed. And if you think you can warn them to leave in time you are incorrect. As we speak, the media and social media are becoming overwhelmed with an anonymous tip. There will be no evacuating anyone."

"You *are* a monster!" Allison said. "You could kill millions."

"As I said, part of the job. You have seven orbits, Major. There will be no debate or negotiations. Good day."

CHAPTER 53

❦

Low Earth Orbit
International Space Station
Tuesday
9:58 A.M. Eastern Time

"YOU HAVE SEVEN ORBITS, MAJOR. THERE WILL BE NO DEBATE OR negotiations. Good day." Vladimir flipped the comm panel switch, closing the channel.

"You actually think that will work, V?" Michael didn't seem very optimistic.

"Of course not. But it will keep her from reentering the atmosphere and letting the warheads burn up. Now, she will stay right where she is until the overly politicized military leaders, or Major Simms herself, decides to do something," Vladimir explained. "Either way, it buys us some time."

"Time for what, V?"

"You saw M's message. First priority is to launch to target number one and that is in two and a half orbits. Then target number two is a few orbits beyond that. I do not intend to waste one of our nukes on some hostage negotiation tactic, but they don't know that. So, we have a bit more than two hours to make certain that we are ready for the first launch. That is all done here and is now on K to finish the software loads," Vladimir said. "And..."

"I knew there was an 'and' in there." Michael smiled then said using his fingers to make air quotes. "What is the 'and'?"

"And, while he prepares for the first launch, we go get our nuclear warheads back!"

"How? We have to leave the Vyrezka attached to run the launch." Michael did his best to shrug while still in the suit.

"In case you didn't notice on the way in, there are two other vessels still attached to the ISS that can fly, my friend." Vladimir raised an eyebrow as if he were surprised Michael hadn't known this?

"What vessels?"

"Michael, just because the Progress modules are for cargo, that doesn't mean humans cannot fly in space in or on them. They just can't reenter the atmosphere while doing so. If we push three meters in that direction, we will be inside one of them and flying in space in it here in the ISS. We will undock it. We will fly it to the Soyuz. And while Major Simms and the generals and politicians are paralyzed in debate, we will take our warheads back."

"Sounds good. Do you have more of a plan than that?"

"Yes. Have you ever seen the old American Cold War movie *Dr. Strangelove*?" Vladimir grinned wildly. "We'll just need the Progress, our space suits, firearms, and perhaps a few hand tools."

"Shoot." Michael grinned knowingly in return. "A fella could have a pretty good weekend in Vegas with all that stuff."

The Progress module on the end of the Russian Service Module had taken no damage from the DSIHM high-voltage discharge attack and was in perfect functioning order. Vladimir had long studied all things Russian and American space. He had done everything within his power for decades to become a Soyuz pilot and cosmonaut. Internal politics of the Russian Federation and various other aspects of his life had managed to keep him from it. But not any longer. Vladimir was in charge of the International Space Station and all it had to offer. He would do any damned thing he wanted to and the Russian Federation could be damned.

"Okay, I have disconnected the Luch Russian relay system and ground station navigation components. Roscosmos cannot take control of it," Vladimir said over their communications link. "GNSS autonomous navigation patch is uploaded. K, can you patch in a code so I can control it through my virtual view?"

"Yes, V. Already done that. You should see a new icon on your desktop that looks like a Progress Module," Keenan said from his island refuge. "And note that I am twenty-three minutes from being able to deploy to the primary target."

"Understood, K. As soon as the system is ready and we enter the launch window, fire at will. Do not wait for us to be done with this mission. Understand?"

"Understood. Firing in twenty-three minutes, then. I have started a virtual clock for us."

"I see the clock."

"Copy on the clock," Michael said.

"I have the code up and running to control the Progress. Looks good. Great work," Vladimir said.

"Of course, comrade," Keenan said. "Now, while you fellas go forth and conquer, I have work to do."

"Right. Get to it, then," Vladimir said.

"Good luck."

"Progress is ready for undocking, M," he said over their commlink. "My view shows that you are in place?"

"Yes. I'm ready to go."

"Very well. Releasing the docking clamps now." Vladimir worked the various controls of the Service Module docking system and released the Progress. He would fly the Progress from there while Michael rode on the outside of the vehicle. There was definitely a *Dr. Strangelove* vibe to the moment.

"Keep your forward view on the Soyuz and your rear view on as well, M. I will use your camera views as my guidance system," Vladimir told him as he backed the Progress slowly away from the station with its first couple of retro-rocket burns.

"Copy that."

The code that Keenan had supplied him was simple and appeared to be almost identical to the code that ran the jets on their space suits and used the auto control application they already had. The only difference was the location of the jets and how the system got the state vectors to feedback into the control algorithm. The Progress typically took that data from GNSS and could fly from point A to point B autonomously, much like modern-day drones. It worked well and that was all that Vladimir cared about.

"On our way, comrade. Ready yourself. All Progress reporting telemetry to Earth has been shut down and we are quiet. Unless

Space Command is giving her radar updates, which I doubt, she'll have no idea we are near her. Perhaps we can sneak up on her and pick her pocket."

✧   ✧   ✧

Michael waited for several minutes as the Progress finally began moving upward away from the ISS and toward the bright spot in the sky above them. The spacecraft slowly closed the gap between them and the bright spot grew much larger until he could make out details of the Soyuz spacecraft. As he approached, Vladimir began slowing him down to a near relative stop about fifty meters away.

Michael disconnected his tether and pushed hard off the front of the spacecraft, propelling him forward. He used the thrusters in his suit to maintain his attitude and to keep the Soyuz locked on target. A moment later he was slowing to a quiet relative stop near the Orbital Module of the Soyuz spacecraft. On the large ball-shaped section of the vehicle were the four nuclear warhead glide bodies tethered to a handhold emplacement. They had been too big to wrangle through the hatch, apparently.

Michael studied the tether attachment and carefully worked it loose. He didn't want to make any undue clanks against the hull to alert the Space Force major that he was out there. A few seconds more and they were free. He carefully jetted backward while tugging the tether with him. About that time the countdown timer in his virtual view counted down to zero. He looked back downward to the ISS and suddenly there was a bright flash and a rocket streaked downward and against the direction of their orbital motion. A new clock appeared, counting down from twenty-nine minutes to detonation.

"Launch one is good!" Vladimir said.

"Looks great from here," Michael added. "Note that I have four packages and I am headed back to the Progress."

"Copy."

CHAPTER 54

⌒∿⌒

Vandenberg Air Force Base, California
Space Launch Complex 3E
Tuesday
8:01 A.M. Pacific Time
11:01 A.M. Eastern Time

"WILL THIS DO?" THE SPACE FORCE CONTRACTOR TECHNICIAN asked Lieutenant Colonel Frank Alvarez after handing him the modified M4.

They had taken the three-dimensional model of the receiver and adjusted the trigger guard to be much larger and open at the bottom so a space-suit gauntlet finger could fit there. They had also made the safety switch mechanism much larger and all of the hasps and pulls made in a way that would accommodate the gloves. Then they rapidly milled them out of aluminum on a computer numerical control router—CNC—machine. They also 3-D printed new stock and forearm parts as needed. The beauty of the M4, and all AR platforms for that matter, was the interchangeability to make quick and easy changes to the design, caliber, and build.

"Let's see." Frank pulled the mockup gloves on and inserted the magazine, loaded a round in the chamber, flipped the safety off, and then raised it to ready. He sighted it in on the target down the makeshift indoor test range and fired several rounds. "Works fine. Need to practice it in an actual suit if there's time."

"There won't be any time for that!" Ginny Banks said from behind them looking at the new weapon as she entered the indoor test range. "A nuke just detonated over Kentucky. The massive EMP affected most of the systems on the Eastern seaboard. Power is out across most of the Eastern United States. The launch has been pushed as far up as possible and still maintaining safety protocols. We'll launch at midnight tonight."

"No shit." Frank just hung his head. "Those crazy bastards are actually doing it."

"Yes." Dr. Banks said. "Dr. Grayson predicts they'll hit either Moscow or Paris next. Maybe northern Africa."

"Okay, hang on." Frank turned to the contractor technician. "Thomas, this is awesome. Can you make us, like, twelve of them within the next couple of hours and reassemble the weapons?"

"Yes. I think we can get them done in that kind of time. I'll get right to work."

"They have the news feed up in the break area, if you want to see," Banks said.

"Yeah." Frank followed her back into the main hall and toward the break area. Several Space Force enlisted and a few of the United Launch Alliance rocket engineers were having coffee and watching the morning newscasts.

> "...It is clear from this disturbing video that we just received that a nuclear weapon has detonated some-where about fifty kilometers above northern Kentucky. There are currently no reported casualties, but the level of devastation to the communications and power grids is still unknown at this time and likely will be for days to weeks. We are expecting the president to address the nation soon..."

"Somehow, they knew who the astronaut was," Toby told Frank over the secure VTC between Tampa and Vandenberg. "At the time, as best I can tell, only the Chiefs and their staffers were online on our end. No way to know who on the Russia end was on."

"We have a mole somewhere, then?" Frank frowned at that. "Somebody at the Chiefs level. Jesus Christ."

"Brings us back around to our three assassins. Who tipped them off about Watkins? The forensics on the computer at his house shows a link to an IP address leading back to the Pentagon. I don't like this, Frank," Toby told him. "You better watch your ass doing whatever it is that you are doing."

"Yeah. Keep digging, Toby."

"It's not a sword, Kenny," Mac argued with the Delta Force major. "It's a very long knife. I'm guessing we might have to stab someone in a suit or something."

"Why don't we just shoot them from a long way off?"

"Maybe. But the ISS is designed to withstand micrometeorite impacts that hit faster than any bullet. We'd have to use a shaped charge or uranium-tipped, armor-piercing, high-caliber rounds to shoot through it, maybe. I'm not sure, maybe a fifty cal would do it. This is going to be hand-to-hand," Mac explained.

"Shit," Kenny replied with a chuckle. "I hate it when Squids are right. We should see how Dugan and Frank are doing with the rest of the gear."

"Yeah."

"My heart?" Dr. Banks was shouting hysterically. "My heart is fine! I ran a damned marathon four weeks ago."

"I'm sorry, Dr. Banks," the flight surgeon tried to calm her down. "I cannot clear you for flight at this time."

"These are your flight crew." General Cates introduced them. "You know Captain Ames. For security purposes, you will refer to her only as 'Commander' from here forward. This is your copilot and will be referred to only as 'Copilot.' This is your flight engineer and will be referred to as 'Engineer.' No names will be briefed further for their protection. Is that understood?"

"Sir," Frank, Kenny, and Casey said in unison. Mac merely nodded. Warrants were just that way.

"This is Captain Stevens, U.S. Space Force. Not his real name. He has volunteered to replace Dr. Banks and will be your fifth team member," Cates said.

"Sir, if I may..." Frank started to protest but was shut down.

"There is no discussion, Colonel. Captain Stevens is on your team and that comes from the Chiefs. Moving forward, this mission will be referred to as 'Hot Eagle One,'" Cates said.

"The commander of the mission will brief you on protocols

and procedures and you will not move forward without their permission. We've already had one nuclear detonation, ladies and gentlemen. Let's stop the bastards from doing more."

"Hoo-ah," Casey and Kenny said in unison.

"Uhrah," Frank grunted.

"Hoo-yay!" they finally got out of Mac.

The Space Force members said nothing but nodded and saluted from an attention posture.

"Launch sequence is T-minus seven hours. With built-in holds that will put the launch around twenty-three hundred. We'll load in at T-minus one hour and forty minutes at a scheduled hold. Final preps and loads on your gear and suits. And start making last actions now. No calls out."

CHAPTER 55

❧

Low Earth Orbit
Tuesday
12:01 P.M. Pacific Time
3:01 P.M. Eastern Time

"OKAY, THAT'S CLOSE ENOUGH, V." MICHAEL AND VLADIMIR WERE absolutely exhausted. Adrenaline and stimulants could only take them so far. The two of them had been truly burning the candle from both ends and the middle for several days. Instead of redocking the Progress Vladimir had brought it around adjacent to the Vyrezka and parked it there while they off-loaded the glide bodies into place on the DSHIM. Michael tethered them close so it would minimize the effort of installing them. Once Michael and the warheads were off the spacecraft, Vladimir had brought it back around to the Service Module side and ran the automated docking software.

"I'll be right there, M." Vladimir had already begun cycling through the airlock and was on his way to support the installation process. It had taken another two hours to bolt them into place and then plug in the command line umbilicals.

"I'm wiped out, V." Michael was exhausted beyond being useful.

"Agreed, comrade." Vladimir helped him with the last of the warhead connections and let out a very long exhale. "As much as

I enjoy being a cosmonaut, it would be nice to pee in something other than this suit."

"Let's take the time, then," Michael said. "K, how much time before you would need more from us?"

"I have connectivity with the remaining five warheads. Target two launch window is in three hours and thirteen minutes. I can take it from here if you guys need a rest."

"We have to take a rest cycle. Should we alternate or both sleep?" Vladimir asked.

"We'll let K be our eyes and ears. You heard that right, K? You will be our eyes and ears?"

"Copy that, fellas. I'll keep a watch on the multipath and on the other alerts we have in place. If something is coming, I'll let you know."

"Let's get some rest for a few hours, then," Vladimir said.

"If there is any movement from the Soyuz, you let us know," Michael said. "We have a camera fixed on it now so you should be able to track it."

"Get some rest guys. I have it under control."

M,

I hope you are happy so far. Target one accomplished.
Close to two.

V

"Major, we have a report from Space Command that there was a large object anomaly that approached you a couple hours ago. We were just now fed the report. For whatever reason nobody from Russia said anything either," the current U.S. CAPCOM told her on a secure channel.

"What was it?" Allison had drifted off to sleep as she awaited her burn package to go home. She realized way more time had passed than it should have. She checked her watch. "I've been asleep for two hours!"

"Roscosmos says they didn't see anything in their live feeds, but they now confirm. It was a Progress Module."

"Progress? From ISS?"

"Copy that, Major Simms."

"No! NO!" Allison immediately flipped the docking camera

toggle with the long metal pistol grip rod. She couldn't see the tethered nukes. She toggled the periscope and didn't see them. She leaned as best she could to the window and looked out. She didn't see them or the shadow they had been casting across the solar panels of the Soyuz. "Shit!"

"Major?"

"They took the nukes back!"

"What was that?" Michael jumped awake from a deep sleep. Hanging in the sleeping system in the main executive suite in the DSIHM had him confused at first until his tired mind and body caught up with the fact that he was in space. He was on the taken ISS. He was in the DSIHM. And he had a good idea of what had just awakened him. He scrambled through his pouch and pulled his glasses from there. They *ding-dong*ed his implants as he put them on.

"K, you there?"

"Yes, M. Did the launch wake you?"

"So, you did just launch number two?"

"Yes. It is away and so far, looks good. Detonation clock is ticking away. In nineteen minutes the lights in Moscow go out."

"Great. V, you hearing this?" Michael asked. There was no response. "He slept through it, probably."

"Probably."

"Next launch window is when?" Michael asked.

"We have to make it eight orbits to get to the right location over Africa. But when we get on that one orbit, we can launch three of the remaining four." Keenan showed him a graphic of the orbital tracks of the space station in his virtual view with the remaining launch windows marked in red dots with times. The first time was about eight in the morning Eastern Time Zone. "Everything is still moving along."

"Any movement from our friend in the Soyuz?"

"Nothing so far. I wonder if they even know you picked her pocket yet?"

"I'm sure NORAD saw us and tracked us."

"Hmmm, maybe I can hack in there..."

"Don't waste your time. Focus on what we're doing now. Keep a watch out for anything we need to know and keep the software updates for the warheads going," Michael told him.

"That is mostly automatic now. I'm pulling the ephemeris data from the ISS directly and reloading the Kalman filters. They recalculate burns to target every minute," Keenan told him.

"Can you keep watch so I can sleep a bit more?"

"Sure. Rest. I'll wake you if anything changes."

"Great. Thanks."

CHAPTER 56

❦

Vandenberg Air Force Base, California
Space Launch Complex 3E
Tuesday
9:01 P.M. Pacific Time
Wednesday
12:01 A.M. Eastern Time

"STILL ON SCHEDULED HOLD SHOWING CREW AND COMPLEMENT fully boarded," the X-37D flight controller said. Captain Shelly Ames wiggled a bit in her suit, getting comfortable in her pilot's seat. She checked the view from her screens and had camera shots of each of the crew and Task Force. The last access hatch was closing and being buttoned up. They were very close to launching.

"Copy, Flight. Hot Eagle One is locked and loaded," she said. "Any further word on Moscow?"

"Very little, HE1. What we are getting is that the EMP has created massive blackouts across the western portion of the country. Moscow is blacked out also."

"Thanks, Flight."

Captain Ames checked each seat view to make certain the crew were not freaking out on her. Dugan and Thompson seemed alert and their heart rates were nominal if a little elevated. McKagan sat beside Alvarez and she couldn't tell if both of them were actually asleep or just playing opossum as some sort of bravado thing. Captain Stevens sat beside the Engineer. He seemed calm enough.

"Okay, HE1, initiate onboard life support monitor and internal vehicle health status dashboard."

"Roger that. LSM and IVHS dashboard is on and we have a green light on the circuit breaker menu," Shelly said.

"Copilot, what is the status of the transfer line chill-down?"

"Status is green, Flight."

"Copy that status is green. Preparing for LOX flow-down on Centaur upper stage."

"Uh, roger Flight. Copilot is showing flow-down on upper stage."

"Commander, please inform us when the fast-fill light goes from red to green on the Hydrogen tank."

"Roger, Flight. Pilot will inform. Breaker current status is red." Ames held calm and continued to follow the checks and the cryogenic fast tank fill light for the hydrogen fuel of the upper stage flashed green. "Flight, be advised the fast-fill fuel light is green."

"Copy that, Commander. Fast-fill is green."

There was a fairly loud snoring suddenly through her headset that jarred her train of thought. Shelly quickly toggled through the menu, looking and listening to each of the seat cameras. Both Alvarez and McKagan were sound asleep and both of them were snoring. She turned their mics down with a chuckle. She knew they had been going around the clock. For the next almost two hours, there was nothing for them to do. Seasoned combat soldiers knew to sleep when they could. Now was as good a time as any.

"HE1 countdown restart in three, two, one...T-minus one hour forty minutes and counting."

"Copy, Flight."

"Jesus Christ!" Frank said through gritted teeth.

The Atlas V rocket's first stage fired the RD-180s shaking him about like he'd never been shaken before. Frank thought the teeth would rattle from his head. Then he was pushed into his seat with three times the force of gravity or more and it felt like a giant rock was lying against his chest. He focused on his breathing and just prayed that Captain Ames knew what she was doing. Then he prayed that all the scientists, engineers, and technicians in Decatur, Alabama, who had built the rocket knew what they were doing. He had no idea the motors were built in Russia or he would have prayed for them too.

"I hope this wasn't a really bad idea," McKagan said quietly, looking over at him through a slight turn of his head.

"Me too, Mac."

"HE1, Flight. We're showing MECO and staging burn."

"Copy, Flight. Main Engine Cut-Off. We have second stage ignition."

"HE1 we show you circularized at fifty-one point six degrees inclination. Phasing burns being calculated now."

"Copy, Flight. How long to intercept?"

"Give us a minute on that one, HE1." There was a bit of delay and then Mission Control responded. "We show intercept in four hours, thirty-seven minutes."

CHAPTER 57

⚬

Low Earth Orbit
Wednesday
4:50 P.M. Pacific Time
7:50 P.M. Eastern Time

> *M,*
>
> *Just got word. Top Secret launch. Soldiers. Will inter-cept ISS around 8AM Eastern.*
>
> *A*

> *K,V,M,*
>
> *Soldiers coming 8AM Eastern on secret launch!*
>
> *M*

✧　　✧　　✧

"Why haven't I been given a burn package to go home?" Allison asked the CAPCOM for Roscosmos. She had fallen back to sleep and had mostly slept through the entire night.

"Major, please stand by." There was a pause and then a familiar voice.

"Major, this is General Hastings and the rest of the Chiefs are listening. We have an operation ongoing presently with a Top Secret asset. A team is moving into place any moment now

349

to intercept and retake the ISS. We would like for you to move closer for live reconnaissance. I'm told you were just sent the burn package."

"Understood, General," Allison said but she was confused. She had never heard of a Top Secret manned vehicle and now she had just told the Russians all about it. The software downloaded and she initiated it. There were several retro-rocket burns and she slowly approached the ISS with her periscope view, staying locked on target. "Do you have the video feed, General?"

"Yes, we see it now, Major."

To Allison's amazement, she saw a spacecraft approach that looked like a small version of the old space shuttle. It was an X-37 variant. The payload bay doors were open and she could clearly see several astronauts on board it. The spacecraft did several roll, pitch, and yaw maneuvers and then reached a near zero relative velocity with the ISS near the Quest Airlock.

"So, I guess the rumors of the X-37D are real?" she said to no one in particular.

✧   ✧   ✧

"V! Get up!" Michael slapped him across the face.

Vladimir jumped and kicked within his floating sleeping bag system. "What?"

"We have a boarding party almost on top of us!" Michael was already half the way in his suit and continued to pull at it from all different directions, cinching it tight. Fortunately, the Dorman suits were fairly easy to don. "Get your fucking suit on!"

"Where are they, K?"

"They are five thousand meters and closing according to the multipath. I don't have them in cameras yet, but they are approaching from the RAM side and it looks like they might be headed for the Quest Airlock Module," Keenan told them.

"Get me a goddamned exterior camera view!" Michael shouted as he and Vladimir scrambled about.

Michael had managed to get his suit donned but had waited about putting on his gauntlets so he could prep his and Vladimir's firearms. He checked them. Made certain there were rounds in the chambers. And then he set the safeties off.

"K, how long to the launch window for our next warhead?"

"Nine minutes."

"Launch it early if you have to. A lesser effect will still be an effect," Vladimir said. "If we get overrun and taken or killed, launch them all on backup targets of choice."

"I understand."

There was a clanging against the hull not far from them. It was near the airlock. That is where they would come through.

"Come on, V! I have a plan."

The X-37D carrying the HE1 mission team came to a relative stop with the ISS just a few meters from the Quest Airlock Module hatch. Frank could see the space between them and the Earth below them and the heavens above them and the large space station all around them and it frightened the shit out of him.

"I recommend not to look about too much, Colonel," Ames told him from her pilot's seat. "It takes a bit to get used to it."

"No time for that, I guess."

"We'll hold here until you are clear. Then we will back off a bit to make certain not to be in any lines of fire," she told him. "Go!"

"Let's go, guys." Frank held onto the gadget they had been rapidly trained on called a personal maneuvering unit. The PMU was a large horseshoe-shaped object with multiple jets on it that could be fired by a thumb lever. The unit was tethered to their suits at the waist so they could drop it as they needed. Frank led followed by Mac, then Casey, then Kenny. Captain Stevens was getting prepared to follow behind them.

"Shit!" Stevens said. "I'm tangled. I'll be right behind you, Colonel."

"Don't dally about, Stevens. You cover our six as we breach. I doubt there is a need but you win that by default now," Frank ordered him.

"Yes, sir."

"It looks like the operation is started, General." Major Simms had brought the Soyuz to within a thousand meters and had a full view from multiple cameras on the spacecraft. She watched as four of the team egressed from the X-37D. A fifth astronaut seemed to begin to move but then stopped. She zoomed in on him more closely. She wasn't sure if he was tangled up or what. Then she saw him pull his firearm and shoot the astronaut in the seat next to him in the head, turn and fire into the seat in front of him.

"Oh my God!" Allison shouted. "There's an enemy on the team! He just fired on the pilots!"

"We see that, Major." General Hastings was shocked. There was nothing they could do from Earth.

Allison didn't hesitate. She dropped her faceplate and evacuated the Soyuz capsule, then fired a burn to push her closer. Once the outer hatch was released and the capsule had fired a braking burn, she unbuckled her harness and pulled her way through the Orbital Module, grabbing the gun she had taken and her last fire extinguisher along the way. She flung herself outward from the opening toward the X-37D and started floating across the several-hundred-meter gap between them. She pulled the fire extinguisher tether, bringing one of them up to her body, and fired it in the opposite direction accelerating her even faster.

Suddenly, one of the glide bodies fired from the hotel module in a bright white flare and rocketed away from them toward the Earth below. Allison tried not to think about it because there was nothing she could do about it at the moment. But she could do something about the asshole she was zooming toward. She held the shiny metal extinguisher lever until it ran dry and then she brought up the gun she had taken from the man she had killed. She activated the laser sight and brought it down in front of her and tracked it across the X-37D payload bay. The man who had just shot the other astronauts had yet to realize she was even in the universe with him. It looked as if he was trying to remove the bodies from the copilot seat or maybe, maybe, he was fighting with somebody still alive there.

Allison put the green dot on his head and pressed the trigger. His suit deflated and he spun slightly forward, bounced off the seatback in front of him, and then floated slowly away from the payload bay. Allison scrambled with the tether for the last extinguisher but couldn't get to it in time. She slammed into the open payload bay stomach-first over the back of one of the seats. The suit absorbed most of the impact but it was enough to knock the wind from her. She grasped for air and a handhold but she found neither. She tumbled feet over head and was certain she was about to tumble outward and away when a hand grabbed her by the fire extinguisher harness and started to reel her in.

She was bleeding air and blood from her left shoulder. Quickly, the pilot pulled a patch and slapped it to her suit. Allison pulled a roll of tape from her waist pouch and wrapped it over and around the patch. The air leak had been stopped at least. Then the pilot of the X-37D grabbed her arm and tapped at her wristband transceiver, tuning her to their channel.

"Captain, name classified. United States Space Force," the woman there said.

"Major Allison Simms. United States Space Force," Allison said.

"Thanks for the help, Major."

CHAPTER 58

ᦉ

Low Earth Orbit
Wednesday
5:11 P.M. Pacific Time
8:11 P.M. Eastern Time

"BLOW THE HATCH!" FRANK DUCKED BEHIND THE EDGE OF THE module with the rest of the team. Mac released the charge igniter and the outer hatch door to the airlock was blown. They hadn't expected the inner door to be open. The International Space Station depressurized explosively and various pieces of debris and equipment flew out into space along with the atmosphere. "Go! Heads on a swivel. Watch each other's blind spots."

Using the PMU, the four of them fired jets and used handholds as needed until they managed to pull themselves into Node 1. They did their best to keep one another covered, but being astronauts was not what they had been trained for.

"First corner, clear!" Thompson said. He pulled himself through with Mac and Casey behind him. Frank scanned behind him, wondering what had happened to Stevens. That made him very nervous.

"Okay, move slowly." Frank followed in. He sent Dugan to the left, down the Russian segment, and Thompson to the right, down toward the JEM. He and Mac would move forward toward Node 3, the BEAM, and the DSIHM.

Suddenly the lights to the module went out. Then lights through the entire station went out. Frank noticed that Mac's headlamps turned themselves on and, likewise, he realized his had come on as well.

"Shit! That's not a good feature." Mac looked at him. "Do you know how to turn them off?"

"No. Hold on. Commander, do you copy?"

"HE1 team. Stevens was a traitor but has been dealt with. We have two dead, one wounded. Me. We have a new team member in a Russian Orlan space suit. She is a friendly. Copy?"

"Copy. Shit. Commander, how do we turn these damned helmet lights off?"

"Sorry, sir, I don't think you can."

"What a shit show," Mac said. "Keep moving?"

"Have to."

"Yeah, I knew you were gonna say that."

The two of them very slowly moved through Node 3 to the entrance to the BEAM. As soon as Mac leaned around the corner, a green dot lit up the wall near him and tracked in his direction. Frank pressed his legs against the bulkhead, flinging him forward into him.

"Mac, look out!"

Several holes suddenly appeared silently in the bulkhead around them and they did all they could to scramble away from the opened hatchway to take cover. Frank bounced off the opposite bulkhead but managed to grab one of the blue handhold bars. He leaned his modified M4 around the corner and began firing it in short bursts in random directions. There was no familiarity to the action as in space there was no sound and only the flashes of light. It was odd. But Frank didn't let up until he was certain that Mac was in a position to fire back as well.

"Thompson! Dugan! Taking fire. Node Three now!" Frank shouted over the comm.

✧   ✧   ✧

"Shit!" Michael did his best to hold cover for Vladimir, but fighting in microgravity was damned near impossible. Fortunately, the Dorman suits stabilized their attitude and they could fly using the mental mouse.

"I'm hit, comrade," Vladimir said. "I have a quick patch on it. I'm not leaking air. Not sure about blood."

"Okay, we're getting the fuck out of here." Michael used the virtual view controls and cycled the hatch for the DSIHM airlock. Then Vladimir jetted to it and pushed it open. "Let's go. Get to the Vyrezka."

More holes suddenly appeared in the bulkheads directly in line with the hatch through the BEAM to Node 3. The assault team was coming fast. They had to go. Michael pushed Vladimir through the hatch and followed him. He reached into a pouch on his thigh and pulled a cylindrical-shaped container about the size of a soda can from within. He tapped at the buttons on the surface entering a code.

"Shit, I didn't want to do this!" He pressed the activate button and then threw it across and through the BEAM hatchway. He closed the airlock door behind him. "Go, V! Go!"

The two of them jetted across to the Vyrezka as fast as their jets would take them.

✧   ✧   ✧

Frank and Mac worked their helmet lights back and forth, watching for any motion coming from in front of them. Dugan and Thompson had made their way into Node 1 behind them. The gunfire seemed to have stopped for a moment and Frank wasn't sure that was a good thing or a bad thing. At least with the gunfire, he knew where the bad guys were and what they were doing. Frank suddenly caught a flicker of something out of the corner of his eye and turned his helmet in time to see a little black cylinder with some blinking lights and buttons on it. He knew an explosive when he saw one. He swatted at it but missed.

"Grenade!" he shouted.

"Shit!" Mac dropped his weapon, fired his PMU with his left hand, and grabbed the explosive with his right in an amazingly athletic catch. The PMU cold gasses sprayed out, jetting him forward into and through the BEAM all the way through the hatch to the hotel, and slammed him into the giant window of the DSIHM with the grenade between the window and his body. He saw the two men jetting by, making their escape, and one of the warheads ignited just as the explosive detonated.

The grenade was designed for space with antipersonnel pellets surrounding the charge. The metal balls tore through everything—including the bulkheads and Mac. Several of the pellets pierced the hull and partially severed the main umbilical between the Vyrezka and the DSIHM, cutting the command line. Others zipped into the rear of the igniting warhead, damaging the rocket motor and causing it to explode out one side, throwing shrapnel into the other two. The DSIHM was torn to shreds and most things in it or attached to were as well.

CHAPTER 59

෬

Low Earth Orbit
Retaken International Space Station
Wednesday
8:33 P.M. Eastern Time

"JESUS, MAC, WHAT DID YOU DO?" FRANK LOOKED OVER WHAT was left of the man's body. Blood had boiled away and frozen. He was a mess.

"Goddamnit, Mac," Dugan said.

"Colonel, our bad guys have fired deorbit burns on their spaceship. They're gone. We took a few shots at them but I'm not certain we hit anything useful. Maybe the Navy or somebody can get them, depending where they hit. But my guess is, they just got away from us," Captain Ames said. "The fourth warhead fired right as whatever happened in there happened. Some debris came through the bulkhead and went careening out of control. By the tumbling of it, I suspect it will burn up on reentry. Be advised there are two more warheads active and connected."

"We need to disconnect them or make them inert somehow," Frank said. "We're coming out."

"Here, Colonel." Kenny worked the mechanical hatch controls on the DSIHM airlock the two terrorists, or whatever they were, had escaped through. "Go. I'll get Mac."

Frank worked his way out toward the exterior ring around the

DSIHM that the warheads had been fastened to. Dugan wasn't far behind him. The two of them studied the glide bodies and their connection flange closely with hopes of coming up with a plan. Neither of them wanted to say the obvious thing: What if they just detonated them where they were? Their ship was gone and so were the umbilical lines running to the warheads. Frank hoped they were not autonomous or wireless. There were multiple holes in the sides of both reentry vehicles—Frank pointed them out with the barrel of his weapon.

"Think that broke them?" Frank checked the gamma ray detector on his left wristband and didn't see anything unusual.

"I dunno. Hopefully?" Casey studied them closely by grabbing a handhold near the base of one of them and pulling himself down to it.

"You're the Sapper. You tell me what to do."

"The bolts are cheap breakaway bolts. Probably rated for a certain thrust or something." Dugan studied them closer. "If I had the right tools—but, damn. Looks like a thirteen-millimeter socket-head cap bolt. Probably need some kind of special astronaut drill or something. Not prepared for that. Other than shooting them off of there, I have no ideas."

"That would be a difficult shot from a minimum safe distance. We'd need a laser sight at a minimum."

"Did somebody say laser sight?" a new voice said. It was the friendly that Ames had found. "I have one. Hold on a minute."

It had taken the better part of the next hour to carefully shoot the heads off the bolts with the laser-sighted gun that Allison had taken from the dead bad guy. Allison had first looked for the right tool, and they had even tried pliers. In the end, it had become easier to shoot the heads off the bolts. While she and Dugan worked that, he and Thompson gathered up the dead cosmonaut, Mac, and the dead bad guy, and loaded them into the X-37D. Once the warheads were clear, they were ordered to put them in the Progress and deorbit it so they would burn up on reentry. That had taken an hour or so as well.

Allison and the commander, Ms. Captain Classified, brought the propulsion modules back online and reconnected the satellite communication and control uplink to the Russian Service Module. NASA and Roscosmos would be able to keep the ISS in orbit for at least long enough to send up repair crews or decide to deorbit it.

"Thanks for the assist, Major," the lieutenant colonel told her. "You slowed them down enough to give us time to get here."

"Why did they do this?"

"We may never know unless we catch them. We'll see," Frank told her. "You ready?"

"Yes. Will I see you guys again? I'd like to join, whatever this team is," Allison told him.

"Not sure *we* know whatever this is, and the mission name is classified."

The X-37D slowed to zero relative velocity only two meters from the Soyuz capsule. With the help of the soldiers, she loaded Major Nolvany's body inside and strapped him in.

"Thanks for the ride and the help. Maybe I'll see you again soon?" Allison said.

"Do you drink alcohol, Major?" Thompson asked her. "We have a tradition of toasting our fallen."

"Let me know when and where." Allison saluted them. Then she closed the Soyuz up and climbed into the commander's seat.

"Roscosmos CAPCOM, this is Soyuz MS-53, do you copy?"

CHAPTER 60

∽

Indian Ocean
Thursday
4:33 P.M. Local Time

THE VYREZKA HAD PERFORMED FLAWLESSLY. THE PARACHUTES
had deployed without a hitch, slowing the descent down. The squatty
space capsule splashed down in the middle of the Indian Ocean
as previously planned. The inflation devices deployed and the ship
surfaced and bobbled up and down on the waves like a buoy.

It had been an endeavor to get Vladimir out of his suit. His
left arm was shot up pretty badly and had stuck to the adhesive
of the safety patch he'd applied during the fight. Michael had to
cut most of the suit material away. He'd lost a lot of blood, but
he would survive.

They had waited for hours watching through the satellite feed
of the progress of the Russian and American naval ships coming
for them. They were only a matter of hours away. A few times
both countries had flown fighter jets over in search patterns and
Michael was certain that they had been spotted.

M and V,

Time to swim.

R

Michael popped the hatch of the Vyrezka for the last time and helped Vladimir out. About ten meters away a long, gray, concrete cylinder emerged from the calm seas. The concrete submarine the multibillionaire drug lord Roberto Ibanez had built for smuggling drugs, guns, and people continued to rise to the surface. A hatch on top opened and Roberto climbed atop, waving at them.

"Time to go, gentlemen. We must hurry before company arrives!"

Michael and Vladimir jumped from the Vyrezka, falling into the small, inflated yellow life raft. Once they were clear of the spacecraft and were moored to the submarine, Michael opened a menu in his virtual view and flipped an icon from red to green.

"She was a good ship, V," he said as an explosive charge detonated within it, blowing out the bottom.

"Yes, comrade. There will be more."

The two men watched for a moment as the spacecraft sunk beneath the surface. They climbed aboard the submarine and greeted Roberto with handshakes.

"Congratulations! Men, you have done the impossible."

CHAPTER 61

∾

Huntsville, Alabama
Temporary FBI Headquarters
Monday
11:45 P.M. Central Time

"WE HAD THE BODY AND THE SPACE SUIT RUSHED HERE OVER the weekend. With the mass blackout in D.C. and all the chaos, coming here to the temporary HQ made the most sense." Dr. Ginny Banks stood next to the medical examiner and the FBI computer forensics expert Vineet Mathur. Special Agent Toby Montgomery watched and listened cautiously. He had about decided he could trust Dr. Banks, but from his past experience, full trust was hard to give to anyone.

"So, why are we here?" Toby asked.

"First, man, this space suit is sweet," Vineet said. "It has a computer network running all through it and there's some sort of wireless control system that runs it."

"Wireless?" Toby asked.

"Yeah, the actual control computer isn't part of the space suit. Well, it is, and it isn't," Vineet said excitedly. "This is beyond state-of-the-art stuff here."

"What is?" Toby prodded the scientist along.

"It took me a bit, but once we powered on the suit, I realized the helmet visor was smart-glass." Vineet pointed at the faceplate on the helmet he was holding up in his hands. "It's so encrypted we'll never hack it. But that's not the important part."

"Never hack it?"

"I have put some assets at the Agency on it and Dr. Grayson is setting up a program to run it through Bumblehive, but for now, it doesn't look like even the U.S. intelligence community has the ability to break this encryption," Ginny added. Toby just nodded in understanding.

"Yeah, but the big thing here is, how on Earth was this guy controlling the virtual glass?" Vineet shrugged with his palms upward. Then he nodded to the medical examiner. "That was the big question. Show him, Doc."

The medical examiner, Dr. Michon Smith—Toby wondered if that was her real name, but decided it probably was and put his undercover agent paranoia aside for the moment—smiled at him with a raised eyebrow. Then she pulled the cover back from the dead man's head.

"Sorry for the gruesome nature of this. Per the report, he was indeed killed by a high-temperature flare being fired into his face. There was little left there. Fortunately, he didn't burn up because of being in the vacuum of space. Had it not been for that, there would have been nothing to see here," Dr. Smith explained. "The first thing we did was a full course of X-rays of the body."

"We did the suit too," Dr. Banks added.

"Special Agent, you simply can't grasp how dope this suit is," Vineet interrupted. "The Space Force guys want it back as soon as the investigation is over so they can reverse engineer it."

"What did the X-rays show, Dr. Smith?" Toby was getting impatient for the punch line.

"They showed this." She pointed at the X-ray display screen across the room. "D'ya see these white spots here and here on either side of his ears?"

"Yes."

"Well, we pulled one of them." She turned the dead man's head over and pointed out the incision point behind his left ear. "It was some sort of magnetic implant."

"It was a neural link implant!" Vineet couldn't help himself.

"A what?"

"This guy was talking to his space suit, and probably other people, through a brain-to-machine interface. This is stuff DARPA has been working on for years. NASA wishes they could have a suit like this. I bet he could fire his jets about just by thinking commands." Vineet was all the while waving his arms about and pointing and acting like a geek at a computer expo.

"Wait a minute." Toby had to think that through a minute. "You are telling me that our bad guys have implants behind the ears that allow them to control their space suits with their brains. You mean literally by thinking control commands to it?"

"Well, without being able to hack into it we'll never know how complex the system was. But even if there were just virtual buttons, a virtual keyboard, or a virtual mouse or something, they could just think of pressing the keys or buttons or moving the mouse to control it like any other computer. That is still, well, a decade away for us?" Vineet explained. "I've never seen anything like it other than in science fiction."

"I have requested access to programs regarding this type of technology at all classification levels," Banks added. "Nothing back yet."

"Okay, so why behind the ears?" Toby asked.

"Aha!" Dr. Smith clapped her hands together. "I thought you would never ask."

"So, you do know why?"

"I have an idea," she said. "I looked more closely at the skin of the other ear without disturbing it. Under the microscope you can see here there is a depression in the skin and fatty tissue indicative of someone who wears glasses regularly. Unfortunately, there was only one eyeball left and it was damaged too badly to test the man's visual acuity. However, it is my hypothesis that the reason the implants are magnetic is that they hold glasses in place."

"The implants could be using a magnetic induction process to connect to a pair of virtual display glasses," Vineet said. "They might have glasses they can wear around that work like the space helmet does."

"Why would somebody want that?"

"Communications, sensor network data, because it is cool—hell, there are all sorts of reasons I'd want them." Vineet grinned. "I mean, that is some real sci-fi shit, Special Agent. Who knows what advantages it would give you? You could cheat at almost anything with them."

"Okay, glasses then—" Toby started but was interrupted by Dr. Banks.

"Toby, can we speak in private a moment?" She held up a blue neoprene locked bag about the size of a large legal envelope. "In a secure area."

"Okay, sure." Toby turned to Vineet and the doctor. "Great work. Let me know if you find anything else."

❖   ❖   ❖

"Airman First Class Shannon continued to look for a way out of Russia that Lytokov could have taken the nukes. She took the challenge Frank gave her seriously," Banks explained as she unlocked the bag and pulled an envelope marked TOP SECRET from it.

"So, she found something?"

"Yes, she did." Banks nodded. "There is an oil pipeline that runs all the way to the Black Sea there. The line has a security and maintenance road running alongside it with controlled access. It was the perfect egress route."

"We know for sure this is how they got the nukes out?" Toby asked.

"Yes. Dr. Grayson put the full might of the Bumblehive on it and managed to hack into the security cameras along the path. Look here in these pictures. Here are guys in these vehicles here. We know it's them from this one." Banks shuffled to the next printout. It was a picture through the windshield of two men. The man in the passenger seat was Lytokov. Both men were wearing sunglasses.

"Damned good thing the power in Utah wasn't knocked out, then. Have you shown this to Frank yet?" Toby asked.

"No. He should be landing in Tampa soon." Banks then pointed at the glasses. "Notice these?"

"Yes. I do." Toby agreed.

❖   ❖   ❖

"That's it, Vineet. Can you print that out for me and send it to the evidence folder?" Toby and Ginny had watched as the computer wizard white hat hacked the Pentagon security gate cameras and scrolled back through the previous week.

"Will do. Do you want my algorithm to keep looking for others with sunglasses as they entered or what?"

"Only those connected to the Joint Chiefs and this investigation.

Any more than that and we'll likely have a problem with the FISA judge." Toby turned to Banks and grinned. "We got the bastard. Let's go get a warrant."

"It would be nice to actually get a pair of those so I can reverse hack 'em," Vineet added. "I'm just sayin'. It would be nice."

"We'll see what we can do," Toby replied.

CHAPTER 62

∽

Washington, D.C.
The Pentagon
Tuesday
7:45 A.M. Eastern Time

"SIR, THEY HAVE A WARRANT, FBI AGENTS, A FEDERAL MARSHAL, Pentagon Security, and Military Police," the young Army lieutenant said from behind several men and women as they bustled hurriedly into the room. "They have a warrant, sir. I couldn't stop them."

Colonel Allan Vinderman looked up from his desk. While the backup generators were supplying power to the Pentagon, they were minimizing usage so only his desk lamp was on. The office was fairly dark and he couldn't make out exactly who the people were rushing toward him. Vinderman froze like a deer in headlights.

"Colonel Allan Vinderman?" a man in a ski mask asked him. When he turned in the light, the colonel could see the letters FBI written in yellow across his body armor. Another man wearing the Military Police insignia quickly flanked Vinderman from the other side and produced a set of handcuffs. The shiny metal glinted against the desk lamp's lighting.

"Yes." Vinderman swallowed a lump in his throat. "What is this? Who wants to know?"

"FBI. You are under arrest for conspiracy to commit mass murder; conspiracy in the theft of and use of weapons of mass destruction; treason; and espionage. You have the right to remain silent. Anything you say can and will be used against you..."

CHAPTER 63

〜

Near Tampa, Florida
Wednesday
2:33 P.M. Eastern Time

"A1C SHANNON DID JUST WHAT YOU TOLD HER TO DO, FRANK." TOBY told him. "She continued to look for a way to get those nukes from where they were in Russia to the Black Sea. And she found it."

"Yep, never underestimate tenacity and drive to do a good job." Frank grinned proudly. "Shannon has that drive. She's a good soldier. So, exactly how'd they do it? What did she find?"

"The Atyrau-Samara pipeline. The thing has a privately guarded road all the way from just a few kilometers from where they took the nukes straight to the Black Sea. No police to stop or bother them."

"Hell of a good plan," Frank said.

"You know who paid for most of it?"

"What? The pipeline?" Frank asked.

"Yes. Well, that and the road," Toby said.

"No. But I suspect you are going to tell me."

"Yes, I am." Toby paused for dramatic effect. "Marcus Dorman."

"The billionaire guy?"

"Yes."

"So."

"Did you see the news this morning or last night?"

"Other than a mased FBI agent arresting a colonel at the Pentagon? Um, honestly, no. Was busy with Space Force security

373

stuff, then tired. Then I got drunk." Frank laughed halfheartedly. "Why?"

"Dorman has just worked a deal with both the U.S. government and the Russians to help rebuild the energy infrastructure at a steal of a price. It will be worth trillions to him over the next decade. Literally trillions. Several of the governments of Africa are in negotiations with him also. He is projected to become the richest man in history and likely ever. He will probably be the first-ever trillionaire."

"What? You think he did this for the money?"

"Maybe. I don't know. Partly. But guess who the biggest campaign contributor to various senators, congressmen, and governors on the right energy and infrastructure committees and states was?" Toby asked him rhetorically.

"Let me guess, Dorman."

"Ding-ding! You win the prize."

"There has to be more. What was his connection to the Pentagon?"

"You mean, was he connected to Vinderman?"

"I guess that is what I mean. I'm not sure exactly what I mean. Do you?"

"Well, the lead to Vinderman was the pair of sunglasses he wore everywhere, even inside on occasions. We've got lots of security camera footage of his daily life where he is wearing them when it isn't sunny."

"So?"

"Lytokov and this other guy driving the truck were wearing them in every picture. The space helmet had a visor that was similar. The glasses are electronic devices, Frank, and so was the space-suit helmet's visor. The dead astronaut you guys brought back had these brain-implant things. They connect their brains to the glasses wirelessly."

"What?"

"It's all in the secure folder, Frank. Jesus, you need to get caught up on this."

"High-tech glasses? Like VR glasses?"

"My computer guy says beyond anything he's ever seen before. You know who makes high technology computers, internet, gaming systems, and who also has a spacecraft and a rocket?"

"Dorman."

"Right again!" Toby leaned back in the chair, almost making

it tip over. He reflexively grabbed at the side of Frank's desk to catch himself. "Damn. Look, Frank, I don't know who Vinderman was answering to at the Pentagon yet, or if he was acting alone and reporting to Dorman, but we'll find it. A guy that wealthy with all the Silicon Valley influence he has must be tied into the military-industrial complex at levels higher than just a colonel."

"I have to agree with that. Colonels usually answer to generals," Frank said. "But which general? Talk about high treason."

"This is big, Frank. And whoever it is will be so connected as to be damned near untouchable."

"Toby, you can't tell anyone about this. You'll never know who might be on the other side of it. This is very dangerous," Frank warned him.

"Not just on the other side of it Frank. Who's on the inside of it? This is deep treason we are talking about," Toby said. "There are estimates that tens of thousands are dead already from the chaos in the blackout areas. There was economic loss on a scale never before seen, and we still don't even understand the full extent of our current situation."

"This is mass murder that might end up worse than any of the pandemics. No telling how many will die in the next few months because of these blackouts," Frank added. "And the trail of bodies left behind already... Jesus."

"I don't know what the plan was! I don't know if it is done or not. But I'm not giving up until we find out and catch these bastards. Whoever they are," Toby said.

"I want to know who the two astronauts were that killed Mac. I want them. It is highly likely one of them is Lytokov. I'm going to kill him and his pal someday." Frank tapped the picture of the two men in the truck. "Someday soon."

"Forensics is still going over the dead astronaut. No ID yet. But maybe there will be more clues."

"Any word on Thomas Sing?"

"No, Sing is still vanished, probably with your astronauts. We'll find them. Vinderman is a patsy. Maybe he'll talk and give us something useful." Toby started to say more but there was a knock at the door.

"Come in?" Frank said.

"Colonel Alvarez, you have a visitor here, sir," A1C Shannon told him.

"I'll be right out." He turned to Toby. "Nobody, and I mean nobody, hears this but us. You, me, Kenny, Casey, and that's it."

"What about Banks?"

"Maybe. I trust her, but not who she has to report to."

"Understood, Frank."

Frank stepped from his office in the hangar and out into the high bay area. There was a woman standing there in a Space Force uniform, a lieutenant colonel. SIMMS was on her nametag.

"Lieutenant Colonel Simms?"

"They gave me a field promotion yesterday," Allison said.

"Congratulations, Colonel Simms." Frank shook her hand. "You here for that drink?"

"Yes and no."

"Yes and no?"

"Yes, in that I am ready for that drink to our fallen. I lost two and one, Dr. Denton, might not pull through. He's still in a coma," she said somberly. "But no, because I'm here on my new assignment."

"New assignment?"

"This." She handed Frank an envelope with a red-and-white cover and the words TOP SECRET on it. It seemed to Frank like he'd seen more of those classified covers in the past week than he had his entire career. Frank opened the folder and there was a sticky note in it next to a full-bird colonel uniform patch.

> *Welcome to your new assignment. Good job, Frank.*
> *Oh, and don't give me any lip about it.*
>
> *Alton*

Under the sticky note was a cover page. Written there was something Frank hadn't expected, but who was he to argue with the chief of the Marine Corps?

> *Hot Eagle Task Force Operational Orders Command-*
> *ing Officer O5 Colonel Francisco Alvarez. Operations*
> *to begin immediately.*

"Congratulations, sir. And, Lieutenant Colonel Simms reporting for duty." She saluted.

"I guess I can't argue with that either." Frank returned the salute.

EPILOGUE

〜

M,

*M and V are safe. We will meet S, G, T, K and K
on the island to begin Phase II. Talk soon. Cheers!*

R